T0149632

Living on Powdered Sugar

Living on Powdered Sugar

Barely Living. Maurice Fortune

Maurice P. Fortune

Living on Powdered Sugar
Barely Living. Maurice Fortune

iUniverse books may be ordered through booksellers or by contacting:

iUniverse
1663 Liberty Drive
Bloomington, IN 47403
www.iuniverse.com
1-800-Authors (1-800-288-4677)

ISBN: 978-1-5320-6461-6 (sc)
ISBN: 978-1-5320-6462-3 (e)

Print information available on the last page.

iUniverse rev. date: 03/22/2019

Contents

Ode to A Tree 1

Carefree Roses for A Funeral ****** 3

The Cat's Out of The Bag 62

An Envoy from P. O. T. S. (Power of Thoughts Suggested) 112

The Last Guest 129

Not Maid for Mayhem 170

The Humannequins 236

Riddles and Time 273

Two Undocumented 294

Message On The Subway M.O.T.S. 317

Ode to A Tree

Maurice P. Fortune

It's winter now the tree is gone. The roses sleep their slumber.

The benches sit in silence across the rain-swept stones, while remnants of dried bushes hide wistfully from sight.

I alone walk aimlessly in Sunday morning's light.

Beneath a sky of billowed clouds I brave the frigid air, to listen to the cry of birds: their voices petrified.

I hear, I watch, I think, I live. I try to understand.

It's winter now the tree has gone, the carefree roses snore. Their beauty but a memory, their thorns a threat no more.

A mind no longer stagnant, its absence not ignored.

My tree has joined the birds and winds with wings that God lets soar!

For Dad and for Faye.

Carefree Roses for A Funeral ✼✼✼✼✼✼

I have always loved history. Not because the accounts given are accurate but because the stories passed from generation to generation by those who were too young to remember them or were not there at all are so much more colorful than the mundane truth. I guess that is why it's called his story. – M. Fortune

"Donnellan Square is dying in the filth and all the trash that's left behind. Underneath the benches and the trees are old newspapers, cans and grime."

*Meter from Jimmy Webb's
Mac Arthur's Park *

MAY 28th, 2010

To Gail Wittner, who designed the setting, it must have seemed a good idea. Even now, the decision to place the roses behind the yews, and just under the Norway spruce that would serve in winter as the community Christmas tree was the logical choice. It's difficult to argue with a professional eye. The roses bloom but once a year, and when they are in the fullness of bloom they certainly break the monotony of the continuous carpet of green that otherwise dominates the square's main entrance. In spring and early summer the backdrop of the towering green drapery of the spruce and the full rounded skirt of the yews are impressive. To the viewer driving a car uptown on St. Nicholas Avenue it must have made a pretty picture. It still does. It is all nice and symmetrical. One can sit in an automobile and take in the scene from three different perspectives. If you turn west instead of east down the one way street that is 150th and it happens all the time, a closer look leaves you with the uncomfortable feeling that something is not quite right here. It's kind of like being in a size fourteen shirt when you actually need a neck size of sixteen.

A few years have gone by since the plantings. Nowadays, just looking at the roses it is apparent that they are struggling to survive. There are still enough of the bushes. That isn't the problem. The trouble appears to be that there is little room remaining for their numbers to expand. And so they, like the upright yews and the branches of the spruce, must fight for every inch of space available. Unbridled, at least the spruce can grow upwards. This is a blessing that the other two occupants of the small plot do not enjoy. As the rose bushes grow they poke their heads through the yews. Uninvited, they scratch and climb the branches of the tree, clawing their way upwards against its unwilling arms. This is survival by any means necessary and for one of them it's a losing battle. Even the temporary splash of color the roses bring to the setting is hugely outweighed by the spectacle of them scratching and gasping for sunlight. Years ago, they hadn't had to fight in this way. At least that's what I'd like to believe.

The spectacle is rivaled only by the exploding populations of sparrows and pigeons fighting each other for every scrap and crumb dropped here. It seems an unnecessary war with all the garbage left lying around. No space seems off limits to the trash left behind by careless park visitors. It is a shame to see the rose bushes dotted with plastic cups and various disposable items, as though there wasn't enough of a survival struggle going on within their little prison. Once upon a time someone tended the little memorial garden and made the other occupants behave. I would hear from a few of the older residents in the area that a concerned woman in the neighborhood took it upon herself to tend the rose bushes and trim them when necessary. She also cleaned the park on a regular schedule and her show of citizenship inspired the other residents to do their part. The little square was much cleaner back then they say; despite those times of turmoil and uncertainty that surrounded it. Sadly, it is said that even this Good Samaritan eventually gave up all hope of keeping the place clean. Of course this is only rumor, but it might have been this way. Although even an eternal optimist like me would be hard pressed to believe that this was the way it was planned, or that somewhere, in the drawer of an old file cabinet, faded yellow notes bear this out. Without more evidence, it would be difficult to prove because like most of the good things about this section of the City, along the way, somebody dropped the ball.

How regrettable it is to now see the roses pushing against the yews from within and the yews leaning and straining against the iron rails of the enclosure like prisoners. Faces and arms tense, theirs is a futile effort to make contact with a world that lies beckoning just out of reach. Ironically, if they had but a mirror they would see that the world they reach for outside this prison is but a reflection of their own private hell. It is almost incongruous that those times on Sugar Hill they seem so desperately re-seeking are long gone. Exempting the surveillance camera that is conspicuously mounted a good distance away ostensibly to regulate traffic violators but whose lens undoubtedly overlook the park, only the Norway Spruce, looming high enough to look the length of the little square and beyond to the surrounding streets knows the truth. It stands there mute. At times like a guard hovering over detainees. But mostly like a disinterested parent whose children, protected beneath its skirt, beg to be let outdoors to play. Wisely, the spruce knows that there is precious little space outside for any of them.

The era, of the park's inauguration, although only eight years past, seems innocent by today's measurements. I would hear this theme repeated over and over by the few remaining residents who were fortunate enough to remember the good old days. Like Ms. Lila. Nowadays, she complains of the painful carpal-tunnel syndrome in her hands and reminisces of the times when her brother and uncle owned newsstands across from the now Sugar Hill Pharmacy and when the now present Food Town Market did not exist.

These were the days when Jackie Robinson came here often, and Duke Ellington visited number 805, better known as the St. Nicholas Hotel. "Celebrities often sat in the Sugar Hill Bar all night long," she says. They'd emerge in the early morning light with the rush hour crowd." She seems nostalgic when she looks in the distance remembering that until just four or five years ago summer bands played in the very spot where we now sat talking. Bitterly, she says it was the drugs and guns that ran everyone away.

I doubt that even then there had been much hope left here. If there was it has faded with each passing year. Like the sparse crowd of residents who were no doubt present that June Day in 2002. Anyone who could leave had already left for other places.

The exodus happened here beginning in the 1960's. I suppose there was no single reason for it. Today, some mention the collapse of the Civil Rights Movement after modest achievements were made. Even the urban riots of the 60's and the deaths of Martin Luther King and Malcomb X are mentioned. Any one of these events may or may not have contributed to the blight that ensued but one thing is certain. As the area deteriorated many residents simply followed their forbearers who'd begun the trek years earlier. Many of them moved back to the south. They were more willing to bear the under -currents of lingering racial discrimination than stay and face the constant daggers of living in a place that had once welcomed them with a modicum of safety, if not open arms. This hope of returning to the place of birth is still a lingering one for some of the older residents on Sugar Hill. Only now, rather than the south of the United States, it is more often distant lands that are longed for in the dreams of the immigrants. The young Black Americans do not seem preoccupied with any such pining and the older ones appear tired of all the fighting, the political promises and of course the drugs. Some are even weary of talking about the historical Sugar Hill. That was in the past they'll tell you quickly. "We have to live for today and tomorrow." Of course, they're partially right. There is little satisfaction and glory in celebrating yesterday when today and tomorrow seem so uncertain.

But all of Sugar Hill's residents don't feel this way and as I sit reading I am approached by a quite grey- haired, aged white man. After inquiring about my reading material he informs me that he and his wife are the personal custodians of a library of some three thousand books. They are all of the subject of Black American history and he tells me of his search for more volumes. His enthusiasm is infectious as he relates to me several stories. As a teenager he remembers going to the home of a meticulously dressed, brown suited man who wore a gold medallion around his neck. Each Sunday the man taught African history from his apartment on Edgecombe Avenue. His name: W. E. B. Du Bois. The glow in his eyes continues as he relates to me the story of another famous person and how while hospitalized he'd met his wife - a white nurse. I'd wanted to ask him more about Paul Robeson but I didn't dare interrupt him as his conversation changed slightly to include the first school in America. Built and founded by Libyans in the Second

Century. And then of the King from the Kingdom of Mali who, having abdicated his throne there, set sail for these shores, arriving with a flotilla of 1,000 boats. Shades of Ivan Van Sertima and "They Came Before Columbus." Alas, before I could ask questions the gentleman informed me that he was off to the Chinese Restaurant on the corner. It seems he wanted to get there before the menu changed for the day.

As he walked away, leaving me to ponder this new information, I am jolted by the spectacle of a police van parked near the Dawn Hotel. There has been a drug bust and the van is being filled with several handcuffed young men and women. I watch with curiosity and as I look closer at the young people being herded into the van I am struck by their expressionless faces. The faces, matched only by the business as usual attitude of the police officers speaks volumes about how far we've come since the days when teachers such as Du Bois used their spacious abodes to bring wisdom and knowledge to a struggling populace on Sugar Hill. One by one, all of the old grand structures that line St. Nicholas, Edgecombe, Eighth and Bradhurst Avenues have witnessed the scourge of heroin, cocaine and weed. Of course, the young don't remember. And most are too busy to care but there are still many of the 50 plus group who know the truth. They and their parents had once been proud to live in buildings once occupied by the likes of Cab Calloway and Bo Jangles, Duke Ellington, Thurgood Marshall, Ruth Brown, and so many other well-known Black Americans. The list of the greats who lived on Sugar Hill is endless.

As a young person I can remember driving through 145th Street and being shown the building where the legendary singer Dinah Washington had been a resident. She's been dead for decades and her name is still the first that arises by residents of the area whenever the building 345 is mentioned. But it all came screeching to a halt sometime in the 1960's. At least that is the period that I hear most often referred to. Now, even much lesser known personalities steer clear of the place once referred to as "Sugar Hill".

The only sugar remaining here is that of the processed cane variety that is sold in the local delis and where the shopkeepers shamelessly change prices from one customer to the next. When they are caught they simply smile and say, "thank you, brother." It's an old game but they get away with the disarming ploy. At least for the moment. Much to the chagrin of the diminishing Black American population who are old enough to remember the hay days when every store was not immigrant owned. Blacks own few businesses here now unless one counts the illegal drugs. And even here there is territorial infringement of a sort. Even so, there are enough clients to go around as all street drugs are here -in abundance. They are, to borrow a street term, represented. In fact, there are so many small time pushers on Sugar Hill that even during the daylight hours it is difficult to walk the streets along St. Nicolas Avenue from 145th to 155th Streets without passing half dozen. And just in case you miss them in the street you will rub elbows with one or two as they, fresh from delivering drugs to home-bound customers enter or exit buildings. They are not difficult to spot. Their faces and their routes are well known even to the disinterested. Even during a visit to the local laundromat one can, between wash and dry witness several money and drug exchanges taking place right in the open area next to the door and the plate glass window. One brazen drug client, instead of placing his newly acquired drugs in his sock dropped the plastic baggie on the floor and walked out only to return a few minutes later to find it lying where it had fallen. Without a word or look around he picked up his errant goods and walked out again. A few of the sellers are no more than hold- over's from the 1980's and 90's. At least one I hear has simply inherited the family business from his father and I suspect there are other such infamous examples.

Many are no longer young and except for the revolving door of the criminal justice system, they've been around doing the same thing since they were little more than teenagers. Perhaps this is the reason that most of them are respected and liked in the community. They still strut around like the two dollar drug pimps they are. Balding, graying and losing teeth. They dress and behave as if they're still eighteen years old. Despoiling the innocence of the current crop of young people in any way they can. This usually means by enticing the young men into the local drug business and raping the young women of their bodies through drug addiction or the promise of new clothes and/or a fist full of dollars. Still, in this way, they are no worse than the old men who sit around drinking alcohol, smoking marijuana and cigarettes and chugging beer all day long. Tongues hanging, eyes bulging, heads turning and making senseless comments about every female who passes within 50 feet. Some of the younger women live for the "check" days of these old men. The first day of the month never coming fast enough; when money flows as freely as the alcohol these men consume. For the most part it's all about dreams for the older men. And chasing women is mostly about the hunt. There is little action. Never have so few, done so little, to so many!

Besides the many folks who have left willingly, so many others have simply died. Most people I speak with have lost count of their personal and casual tragedies. Almost as a past - time activity the older folks sit around bemoaning the passing of a friend or colleague they've known for decades and the younger people give memorial parties. Parties that go on for hours and into the wee hours of the morning. These parties leave the park strewn with pounds and pounds of garbage. Trash, empty beer cans and bottles and of course the omnipresent liquor bottles. The cigar tobacco is poignant reminder of the marijuana smoke blown into the air like dissipated lives. Here, just like in so many once predominant African American Communities across the city H.I.V. and A.I.D.S. have taken its toll. Amid the myriad other sicknesses such as diabetes, hypertension, heart disease and stroke are added alcoholism, drug addiction and violence. It has thinned the population. I am surprised by the numbers of young people walking with canes and what by what seems to my untrained eye more than a small number of mentally challenged people. All have linked arms with hopelessness, sheer exhaustion, broken spirits and again -drugs. So much promise thrown to the ground like the pink rose petals of the Carefree Roses that now lie trampled on the flagstones of Donnellan Square.

It was spring again and the roses were in the fullness of bloom. Sitting there on one of the fourteen benches that line the park of less than a third of an acre; I try to imagine how proud the residents of 150th Street and St. Nicholas Avenue must have been the day of the inauguration ceremonies. I will later be told by a resident that the ceremony took place at the 149th Street entrance to the park. There were probably local and state dignitaries present. Perhaps a representative from the Veteran's Administration. Certainly someone from the Park's Department. Someone always comes from that Agency to claim a share of the credit but they're never present to take responsibility for the lack of maintenance. My thought that maybe long- time and legendary Congressman Charles Rangel was here or perhaps even one of the speakers on that day persisted for only a brief period. I spoke with a man who was present. He quickly debunked that notion, looking at me with a smirk on his face he simply said, "Oh, he didn't show. He never shows." But he added quickly that there were indeed other politicians present including a Congressman from Brooklyn. I didn't press him further about the red carpet crowd who'd come for the little park's dedication. Preferring in some foolish way to construct my own imaginary list which included a representative from Governor's Office and one from the Mayor's Mansion. The Mayor's commitment is not respected very much in this part of town - although his wealth is often the topic of admiration. Incredibly, people here say he's planning to run again for office in three years. To bend the rules one last time and with his dollars, make a mockery of the democratic election process. Of course I have no records or information to prove my little flights of fantasy and few of the older people I talk with on later occasions can remember that day. None are aware of the bronze plaque that hangs on the north façade proclaiming the existence of the man for whom the park was named: Private First Class Timothy Donnellan, the Irish Immigrant born in 1895. A war casualty at 21, the memorial pays homage to the ultimate sacrifice he paid for his adopted country. It is not to take anything away from the man when residents shrug their shoulders or place tongue -in- cheek when his name is mentioned. They simply don't make the connection if there is one to make. Did the man reside in Harlem at some point in his short life? Or did he have relatives here? I look for something to hang my hat on and I dream on.

At the inauguration someone probably ventured that the reconstruction of the park symbolized hope, achievement, sacrifice and dedication. Peering out of the windows of the buildings that line St. Nicholas Avenue people must have looked out over the dignitaries and the bunting. They surely applauded as they listened to the litany of kind words and superlatives used to describe Donnellan. There was and is no question that the man was a hero and this small expression was one more token of a city's gratitude. One final way to say thanks for a job well done and to mark forever a spot for Pfc. Timothy Donnellan as a New Yorker of great distinction and honor. Of course, these are only my imaginations. The truth is that in the coming days I will hear a much different version of the feelings of the residents about the upgrading of the park. Knowing the wisdom and the caution that is ingrained in my people the facts are probably somewhere in between. I will hear from a few who were here on that day what most were thinking as they looked south beyond 149th Street or even north to 155th.

To begin with there were many who felt that there was nothing wrong with the old park that stood at this spot. The old park sat on an embankment that required users to climb 4 steps to reach it. There was an old mountain of a tree that sat in the center of the park and reminded folks of the old tree in the yard when they were kids in the south or of pictures they'd seen of outdoor gatherings in Africa: always under a huge shade tree. There were smaller trees too and more grass. And tables where men played cards, checkers and chess. Their bottoms plastered to flat red painted benches, they held their drinks and sipped them in an upright position without spillage. Old timers remember and are quick to point out that the old seats were more comfortable than today's high-backed replacements. I get the point that despite the violence that occasionally erupted there the old park was a comfortable and welcoming place for anyone. Anyone looking for shade in summer or just company year- round.

No one denies that there were drugs but a new square would not change this. It simply gave the dealers a more uncomfortable place to sit while they transacted their business. It also gave them an edge when it came to getting away from the police. The park was open without the encumbrance of an iron fence. They could see the cops before they themselves were spotted. One gentleman I spoke with said that back then he always knew where to find his father. His dad could be located in the old park drinking beer or wine with his friends. A newer park would not alter his dad's beer drinking habit either. Only death would bring this pattern to a final halt. Secondly, few kind words could have been spared to give justice to the despair most knew lurked there in silence. The redundant cycle of desperation that loitered in the lobbies and spilled out onto the sidewalks of the very buildings they inhabited, polluting their kids and their kid's kids. But equally disappointing was the feeling that they had once again been sold out. Not to discredit Pfc. Donnellan in any way but many were asking the question. Who is he? Unhappy with the answer, they asked another. With all the Black veteran soldiers of wars, couldn't they find a black face to give honor to in this small park smack in the middle of Harlem? Someone, somewhere had no doubt cut a deal. That was the talk then and the questions still persist. There are no answers and probably will never be. I am reminded briefly of the monument of England's Black Prince of the tumultuous 14th Century in Canterbury Cathedral proclaiming to posterity and succeeding generations of visitors: "Such as thou art, so once was I, as I am now, so shalt thou be."

But all of that was then, June 2002. This is now, June, 2010 and nothing has changed. At least not for the betterment of the park. Most residents call the park by a new moniker - 'dirty park'. Only eight years since the place was completed and already it looks as though it is a relic from another age. It may as well have been constructed the year Pfc. Donnellan was killed in battle. Back then, the country and most of Europe were engaged in WWI. The war to end all wars. It was a noble idea and an even nobler effort. Yet, some six or seven wars, and many conflicts later, the world is still waiting. Waiting and counting, wars haven't ended in the world; they've increased in number if that is possible. Only now they're not always referred to as wars. They are civil disobediences or conflicts, sometimes disagreement and uprisings. Even worse, here at home in the U.S. we have yet to begin fully recognizing that there are multiple social wars to be waged. Perhaps it's the same in most other so-called capitalist's nations of the First World. I wonder what Donnellan would think about that if he were still alive. I wonder if he'd even care. I mean of course, about the wars that need to be fought here in the Black community of Harlem, New York where he is immortalized. After all, he was Irish American and at the time of his death there were few Blacks in Harlem. Almost certainly none in the 165th Division in which he fought. For a moment my own thoughts return to the photograph of my own grandfather. Dressed in a WWI Army uniform, he stands looking into eternity from behind the glass frame that sat on the mantle in his dining room. I wonder if he saw action in any of the battles. Or, as a Black soldier, if he was allowed to do anything more that menial chores. Had he even gone abroad? My grandmother claimed he hadn't although he disputed her most vehemently.

One thing I know for certain, others followed him into the military. His sons, and grandsons, his grand -daughter and great grandsons and daughters. Even myself. All serving honorably.

Although I spent the least amount of time in uniform. One of his sons Carroll, mysteriously died while a soldier, and my namesake, his great grandson, Maurice Keith Fortune was killed in a road-side explosion in Iraq. A young man I'd never had an opportunity to meet. He left behind a young wife and an unborn child. He'd never see that child grow to become an adult, never hear her laughter. At least he won't hurt. There are much sadder prospects for his child: she'll never know him! The war to end all wars. Indeed!

I sat scolding myself for thinking these thoughts. You are, after all, not an historian or a scholar, I admonished myself. Not by any stretch. In fact, I chided. You are only just beginning to put thoughts to paper and you're not sure you are doing that much right. It was true. I could deny neither. But there is one thing of which I am certain. The Carefree Roses planted in Donnellan Square eight short years ago are no longer carefree. They are dying and they need attention. And the roses, as real and in need of proper care as they are, simply stand as a metaphor for the real victims on Sugar Hill. Even to a novice such as I, this is not a difficult thing to see. Planted behind the hedges, they were intended to grow for decades. To fade in winter and to reappear with the renewal of nature each spring. I doubt it was ever intended that they should struggle for that survival. Even to suggest that premise would be wrong. I am no horticulturist, but I suppose someone could extend the life of the roses and the yews. My thoughts return momentarily to long ago on Maryland's Eastern Shore. Back to the stretch of property owned and cultivated by my maternal grandfather. He grew roses of different varieties. More than a few bushes lined the 100 ft. wire fence of the property. As a young person I paid little attention to the beautiful red, pink and white flowers. There were large ones and smaller ones. Even a few bushes of medium size planted around the house. There were lots of other flowers too. I couldn't be blamed for not noticing anything special about the roses. Saving their fragrance, perhaps the most significant thing about them was the abundance of bumble bees and yellow jackets their sweet nectar never failed to attract. More than any of the other flowers, to touch a rose meant that one risked getting pricked by the thorns or stung for the effort. Moreover, it was always taken for granted that the roses would appear each May or June to bring their special perfumes to the road known as Pine Lane. Papa would do his share to see that they did just that. He tended them. He pruned the bushes and the trees on his land with expertise. Such things have a way of clinging to one's inner soul and I knew instinctively that although the arms of the spruce tree could benefit from this simple act of kindness, this alone could not now help the roses. But without help they will never fulfill the task for which they were planted. The sad fact is that they are being out-muscled here in the little garden and only re-planting and relocation will help them. Maybe a few of them can stay on if only to bring a hint of color and soul to the place, but not in the numbers that were once intended.

That is the predicament in which the roses now find themselves and it is the way things seem to be moving for the other group here on Sugar Hill. The situation is almost identical to the one facing so many Black American residents of the area. They won't tell this to a white face but they grumble loudly about it among themselves on the street, in their homes, or as they sit along the benches of the Jackie Robinson Park on Edgecombe Avenue. I've heard the same argument made in other areas of the city where I have lived or visited but this time things seem especially poignant. Someone once said that you know things are bad when even the young begin to complain that nothing is the same as it once was. Here, in Donnellan Square, even teenagers pine for the way we were. Some of the older residents and people who come to sit in the square blame it on the influx of white people into the area. I've heard it more than once. As nice as the renovation and reconstruction of the area has been many preferred things the way they used to be. "When we could sit here in the park and roll our reefers and drink our liquor without intervention even from the police cars riding past." Before the presence of white faces changed things and in most cases ruined the fun." I listen, taking it all in with the proverbial grain of salt. Something inside tells me that the 'fun' was ruined long before the whites started moving back to The Hill. Not that there aren't lots of whites here now.

Some estimates put the figure at about one third the present population. Some residents claim that as the Blacks are willingly or forcibly removed from their dwellings some unscrupulous landlords clandestinely rent to whites only, or to an oriental, if a white occupant is not forthcoming. Mixed gay couples seem popular with the building owners. There is the notion that they can pay the exorbitant rent and besides, they never complain. How farcical! But these groups appear to go about their business unimpeded and disinterested. They seem friendly enough and the several religious sects that are present also make an effort to be friendly with their neighbors. That is, those neighbors who are not put off by the dress codes of the various sects. The black trousers and white shirts of one such sect are out of touch and as they walk by in small groups they almost shout out to all they pass, "Yes we're here but don't draw too near." But I suppose their attire is no more out- dated than that of the sect whose women wear the traditional long dresses that were popular in the 1940's and 50's. I can't help thinking that if they ever hope to make converts here among this population of flesh-baring souls and three inch heels they're going to need Divine intervention. But even I admit that the group I witnessed sitting on the stoop outside their mission building were an attractive lot. Not to be outdone, there are plenty of sidewalk ministers here among our own people. It is not unusual to be asked to be prayed for while sitting on a bench in the little park. Or, to find oneself engaged in conversation about the meaning of sin, who and what is the devil, God's plan and if the earth is coming to an end. More often it is a woman who does the conversion or the praying. One woman I saw praying for someone spoke in tongues and laid her hands on the forehead of the sinner as she prayed. She then asked him for a donation and as he walked away she ran after him explaining that she couldn't allow evil people to walk in front of her as she'd just witnessed a family of immigrants do. She then crossed in front of the sinner leaving him and I bewildered. Walking the streets of Sugar Hill one can feel the tension permeating the air. It is a kind of cornucopia of people and cultures. All of them struggling to get to know one another without getting to know one other's customs and ways. To be fair, they haven't had much time to do it. It has come upon everyone with the suddenness of an earthquake or a summer storm. Although the handwriting has been on the wall for years no one thought it would happen in their life time. No one really thought whites would ever return to Harlem in these numbers and to their credit everyone has made an effort to adjust. But it is a modus vivendi brought on by necessity and most of the Black residents feel they are being out-numbered, out-spent and squeezed out by landlords and by the new flux of immigrants pouring into the area. We own few store front businesses, where once we were proprietors of many. Our people complain about the prices, but still patronize the many stores owned by those who don't live in the community. They take the money and they call us "brother' nowadays. Sometimes an irate patron will balk at the exorbitant prices or the pervasive practice of charging a different price every day for the same article. Sometimes it depends on which 'brother' takes your charge. The shopkeepers do whatever they can to make a few extra cents by cheating customers here and there and if they are challenged or caught they'll laugh good naturedly but unabashed and correct themselves. They know that at the end of the day they'll get paid and flee the scene.

Still complaining, most residents vow to hold on to the old and occasionally remodeled apartments some have lived in for decades or at least have been in their families for that long. They reach out to the city and state agencies for help. SCRIE and Section 8 or Human Resources. But these agencies have become so huge that they've outgrown their ability to offer much help. Not to diminish the good they've done but in the current climate of financial despair there is simply not enough money to go around to fund them.

There is a backlog and a waiting list of years. Some hopefuls will tell you they've been waiting for affordable housing or to get into an apartment in 'the projects' for more than five years. For the moment they will tell you that the application process for Section 8 is frozen. It's no wonder. So many applicants. So few resources. By law these agencies must help ALL the city's residents and with the new influx of people moving to Harlem: immigrants from the four corners of the world …well, by definition, the Black Americans lose.

Despite the foul odor that seems to seep from the flagstone floor, on this day the park is full. At least the area that is furthest northwest or at the main entrance to the square. In early afternoon it is the only spot that is not drenched in sunlight and everyone wants to sit here. But there is a price to pay for this small comfort zone. The tree top here is the afternoon habitat of sparrows that apparently have not yet been toilet trained. Although the flash rain that fell the day before lasted more than an hour was at times torrential it seems to have made things worse. It is more humid and the square stinks to high heavens. Taking a seat on one of the shaded benches I look around at the faces of my bench friends. This is a term I've picked up in the few days I've been coming here. I use it, but it doesn't quite fit. It's uncomfortable: like the infamous O.J. Simpson glove.

There are a few old ladies, one in a wheel chair is an ex-professional singer I hear and as many older men watching their watches and looking bored. There are at least two home care attendants. The wheel chair bound woman is toothless and wise, and although she must take dialysis treatments three times a week she seems strong enough for her age. I laugh when I hear her say she doesn't desire a man in her life. She is stage 2 diabetic but she says the doctor has not begun to give her medication for this illness. Originally from somewhere in Alabama, she's lived a full life that she is by no means shy to speak of to anyone who will take time to listen. I take time to listen as she speaks of her youth and of course of the way things used to be here in the park before the makeover.

Before "they" started to come to Harlem. It is not difficult to figure out who "they" are. Others sit talking about the problem of their grand kids and anything else they can think to gossip about. It's a routine they will repeat day after day. There are three homeless men here today. I've never seen this in the park. At least not so many in a group and I turn my attention to them when I hear one of the older women mention that a huge Black man has been asleep since 8 a.m. She knows this because it was the time she left her apartment to go to the mailbox at the corner. Her story is backed up immediately by someone else who saw the man asleep as she walked her dog. Just then a police officer walks through and nudges the sleeping giant at the shoulder. "Get up buddy," he says. "You can't stretch out like that here." The cop is the first I've ever seen in the park and he looks almost apologetic for his intrusion.

He waits until the man sits up and moves on. All eyes follow him with anathema as he leaves walking with the familiar saunter that is trademark for New York City Police Officers and with his departure most of us get a good look at the indigent who moments before had been sleeping as though he hadn't a care in the world. Only then I see just how large the sleeping giant really is: about 6 feet 3 inches tall, with a huge belly and a short beard. About 40 years old, he has a shock of jet black hair to be envied by anyone balding such as me. The hair looks as if it hasn't been combed in weeks and I watch as this goliath silently gathers his shopping cart and three bags. Slowly, he shuffles off in his shower 'flip-flops'. He is supported by a cane. One look at his feet makes me wonder how he manages to walk at all. They resemble the feet of a child's doll. They are swollen and have the look of dark brown plastic. The nails are thick and yellow: the telltale sign of onychomycosis. It is a common infection.

As soon as the coast is clear of police intervention one of the other two homeless men begins to empty a large black garbage bag. He has a sweat suit and an extra-large T-shirt that he hands to his friend. "Here," he tells him. "Take it man." I note that the sweat suit is colorful and it looks new. The T-shirt still has a price tag which the man peels away. It drops to the ground. "It's nice but it's hot as hell," his friend tells him. "You can wear it in the evening, when it gets cool." His friend replies. The man nods and continues emptying the bag of other goods which he places on the iron raining between our two benches. "They're wet and they need air," he explains to me without looking up. I can see that these too are new clothes and are meant to be worn by a female. There are two pairs of pants and a blouse of sorts. The goods have obviously been stolen from a clothing store and I conclude that the two men are boosters. The younger man also is a drug user: probably heroin. He takes his time removing the filthy socks he is wearing and hangs them on the fence behind him. It is then that I notice his pants are rolled up to the knee. The left leg is heavily bandaged and the injury appears to be severe. After a few minutes he turns to his friend and asks for money. But the friend is reluctant to give it so he says rather tartly, "I can't keep doing this- begging you for money, you want to pay for everything but if I had my own money I you wouldn't have to." I watch as his friend digs into his pocket and unravels a small wad of paper bills. He then turns to his left to offer the money but his companion is reluctant to take it. Apparently it is not enough. I count two twenty dollar bills and a few fives but I turn my head quickly, trying not to be too observant and when I look again it is just in time to see the first man counting. He has in his hand a ten dollar bill and three or four one dollar bills. Although he seems dissatisfied, he puts the money inside the bandages on his leg.

My thoughts are momentarily interrupted by the presence of a cat. It's an adult female and she appears from behind the curtain of bushes and trees that lead to the street. Walking cautiously toward the iron railings that ring the memorial which is meant to be the centerpiece of the square she stops for an instant, peering into the labyrinth of yews and rose bushes. Then, spotting something, she disappears behind the screen of foliage.

I wait for her to reappear but she takes her time, remaining inside the bush stalking her prey. Perhaps she's found something or someone to eat I surmise. In another 10 minutes or so she reappears. Hesitating, she looks at me with deliberation. Her green eyes are as clear. They appear as beautiful as they have ever been. She is dirty. It is undignified of her and she appears abashed by this lapse of proper hygiene. I pretend not to notice her discomfort but it isn't easy. Long ago she'd been abandoned by someone unwilling or unable to continue her upkeep. She purrs, and she seemed to be trying to explain herself. As if it is a requirement that she offer me her excuses. Then, satisfied that I've forgiven her present condition as an alley cat she walks on. I was momentarily transfixed by her decorum. Dirty or not she has lost none of her elegance and with defiance she walks with the gait of her royal ancestors.

Her coat is multi-colored with a mixture of gold, white and grey fur. It resembles a tiny patch-work quilt someone has taken great pains to design. On any other creature her colors would be almost comical or cruel. But the head of gold with the spot of dark ash on the crown is rivaled only by a magnificent stripped ash tail. These marry well with the golden splashes of fur on both hips and legs of snow white. It seemed an intentional design created to mimic the makeup of the immigrant community in which she now finds herself a chief resident. No painter could have dreamt her up. She looks around her for a long moment before proceeding to the other side of the square. Here she repeats her disappearing act among the trees and bushes. I can see that this is all a part of her daily routine and that she makes her rounds this way a few times during the day and night. I wait once more for her reappearance.

It is almost thirty minutes later that I hear something in the bushes behind my bench. Turning to my right I look into the slanted eyes of the cat. She is holding something in her mouth and it looked like the remains of a half-eaten mouse. She could have gone the other way around. It would have been easy to leave the park without me noticing. But I think she wanted me to see, needed me to take note that despite her slightly unkempt appearance, she had lost none of her independence or her regality. "You see sir," she seemed to say, "I can fend for myself quite well. I am not a beggar." I take note. I notice something else too. Something I hadn't seen from a distance. There is the clear imprint of unborn youngsters showing through her belly. She is to become a mother.

I watch the cat as she crosses the street negotiating the traffic as only a seasoned veteran of the city can do and after she is of sight I sit there for a long time taking in my surroundings. The place is filthy. I hadn't noticed before just how bad it was but my eyes now focus on an ant crawling along the flagstone with a bit of food in its mandible. The insect almost blends in with the grey and the filth, and I am sure it is not intentional. I next notice the dozens of cigarette butts littering the ground. They have all been smoked down to the filter save one or two. Thinking of those television ads showing the faces and limbs of habitual smokers, I shudder. My father had died of lung cancer and for a moment I recalled years before his death how apologetic he'd been just sitting in the front seat of my car between me and a friend. He'd said he could smell the cigarette smoke emanating from his pores. To my nose, he just smelled like my dad and I didn't mind at all. But he was embarrassed. Uncannily, my friend would also die of lung cancer. He'd been a smoker too.

As bad as they were, cigarette butts were not the only remains being left behind in the Square. There were dozens of cans and bottles pushed under the benches. Newspapers and candy wrappers, Styrofoam containers from Chinese Restaurants, pizza boxes, junk food wrappers and boxes. All just lying there beneath the benches, pushed in corners, spilling over the tops of the two garbage cans and sprawled precariously on the only available spots of grass. To make matters worse, the same kind of trash appeared in abundance under the trees. Except here, the worse was saved for last. These places were reserved as a garbage dump for dozens of beer bottles, Red Bull beer cans and of course adding insult to injury: tiny plastic baggies and used condoms.

A city park; there are at least two signs. Both indicating that the park is open from 9 am to 9 pm. But the printed list of don'ts go largely ignored. I suppose the rules are difficult to enforce. It is something the residents and users of the square must do for themselves. No amount of policing can save a public area from carelessness and neglect. The city seems to have given up trying. Maybe because there are too many 'don'ts' on the list and not a single 'do'. Like, 'do remember that the proper maintenance of the park is ultimately the responsibility of all residents who use it.'

It is obvious that there had been no garbage collection or cleanup in days: maybe even weeks.

But it was refreshing to find that I was not the only one taking note. Sitting there I listened to the conversation of two 40 something males as they passed through the square. "They need to do something about this place," one said. "Clean it up or something," The other man replied, "it's not the cleaning up! That's not the problem. These (N's) ought to stop throwing this shit all over the place like they is home!"

I am sure that many such comments were being made by well-meaning folks as they walked through or around the Square.

Good people, kind people, people with the most honorable intentions who would remember how things used to be here or certainly ought to be. Unfortunately, playing the blame game never gets anything accomplished. More than a few times I had been told years earlier by a dear friend: "let's talk solutions!" It took me a minute to get the meaning of her words but I finally understood.

But I still wasn't getting all of it. I was new to the area and though I took in the meaning of the blight I was stubbornly of the mindset that the park was only being used for what I considered good purposes. Used by the kids I saw playing tag as they chased one another around the circle of the memorial or sat at their mother's knee. That is was being used by the young girl I saw playing on the hopscotch squares and as she skipped behind her mother as she wheeled an infant through the center of the square.

Even by the boys of 8 or 10 years old I watched riding their scooters and skate boards. One foot on the ride and the other pumping furiously, propelling them faster and faster along. There were old timers on the benches drinking beer and chatting. Gossiping about everything and yet nothing in particular. Even wheel chair bound people out for fresh air with their mostly bored and disgruntled home attendants. I would be jolted out of my lapse into naiveté by the sudden appearance of the drug men. Of course, I said to myself. Why hadn't I assumed this from the very start?

This place is also a haven for the small time drug lords of the area. Suddenly a fish out of water, I felt foolishly out of my element and I rose to remedy my situation. Making my exit, I crossed the avenue with the nagging feeling that I needed to do something. But what could I do. I could do nothing about the drugs and alcohol use going on there, and I wouldn't even try. Yet, I felt I needed to make a statement: however small. I passed in front of the once majestic Dawn Hotel. The fresh coat of paint over its fine lime stone and natural red brick façade as well as the outer wall of its enclosed garden is almost criminal and deserving of corporal punishment if not of water torture. The once elegant building has again become victim of cheap hardware store paint probably purchased at ten dollars the gallon. And yet even dirty and tattered, her aging green canopy running nearly twenty-five feet from door to street is still an imposing sight. It accomplishes the drop-down of the last two flights in graceful style. I count 16 stairs and remark to myself how well the canopy marries with the faded green window awnings peeking between tree leaves from two of the Hotel's windows along the east side of St. Nicholas Place. Neglected or not The Dawn is still a beautiful place. Is it any wonder that rumor says it was recently purchased by the Russians? Or that the magnificent Bailey House across the street was bought by an Oriental Family for the paltry sum of three million dollars? They say The Bailey will now become a bed and breakfast. I also hear that the handwriting is already on the wall for the occupants of the Dawn which currently houses homeless families.

Turning once more to witness the going's on in the Square my eyes make full contact with a young woman dressed in blue sweats.

Like many others in the city she's adopted the swagger and the demeanor of a teenaged male. Even the pants are worn too low on her hips. Except she has taken things to the extreme and with her underpants showing boldly her entire derriere is on display. Even in this she is in uniform. Her men's Hanes underwear are navy blue. I would see her many times in the coming days on my visits to the park and learn the sad truth. She is a drug seller and a whore.

Whore, a lesbian to be sure but a whore nonetheless and she knows the value of the female anatomy in this neighborhood. The fact that she is different is for her a good selling point and a plus. I'm not shocked by this revelation as I've seen her kind before in Harlem -ten blocks down, twenty years ago. The beautiful young woman and mother of a young son eventually died of A.I.D.S.

The lesbian / prostitute has attracted the attention of someone else. He is a regular here and I've seen his face before. A kindly person, he seems to go out of his way to say hello to me and I invite him to sit and talk. It is only as we talk that I recognize the unmistakable signs that he has been the victim of a stroke. He makes an attempt to apologize for his slurred speech but I wave him off. "You don't have to be sorry. I understand you quite well." With this he relaxes and tells me that although he still has trouble talking and walking, he is doing much better than only a few months ago when he could do neither. He is about 67 years old and married. He and his wife live in the neighborhood and he comes to the dirty park (his words), every day. As a former truck driver, he is used to doing things on his own and he hopes to be able to drive himself from New York to Amarillo, Texas very soon. I find myself silently betting that he'll do it. But on this day he appears a bit weak. Suddenly, he spots a group of teenage boys. "I don't trust these kids," he says. "They'll rob you in a heartbeat." Then turning to look me in the eye he says, "Why do you think I keep this cane with me?" It is a loaded question and although I want to reply that he needs the cane to help him walk, I refrain from saying it. Instead, I nod in agreement, indicating that I understand what he means.

Somehow, taking all this in was more than I could stomach on this day and even though I was new in the area, I felt it was my duty to do something about it. Not that I had ever before done anything as bold as what I was now contemplating. In fact, I felt I was almost being intrusive. Living in the area for less than a year, I only knew a handful of people well enough to say hello or give a nod. It didn't help that I had never been a very outgoing person. I was friendly enough and if someone wanted to talk I was always willing to give them an ear or to exchange views. I could also be depended on to give a hand to a stranger. Whatever that meant. But this was another matter. This involved action. The kind of action that was going to attract attention however much I didn't want it. I asked myself the same questions I was almost certain to hear from the mouths of my new neighbors. Who the heck are you to take matters into your hands and to change things around? These things that have been the same for years and nobody has complained. Now, here you go wanting to shake things up. Well, no one asked you to interfere, sir. Toi, on ne t'as pas sonee.

I sat there imagining all sorts of responses to the action I was contemplating. Maybe they'd be right. Maybe I had no business putting in my two cents, so to speak. I'll try letting it rest for the night. Perhaps, if I sleep on it things will right themselves tomorrow. Let's see if the Sanitation Department comes roaring in like the Cavalry in one of those old western films. And if not, then I'll ask some of the area residents for their input. Or, even their assistance. Together, we could do something. Anything to bring a halt to the murder. To end what everyone around certainly know is going on.

I walked back to the apartment with these thoughts running through my head. I hadn't really decided if I would go ahead with the plan. After all, I told myself. You don't have the equipment, and there are things you are going to need. Eventually you will have to enlist the help of someone. "Good evening ladies," I say as I approach the stoop. Two busy bodies who live in the building are sitting gossiping distributing the latest news. Well, I say to myself. Busy bodies have their good side. They know everything there is to know about this place, I'll ask them. Ladies, I begin meekly, what time does the super usually clean the building in the morning?" Both women looked at me as though I was a talking cow. Then one snickered and replied in a snide way. "Clean what?" "Oh, clean the building and the stoop," I answer. I didn't back down, wanting to let them know I was serious. "I was wondering if he'd let me use a broom and pan. Maybe he'd give me a couple of large garbage bags." "What on earth do you want with those things," one of them asked me in a shocked tone? I didn't hesitate to reply. "I want to clean up the park. You know the little park in the street, up on the hill?" They both laughed and gave a mocked sigh of relief. "Oh, you had us worried for a second. I thought you were talking about that big-assed place across the street. She pointed to the rather massive park known as The Jackie Robinson Park and located just in front of the building. "I knew you hadn't lost your mind." I let them get a good chuckle out of it, joining in the merriment of the moment before I continued. "I just left the place and it's really dirty and nasty.

I hate sitting around in all that filth and since it's a secluded spot and otherwise quiet, it's a nice place to hang out." "You mean, sometimes," one of the women almost yelled at me! "Yeah," the other dead –panned. "And when you finish cleaning it up the dope pushers and the junkies and whores will come right back there and run your behind all the way back down here to Edgecombe." Neither of us said anything for a few seconds but I finally broke the silence. "Well, I'll cross that bridge when I get to it," I said. "No one knows when the sanitation department is coming to do the job so I thought I would just do it and save them the trouble." "Why, don't you call 311 or just meet the truck in the morning. I'm sure they will be happy to give you something to do the job. No sense asking this super, he won't help unless you intend to clean this building and make life easier for him." The ladies threw back their heads and enjoyed another roar but this time I didn't join in. I thanked them for the information and stepped between the small spaces they gave me to climb the three or four steps as I entered the building. "Thanks again for the information ladies and good night to you both," I called. Using my key to unlock the lock I pushed open the heavy glass and metal door. For once the lock wasn't broken and I stepped quickly into the hallway. I was happy to hear the door slam behind me closing out the sound of the idle and malicious chatter that I knew would now continue about me. I was glad to be out of their sight but I knew I wouldn't be out of their minds and off their tongues for a few hours. It'll give them something else to do with their lives as they enjoy a few laughs at my expense, I thought. Uncaring, I walked the single flight of stairs to the apartment.

To be honest, I spent a restless night. A 'motus animi continuus', an uninterrupted motion of thought where, according to the Greek philosopher Cicero, eloquence resides. After a sleepless night of tossing and turning on my little cot I dragged my exhausted body to a sitting position. I had decided that what I had in mind needed to be done. At first I thought of asking family or neighbors for help. Anyone who could tell me where to locate a few necessary materials would do just fine. But when I opened the bedroom door to announce my plans to my brother and his wife, I discovered that they had already left for the Laundromat. Well, I couldn't just take their broom and go off to the park to clean and I wouldn't have money to purchase one for another three or four days. Deciding that things couldn't wait until then I dressed and went out into the morning sun.

It was a glorious morning. The buildings along Edgecombe face east and at ten in the morning only the trees along the park front offer any shade and relief from the blinding sunlight. After a long winter and a very wet and cool spring; the warmth of the sun in early June was welcome and much anticipated. Wasting no time, I headed for St. Nicholas Avenue, hoping that on the way I'd gather enough courage to ask someone to borrow a broom and a pan and maybe a few large black garbage bags.

I could promise to repay the loan in a few days. Surely, I'd see the superintendent of one of the buildings as he washed down the sidewalk with a water hose or stood idly outside. But I didn't see a soul. Not one person. My second plan of action included asking one of the local merchants for assistance. After all, they had businesses here. Certainly they would help. I'd try the Food Town Supermarket, or the Sugar Hill Pharmacy. There was a beauty salon, a dry cleaners and at least half a dozen mom and pop stores in the area. I looked across the street at the once proud Jazz Club- the St. Nick's, its doors closed for the holiday or for vacation. Once there were a half dozen or more such bars in the area. Some of them had live music too. Their names are legendary but they fled during the years of wide- spread crack cocaine usage. Too much violence, the real jazz lovers were afraid to patronize them. I hear there is great music still being played at the St. Nick Pub by some really talented jazz men and women. But even here there is the rumor of open drug sales and usage and the joint is now only a shell of its former self. Blocking the entrance to the club was a painter. He was engaged at his work as he talked to the familiar figure of a neighborhood, a drug pusher seated on the curb next to him. Losing courage I looked about me. Whom could I ask for assistance? Someone had to help. And maybe they would have if I had only the balls to ask. I had taken the precaution of bringing with me two pairs of plastic gloves. The kind that somehow never fit but manage to find themselves included in the box of hair coloring. Now, my nerve having failed, I was resigned to my only remaining choice. I would have to go it alone. It isn't as bad as all that I said to myself. Alone, I've done worse cleaning jobs many times. When an employee of my small business didn't show up for work or got sick on the job or when I was obliged to fire someone on the spot, I'd had to step in an do the work. I used to tell myself in those times that the show must go on, and that I am my own best worker.

I could do this job, collect the garbage or pile it in a corner, and then call 311 to insist on a city trash collection. There! I said as headed toward Donnellan Square. When others see what I'm doing, they'll come in hordes to help. They'll ride in from all directions. Just like in the movies. Right?"

I walked to 149th Street. Crossing at the cross walk, I entered the park from this vantage point.

Whew! I caught my breath and sucked in air. Damn! I said aloud. I should have said it again. I was totally unprepared for what I now saw. There was garbage everywhere. Beer bottles and cans. Empty quarts of Hennessey Cognac, Bacardi Rum and cheap wine. The kind of wine that has sent many drinkers to an early grave with liver or stomach cancers. Just like the Boone Farm, Ripple Wine and even the cheap Pink Champale that I drank as young man in the bars on 125th Street and that I'd hear the park's old-timers speak of on another day. They too had known friends who'd drunk the stuff back in the 1960's. Most of them were now long dead, they'd tell me. And not to be outdone, cigarette containers of every description littered the walkway and the corners of the small enclosure - green and white boxes of the Newport variety- shorts and longs.

Here, like everywhere else in our communities, Newport Cigarettes have a lock on the market. They are the kings of lung destruction. For years, I had refused to smoke this brand. I had foolishly insisted on Marlboro's. They were after all a 'man's' cigarette. I finally got the message when I realized one day that it was becoming more and more difficult to walk up the slight incline to the main avenue. I took the cigarettes from my shirt pocket and tossed them into the nearest trash can and I haven't had the desire to smoke one since. But that was me, I couldn't expect everyone to do this. I was just plain lucky. Here, twenty years later, I stood in the center of the park taking in this impossible scene. On a bench, in the middle of it all, lay a homeless man, sleeping as if an infant. Shoeless, one lone stockinged foot exposing an enormous big dirty toe.

Defeated, I walked the distance of the park, and sat on one of the benches at the foot of the memorial.

I sat there for four hours. Convincing myself over and over that one person CAN make a difference.

If only we are willing to do the work. If only we'd reach out to others for assistance. Ask, interact, and hope and pray. Go kicking and don't go quietly. Make noise, let the world know what's going on here. This is our space. We must confront those who are hell-bent on their modern version of Manifest Destiny. For we are the Carefree Roses and will not be ousted by the upright Yews and the Norwegian Spruces of the world. But first we have to right our own wrongs. Cleanse our own houses and do our own culling. Great words but no action from me on this day. As the Bible says, "Faith without works is dead." As I turned and walked back down the hill, I had to admit that I was not the one to clean Donnellan Square on this day or on any other day. I have plenty of faith but this, even I had to admit was too much work to do.

Although I vowed to stay away from the park, it holds a kind of morbid fascination for me. It's like that for others too I suspect, for we keep coming back. There are other parks around that we could visit. Convent Garden or Park is just 2 blocks north on St. Nicholas Avenue. I hear it is well kept. Cleaned by the mysterious woman who single-handedly ran all the drug dealers out- rumor has it. It is also fenced in and shaded. And even though Jackie Robinson Park lies just one block away on Edgecombe Avenue. It's a clean place, too. There are plenty of shade trees and rocks. There is also the Jackie Robinson swimming pool. It's a humongous work, about a hundred feet. It looks clean too although I hear that things sometimes get out of hand there and the Parks Department will shut it down without a second thought for the crying youngsters seeking relief from the sweltering summer heat. There are benches there with lots of seating and anyone who doesn't want to walk down the several flights of stairs from Edgecombe Avenue can enter the park from the main entrance on Bradhurst Avenue. It seems safe enough. As safe as any park in the city. Even though I have stood at the top of the park along Edgecombe Avenue and witnessed more than once, young men sniffing drugs and rolling "blunts" as they sat on the rocks just forty feet beneath me. Oblivious to my presence just above them, they looked around believing themselves hidden by the thick overgrowth of trees and bushes. How foolish. On one side there are several basketball courts where kids practice 'ballin' year 'round. Someone says it is the spill over home of the annual world famous Rucker's tournament, and that it is used as a practice field for participants of the league. It's a nice rumor but no one I talk with can verify this.

What is clear is that it sports an open-air stage for performances, lots of benches beneath fifty foot trees that act as shelter from the afternoon sun. In the heat of the summer, the swimming pool draws lines of people young and old. The markings announce that it's 3 ft. 6 inches all around and deep enough for the young to dive. To be sure, Jackie Robinson Park is a big place. But maybe that is what is wrong with it. It lacks the warmth and the coziness of Donnellan Square. For all its vastness this place seems devoid of soul, and so unlike my image of the man for whom it is named.

Like the other returnees to the square, I am back yet another day. It's a cloud filled day. There's been the threat of rain since morning.

But just when it appears the deluge will come, the sun breaks through bathing us in generous doses of vitamin D. There is much talk today about the murder that took place one block down on St. Nicholas Avenue. Slowly, I piece together the story. The rather sad tale of another young life who had the good sense to walk away from the chaos but the bad judgment to return. No doubt an effort to prove his manhood maybe it was a necessary thing to do. To return to face his tormentors and to have done otherwise would have meant a loss of prestige and shame. Whatever, it was all a moot point. He had chosen the honorable option and paid the ultimate price for his decision. Now there would be only the outline of the police chalk to mark the spot where he'd fallen and maybe a few candles or a bouquet of flowers. Sometimes a dear friend will bring a drink of liquor or a bit of marijuana to sprinkle over the drying blood but it will all wash away with the next rain fall.

I am struck by the appearance of the young men. A few of years ago the youth seemed of much larger builds.

Now they are almost skinny. They appear leaner and sometimes much meaner. Maybe it's the clothes they are almost wearing. They are not the triple X white T's or the baggy trousers that were the rage back in the day. They call anything older than yesterday back in the day. It's hard to tell that they are meaner too because they're quick to smile. Quick to say thank you and Sir. I know it's mostly a ruse. Their rage has been turned inward and replaced by four- letter words. Even the youngest use them. Toss them about easily. As if they were peanuts being fed to the legions of pigeons and sparrows always present here, forever scavenging and begging for crumbs or anything edible.

I can't help noticing too, the young women. They are fiercely independent but they seem desperate to out-do the fellows in their rage and in their talk. Even in their non-dress, see-thru net tops. Their almost bare breasts and low rise pants have replaced the warm coats and hoodies necessary only a couple of weeks ago. Bare stomachs, bare bottoms squeezed into trousers and short skirts. Everything on display: light skin, dark skin, white skin. The colors that now reflect the multi-national flags present on the Hill.

There are lots of openly gay people in the community. Lesbians and gays, young and old, black, brown and white. Perhaps there are more in the city, or even in the country. Maybe even in the world.

They seem at ease and accepted here. Nobody ever notices them except a few folks who make it a point to continue referring to gay men in derogatory terms. Most will be the first to tell you of the gay people they've known in their lives. Of a gay relative of a next door neighbor. One lady is proud of her brother's photograph. In it he is seated in a tree swing. His legs are crossed like Elizabeth Taylor in a scene from "Cat on a Hot Tin Roof" and he is wearing a dress from those times. She also speaks of a grand daughter who is a lesbian and currently living with her partner somewhere in New Jersey. And of her godson. Even in these times it is not difficult to see that old habits die hard and whenever I listen to her I always think of the once -used phrase: "some of my best friends are Black". Here in Harlem 2010, emboldened by the new laws permitting domestic partnership arrangements and marriages, LGBT's revel in these new-found freedoms of expression. But they must be careful, tenuous freedoms can be snatched from one like soiled clothes from a laundry hamper. Sorted through for the cleanest to be shaken, pressed and worn yet another day. Not recyclable, the dirtiest go back in the hamper. There's a flip side to the slogan, Don't Ask, Don't Tell. It is simply Don't Tell, Don't Ask'!

Three or four times a day people gather in small groups. Not to be too conspicuous they talk on the cell phones or make light conversation with one another. With others in the park one has to look closely to see that these are not here for an outing. Regulars, many are known only by their faces or by the buildings they live in. They mill about in separate groups. Separate but equal in their hunt for drugs. They wait for the drug lord's arrival. And he never disappoints. Almost like clockwork he shows up. For this visit to the office he is accompanied by one of his 'hoes'. She's the flavor of the hour and she trails behind him like one of the several leashed pit bulls that are half dragged into the square. Massive animals, looking dangerous but un-muzzled, their owners delight in repeating to anyone who'll listen that his dog is a killer. That the dog, usually a male, has killed several other pit bulls in fights.

The drug seller and his woman are on foot, and the woman looks at him with a jealous eye as he chats on the latest cell phone gadget. It's always the latest one. The phone with the most features. Features that are never used and sometimes not understood. Years ago he'd have been the cause of much joking. No king pin ever went anywhere without his 'ride.' This crop of dealers don't make enough money to afford the expensive cars and life style of the old-timers. Somehow I can't help thinking that there must be an easier way of making a living than the long hours they can be seen standing and walking the streets in an unending search for drug buying customers. They can occasionally be seen walking with their women to and from the area super markets and 99 cent stores. Even struggling with bags of purchased goods like the bargain sales of 10 rolls of paper towels -too big to fit into today's small plastic grocery bags. It's just as well, stripped of all their valuables, the old-timers now languish in prisons across the country.

On this day in Donnellan Square, his audience of regulars wait patiently for the end of their patron's telephone conversation. But he answers another yet urgent call. "Yo," he calls into the mouth piece. "What up?" Then, "Whereyouat?" Moving out of ear shot it's another ten minutes before he's done with his call. It's like this with the dealers - incessant talk on the cell phones. Ceaseless chatter.

Now, finally, he is about business and after a couple of nods he walks through the park and down the block to his office. From having seen him there on several occasions I know his office is the left hand side of the food counter in a restaurant. Apparently it's a space he shares with others in the business and it is a good spot. Standing there one has the advantage of looking in all directions and staying just out of the arms of the law. Everyone knows the rules. He goes in to prepare the sale. Then, taking it from the stash he keeps in his underpants, and beneath his testicles, he exchanges the 'product' for money. The sale over, he waits for the next customer.

His clients know what to expect. Not to 'play' him too closely, and to give him space to look around for any hint of police presence. If they forget they are sharply and roundly reminded. It's impossible to imagine that the restaurant owners and workers don't know what is going on here.

Back in the park I keep a not too watchful eye on the other visitors. No one seems to tarry here. Except maybe the old. Like the young, some come here to smoke marijuana. But as bad as the habit has become among young people there is something inherently vulgar about an old pot head smoking in public. It seems to say that they've decided not to grow up; that they are willing to pass along their habit and the disdain they have for themselves to those around them.

They go about their business pretending to be unmindful of the goings on around them. But it is all show. They know very well what is happening in the park and most of the old men and some of the women are willing participants. Except for the dyed-in-the-wool reefer smokers, the business of the older men seems to be drink. Liquor and beer. Drink is still their drug of choice, and they come prepared with cups and ice. It's mostly rum chased with a Coke or Pepsi. They keep the liquor hidden in the bags and pass the cup to their friend, hiding it from the prying eyes of the law and from their wives at home. They ignore their body's warning signs of impending danger until it's too late. The tell-tale signs of sclerosis. Many of them have been in the neighborhood for years. Some of them have been here all of their lives. They've grown up and old here. There's a running joke they tell about a friend who appeared healthy one day and showed up the next day with an incredibly extended stomach. "He looked like he was about to have twins and in a few days he was dead," they laugh. "He couldn't even see his shoes beneath him."

They look older than their years. Fifty-two looking sixty-two, sixty-five looking seventy-five. Walking with canes and telling stories of the hard lives they've lived here. It is a tale of street life and they have the scars to prove it. There are stories of multiple surgeries and strokes. An occasional heart attack or gunshot /knife wound. All of the stories are told with just a hint of braggadocio. The scars are worn like medals of Honor from long fought battles and in a way I suppose it is appropriate. But as sad as the tales may be and as frightening, they never seem to have been severe enough to deter them from a life of excess. On this day I am to be treated to a blatant display of disrespect. As two elderly women look on two men in their sixties take a seat on the bench across from us. As they speak, one of them takes out a small package, pinches something between his thumb and fore finger and puts it to his nose where he begins to sniff. He then offers the package to his companion and the act is repeated. It's not difficult to conclude that it is cocaine or a least a mixture of heroin and cocaine. It was the drug of their own heyday and they have never outgrown or kicked this habit. The two women look away and I drop my eyes when the offenders look at me with staring eyes that say in no uncertain terms: f….you! But this is, I suppose, an integral part of human nature: that somehow we never get over the habits of our younger days. As George W. Bush once put it, we always "Dance with the one that brung us."

We also dance with something else. The search that goes on 24/7. Meaning the search for sex. Sex and more sex and the talk of it is the fuel which drives some and propels even the infirm. Young women, not so young women and even the used women.

They pass them around like one of their reefers smoked too short to hold between the thumb and the forefinger. As long as they can get something out of a woman she is a commodity.

I sit listening as one of the part-time dealers talks of pension checks and S.S. I. checks. He admonishes one of his clients for not having had the good sense to open a direct deposit account. "It takes too long for the 'shit 'to come in the mail, he tells the man. Another customer is called stupid for losing his eligibility for S.S.I. "What? You gave up seven hundred a month just because you were too lazy to get up and go to the meeting,"? He further chastises the younger man, "all you had to do was get your ass up and go down there. You didn't have to give up the drugs. It don't matter if your urine was dirty. Dirty urine is what got you there in the first place, you dumb f.... You better not ask me for shit!" But even the offender knows that money is the name of the game here and he will get what he wants as long as there is even a remote chance that he can pay it back. Even if that means with his food stamp allotment. These people are blood suckers. They lend money to the others for profit. They never lend too much. Just enough to purchase another drink. Enough to buy a deli sandwich and soda or a beer. Sometimes they'll lend a woman money and when she can't pay, they will demand their due in sexual favors. The lenders always feel themselves a cut above the others. They look down on the loud mouths and the drunks. Although they never seem to notice that they are as vulgar as everyone else. I give them credit for not wanting to draw attention from passers-by or from the cops. The false pride and 'dignity' that they reserve makes them shy away from anything and anyone who might get them picked up in a sting or handcuffed to one of the rails that line the benches as is sometimes done by the police department. They never consider that true dignity would have long ago driven them from their persistent ways.

It's getting late in the afternoon. I peer at the time on my phone and see that it's 4:05 pm. It still hasn't rained and the sun has forced its way through to shine on the square once more. Just then a group of young, school kids, backpacks strapped to their shoulders come through from 149th Street. Probably on their way home they talk loudly. All are forced to walk with legs spread wide. It's the only way they can keep their trousers from falling to the ground. They stop and ask an older man for a cigarette and he gives them one. It's a Newport 100. What else? I nearly speak out loud.

The young child is there again. I'd seen her there with her mother earlier in the day. She's about six years old and she whines that she wants candy. Her mother scolds her and reminds her that the ice cream she's eating was her choice. Her mother refuses to give her a portion of her own candy, potato chips (two bags) and soda. "I bought these for myself," she screams at the little girl. For a moment my thoughts are glued to the little child and I wonder what kind of life she faces. Her skin is almost chalk white. Her mother is the shade of a medium cup of coffee. Unfairly, I can't quite shake the feeling that she reminds me of a seasoned street walker. I have no proof of this and I feel ashamed. But it is easy to tell that the mother was once a very pretty woman. She is now bordering obesity and her mouth is awash with vulgarities of every genre. She must have been a stunner, I say to myself. At least until the ravages of a hard life took control. For a second or two my mind returns to a classic movie - it starred Lana Turner and Sandra Dee. There was a Black actress in the film who nearly stole the show and of course the incredible voice of Mahalia Jackson. Now that was a real tear-jerker. But I can't remember the name of either the film or the Black woman who played the part of the distraught mother. Only that it was a remake of an earlier film named "Pinkie."

I am watching this mother and child and I can see that the child seems oddly out of place here. Even among her little playmates, she is standoffish and different. Her mother has dressed her in a long dress, as if to maximize that difference. Other than that, the woman doesn't seem to notice the child's discomfort. She is too pre-occupied with her excesses: the street life, too much candy, potato chips, and Chinese food. Too many high fructose sugary soft drinks. Between the foul languages she uses to address her daughter she calls out to two older women sitting near me. "Hi, my park bench friends, nice to see you." They answer her and continue their conversation.

I wonder what kind of life the kid will have. It's appears no secret that her mother is a prostitute. There is a peculiar look. Like recycled jeans in a clothing store. No matter how many times they are cleaned or how many shiny new labels are pinned to them they always look used and washed out. But will this little girl follow in her mother's footsteps. Living just out of reach of danger and disease. Violence and drugs. I cringe as I think of my own god daughter. Just 15 years old and driven from her mother's place in the Bronx. "Go live with your brother," her mother yelled at her. It developed that the mother wanted to rent the child's room to a stranger. Probably to pay for an ongoing drug habit for herself and her newest boyfriend. The 4th or 5th boyfriend in as many years. People are hurting everywhere. Desperate to make money on the backs of even their most cherished friends and loved ones. Even the ones they are duty-bound to protect. Thinking about the situation of my god daughter jolts my memory and I recall at least half of the riddle. The name of the film is, "Imitation of Life." It's a damn good title for the movie, I decide. I still wish I could remember the name of the actress who turned in such a great performance as the mother and housekeeper.

I see again the friend who seeks me out whenever he comes to the park. Indeed he claims he comes here only with the hope of chatting with me. I know it's a lie but I indulge him because he has something to say that my own eyes could never see. He lives in the neighborhood and he too has a story to tell. He is a stroke victim. He says he had three just last year and had to face a couple of spinal taps as well. To make matters worse he has lupus. Although he claims it is not serious. I don't consider lupus non-threatening. My sister died of lupus complications. But I say nothing more on the subject.

As we talk he mentions to me that he is an early riser and often takes a walk at 4 a.m. He insists that the walk is only for exercise purposes but I don't believe him. My doubt grows as he mentions almost as an afterthought that there are gangs in the park at that time of the morning. Especially when the weather is hot and humid. "The bloods and the Cripps are here almost every night," he says. "But I ain't afraid of them. That's the worst thing you can do, show fear." He then mentions that I should come out at that time of the morning and witness first-hand the shenanigans that play out in the park at that hour of the day. It's an offer I have no hesitation about declining. Moreover, he tells me that the surrounding streets in the area are often full at that time of the morning. "There are as many people out and about at 4 a.m. as there are at 4 p.m.," he says. "In fact, the only creatures more numerous than humans at that time of the morning are the rats." "The RATS," I say in disbelief! "Yes," he echoes, "I'm not joking, they overwhelm this dirty place." Given, the garbage here, I don't know why I am surprised but somehow I had never even considered it. He also mentions that there is a cat that dwells somewhere in the undergrowth of the shrubbery. He can't see the animal but it makes a lot of noise. Silently, I hope it's not my cat he speaks of. He claims that people come out to the park at that time of the morning because they have no air conditioning in their rooms and apartments. I doubt this is the case but again, I don't offer any comment. We talk further and he relates that he too is concerned about the amount of violence in this neighborhood. It's the kind of stuff that never makes the news and that most people are unaware of.

"Just two nights ago I was stopped by a plain clothes policeman. It was 5 a.m. and he asked to see my identity. Apparently there were two separate shootings that took place on 148th Street. One between Convent and Amsterdam and the other on Amsterdam Avenue. "One of the victims died and I don't know if the other lived," he told me. He then mentioned that there was a fight in the building where he is a resident. The trouble began when the co-op owners began making unreasonable demands from the renters. Of course, the co-op owners are mostly white. In the end, the Manager of the building was physically assaulted. It was just another example of the turmoil here on Sugar Hill only this time modus Vivendi was cast aside in favor of the area's own special brand of modus operandi.

It suddenly occurs to me that I've forgotten something. I have been here a number of times and each time I forget to check the roses. Do Carefree Roses have thorns? I don't have a clue but I need to know. If they do it might explain why they are so tenaciously holding on to everything around them. I decide to check as I leave the park but as I begin gathering my few possessions an expectant mother enters and sits beside me. She has a black bag containing half a watermelon which she begins digging into with a plastic spoon.

She is well acquainted with the mother of the 5 or 6 year old child and as they talk another woman enters the park with her child of the same age. They are all friends and before I know it another woman has arrived with a little girl. As the kids play and share goodies, one of the mother's sends to the store for more food. Junk food to be certain but soon there is a little party going on. It's refreshing to see and I sit just a bit longer, taking in the little drama. The mother who was so abusive to her child only minutes earlier is now doting on her and giving her all the attention a child deserves. And the little girl is radiant again.

Hope, I say to myself. There is hope here and even the half eaten watermelon that the woman tosses over her shoulder and into the bushes can't dim that hope. It's in stark contrast to the Mexican couple who have finished eating their melon and taken its remains to one of the overflowing garbage cans. Nor can the sight of the man sitting a little farther down from me. I've seen him on the street several times and I am almost certain he is a drug runner. His face wears the tell-tale sign of H.I.V. infection and anyone who has seen this killer disease up close and personal will spot the overly pink lips and the far and distant look in the eyes. I'm not surprised, like many of the young here, there is little knowledge or respect for communicable diseases- A.I.D.S. included. Still, he wears his age well and it is difficult to tell if he's in his thirties or early forties. His expression is pained and even the latest sportswear and gold chains can't mask the obvious.

He has the thinnest legs I've ever seen on anyone who wasn't hospitalized. Still, hope is omnipresent and even the sight of another small time drug dealer digging into his underwear can't dim it. "Product," the client asks? He doesn't reply as he exchanges his marijuana for dollars. A couple walk through pushing their shopping cart as though it's a baby carriage. The cart is filled with cans and bottles peering from the top of blue recycling bags and black can liners. These are the bottle collectors and people move aside for them so that they can ply their trade. Lifting their legs and allowing the man to search under the benches. It's the same thing they do for the other scavengers in the park. The flying rats: the pigeons. But it's growing late now and I'm both thirsty and tired. I rise from the bench to make my exit to the chorus of idle chatter.

The late hour is punctuated by laughter and the squeals of the four kids playing. Innocents. Oblivious to the symphony of ugly words spewing from the mouths of men and women alike, young and old. Niggers, bitches and mother-fuckers are thrown gleefully about. Words that if spoken in my youth, would have earned the offender an invitation to do battle or worse, a trip to the hospital or morgue. But that was far in the distant past and now alcohol, drugs, and the infidelities of both women and men are usually not enough to unleash the rages that lie just beneath the surface of the skin. The rage is still alive and well. It just takes something more to provoke people to let it fly. I think once more of "All God's Children". Of Fox Butterfield's book.

Just before I leave the little park I walk to the other end. I've noticed that there are other roses planted here. Not much care seems to have been taken to provide a place for them and they appear to be almost an afterthought; late arrivals who just made it in the gate. But they too are Carefree Roses and I liken them to the newly arriving African immigrants. Uncertain, still not fully integrated with the others: aloof and clinging to the old ways, the old languages - yet unable to block exposure to the new. Unable to shield themselves or to prevent contamination of their young to the new found American ways, or the seepages of the vulgarities and bad habits. Of course some are not aware that their separation from the original Blacks in the area only serves as a catalyst for further exclusion. Many of the older Blacks feel that they have something to hide or that they feel themselves superior. I've heard said, "When I go to 125th Street, I see 'them' gathered about in groups whispering and speaking their language. It takes only a few minutes to set the record straight. "Let me ask you a question," I respond. "If you were in a foreign country, could not yet speak the language, had no friends and with limited movement, who would you speak with?" Most would have to admit that they've never given it a thought. Never thought it possible that people from another land might be simply terrified. Still, some of the immigrants have other issues too. This includes a distrust of Blacks Americans. They don't understand them either and when I feel like it I do a little prying of my own.

Occasionally, I speak to them in French and having a decent history with certain groups it is not difficult to get from them they are not certain where things are going here or even "back home' on the African Continent where they sometimes feel as distant to the countries surrounding them as they do here. Some of the English speaking countries regard Nigeria as a country that is wasting its natural resources and as a joke. I try to point out that they are all young and newly independent nations, still flexing their muscles. I wonder if my argument that it took Great Britain hundreds of years to develop into a mighty power and that it could be argued that she too wasted her resources has any effect upon my friends. They do seem to get it whenever I mention that the United States just celebrated her bi-centennial a few years back and that there are problems here too. I can understand their quandary. Try as they might to separate themselves and their young it is only a matter of time. Familiarity breeds contempt is only a saying. Soon it will be forgotten amid the more potent forces of sex and drugs and indoctrination. I head for the other end of the Square to make my exit.

As I walk past the memorial I thrust my fingers into the maze, wondering how many more days the sagging roses will last. I feel nothing at first and I am almost disappointed. But I catch a stem between my forefingers and thumb and I squeeze. Feeling the sting of the thorn I withdraw my hand quickly, almost happy that there's a spot of blood trickling from my forefinger. Carefree Roses have thorns!

They have the weapons necessary for the fight. Maybe it's what the square's designer Gail Wittner was trying to say all along. Perhaps she knew that Carefree Roses would find a way to survive somehow, someway. I leave the park at 6 pm. thinking that I'll come no more. I don't want to be here for the Final curtain call of the roses. I've never been a big fan of funerals.

As much as I try to avoid it, I find myself drawn by the magic circus of the little park. I listen to the stories of the old people and I watch the faces and the body language of the youth. There are lots of youngsters here and as the weather grows warmer hey appear more bold and dangerous. I group them according to age and it is easy to see that the young are the most violent prone. They haven't yet learned to be cautious or afraid. Not even of death, although it is always a threat here. There is always talk of someone who was shot, stabbed or beaten. On this day I am driven from my seat on the bench by four 14 to 17 year olds. Not because they are a menace to me but because they seem to have forgotten that pants are meant be worn and tied at the hip by a belt. One young man takes a seat only inches from where I sit speaking on my cell phone. His rear end propped against the iron fence near the top of my head. I don't want to show fear but I reconsider quickly when I realize that people in passing cars behind us would find this a comical sight. I pretend to be searching for something in my pocket and leave him to continue his conversation with his friends. The conversation that is fraught with foul language and talk of violence, death and sex. The conversation that is punctuated by a single expression at the end of each sentence, "my nigger!" Although I leave the park and walk quickly to the deli for a cool drink, I return in a few minutes. Happily, I note that the group has left the park as well. But I will see them passing later- their numbers swollen to seven. I will see several such groups in the street as the days pass. The 18 to 21 year olds and the 22 to 26 year olds. After 26 there seems to be no inclination to hang about in groups although the older men still gather for other reasons.

Before I leave the park I sit listening intently as two older men engage in their favorite conversation: the past. Rumor is rife here on Sugar Hill and these two are full of them.

They speak of an underground "C" train exit that runs beneath Bailey House on the corner of 150th Street and St. Nicholas Avenue. It is supposedly an emergency exit from the subway tunnel below and it was open until twenty years ago or so. More importantly, ostensibly this subway stop served as a quick getaway for German spies who used Bailey House as a strategic meeting place back during the Second World War. I place this rumor along with the others: that a disgraced and jailed former drug lord cut the potency of his drugs with some mysterious and deadly substance. That he, having been released from jail is in a witness protection program and has had numerous operations to make himself over into a female.

I listen a little closer when the older of the two men says he has multiple sclerosis. He speaks of remembering a Sugar Hill that in the 1980's resembled the wild- wild West. The residents here could expect to wake any night to the sound of gunfire. It was, he said, impossible to leave one's apartment building without stepping over dozens of shell casings on the sidewalks. These were the days of crack cocaine and crack wars and his stories are believable. Not because I want to trust his accounts but because I have been told the same thing by so many other people living in so many other sections of the City. And today, I make my final exit when I hear that part of the historical significance of Sugar Hill is not that it once housed blacks who lived the "sweet life" but that Sugar Hill was the last place in New York City where slavery was abolished. It's a fantastic story and I make a note to check it out.

I come each day. Only to keep vigil with the roses. They are dying now. Roses die a slow death. Sometimes, I bring a sandwich or a snack to the wake. Sitting in the sun makes a soul hungry and a famished mind can wander. There are others here too but they don't seem to notice me. Nor I them. I am present and alone in the park one Sunday afternoon when an elderly lady walks through. We nod and she walks on but only seconds later I hear a voice crying, "Please help me, please." I look up to see that the woman has fallen between the benches not twenty feet from where I am seated. I rush to her aid and then, remembering my first aid training I tell her not to move. "Don't try to get up, I say to her softly, and she nods in agreement. Quickly I dial 911 for assistance and after the usual question and answer session that seems to take forever I ask her a few questions of my own. Taking off my light coat and placing it around her to keep off the unusual afternoon chill I discover that she is about 85 years old and a resident of the area for many decades. She lives alone without family and no friends to speak of. She was on her way to purchase her Sunday newspaper and suddenly felt ill. Perhaps it was the medicine she'd been taking for pain, although she couldn't remember why the doctor had prescribed it. I stayed with her until the ambulance arrived and then went across the street and purchased the newspaper for her. The paramedics thought there was more to the story than she was able to remember and took her to the hospital. I never saw her again although I often wonder what became of her.

One thoughtless and selfish woman shows up every afternoon with a tiny pair of shears. She clips a small bouquet of the precious and dying flowers. "No one else wants them," she offers as a poor excuse to anyone who's listening. She doesn't understand that she is defiling a memorial. Although occasionally she'll get a scowl or an audible "Humph" from an older visitor to the place. But she ignores the affront and continues her destruction. Then, she shuffles off to one of the buildings on the west side of the avenue. There's an old man here too. I heard him say one day that it's a crying shame how fast the park went down. It used to be so nice. When they first 'did' it. Before all the barbecuing and the hoodlums took it over. I looked at the old eyes, glassed over now with the tell-tale signs of cataracts. One of the scourges of aging. Will I have them too, someday? I must force myself to look at the roses. I already see death in their faces. Most of them have already dropped their heads and are desperately leaning on the shoulders of their more hardy companions. And the hardiest try to offer one last gasp of support. They don't want to be disrespectful but they know that it is only a matter of a few short days before they too will lean. Their faces will fall on the heads of the poisonous upright Yews or at the feet of the mighty Norwegian Spruce. Those who do not lean will die where they stand. Their petals turning brown and flaky. Defiant to the end, they will not bend their heads. It is true that although heroes die on their feet, they die nonetheless. Soon, only two will stand alone in the garden among the tangled web of the vines. Maybe this year, the community will decorate the Spruce at Christmas time. It won't matter to the roses for they will not be there.

But come spring the roses will try once more to gain control of their space. They'll scratch and claw and climb half way to the sky on the back of the spruce tree. They'll greet their only friend: the green-eyed and graceful pussycat. Maybe she will bring her new litter of kittens to say hello to the newly born crop of roses. They'll ignore the poisons of the Yews and the blue handled shears of the thoughtless woman. I have no doubt that the roses will return for yet another spring and the one after that and for several years to come. These roses will probably out-live many of the residents of the community. Even the transient ones like me. But like the community around her, the open question is: will the roses live or die? Will they not return one such spring? It's almost a certainty that eventually they will be outnumbered and out-muscled. There will always be someone selfish to despoil them and cull their numbers.

But they must survive here. Not because of what they have or have not been given. Not because of the past but because of the future. Not because of Cab Calloway and Thurgood Marshall or Jackie Robinson or Bill "Bojangles" Robinson. Not even because of the memorial to the WWI hero Timothy Donnellan.

They must survive here because of what they are: Carefree Roses!

Epilogue

It's Monday, the 7th of June 2010. It was not my intention to sit in Donnellan Square today. At least not consciously. For one thing the weather can't seem to make up its mind if it will rain or let the brilliance of this day in June shine through. It vacillates between a sun that is almost unpleasantly warm and the dark storm clouds that roll past high in the sky like precursors of doom. As I walk home from the subway and enter the square from the 149th Street side, I am met by the sight of death. All of the roses planted here are now nothing more than dried petals on the vines. There is not the hint of a living flower. Sadly, even in this state they have not been left to their dignity. Someone has thoughtlessly thrown a half-eaten round metal container of takeout food on the ground and directly under the bushes. There is an almost empty garbage can not 12 feet away. It's upsetting but I continue walking through the park. Except for the local one-time prize fighter who has stretched himself on one of the benches, the place is deserted. Continuing to the other end and to the memorial I am surprised to see signs of life among the roses here. More than just a few of the bushes and stems are clinging to the last gasps of life. So many of their colleagues have died to be sure but there is still life here and it's good to see a lone yellow jacket buzzing from flower to flower and the single white butterfly that cannot seem to make up its mind which flower to drink from at this late lunch period. I sit alone and watch the comings and goings of the day. It's a lazy afternoon.

Not many people are in the street and it takes a half hour before a few begin to trickle in to fill a bench or two. There's an older man and he's soon joined by his girlfriend. She's a much younger woman. Two boys of six or seven years, dressed in the black trousers and white shirts and the ties that are mandatory wear in public schools walk through. The uniforms are a great idea, meant to inspire discipline in the kids. But nothing can stop the barrage of naughty words flowing from their mouths - bitches, mother's, and kiss this or that! But they are young and they move through quickly. Back packs swinging as they go. I recognize the faces of two women. They are representatives of the Jehovah Witness Sect and they come to the house often to study the Bible. They sit in the sun just in front of me, and as they do, a rather tall man with a barrel and hairy chest gets up from one of the benches. He's been sunning himself, and he doesn't bother to put his shirt on until one of the men in the square call out to him to cover himself. All eyes in the square are drawn to him in mock disbelief. He pulls his pants down to tuck his shirt inside and displays his totally bare rear end. It is a gesture he delights in and the meaning is clear. He's spoiling for a fight and with a menacing look he waits for further comment. But no one says anything more. Instead, embarrassed and appalled eyes roll toward the ground or in any direction away from the spectacle. Mercifully, he exits the park, turning to give one last threatening stare. As if to spare us all from bodily harm. For a moment there is a strange silence here. It's refreshing for nothing anyone could say will explained away this act of ignorance and disrespect. Then, almost on cue, the air is pierced by the sounds of sirens and wheels as a fire truck and an ambulance come roaring to a halt in front of The Dawn Hotel. There's been some kind of emergency there and we all watch as the firemen from truck number 84 and paramedics from ambulance number 036 jump out of their vehicles with equipment in hand and race up the long stairs and into the doors of the Dawn. But it's just another day on Sugar Hill and something is always happening on the Hill. I sit there long enough to see two more familiar faces. Once again I see the mother of the little fair complexioned girl but today she is alone and she is walking with the support of a cane. She looks better than I've seen her, almost pretty. But she is eating as usual. Still stuffing her face and her body. I also see my cat. But the cat doesn't enter the park. Something in the street attracts its attention and she races under a car and out of sight for a few minutes. When she emerges she walks in the direction of the hotel. Too bad she didn't come to the park today, I say to myself. She'd have found it clean and swept clear of all except one empty can of orange Fanta soda, a single Newport cigarette butt and an empty pint bottle of Wild Irish Rose wine - flavor unknown. The sanitation department has finally done its job, and the place looks almost immaculate.

There's a brother approaching me and he tries to make conversation. "You live 'round here long," he inquires? I answer that I've been here for about a year but that I don't know the area very well. I'm staying another two weeks with my brother and his wife and then I'm moving on, I tell him? I hope this will be enough to discourage him from further conversation but I am wrong. He continues. "Where you from, Maryland?" He has guessed correctly and I admit that I am indeed from Maryland. I don't mention that I haven't lived there in many years but I tell him I am familiar with the name of a town he mentions.

I say I went to grade school and high school in Maryland so it's not a lie. The town he speaks of is in the north near Annapolis I recall. Then, he says something remarkable. "You a writer, or something? You look like you write books and shit," he says, in a matter-of- fact way. Then, he adds that I look like that guy who wrote a lot of books back in the 50's and 60's. He can't recall his name and so I chime in, "do you mean Jimmy Baldwin?" "Yes, yes," he declares. "That's him. Now that was a smart dude." I know that his comparison is a lie and that he knows I look nothing like James Baldwin

But I am curious as to how he guessed I was a writer. I don't ask him any questions about it and his conversation turns to the church across the street. He is talking about the large structure named Bailey House and as we both look in that direction he mentions that it was on the television news just the evening before. He'd watched the coverage as the reporter spoke of the landmark significance of the building and the fact that it is being restored to its former glory. "It's about time, "he adds. "But our people won't be around here once it's completed. You notice how the whites are moving back to Harlem," he asks? They been coming back for a long time. "They tired of living in Jersey." He shakes his head sadly as he continues. "Our people don't even realize how they is pushing us out. All they got to do is keep raising the rent. How we gonna pay two or three thousand a month?" "I wish I could write books," he says unexpectedly. The comment almost catches me off guard but I recover quickly enough to say. "You'd be surprised what you can accomplish if you try." I observe him as he looks off in the distance and says quietly, "I'm not stupid but I can't write." He is almost apologetic and I wish I could say something more to encourage him but I realize it would be false of me. I let it hang and it's only a few seconds before his attention is diverted to one of the women walking past. He tries to talk to her but she ignores him and he takes affront to her attitude. "See how our women are, "he asks me? But I won't bite. I let him continue with his put- downs for a few seconds more and I am rewarded by my silence when another man approaches us and the two begin a conversation that excludes me. I am excluded but I sit there listening with both ears. Incredibly, the stranger has lived and worked in the Annapolis, Maryland area. His family he says owned a home there a few years ago. And the two of them have something else in common. Both men grew up in the Bronx within walking distance of one another. One man is 54 years old and the other just turned 50. I listen intently as the two men discuss the current situation in the neighborhood and in Harlem. They reminisce of the old days on 125th Street. Of A. J. Lester's clothing store, Florsheims and Stacey Adams. Of cheap meat markets and the old fish store with the tank in the window. I am tempted tell them that I was part owner of that fish market, and that I went each day to purchase the fresh fish. That eventually we bought the meat market next door and that I purchased the goods for that store.

Me, with the big ideas. The visions that my people would break the doors down purchasing the fresh fish and gourmet meats/foods that I brought to 125th Street: the expensive cuts of salami, sausages, Virginia hams and the like. Tell them of my extreme disappointment when the customers didn't come. Of, when I was forced to eat crow, and listen to the ridicule of my partners and their untrue and hate-filled words: that I was expecting too much from my people. And finally of how I agonized over the decision to sell the stores for a fraction of the cost. My long hours and labors wasted. My hopes of providing people with different choices, all dashed. I suppose I never once considered that it had all been done before. It is like that for the young. They like to believe that their every thought and idea is a new and un-charted course. Yes, I'd wanted to say to them that I too have dreams of a Harlem I once knew - however briefly - but I say nothing. I just sit there and listen in muted disbelief of their ignorance. What would have been accomplished by my utterances?

I could have put in my two cents but I kept my tongue and I remained silent. Old memories are sometimes better kept in silence. As the two of them talked it became apparent that the first man was drinking heavily from a bag containing several small bottles of alcohol. Nips, they call them and I recognize the brand by its black label: it was the indomitable Black Velvet Canadian whiskey. He was, by most standards practically drunk. The second man was not interested in alcohol. He wanted to buy marijuana but no one showed up to sell any. The two strangers spoke of the decline and fall of Harlem and I couldn't help noticing that they were only talking of the last twenty-five or thirty years. But even more important is the fact that they were not talking about the economic boon that the area has witnessed in recent years. No sane person can deny that there has been tremendous growth here. Like so many others who were around to see it they were speaking of the absence of an all-Black Harlem. "It's just not the same anymore," they lament. They spoke of many other things, most of them negative. The wild days of crack in the 1980's. The crack dens where one of the men said he witnessed several bodies. They had either been killed there or died and cemented into the walls to avoid detection by the authorities. It is an incredible story but I have heard it before and I can't help believing him. It is not much different from that of the ex-valet of a famous singer who it was rumored once asked an acquaintance of mine to help him cut up the body of a young man and when he was refused, did the gruesome work himself. Of course, no one knew for sure if this was true until after his own death and during demolition a body was discovered behind a false wall in a closet of the apartment. I was horrified when I realized that I had spoken on the telephone with the perpetrator at least once and only fate intervened to keep me from attending a party in his apartment.

These were the times when special names were given to street drugs - Panamanian Red and Turkey Black. But they spoke too of the good things that made Harlem- Harlem. The abundant night life, the old Apollo Theatre. And the bars- The Top Club is mentioned several times along with the Baby Grand. There is laughter as they joke about two gay bars that were once on the street. So many gay people trying to get inside that they spilled out onto the curb and partied outside until they could get a spot at a table. It was sad to hear them speaking of the past as though they were old men. These two young people, both in their early fifties. Both of them retired (although one man said he wanted to go back to work). The other mentioned that he receives a social security check on the 3rd of each month. He seemed content with that fact of his life. He said it several times, as though once a month he collected a fortune.

It's a strange afternoon and for a moment all eyes are drawn to a single white man in the park. He is about 30 years old and we watch him as he practices riding his unicycle. He holds on to the iron fence for support and when he gets up enough courage he lets go only to have the unicycle crash to his feet or slip wildly out of control. But he is game and he tries again and again to get the hang of it. Soon there is another white face in the park and he sits quietly on the bench and begins texting on his cell phone. I smile as I see another white head peek into the park. He doesn't enter. I am amused because the scene reminds me of the cliché about Black folks. That in a crowd, we always look for our own kind. Apparently we are not the only ones with this tendency. I suppose there is safety in numbers. Bored with the unicyclist my ears turn once more to the conversation of the two so-called historians but they've exhausted their conversation for the day.

A few more exchanges and the two men bid one another a hasty adieu. The second man walking over to a nearby bench to wake the sleeping figure of a twenty-something year old female he said was his 'cousin.' And although the first man pleaded that he should stay and hear the end of yet another episode in his life his audience disappeared through the park to go in search of weed, and then, without so much as a goodbye to me, the remaining man, drunk from alcohol consumption stood to leave. I watched him as he staggered past the memorial and through the park's exit. Just before he crossed the street he threw the empty nips into a nearby trash can, then grasping the rim of the can with both hands he leaned over it and vomited his guts out. It was the third time he'd done so.

* On Sunday, July Fourth I visited the larger St. Nicholas Park that runs ten or more blocks along St. Nicholas Avenue and ends at 141st Street. There, I encountered one of the Park's Department janitors. Recognizing me, he informed me that the large park was ten times filthier that Donnellen Square. And certainly dirtier than Jackie Robinson Park has ever been. But not to be outdone, Jackie Robinson Park was the victim of arson later that day. As I stood looking at the fun going on in the large and impressive (free) swimming pool, my gaze was attracted to four or five teenagers standing in the bushes just above the pool. Suddenly, one of them lit a firecracker and the explosion sent a shock wave through the swimmers. The group of youngsters scattered and in a minute or so

we all began to smell smoke and notice the fire spreading rapidly through the undergrowth and among the beautiful trees. It was fortunate that the time was just 5:04 pm and in minutes the fire department had arrived to put out the blaze and to avert a disaster, the outside temperature being a steamy 90 plus degrees. But not before damage had been done to an area as large as a basketball court. Two days later the pool would be closed early because of violence. Two young men got into an argument about a place in the long line of bathers waiting to enter the pool. One pulled out a gun and shot the other. Sitting in the adjoining park I heard the announcement and made my way up the long flight of steps to the street. As I walked I noticed an Oriental mother with a young son. The boy was crying because after waiting for more than an hour he hadn't had a chance to get in the pool and he was disbelieving of the promise his mother was making to bring him back on the following day and of the reason he was being spirited away. In one last desperate attempt to garner support for his position he turned around and looked at me. "Is the pool really closed,' he tried to say through his sobs. "Yes," I told him observing that his face was almost perfectly moon-shaped. "They've closed the pool because someone threw something into the water," I lied. "They have to clean it so kids won't get sick but it will open again tomorrow." I didn't have the heart to tell him the truth. As it turned out even I didn't know the full truth. This was only the second incident of the day. The first happened when cops were 'forced' to use mace on two unruly mothers and their kids who were fighting over a place in line. Yes, the kids were sprayed with mace. I had no way to know at this point but New York City and the rest of the nation were in the throes of the hottest summer on record and on Sugar Hill, as well as in the rest of this town we were in for a violent summer as well.

Realizing that each day could be my last day in the park I have developed the ritual of saying goodnight to the few friends I see. There is the elderly retired woman in the wheel chair and another lady who comes each day to sit nearby. She says she has an allergy and the pollen of the park's fauna makes her eyes puffy and tear but she comes anyhow. She tells me it's just to sit and talk with me but I doubt her sincerity. She's been coming here for years and it is through her that I learn that during periods of the 1960's and 1970's the place was almost deserted. "No one wanted to come here. We was scared to come anywhere near this place, it was so bad with the guns and shootin' and stabbin' going on every other day." She was a young woman of twenty-something at the time and her memory of events seems credible enough although she was difficult to talk with for long periods of time. Like most people I meet she has a negative attitude. But at least she's consistent, she doesn't trust Spanish speaking people, Arabs, whites or young Black Americans. I would run into her a month or so later and she'd tell me that she'd been the victim of a car accident since we'd last spoken. I also say goodbye to an older man I have come to like. I try to have a dollar for him whenever I come to the park or enough to buy him a sandwich. He doesn't speak except to mumble a greeting or a 'thank you.' I am told that he is a recent prison parolee and that he was there for three years and although I don't know his crime I learn that he was once a crack cocaine seller and a heavy user (I suspect he still uses the stuff). There is a man who comes to the park nearly every day looking for him. He brings two children and sitting nearby I've heard the man tell him that "mom" wants to talk with him. I've seen him reach for the cell phone and speak into it and then return the phone to the man almost nonchalantly. As I depart and shake his hand. I look into the sad eyes. I place the money in his fingers. They are long fingers with dirty nails but they in no way detract from his sincerity or his toothless smile. I try to say with my eyes what I cannot utter with my tongue. That I understand. That I don't care what he has done in the past and that I feel for him and wish him well. I search my head and heart for a phrase or just a word that will give him hope for one more night to get through his private hell but I find nothing, finally concluding that perhaps it is best this way. That whatever I might have said aloud I had already said with my eyes.

Walking back to the apartment I spot my cat. She races between the cars on 150th Street and Edgecombe and stops to take a look around her. When she spots me she looked into my eyes. She seemed embarrassed, like a lady who'd been caught exiting the shower without her robe or a towel. There was something peculiar about her, I thought. She seemed different and more resigned to her condition. We had parted ways when I turned at the corner to catch one last glimpse of her. It was no wonder she was forlorn. Someone or something had robbed her of her beautiful tail. I was a butcher's job. It looked as if the wound was having a hard time healing in the heat of 100 degree weather we were having. She had become the victim of violence for yet another time in her miserable life. How sad, I thought. How terribly regrettable and unnecessary. It's like that here. Everything is over the top. Every situation gets a little more than necessary. Like cell phone usage. Each second over a minute being charged as an extra minute. As if technology somehow hasn't advanced enough to charge for seconds. A few extra cents charged at the super market for goods that always seem to have only a few days left before the expiration date. More energy required to argue with shop keepers and sales and counter clerks, bus drivers, subways token clerks and even neighbors.

It's no wonder people here seem always on edge. But then, I'm Living on Powdered Sugar and every situation is confrontational here usually terminating in the usage of vulgarity and sometimes violence. It's the truth but still I chide myself for the juvenile and intended pun. There is so much time wasted proving who is best. People are always striving to prove "one-upmanship": if there is such a word. Long ago I decided that I would not do "ugly", which is what I consider all things combative and violent. And in my humble opinion even arguments can be non - productive and a waste of time and energy. Unfortunately, I fear there is little room for this attitude in the year 2010 on the streets of Powdered Sugar.

Addendum

Almost two years have passed since I was last on the Hill. My departure had been rather hasty and I had not left my brother's place under the best of circumstances. It wasn't anything that I'd said or done. Things simply had gotten out of control and unable to do anything to make a difference I'd finally realized that it was time to leave. I moved on and I rarely thought of those turbulent days but I would never forget the days I'd spent sitting in the sunlight of the little park known as Donnellan Square. On this sunny day in late spring I'd taken the subway to 145th Street. Concluding my business there I decided to walk the few short blocks on St. Nicholas Avenue to say hello to a few of the souls I'd met there. Maybe I would catch a glimpse of my favorite cat and say a word or two to anyone willing to give me news of the important events that had occurred over the last 20 months or so. I walked northward on the nearly empty street and chided myself for expecting anyone to be outdoors at 11 o'clock on a Thursday morning.

I pressed on. Suddenly, my footsteps slowed. Something was not quite right. As I drew nearer to 150th Street and the Dawn Hotel it occurred to me that the Norwegian Spruce was not there. At first I thought I'd made a mistake. I knew I had not been walking in the wrong direction. I was still on St. Nicholas Avenue and I was across the street from the "dirty' park. Yes, the tree was gone and as I crossed at the corner and entered the square I could see quite clearly that there was a hole dug into the ground where it should have been. The roses were there and still blooming in profusion. And the yews had been thinned and trimmed to a more manageable state of existence but there was only the open space and the brown-colored earth in the spot where once existed the seven or eight foot fir tree. I walked to the outside of the concrete barrier. Perhaps there was a sign there a announcing the future plans of the park or some explanation as to why the tree had been removed. But in the place that had once proudly boasted that the park was dedicated to Pfc. Donnellan there was nothing. The sign had been removed. The park itself seemed almost untouched from the last I'd seen it. But the Carefree Roses were in abundance.

I sat down a minute on the bench nearest the entrance and then I recalled the brown tell-tale signs of the branches of the fir when last I'd seen it. I recalled the tenacious thorns of the roses as they climbed branch upon branch and as they clawed their way to the top of the hill. Determined to outlast the tree. Determined to survive to the final rose. And then it hit me! The Carefree Roses had never been in danger. They were not facing demise. The winner of the battle had already been decided months before I'd moved to the area and it was just a matter of time before the Fir tree would give up the fight. As for the removal of the sign? I did not know but I could bet that it was the idea of someone in the community to take it down and not knowing what else to do the Park's Department had decided that if Pfc. Donnellan could not be honored here then no one else would be so.

I walked slowly as I left the park. There was a lot going on in my head and I wondered if this victory of the Carefree Roses also symbolizes the plight of the community at large. In other words it begs the questions: Has the community given up the fight too soon. Can they hang on long enough to win the fight against the influx of outsiders with their megabucks and new lifestyles? With their skinny jeans and wine goblets? With their Brooks Brother ties and designer dresses? Only time will tell of course but in the end the Carefree Roses on the Hill have thorns!

The Cat's Out of The Bag

By Maurice P. Fortune

Viscomtesse Philomene Marguerite de Larchmont was a feline and of that she was inordinately proud. For she was not just any cat. She was a felines de premiere class she told anyone who would listen. Yes, you could say she was stuck up if you wanted to be unkind but she didn't care. Not one whit. She was of the finest pedigree and she flaunted her superiority as she pranced about seemingly unaware of the envious stares of others around her. She'd learnt from the best. And following her mother's example she knew how to put on the Ritz, to put it mildly, as she took her own good time stretching and preening to get the most from the attention she'd draw. She knew exactly what she was doing and she felt not the least bit ashamed to be milking it - no pun intended.

From the small tuffs of white fur that lined her front feet, not paws as some commonly called them, to the fluffy striped tail on her derriere; even up to her beautiful eyes of bleu ceil she looked good! Of course those were not her words, she reminded folks. Everyone said so and she was not one to argue with popular opinion.

Yes, she was a cat and she knew her lineage. At least that on her mother's side. Although she didn't have many opportunities to speak with her mother, she knew very well where her mother lived. She also knew that one of her siblings lived in the same house with her mother. There! Over there in that English Tudor house across the street. Her mother was what was commonly referred to as 'grimalkin' or an old female cat. It was a term she detested and took personal offense to the reference, as she reminded everyone she certainly didn't feel old. But there was no denying that her sister was kind of crazy.

She told everyone she'd got that way after they'd forced her to breed with that, that Mongrel. She had been so traumatized that she had leapt from the window sill in a failed effort to end it all. Of course, her sister never mentioned that the window was on the first floor of the house. Well, those are the breaks, aren't they? Philomene would gently remind her that she too had been a child bride. And it mattered none at all that her husband of just two short months had died. He had been kind and more like a father figure and he'd respected the fact that she was but a mere kitten when they'd married. It too had been an arranged marriage. The arrangement had been made by her very own mother who knew full well that Philomene was months away from being able to produce offspring. But she'd been so focused on taking advantage of his name and prestige; he'd been with the family a few years and they absolutely adored him. He was called Count Vladimir Romanov.

It had all come to a sad end. While trying to flee the wheels of a delivery truck he'd been run over. Apparently, he had been less than truthful about his real age too because it after his demise it was discovered that he had exhausted all of his lives. All nine of them. Mother had told her not to worry. At least she'd inherited his title and could now be referred to as Viscomtess with a special position in the house. Her sister had been beside herself with rage. She hadn't had much use for Philomene after that and she hadn't tried to hide it. Especially after Philomene was officially adopted by the well - to - do Phelps'. She felt that as the eldest, she, Jeanette Bastet should have been the first to leave home. At least the first girl.

Mother had a mind for history and had given her sister the name 'Bastet' in honor of the great Egyptian Cat goddess of antiquity. Of course Philomene thought the name misplaced but she kept her mouth shut about it. Two of the boys had also been adopted and no one had heard from them since. At least no one Philomene knew. Although she was sure she had seen one of her brothers when she visited her primary care physician (not Vet) a couple of months ago for her annual checkup. They looked so much alike that the nurses said they could be mistaken for identical twins. Philomene thought this a ridiculous comparison as he was much bigger than she and any fool should have been able to tell they had vastly different anatomies. Even so, she couldn't deny that he was handsome young man. Maybe a bit of a prude, she observed. She had been happy when he'd made such a fuss about being placed in a box next to hers that her primary care doctor had advised her mistress to move her to another spot away from him in the waiting room. She certainly did not want to get to know anyone as pretentious as he appeared to be.

She, of all felines knew the difference between being proud and just being a bore. Even so, she had been tempted to ask him if his given name was Smilodon. That was the name mother had given him in her attempt to recognize that we are all are descended from the first pre-historic tigers that roamed the Earth zillions of years ago. The name fit him to a Tee but she'd thought better of questioning him. He might have thought she had something else in mind and

Lord knows she wasn't thinking THAT. Oh well, some things are better off left unmentioned. She wasn't just saying that because she was being insensitive or didn't want to be close to anyone.

After all is said and done cats do grow attached to one another. They grow as attached as those brutish canines have led everyone to believe for centuries that only THEY can do. "When was the last time you heard of a cat biting or mauling someone to death?" She asked folks! Philomene lay there in the large living room window enjoying the afternoon sun. The Phelps' owned the spacious corner property and she had a bird's - eye view of all traffic coming and going. Just then an impressive looking automobile moved slowly down the street as if its driver was looking for an address and Philomene rolled over onto her back and lifted her front paws in mocked playfulness. She smiled as she did this, knowing that the patch of white fur on her belly was showing to its best advantage. She was reminded of her mother's words. "Who knows when a big Hollywood producer might be driving by?" But the car didn't stop and once again Philomene was left alone with her thoughts.

As she lay there looking out the window she looked around at all the luxurious things she enjoyed in her life and she felt uneasy. She knew that it would only be a matter of time before she too would be bred. Her Mistress liked to call it "getting married." Whatever! It was the least she could do for these kind folks.

"You certainly don't want to end up like your sister," her mother said on the few occasions they were together. Mother was always comparing her with her sibling. Philomene didn't like the comparison and she definitely thought it unfair of mother. It wasn't her fault that she and not Jeanette had been chosen to grace the halls of the grandest home on the block.

It was a Victorian Home and it was truly fit for a family of noble heritage. Of course, that was the reason they chose her. They could tell she fit the bill. She and not her sister had that special air and elegance necessary to walk the majestic corridors and rooms of La Maison Anglaise. Yes, she rarely saw her mother but on those few occasions her mother seemed genuinely happy to see her youngest daughter and they purred together and talked for hours if time allowed. On one such occasion, her mother, Claire, that's her name now, told her that she too had been adopted as an infant and that her name had originally been just plain Clara. She had once lived in an apartment on New York City's Fifth Avenue.

It sounded so rich and romantic. Philomene had heard that Jackie Kennedy Onassis once lived there. She fantasized that it was even in the same building. Wouldn't that be upscale if I could prove that connection, she often said to friends? In any event, her mother said they were actually a mixed breed, although people couldn't tell it. Not ordinary laymen anyway. Her grandfather had been of the Mongolian stock or chat de Mongolie and her grandmother was pure chat de Marguerite. That's the reason she had given her daughter that name. Over time it All had been forgotten and now even Claire was not sure which breed was listed on her original papers of authenticity that were kept upstairs in the safe of her owners, the Seymours of Larchmont, New York. Philomene didn't know either. She didn't have a clue but just to make her mother happy she'd promised to look in to it to see if she could find out anything. She'd said this as she was licking and arranging her beautiful snow- leopard colored fur and mother had been annoyed that she didn't seem to be paying attention. She had done everything to try to convince her that it was just her way but the day had soured and mother stormed back into the house in a huff, comparing her with her father whom mother often called pompous. It was just her good luck to have his hair color. It wasn't anything anyone could choose she had explained to the woman. She preferred the other term of course. Panthere des Neiges.

As for her sister, she didn't have anything against the girl. In fact, she was pretty in a strange sort of way. And Philomene had tried to get to know her. To be closer; just as sisters should. After all, she wasn't the type to hold a grudge but Jeanette never wanted to say more than a few words. They'd speak and there would be a stony silence as the girl returned to her habit of twitching her ears and staring in space as though she was waiting for news of an alien mouse invasion or something equally horrid like the burning and persecution of her species during ancient times and again in the middle ages in Europe. Back then cats were burned to death in great numbers once each year just for being cats. Unfortunately, there were other reasons why Jeanette didn't like her sister Philomene.

Oh yes, Jeanette was jealous.

She was jealous of her own sister! She detested the fact that Philomene traveled 'everywhere' with her Mistress. She had been to Europe several times and especially to Paris. The lady of the house loved Paris and any other capital city where French was spoken. This included Brussels and Geneva and even Kinshasa. Yes, they had even been to the exotic heart of Africa. Philomene had absolutely adored Kinshasa. It was so colorful and the weather had been just purrfect. And even if the Congolese didn't particularly care for what they called les chats domestique she cared a great deal for the Congo.

But she had been truly afraid when her Mistress had visited an outdoor market and she had seen all those carcasses of wild animals on display. One of the shop keepers had tried to sell Mistress what he termed a Cousin.

It was the disemboweled body of a green monkey and it was ready for the pot. Philomene had thanked her stars when her mistress had politely refused. Then, there had been the time when an unscrupulous shopkeeper had actually asked if he could buy Philomena. He'd thought that Mistress was destitute and needed money to purchase a ticket back to the United States. The impertinence of some people! He'd looked really stupid when Mistress read him the Bill of Animal Rights. Indeed she could truly say she had traveled abroad. And when Philomene came back with her tales of travel, well Jeanette had simply died at least three times and that left her with only six lives. Philomene told of her days and nights in the beautiful city of Paris. It was all soo romatic, even though she could only see much of it from the hotel window, but that didn't make it any less exciting. She loved the way the French ate and sat in the outdoor cafes. She loved their music and she even said she loved the metro although it was hard to understand how someone could ride around in Paris in an underground train.

The only unpleasantness of her travels Philomene said, were the planes. Oh, it wasn't those big cars in the sky that she disliked. It had been her accommodations.

She had had to ride in the luggage compartment or something close to it. On her vacation last year Philomene told her mother that she had spent six hours confined in a small space with 3 parrots, four dogs, two other felines of the ordinary variety and a python. She was petrified of the python.

It reminded her of that movie with that handsome Black actor Samuel L. Jackson. What was it called? Snakes on a Plane, or something to that effect! The Cat who was closest to her said that there was nothing to worry about because it was a harmless creature and that it was tame. That's like saying that those pit bulls are harmless and tame. Or, that they won't bite. That's a ridiculous assumption to make Philomene always reminded others. Anything that has teeth will bite she said. Even humans. Why that's the reason they have teeth. For a second she thought back to her sister.

Philomene was certain that the other reason her sister envied her had to do with something far deeper and more sinister. Philomene

Living on Powdered Sugar

didn't mean anything by it but just for clarification purpose she often brought up the fact that she and Jeanette were half-sisters. Philomene knew that father, God rest his soul, was of pure bred Mongolian stock. Her mother said that he had been her first love match and that he could trace his lineage back to an uncle who came from the Middle East during the Neolithic Age. And that was 10,000 years ago. No kidding! But poor Jeanette's father had been an arranged marriage. Mother didn't like him one bit but what could she do? The head of the family wanted kittens around the old house. And all because they had those awful mice. They knew nothing about felines Clara had told her. Why cats were hunters of birds and that's why they climb so well. It was humans who bred them to catch those, those rodents.

No, she was no ordinary pet and she was not ever to be confused with that creature called a dog. They were despicable and they were considered tame. Philomene was nobody's pet. Why even the mere mention of the word sent icy shivers up her flexible spine. To begin with she abhorred being called anything except her rightful full-titled name. And of course it was not necessary to use the word Viscomtess if you'd prefer. Few people pronounced it correctly anyway. Especially Americans, with their terrible French accents. But never, ever call her Philly, or Margie. These we no, no's. And don't you dare try disgrace me with the words Fifi or Kitty, she would tell that stupid hound she lived with. His name was Phillip. He allowed people to call him Pippy. Why they may as well be saying Pee Pee or Fido, heaven forbid!

She stopped. Her thoughts were in abeyance just as Phillip walked past. She was glad she had decided to sit on the sofa back because this forced the dog to walk beneath her, which in her estimation, was where he belonged: beneath her. Phillip glanced up at her and barked in that god-awful gruff voice of his but she just sat there glowering at him, as though he was just a picture on the wall. He didn't even merit that much attention. What impudence! Speaking to her! She stared straight ahead as she often did when strangers wanted to take her picture. Oh yes, she sometimes allowed them that liberty. It's the kindly thing to do, she always reminded herself. It might pay dividends one day. She never refused anyone. Even when she was in a hideous mood she would allow them that much. She'd sit still and put her best personality forward. Especially showing her eyes to their best advantage. They say a camera never lies and anyway it was good for all kinds of things like local newspaper stories. Photo opts are good publicity and she had been in the newspapers more than a few times. Anyway, one never knows if some Hollywood producer of someone of importance might see the pictures. Besides, these times are not like when her mother and grandmother were young.

There IS dignity in being a movie star. Grace Kelly proved that much! And so had a few others like Dandridge. Hepburn and Loren. She had heard that there was talk about making Princess Di an actress but she died so prematurely. Philomene thought for a moment and then continued, "I watched the tribute to her when her friend Elton John sang that song he'd originally written for Marilyn Monroe. I don't have to tell you that during those few minutes I died at least twice. And there were many other examples too. Although some mean folks say Paris Hilton had knocked people of money and class back a peg or so.

Once Phillip passed the sofa Philomene got down from the queenly position she had taken and walked toward the kitchen. She was hungry but she would not lower herself by purring and begging for food like that awful brute in the parlor. No, she would wait. Meals were served at dinner time; not between. It was not quite six P.M. and her crystal plate had not yet been set for her. Although she could see that there was some sort of foolishness in Phillips bowl. It was made of plastic and it had his initials written in red on its side. Whatever was in his bowl had been there for a few hours and it looked old and horrid. It's a bone she thought to herself. Someone has thrown him a bone. How ghastly!

It was then she realized that there was some commotion coming from the direction of the pantry and although her instincts told her what it was she felt she had the right to investigate and confirm it with her own sky blue eyes. Lord knows that stupid Phillip could not be depended upon to do it. And even if he had seen what was going on he would do no more that sniff around and get in the way. She hated his habit of sniffing everything in sight and of being so indiscreet about things. Everyone on this planet knows that canines have a terrific sense of smell she had told the idiot. But you can still have some class and decorum about yourself. One would think he'd listen to something she had to say but oh no, not that blockhead. He had just lay there panting, with his tongue half out of his mouth, unable to give a sensible answer. Just before she entered the pantry she purred to let the occupants know that they were not alone but either they didn't hear her or simply ignored her royal presence. So she stood there in the doorway looking at them.

Amazed by their daring and their audacity. Just as she suspected! Mr. Phelps was there with the cook and they were engaged in some disgraceful behavior. Not wanting to look like she had the faintest notion of what they were doing she had purred again and this time Mr. Phelps interrupted himself and looked down at her with a smile. "Oh," he said. "It's just the cat." JUST THE CAT! The nerve of some people. Here he is, kissing and pawing all over a lowly employee like a caveman and he has the unmitigated gall to say I am just a cat. Well, I put my head up in the air, raised my tail and stormed out of there while I still had my dignity intact. I knew what they were doing. I had caught them in the same position before and even worse. Well, Mr. Phelps I am filing this one away just like I have all the others and I promise you that you won't get away with it. I'll teach you to break your marriage vows, Sir!

Philomene walked back into the outer grand hall. She purposely took the long route to avoid having anything to do or say to Phillip. There, she bounded up the spiral stairs and into one of the plush chairs placed near the fine lamp and table. This was the best spot in the house she decided. Save perhaps the kitchen window or the small balcony outside her mistress's bedroom. From this vantage point of fine furniture grouping overlooking the stairs she could see the comings and goings of the house. And believe me she thought, there is a lot to keep track of. Now, she didn't consider herself nosey.

That was not her job, meddling in everybody's business. But somebody around here has to do it, she always said. Some soul needed to take some action to avoid the inevitable disaster that she knew could occur in these situations. She knew of more than one instance in which there had been a nasty scandal and had ended in the dreaded "D" word. And all because someone had not been paying close enough attention to the warning signs. She shuddered when she thought of her friend Dame Tabitha around the corner. It had been a real trauma to lose such a close neighbor but Tabitha had chosen the wrong hanger to hang her coat on, so to speak. She had made the terrible mistake of becoming too friendly with the maid.

When the divorce came and the house was divided Tabitha was given to the maid and the Master of the house. Except, he didn't have any real money. Soon they were all living in a one bedroom apartment
In the Bronx, of all places and reports have it that Tabitha had given birth to several litters of half-bred Alleys. We all know that is short for alley cats. It appears that at least on this occasion the dog of the house had made the right choice and remained with the rightful owner of the house. But the dog was little more than a lap pet so where could it go? Poor thing!

Oh no, I have no intention of letting that same fate befall me, Philomene had told her sister when they were still on speaking terms. She would never even accept food from the hands of anyone except Madame Phelps. She and she alone could prepare the delicious morsels that filled the plate of her "Precious." It was the nickname Mrs. Phelps had given her and she gracefully accepted the moniker. Philomene would not answer to any other. And if the cook tried to call her by that name she just sat there unmoving and staring ahead in space.

Eventually the cook would give up and just let her be. It was a cruel trick Philomene conceded but it always worked like a charm. It wasn't that she tried to put on airs or was conceited. Not in the least. She knew that the cook would not take the time to feed her from the proper crystal or decorate her plate with a small rose. And although the rose was made of no more than plastic it made a pretty picture. She knew it was not to be eaten. Unlike some people she knew who tried to chew on almost anything that mildly resembled food. Not she. She wanted only the best as her name and title called for and she would NOT settle for anything less.

She certainly could not be just tossed a bone or some scraps from the table that someone else had begun eating. How gross! And she could not think of anything more disgusting than going around the dining table and accepting bits of food from everyone's plate. Why just think of the germs. No wonder he always had a runny nose and hacked incessantly. She couldn't count the numbers of times she had seen food thrown to Phillip land on the floor. He just licked it up and pretended it was no big deal. She had wanted to scream at him and remind him that everyone WALKED on the floor with shoes and BARE feet but she had contained her emotions and kept her thoughts to herself.

Just then there was the sound of the main door opening and in walked her Mistress. In her black business suit and white blouse she cut a stunning figure. Philomene especially liked the matching shoes and bag she had worn to work that day. She was a very good Attorney and she had been so long before she met Dr. Phelps. Actually, that was how she had met him. Even he confessed to that point. He had been her client and was involved in a lawsuit that required good counsel. One of his cosmetic surgery patients had suffered a bad reaction to some medication he'd prescribed and she had nearly died. Well, he had found a good lawyer in Mrs. Veronica Nelson Butler. She had been the recommendation of a business friend and she had not been a disappointment. She had helped him seal the deal and the rest, as they say, is history.

Philomene bounded down the stairs and stopped at the bottom to collect herself before her Mistress noticed she was there. She didn't want to appear over eager or too laid back and she definitely wanted to get there before the brute of the family arrived to greet her. Calmly walking over, she waited until the woman had placed her bag in the usual spot and reached down to gather her in her arms. Ahhhh, the best time of the day. At last I get my proper recognition and attention around here she purred to herself. She was still there when out of nowhere Phillip came racing toward Veronica. But Philomene turned and gave him a long icy stare. "You wouldn't dare," it said. "Not on my watch!" Wagging his tail furiously, the dog backed down and made no attempt to jump up. And now Philomene, firmly wrapped in Veronica's arms was headed toward the huge living room and her favorite spot on the sofa where she knew she would be pampered and spoken to for a few minutes with much love.

The night passed without event and Saturday morning dawned at Maison Anglaise with much anticipation. At least as far as Philomene was concerned. Every 1st Saturday of the month, she was driven to the little village shop of Monsieur Andre where she was bathed, combed and clipped most adoringly. His shop was really called Les Petites Fours but everyone referred to it using his name. Monsieur Andre. He was a nice man and a wealthy one too she had been informed, again by her mother. His wife was just as wealthy in her own right. They had property, inherited property and they didn't live in this town. Oh no, they lived in New Rochelle or on a secluded spot near there with their own private beach.

One of their President's, Nixon she remembered mother saying, had liked the place so much he'd wanted it as one of his retirement homes. Of course, that was before scandal that drove him unfairly from the White House mother had said. It was YEARS before mother's birth so it had to be Centuries ago in cat years. She had never been to New Rochelle but the name sounded important and it must have been a special place for Monsieur Andre to have chosen it as his official residence. He was after all, a very important citizen. This would explain why each day he was driven to the spa by a uniformed chauffeur. And in a Rolls Royce too. How, dramatic Philomene thought. How positively a propos.

After breakfast everyone collected themselves to begin the day. Philomene too prepared herself for what she knew would be an eventful day. She always liked going into town with her mistress. It gave them time to be alone and free of certain creatures and although she positively abhorred being forced into a cat cage like a common house pet she had come to accept it as a necessary evil. Mistress Veronique, As Philomene liked to refer to her, was careful to place the thing in a secure spot on the back seat of the car. She placed it high enough so that Philomene could see out of the windows and not give outsiders the impression that she was transporting a beast. Like a horse or something. Mother said it was the law. Pets had to be caged while driving and some animals required a license to go from place to place. Well, she certainly did not want to break the law but she, Philomene was nobody's pet. And for this much she was grateful to her Mistress. Even so, she had once stopped at a gas station for petrol and Philomene noticed that the woman in the car on the far side of the pump was looking at her with much curiosity. Like she was a circus freak. It was so embarrassing. She felt like it would be the end of her. She already had two strikes against her with Princess Di's funeral and all. Lives were too short and she couldn't waste them unnecessarily.

Driving to town that morning to care for her beauty needs Veronica Nelson Phelps felt as if she too would die. Or more like it, that someone else would die and that she would be responsible for his death. She was thinking of her husband Hugh. He was going to regret the hurt he was causing her and she knew just how to make it hurt in the right place. In his wallet! No, she didn't particularly care that he was having an affair with the cook.

She had expected no more of him. After all, this was the second time this sort of thing had happened. The first time had been with the maid whose job it was to come in four times each week. Actually there were two maids, as the house was too large for one person to do all the cleaning. Even she had to concede that point. Of course it was costly. She knew that most of the work was being done by that tramp Hugh was entangled with and she had tried her best to divide the work evenly. The two were illegal and when that impudent and ungrateful foreigner received her walking papers she had the chutzpah to say that someone had informed her that she could go to the authorities and get her, Veronica, in trouble. The maid stood there in her face with hands on her hips announcing to the world that she didn't care if it all ended in her own deportation. She missed HER COUNTRY anyway. Thinking fast Veronica had been forced to give the woman a huge severance settlement of nearly $15,000 dollars in cash. She had been furious but what else could she do. She knew that she could not afford a scandal. She would just made certain that there were no more illegal maids in her future. She hired a professional cleaning company to do the work. It was cleaner, simpler and above board. Besides they sent men to do the work, so she didn't have to worry on that score.

But they still needed a cook. She couldn't be expected to go to a kitchen and cook! Well, she sometimes went there for a quick sandwich or for something cool or warm to drink. She even knew how to put a few things in the microwave oven, thank the lesser gods for that invention. But cooking was out of her league. Why she would have been lost in there. It was a big and scary place and her nails could not survive the rigors of chopping and peeling and keeping things from burning. She was nobody's cook and she promptly hired a mature person to do the job. A matronly type with roots in Georgia. Miss Georgia Allen turned out to be a very special person. And she was a Black woman.

Not that that meant anything to her husband. He wanted a woman and he wouldn't have cared if she was chartreuse or from the planet Neptune. All he cared about was whether or not a human being was male or female. He preferred the latter gender. Of course, he wasn't prepared for Mrs. Allen's dignity or her spirituality and when they saw her for the first time Veronica could have jumped for joy at his disappointment. Still, as special as Ms. Allen was it had all ended badly for all concerned when after two years she suddenly announced the death of her sister in the south. Ms. Allen said she had no choice but to leave New York and go there to care for her elderly father and although Veronica had asked her, begged her to stay. She remained firm. Saying it was her inherent duty to care for the elderly in her family, and that is was the Christian thing to do.

After all, what would she say when she arrived at the Pearly Gates of Heaven and it was discovered that she had neglected that responsibility. Despite Veronica's protestations Ms. Georgia Allen left and returned to Georgia, all the richer for her experience because a still repentant Hugh Phelps gave her a sendoff check of $10,000 for her troubles and for her good services. Now, without a cook in the house they were either going to have to eat out every day of the week or starve to death. She had chosen to hire another cook and she hired unseen a relatively new house cook in the person of Ms. Jennifer Roethlisberger. Veronica was away at the time visiting friends and when the news came that the employment agency had found the right person for the job she called them right away. She always suspected that Dr. Hugh Nelson had something to do with getting her the job at Maison Anglaise. Jennifer had graduated from one of those cooking schools and had taken her apprenticeship under a well-known French chef who specialized in salads and desserts.

To be sure she knew how to do all the other things but it all sounded kind of interesting to Veronica. Besides she was watching her weight now that Miss Allen was gone. Ms. Allen had insisted on cooking what she called 'REAL MEALS' for HER family. The kind of meals that 'stick to the ribs' as she'd put it. The meals had not only stuck to the ribs. In Veronica's case they had stuck in other places and she was having trouble getting them unglued. Beaucoup de difficulte! It was settled in her mind. Jennifer could have the job. It had all worked out to everyone's advantage too. Her meals were light and nutritious and both she and Hugh lost much needed pounds. In fact, she had stopped going to the gym and settled for the light meals and just walking a couple of miles three times a week.

In three months she had trimmed down and was wearing her old outfits once again. Even Hugh lost weight and was feeling good about himself. Veronica felt like she had pulled off a Coup so to speak, and saved herself a ton of money in the process. New outfits were not necessary, how clever of her. But just when she thought all was going well, she began to notice that Hugh was spending a great deal of time in the kitchen. He didn't want to go with her on her walks anymore. Certainly, he tried to cover himself by saying that he was trying to learn to cook just in case something unforeseen happened to "Jen," as he had begun calling Jennifer. "People do get sick or need to take vacations," he reminded her. Veronica wasn't fooled and it was the Viscomtesse who confirmed Veronica's suspicions. She had just returned from her morning walk and when she came in the door the cat was not in her usual place near the stairs. When she didn't come to Veronica to be petted and cuddled, her mistress was alarmed. She thought something had happened to her darling kitty. But a quick search of the house revealed the problem.

There sat the Viscomtesse in the kitchen, on a chair. And she would not move. At first Veronica though she had forgotten to feed her. But when she looked n top of the fridge she saw that there was no more of the special cat food she always used for her darling Philomene's breakfast and that meant she had already fed her before taking her exercise. She was becoming so forgetful again. It could only mean she was working too hard or not getting enough sleep at nights. Veronica was meticulous about Philomene's meals and when and how she ate them. She insisted that Jennifer prepare a special meal of liver or chicken hearts, pate or fresh fish for her cat's dinner. Bending to pick her up, Philomene wouldn't let herself be petted. Instead she scampered into the area of the pantry and although Veronica called and called Philomene would not budge.

Suspicious now, Veronica announced in a loud voice, "well, you can just sit there darling cat, I'm going upstairs to my boudoire, where I'll have my shower and change into something pretty." She knew that just putting it that way would make Philomene come running behind her and when the cat still did not move Veronica walked out of the kitchen and went upstairs. But not before she took notice that the pantry door was slightly ajar and that there was no sign of Jennifer whom at that hour should have been preparing the evening menu. Once upstairs, Veronica did not go into her bedroom. Not right away. She waited at the top of the stairs until she heard her husband Hugh come into the outer hall. He was calling her name. Calling as though he had something important to say. And he was coming from the kitchen. Starting back down the stairs as though she was still trying to get Philomene to follow her, Veronica could see that Hugh was still wearing his P.J.'s. It was his habit to never leave the house in his pajamas. Not even to go out the back door even though no one could see him. But there he was calling his wife's name. And the only thing he had to say was that both the cat and the dog must have run away together. It was a good try but a poor choice for an excuse. In fact, it was downright laughable. To begin with, her Philomene would not go to a dog race with that hound Phillip. He didn't have the brains to cross the street alone. Just then, Phillip came dashing out of the living room where he had been lying with his head across his front paws and Philomene, elegant and in her usual manner strutted past Hugh Phelps with her head in the air. On her way up the staircase.

Just to be certain she was correct Veronica walked down the stairs, scooped Philomene up in her arms and headed straight for the kitchen to tell Jennifer she wanted something special for the evening meal. It was to be chicken cordon bleu with asparagus tips and a baked potato. No dessert was necessary. The girl was standing at the sink pretending to be busy and she didn't even have the courtesy to turn around and acknowledge her employer. After a few words Veronica realized that Jennifer was doing everything she could not to look in her direction. The nape of her neck was as red as a beet. Without another word, Veronica turned and walked away and up the spiral staircase to her bedroom. She had tears in her eyes as she closed her door, locking it behind herself. She sat there with the only true friend she had in the world! Viscomtess Philomene Marguerite de Larchmont.

They were there! They had arrived at the shop and with the car parked at the curb Philomene was carried in the door. She positively lived for these moments. She knew that Mr. Andre was already there and would soon come from the rear to great them. Then, he would unlatch the box lifting her gently while he called her name. "Bonjour Comtesse, he would say." Then, realizing his faux pas he would recover quickly and correct himself. "Bonjour, Viscomtesse Philomene. Comment va tu ce matin?" She would simply melt. She would be in her element, in seventh Heaven. No one. No one on this Earth ever spoke to her or pronounced her name like Monsieur Andre. Not even her Mistress, although she tried hard. But when Monsieur Andre spoke those words, bells pealed and fireworks went off in her head. Monsieur Andre would turn to Mme. Phelps and again offer to give her a fair price for her fantastic creature. No, he would pay her double what she asked.

But her Mistress always gave the same answer. The one that made Philomene the proudest and most important cat in the entire universe. That is, if there are cats anywhere except on Earth. Veronique would reply in her haughty way. "Why Monsieur Andre, I would not sell this darling creature for all the money in the world." And hearing that Philomene would pray for the end of her life at that very moment. Pray that she would be dead of some glamorous disease like sudden and instant brain cancer or an instant death in a limousine sort of like her idol Princess Diana. She would then be transported up to cat heaven to mingle with all the great cat saints who ever lived. Like the ones whose bodies were kept in urns by the Egyptians during the time of the great Pharaohs. Naturally, they would all be jealous! They would wish they could die again and be reborn in her exact image.

Shaken from her day dream by Monsieur Andre's footsteps, Philomene tried to sit as upright and correctly as possible. In a few seconds he had lifted her from the box and gone through the usual rituals but when he got to the part about offering to buy her Veronica Phelps smiled and said, "We'll talk!" With that she told Monsieur Andre that she would be back around one o'clock if she was able to have her appointment at the hair and nail salon completed by then. They shook hands. That's when Philomene noticed something strange. Something she had never before seen her Mistress do with anyone. She noticed that when Monsieur Andre kissed her hand Veronica's eyes lifted to look him squarely in the face. She not only smiled. Why, she had winked! Winked! Her Mistress had winked at Monsieur Andre. Philomene also wondered what Veronica had meant by, "we'll talk." Well, she couldn't worry about such mundane things. She, Philomene was soon to become transformed once more. Like a butterfly she would metamorphose into the envy of everyone who walked on four feet. Without exception, it happened to her once each month and on every special occasions.

It wasn't long before she had been washed, clipped, shampooed, blown dry and combed. To her absolute delight Monsieur Andre had personally overseen the entire operation. Even though it was somewhat embarrassing and immodest to be seen undressed by such a dashing man, Philomene knew that such immodesty had its advantages. For one thing, it gave her the opportunity to show off the fine bone structure that she had no doubt inherited from her own father. Then too, it made her all the more appealing when they were finished with the bathing and grooming duties she took her special place in the window to the envy of all the other patrons.

Monsieur Andre placed her there with his own polished fingernails that showed to their best advantage the diamond rings and the fine Rolex watch he wore on his right wrist. She would lie there, shielded from the afternoon sun by the tinted windows and the cool temperature of the air conditioning. She always pretended to be oblivious to the small crowd that gathered at the window looking in on her as she lay there on the red velvet cushion he placed next to her to demonstrate at its best to all of Larchmont her fine color.

Sometimes, she'd roll over on her back and make believe she was lying on the beaches of the French Riviera or of the Mauritius or Andaman Islands. She had heard there were no snakes in those places and it was all very comforting news to her. She couldn't stand snakes. They were, in her humble opinion, the vilest things on the planet. She could understand how the Egyptians had chosen her species to venerate and to hold in highest esteem. But Snakes! Well, human beings are strange. They have always been strange, she consoled herself. Ever since they became civilized they have been somewhat weird. And that hasn't been such a long time at all.

Just a paltry 10,000 years, give or take a couple of hundred years. To think they have the unmitigated gall to make the claim that THEY civilized CATS. Oh no dearie! It was the other way around. My ancestors were already civilized and living in groups with our own laws and code of ethics when you came out of the trees or wherever. Don't get it twisted, it was 'You' who insisted on trying to tame us. As if that was possible. Even with your weapons and cages some of us are still not tame and will NEVER be. I just don't get it. Did you know that in some societies your species eat us! That's, right, skin us and eat us! Oh, I'll admit that on occasion we have been brutal and territorial.

Occasionally, there's a story in one of the newspapers, you know the kind I mean, where a member of our species has maimed or killed a human. I can't read well but I'm not stupid. I hear things. But whatever we do we don't eat humans. Not unless we are very, very hungry. I don't feel so bad about that because humans do the same. Yes, you have been known to eat your own kind. Why, did you never hear of the movie about the Donner party? It happened simply ages ago out west but it happened. And even more recently there was this movie about a plane crash and people eating people. Although some denied it ever happened. But I don't want to think about that anymore today because it reminds me of the other movie about snakes on an airplanes. You know, Westley Snipes was in it. I watched it one night with my Mistress. I was a nervous wreck for two hours after. Although I must admit that I thought Snipes was cute. Even for a human.

Philomene lifted her head and stretched, getting up from the cushion in one graceful movement. She just wanted the people who had gathered outside the shop window to get a thorough look at her perfectly radiant coat. She knew she was dazzling the crowd and she sauntered over to the little velvet ball that had been placed in the window for her amusement. She put it between her front paws and rested her head on it. It was all for show. She detested balls. She was, in the end, a feline, not a canine. It was no secret at Maison Anglaise that Philomene Phelps of Larchmont, New York did not like balls or games of any kind. Games were to be played by children. Sweet little creatures. Or by Professional athletes or those trying to become such. Unless one included dogs like that hideous imbecile Phillip Phelps. He was always being played with and told to go fetch this or that. Once Peter J. Nelson, you can add Phelps if you want to, even though it makes Peter angry to be called by the last name of his step farther. He is Mistresses son by her first husband you know. Well, he is always joking around and playing with Phillip whom he calls 'his boy'. Can you imagine? HIS boy!

I laugh every time he says that and I'd do so now but laughing musses the fur around my whiskers. And we mustn't have that. Must we? Once Peter had a group of his friends over. His so-called friends that is. He was trying to be impressive as is his usual pattern. He had two ball and he would throw one and then without waiting for Phillip to return with it, he'd throw the other.

"Fetch it Phillip, fetch it boy," he'd called. This went on for a few minutes and poor Phillip, obviously out breath, came to a full stop at Peter's feet. He was tired but Peter wasn't done with his shenanigans. Being stupid he turned to me and said, "You get it. You fetch it Fifi!" WHAT, I nearly screamed at him? Me? Fi who, fetch something dear? Not on your life, you low bred …. Have you taken total leave of your sanity, my boy? Why, I don't even like hair balls and they are a necessity to felines! I nearly lost it. I nearly lost my mind. I mean, flipped my wig! I did! I did! I almost passed out from disgust. Imagine me! Viscomtesse Philomene, FETCHING something. Imagine me picking up in MY mouth an object. Any object that that mongrel Phillip has slobbered and dribbled over. I was sick to my stomach but not wanting to be classless in front of strangers I jumped down from the window ledge I was seated on and without missing a beat I walked right past Peter without looking up. I didn't turn around but I gave him a word or two. "Meee Noo," I said as I passed him. His friends laughed and they thought I'd said "meow" but I never looked back, I walked sraight up to the house and sat right there until Mistress opened the door to let me in. I suppose they never realized that I, Philomene would never use such a term as meow. What does that mean anyway? I don't know anyone who knows the answer to that but it sounds positively classless!

Finally, realizing she had been lost in thought Philomene stood and posed for the crowd once more. She had her back to everyone inside the shop and she couldn't see their faces but with her slanted eyes she could see from the reflection in the window glass that their attention was riveted on her. All the other cats were absolutely dying with envy and jealousy. Philomene played to her audience outside the window. She ignored everyone else. It was the audience that mattered. Always the audience. Wasn't it Marlene Dietrich who said that? Or maybe it was Eartha Kitt! Now those two were a credit to cats everywhere. Weren't they? I mean, even if they weren't really felines they made us all proud.

As he drove his convertible sports car into the driveway Peter J. Nelson Phelps turned off the ignition and sat there listening to the radio. It had been a short drive in from Manhattan's West Side and he was in no hurry to enter the house. The spring air felt good on his head and he hadn't bothered to put on a hat to cover the bald spot now growing quickly in the center of his skull. He hated the fact that he was losing his hair. He had tried everything he could try to stop the fall out that appeared on his pillow each morning.

There was no mistaking the fact that his hair loss was spreading and that the daily applications of a topical drug wasn't producing any meaningful results. He had never known anyone who regrew hair using that stuff and after seven month of trying he was ready to pack it in and let nature take its course. He could always get a wig or some other cover up he told folks. Or, there was one other thing. It was called, Hair Today? Comb tomorrow or something. If that didn't work he would consider a transplant or just let it go and shave his head sort of like Michael Jordon. He had made bald respectable and so it was no big deal any longer.

He didn't see his mother's car in the driveway or in the garage and he was in no hurry to go inside the house. And he didn't want to seem too eager. After all, he was going to meet with Jen later on that evening and he knew his step father, Mr. Phelps would be in the kitchen taking cooking lessons. He always took a few pointers from Jen on Saturday's after his mother had taken her cat to be fawned over and made to look like a figment of somebody's imagination. Peter hated cats and as far as he was concerned people made far too much of them. If he had his way the world would be rid of cats. But not dogs. Especially not dogs like his boy, Phillip He was a golden Lab and the animal was so smart and strong. He had insisted on having him the moment he'd seen him as a puppy in the window of the pet store. The store was no longer in town. It had moved, along with several other shops to the big mall on the outskirts of Larchmont.

But all this had occurred a couple of years ago. Before he'd dropped out of college and decided to go into the restaurant business with his friends. His mother Vern, as he called her, hadn't approved then and she still didn't like him being so carefree with his life and so careless with her money but she was glad to be rid of him and she would pay almost any sum for the privilege of being alone with that gigolo Phelps. Of course, there was Jen, the cook. He was in love with Jen and he believed she loved him just as much. Peter wanted her to quit this job and come live with him in Manhattan but she was always putting him off. Always saying that she made too much money working for his mother and step farther. She'd said that she was just out of apprenticeship school

And if she walked away from this job it would be a long time before she got another. She would not even be permitted the job of 2nd Chef on a luxury liner. What could he say? He couldn't promise her security just yet. Although he hoped to start a new venture with new partners. The idea was still in the planning stages. It would be called, 'Food For Thought' and it would be located near a college or University. They would cater to the gourmet preferences of the university crowd. Of course, they would need to serve wine and beer. But no hard liquor would be sold. Jen had liked the idea and offered to be of assistance when all the kinks were finally worked out.

Well, here goes Peter thought to himself as he stepped from his automobile and entered the back door. Once in the kitchen he looked immediately for Jennifer. He was a bit earlier than he was expected but traffic had been surprisingly light driving up and he had made good time. He looked around for signs of Jen and his stepfather but the only greeting he got was from Phillip who came at him rushing like a crazed beast? "Hold on, hold on Phil," he shouted! He covered his face from the assault of Phillip's front feet and long nasty tongue. "I'm glad to see you too buddy but, I sure as hell don't want to kiss you," he protested to the dog.

Finally, he gave in and just let Phillip tire himself out. He was just about to walk out of the kitchen when it came to him that Jen might be in the pantry. Yes, she might be there hiding from him as she often did. Then, in a mad rush of passion, she would attack him like he was a long lost hero returning from war and they would wrestle right there on the kitchen floor. Laughing until their sides ached and their stomach's hurt. He tiptoed to the pantry and with his left hand he pushed the door open. As it swung open he stepped back and poked his head in the room.

Peter's face turned crimson. There stood Mr. Phelps with his hand covering himself. And behind him was the innocent Jennifer Roethlisberger house cook. Hugh Phelps was as naked as a plucked goose at Christmas. And so was she.

Peter Nelson went quickly to his room on the third floor of the grand house. He had deliberately chosen the attic as his personal space when he was in college and it had served him well. He was determined to grab a few things and get out of that house before his mother came back from town and his step sister arrived home from University to begin her summer vacation. Mercedes was due at any moment and he knew he would have to hurry.

Peter didn't want to be rude to her. Not To Mercedes. She was one of the few bright spots in his life and they got along famously. They had shared more than a few secrets with one another. And it didn't matter to him that she confessed to being bi-sexual. That was like admitting she was a Lesbian. Well, lesbian, thespian, it mattered not to him. To him she was his sweet sister, albeit, half-sister. And they were determined to stay close forever. Throwing a few things in an overnight bag he was almost out of his room when Hugh Phelps came up the narrow stairs leading to the attic space.

"Peter, I want to talk to you," he began. "Well, I sure as the devil don't want to listen," Peter replied! "Save it to explain to my mother when I call her and tell her what I just saw." "Come on Pete." His step father was now pleading. "Come on, come on? Where are we going," Peter demanded? "You want me to be a witness in my mother's divorce case against you? Well, you don't have to worry Mr. because I am going to oblige you. You see, my mother's a lawyer and she taught me well. I'm very, very good at giving testimony. In fact, I was star witness against my OWN father when she divorced him." Peter was shouting at the top of his lungs. "SO WHAT SYMPATHY DO YOU THINK I'M GOING TO HAVE FOR YOU?"

With that said Hugh Phelps began to whimper. "Pete son," he said, "you'll make me lose EVERYTHING I'VE GOT. Everything I've worked so hard for. Please don't do this to me." But Peter remained unmoved, He stood there gloating. As personally hurt as he was over Jen's infidelity he was at happy to have something to hang over his stepfather's head. It was called revenge and Peter Nelson was enjoying every bit of it.

In a one final effort to convince his step son to be silent about what he had just seen Hugh said, "How much is it worth to you to shut up about this? Go ahead Peter tell me, what do you want **twenty**, thirty grand? How much?" Peter wasn't expecting that one. He needed money. Oh, did he need cash! There was the new restaurant venture and then there was his summer vacation to be considered. He was only working part-time. Cash would solve all his problems, at least for the immediate future.

Without thinking too much about it he finally blurted out- "fifty!" "I want fifty grand and I want it by next Tuesday. That's Tuesday, the 14th and if I don't get it I'll tell Vern, I promise you that." "Okay Pete my boy, it's yours. You got it." Hugh Phelps backed out the door with his head hung in shame. He turned to walk back downstairs, leaving Peter to unpack his bag and to gloat in the juices of his coup. Neither of the two men had noticed that there was another person at the bottom of the stairs. No one saw her hiding in the bathroom that Peter's mother had installed for him as a special present. It was designed to save him the trouble of going all the way to the 2nd floor. Although tiny it was fully equipped and it served as his special and private loo or salle de toilette as Veronica called it. But Mercedes, just home from college stood in its doorway in disbelief. Her father: again involved in a scandal with yet another woman and blackmailing her half-brother to keep him silent. He was so selfish- that man. He only thought of himself. Here she was, home for the summer and looking forward to a nice quiet vacation. What does she find at home but this chaos and turmoil! And with one more year to go before her graduation who knows would happen or what would become of her? What would she do? Go crawling back to her mother whom she never could get along with for more than five minutes? It was all so unfair of daddy. So cruel and selfish. Well, they could make all the deals they wanted but this time Mercedes would look out for Mercedes. She would come down on the right side of this airplane so help her. She would go to Veronica and tell her what she had overheard. Every single word of it. Yes, she knew where she would get the money to continue her education. All the way through grad school!

She stood there in the bathroom she waited until all was quiet and then she crept down the thickly carpeted hall to her own room and quietly closed her door. She wouldn't wait until Veronica came home. She would call her forthwith and reveal every single word. Drama! There was always some drama when she came home.

Veronica arrived to collect Philomene at precisely one o'clock. It was earlier than expected but the appointment ahead of hers had been cancelled and Mr. Renee had taken her at once. As she entered Monsieur Andre was leaving the shop and they nearly collided. Monsieur Andre said he was going out to run a few errands and he had not noticed that Mme. Phelps was standing there looking in the window admiring her beautiful cat. "She is gorgeous n'est ce pas, Madame Phelps? You haven't changed your mind about leaving her with me. Non?" "Well, Monsieur Andre, I've been giving that careful consideration and I'd like to keep her at home until I'm ready to go on vacation this year.

I don't know how she'll take to being left behind and all." "Well, if you'd like," he said, "I could keep her for a few weekends. Just to get her accustomed to being with me and then." Veronica interrupted him. "I will certainly give that careful consideration and if you like her and if she likes you then maybe. Perhaps I would consider letting her stay for a month or so while I take myself a much needed summer vacation. Perhaps I'll go again to Rome or Paris and then visit my parents in Milwaukee. Oh, I must go to Paris this year and I won't forget those specialty items you asked me to bring back. What do you think?" Suddenly, Andre was not in such a hurry to leave. "Why, Mme. Phelps, what a wonderful idea," he cooed. "And when you come back we can talk more. Non?" "Why certainly, that is if she works out for your purposes and you still want her. We might settle on something to our mutual satisfaction," Veronica replied. "But I'm not promising her to you. I wish to be perfectly clear on that score," she said- being ever the lawyer. "Wonderful, Mme. Then it's all settled. I'll just run along now, I'm already late and I wanted to pick up a surprise for you know who." He walked to the curb and slipped into the back seat. His chauffeur gently closed the door behind him, went around to the driver's side of the limo and drove off down the street. In his heart he knew that Madame Phelps would never part with the cat and he didn't fault her. The entire scene had been an act for the prying eyes and ears of his nosy clients.

Philomene had been watching all of this from the store's window. She had seen it all but she had not been able to hear a word being uttered. She was bothered by this but she consoled herself, watching Monsieur Andre as he stepped into the limousine and was whisked away to some exciting adventure. He was so romantic. Within minutes she too had been swept up by her Mistress, placed in the awful cat box and was being swung like a shopping bag from Macy's basement. Once again she was placed on the back seat of the car. She didn't understand why Mistress was being so gruff with her. She hadn't done anything to deserve this kind of treatment. Well, she had knocked over that silly umbrella stand but they had all held Phillip responsible and she'd let him take the blame. After all they knew SHE wouldn't do such a clumsy thing. Philomene couldn't wait to get home. Perhaps she would spend the rest of the afternoon lying in bed or maybe she would walk over to her mother's house, just to show off. Her mother and sister always liked to hear about Philomene's adventures in town and whatever news she'd been able to pick up in the shop from the other cats. She didn't understand why they were taken to the shop so seldom, it was criminal the way they were treated by the Stewarts', like wild animals with no rights.

As she gunned the car down the roadway, finally arriving into her driveway Veronica Nelson had every reason to be gruff. The entire scene with Monsieur Andre had been an act. Just one more reason to be upset. She was not upset about parting with Philomene. It was only for one weekend and she had no intention of ever selling her precious creature. But she was upset because she knew that Andre was not just going on errands. Veronica knew exactly where he was going and it wasn't to pick up a gift for her either.

He was going to that other woman's house. The widow Martha Bennington who lived out on the Drive and who did not appear to have any morals at all since the death of her husband Robbie.

It was common knowledge. She had heard the rumors over and over again. Even at the cocktail reception that had been given to thank those who contributed so generously to Lupus Research, there had been talk.

Besides, Andre knew that Saturday afternoons was THEIR time. She was nobody's idiot. That is why he was rushing out of the shop. He had meant to avoid her but she had returned much earlier than expected and now she'd have to spend the afternoon at home with Hugh. Veronica and Monsieur Andre were lovers. They had been so for more than a year. To make matters worse there had been that annoying call from her step daughter Mercedes. She just couldn't wait until Veronica got home to tell her what she had overheard between Peter and Hugh. That was too much to ask. No, Mercedes had called to inform her of the entire conversation she'd overheard. Well, she KNEW about it all. Every last bit of it, she knew. And she was planning to do something about in her own sweet time. But now her hand had been forced and she was going to have to put on an act as the wronged and distraught wife in order to make her point. In order to achieve her goal.

And her goal was nothing short of retaining her marriage with Dr. Hugh Nelson and her good name. What difference did it make that they were no longer in love. They made a nice looking couple. And that was rare. Why their relationship was the envy of all who met them, the medical doctor and his lawyer wife. She could have a worse existence. It was a kind of arrangement. But, there were times when she needed to put her foot down. Just to show him who was in control. Who had the real money and power in this family! To start she would take that vacation. Secondly, she would put an end to her shaky relationship with that gadabout Andre. There were plenty others who would be delighted to take his place and they could be just as discreet about it. After her brief vacation she'd pay for her peace and quiet by giving Peter the money he needed to restart his business in the City. If it failed this time she would do it again and again as long as he stayed away from her house and did not go crying to his father. And of course she had already guessed what Mercedes' real intentions were about. Mercedes didn't realize that she'd planned to keep her in college as long as she wished to attend. She liked the girl but she could be a real pain at times. A pain in the, you know where!

Veronica Nelson cut off the engine, stepped out of her car with her precious cat Philomene and entered the front door. She never used the rear or side doors leading to the patio and swimming pool.

It was un-lady like and she didn't like the noise that the bushes made as they brushed against her dress or slacks. She never wore jeans or pants. That too, was un-lady like. The instant she entered the front door she began moaning and crying as though she had been attacked on the way home. Handing Philomene, still in her box to Peter, she hurried up to her room and locked the door. Veronica sat at her dressing table and took off her shoes. Then, she reclined on her silk chaise longue and picked up a magazine to leaf through. She was worn out by all of this drama and she needed to take a nap before she began the second act of the play, she decided. After all, how long could she keep up the pretense of crying? That was the hardest part. She could do a good job feigning anger but it took a special kind of actress to cry on cue and she wasn't that good at it.

The moment Philomene heard her Mistress crying she understood that she had to take matters into her own hands. She was going straight to that dingbat Phillip and find out what he knew. If he had bothered to pay attention at all. And then, depending on what he told her she would put a stop to all of this nonsense once and for all. She wasn't going to lose her home and what was rightfully her inheritance simply because certain people chose to act like dogs. Philomene jumped down from her position on the sofa and walked into the kitchen. There, she found Phillip engrossed in his favorite past time-eating.

"Phillip what do you know and how long have you known it," she asked him straight away. "What ya Talkin' 'bout," he replied? "Don't you keep your eyes open at all Phillip," she demanded. "Oh, you mean with 'em peoples in da house" he finally asked between gulps of Alpo beef and chicken parts? "With THOSE PEOPLE in THE house," she corrected him and then she added –"Jerk." "Well, I ain't sayin' nothin' if you gonna treat me like a dog," an offended Phillip said sheepishly. "I'm sorry, I had no intentions of hurting your feelings Phillip but SOMEONE around here has to step up to the plate and I don't mean the dinner plate." Philomene was proud of herself. She had used that expression on purpose. It was an expression she had learned from him and he took the bait. He smiled and then began to spill his guts. After he was through he suddenly ran to the door barking wildly and Philomene realized she'd get no more from him because Peter was coming down the stairs holding his leash. Alright, she thought. I've got the facts I need but what to do about them? It was more complicated than she ever imagined. If Phillip was to be believed. Everyone was mad at everyone. She needed something, some event or crisis to divert the attention of all in the house. Yes, she thought at last. That's it. There is but one thing to do. I must disappear. I, Viscomtesse Philomene, will have to make the supreme sacrifice for the good of Maison Anglaise.

Resigned to that fact, she walked slowly up the stairs to spend the evening with her Mistress. She wasn't hungry, not in the least. She had other things to worry about. More important things. Taking her time, she slowly climbed the staircase. This will probably be the last time I do this she said to herself. When I descend these stairs it will be to leave this grand place. And with that thought she stopped at the very top of the stairs and wiped away a single tear. She hated crying, it always reddened her eyes and there was nothing worse than sky blue eyes with red pupils. It was demonic, she always said. Absolutely demonic! Like a Halloween mask or an intoxicated Frank Sinatra. When she thought of his music she let her head sway gently back and forth. He was soo romantic. Soo dreamy and smooth. Not at all like the singers of today. It was the one reason she liked to visit her mother. They'd sit there under the living room window, smelling the roses and listening to the sounds of Sinatra's voice as it drifted out into the garden, surrounding them with romance.

Of course, the garden was not as large or as well tended as her garden but this was a small distraction when HE was singing weaving his web of magic. She was still thinking romantic thoughts when she walked into Veronica's bedroom. She hadn't realized it was now past 7 P.M. and she had not been served her dinner. Veronica was sprawled across the bed and she had the lights off. This was so untypical of Mistress. She NEVER forgot Philomene's meals. She was tempted to jump on the bed and remind her but she stopped short when she realized that this would be an ugly act. After all, she couldn't beg for dinner like a common House cat! There must be something horribly wrong, she thought. There wasn't a sound in the room. SHE'S DEAD. Philomene thought. This has all been too much of a strain and she's committed suicide. Oh no! I'm too late! What on earth will I do now? With that she jumped up on the bed just as the telephone rang. Veronica, half-awake reached over and grabbed the phone in her left hand, switching it to the right hand almost in a single motion. "Hello," she said, "Veronica Nelson speaking." Mistress, Philomene thought. Thank cat heavens. You scared me half to death. If anyone is going to commit hara - kiri around here it's going to be me. Not You. You don't deserve to die, you have only one life to live while I have seven more. By my latest count she thought. She took a minute to count them carefully before deciding that maybe there were only six remaining.

Philomene lay there perfectly still, trying to glean as much from her Mistress' telephone conversation as possible. This might be important, something I need to know, she reasoned. Almost immediately she realized that it was the voice of Monsieur Andre on the other end. She listened to her Mistress say that she knew she had promised to leave Philomene in his shop. She heard her tell Andre not to worry about giving her any more money. But she didn't realize they had agreed that Philomene would only be there until Veronica for the weekend and then again during her vacation. And she had no idea that the money they were speaking of referred to the purchase of high end cat collars and chains that Veronica would purchase at the specialty store while she was in Paris and that would not happen until later that summer, still 2 months away. She understood however that her Mistress was going abroad without her. And that meant certainly to Paris. It had happened but once before.

But she had been an infant at the time and had not understood the magic of Paris so she hadn't been at all bothered.

Philomene was distraught and heartbroken. The only friend she had in the world had abandoned her. She was being tossed out of the house like an old shoe. Sold as if she was a white slave to some harem in the Middle East. It was disgraceful. She would NEE- VER live this down. She quickly decided she didn't need to hear any more and she ran down the staircase to speak with that brute Phillip. HE AND ONLY HE had planned this. Oh, he was a schemer that one. He had threatened and threatened her and he was finally getting his wish.

She was out and he was in. And after all she had done for the family. He had done nothing but cause trouble since they were both toddlers. And now it was he who would be rewarded for his stupidity while she, the brains of the pair was being shown the door. Getting the axe, so to speak. Philomene marched right into the kitchen to confront him. But instead of finding the dog there she encountered Hugh Nelson. He was stirring something into a glass. It was her mistress's favorite glass. The one she asked him to bring her whenever she couldn't sleep and wanted to take a sedative. So THAT's his plan, Philomene thought. He plans to give her a sedative when she calls for it and when they find her dead in her bed he can claim she took an over dose. That done, he will inherit all the money, gain control of Maison Anglaise and win the favor of one Ms. Jennifer Roethlisberger all in one fell swoop. Well, it isn't going to happen!

Not in my fourth lifetime! If I'm correct in my count. And not as long as I'm still in this house, even though it's only going to be for a few hours more, she lamented.

Poor Philomene had no way to know that Veronica had asked her husband to bring her only a glass of water. "No sedatives tonight, dear." She had a headache and she wanted to retire early. "And by the way sweetie, she had added, could you put a little lemon juice in the water? Just a spritz so it won't taste like I'm drinking plain old unfiltered water from the tap. It tastes so nasty sometimes." No, Philomene had no way to know that as Hugh Nelson went back up the stair to his wife's bedroom. He found his wife in bed already in her pajamas. She'd drawn the blinds and in the darkened room, left the night light on for him. Veronica was fast asleep. Leaving the glass on the table beside her, Hugh went back downstairs to the parlor. He was still thinking about the excuse he needed to get his wife to write a check for fifty grand. He didn't have that kind of hush money.

Surely Peter realized how much Hugh needed Veronica. He wouldn't trade her for a poor house cook. No matter how attractive and willing she was. He, Peter could have that young tramp. But he needed his Veronica and the security her money and position bought. What kind of fool did the boy think he was? Hugh made up his mind to speak with Peter one last time and if that didn't work then he would break the news to his wife himself. On Hugh Nelson's own terms. He would then let the chips fall where they May. After all, he had talked her out of divorce one time. Certainly he could do it again. She'd listen to him. She just HAD to listen.

It took only a matter of seconds for Philomene to get up the stairs and into her Mistress' Chamber. There stood the glass on the table where her husband had left it. And it was still full. I made it, Philomene nearly screamed. She was in time to prevent this murder that would bring shame and disgrace to her name and that of her mother and sister. Not that she cared much for her sister, but she had brothers, wherever they were in this world and their names would be besmirched by the scandal of a poisoning. In one leap she was on the table and off. She almost broke the glass as it came crashing from the table onto the carpet. The contents spilling as it fell. But it didn't break and Veronica barely moved from her position of rest.

Hugh would find her still laying there in the same spot when he too went to bed.

But that was not until 4 A.M. He'd waited up for Peter but the boy had not come home. Deciding the whole thing could wait until the next day he climbed the stairs and entered his wife's bedroom. There he turned off the light on the table and noted that she had spilled the glass of water. The glass was still lying on the floor and the carpet beneath it was wet to the touch.

When he picked it up. He smiled. Veronica hadn't needed anything but a good night's sleep, he thought. She was tired. He bent over the sleeping wife and kissed her gently on the cheek. Then, Hugh tip-toed Across the carpet and left the room. He left her door open slightly so that her beloved cat could come and go as it pleased. Philomene was elated with herself. She had saved the day and the life of her mistress. It was to be her final act of bravery and courage in the house. She had put on an Oscar winning performance. People would speak of it for years and years. Ranking it right up there with Leigh in "Gone With The Wind," "Haywood in "I Want To Live "and Davis and Crawford in "Whatever Happened to Baby Jane?" And now she would do one last thing for the family. Something that would write her name in the annals of her family's history. She would leave behind these hallowed halls of brick and mortar. Leave these fine rooms of Italian, Chinese, Louis Quinze and Louis Seize furnishings and she would go on to live out her days amongst strangers, albeit very rich Strangers in New Rochelle's most exclusive suburbia.

The moment she heard Hugh's bedroom door close she sprang into action. She had only a few minutes and she mustn't be late in her intentions. Walking quickly and with dignity down the winding staircase she hurried to the back door. She knew she had to be there when Peter came in the house. Whenever he was there he stayed out late with his friends. He visited the old haunts in Larchmont and always came back to the house around five in the morning. He was always drunk when he arrived. She could smell the alcohol and the marijuana. Oh yes, I know Mr. Peter Nelson, she thought.

Philomene has your number! She sat there alongside the hulking frame of Phillip. Well, as close as she dared. Phillip stank, she observed. He hadn't had a bath in a month. As if he could read her mind Phillip glanced at her like he had seen a ghost and then he said, "You must gotta go too." She didn't bother to respond. She had not even thought of that urge. But she was now reminded that whenever Peter came in late he let the dog out into the back yard for a few minutes to do his business. She started to answer with meee nooo, but thinking better of it, she didn't say a word to Phillip. You'd think he'd have noticed by now that I don't have to be let out in the yard to take care of my toilet in full view of the populace. I have my own private bathroom and it is right there behind the door where you sit. You idiot. Can't he smell that? It's the first thing the cook takes care of when she comes to work in the mornings. She was tempted to respond to the slight but she didn't want to argue with anyone at that time of the morning, it was bad for the nerves.

Suddenly, she saw Phillip stand and begin wagging his tail in a furious manner. Realizing that he'd sensed Peter was in the driveway she stood as near the door as she could. But she nearly miscalculated. For as Peter entered the door Phillip jumped on him and the pair began tussling and playing. "You ready to go boy. You waitin' up for ole Pete ta let you out. Huh boy?" Philomene could have brought up a hair ball but it wasn't yet time. So she just sat there; rolling her eyes to the heavens in utter disgust and contempt at the childishness of the two boys.

Oh, grow up, she wanted to scream. But she restrained herself.

This went on for a few seconds and then Peter opened the door and stood there. In her path! She almost lost heart. If she walked out now he had only to reach down and pick her up. She waited until he closed the door but then, remembering something he'd left on the car seat, he opened it again and walked out.

He didn't go out alone. Philomene scampered right between his legs and into the yard. She ran to the opposite side of his car and then, collecting herself, she moved with stealth and purpose. Right past Phillip and under the hedges. She thought she heard Phillip call to her in his brutish voice, "ruff, ruff." But Philomene didn't bother to look back at him. She was keenly aware that it's a rough world out there. How many times had Claire told her that? And she didn't need to be reminded of it by some oafish lout who still insisted upon saying 'ruff' instead of the proper spelling and pronunciation 'rough'. Under the hedges she ran and then onto the sidewalk. Observing all the rules she'd been taught early in her life she safely crossed to the other side. She knew she needed to pass her mother's home and she dreaded doing that. Claire might be up, even at this hour. After all it was Sunday morning and mother liked to attend Church around the corner for early Mass. But it was only a little after five and her mother was still in bed. Philomene walked in the direction of town and Monsieur Andre's shop.

She would sit there in the doorway if she had to. She'd wait until Monday morning. Even though she had not had a thing to eat since breakfast she didn't feel hungry. They say at times like this you don't feel the need for nourishment, she thought to herself. She was glad she didn't have time to say goodbye to her mother and her sister. Oh, Jeanette wouldn't care. The girl WANTED Philomene gone and out of the way. She was totally jealous of her.

But Viscomtesse Claire would have been distraught to no end. She'd have tried to talk her out of leaving. Reminding her of her familial obligations. Namely, to marry and produce offspring.

And, she fully intended to marry but she wasn't so sure about the other part. They say that pregnancy causes one to lose figure and I'm having none of that. At the thought she smiled to herself. I'll get word to mother on tomorrow by messenger. That's what such services are for and I wouldn't like to be the cause of her worries. She'd worry herself into bad health, Philomene thought. She continued to the corner and then stopped briefly to get her bearings. Looking up at the signs hanging above her she was Upset with herself that she had never bothered to learn to read at a higher level. She had ignored her mother's warnings. It wasn't totally her fault. She'd listened to her Mistress and Mistress always said she didn't trust those schools that trained pets to be obedient.

But Mother had told her that there are more important things to be learnt in those classes and that Mistress was unaware of that. By "important things" she now knew Claire had been speaking of academics. She was learning the hard way that mothers really do know best after all, and she was foolish to have ignored her warning that just having that name tag around one's neck was not enough. "You need to KNOW where you are and what you are doing in this world," she'd been told. "Our species have never seen times like this, when we've fallen so low in numbers and are so loathed and despised."

"Not since the 17th Century during the Salem witch hunts!" And she was right. After all, Claire could read quite well and she could write too. She had not believed it when Claire told her that she read the New York Times when it was delivered each morning by the newspaper man. Or, at least she read all of the front page and as much as she could read of it before it was taken into the house. By the time he Seymours' read it over their coffee it was old news to Claire. And the old girl had demonstrated her ability to write too. Sitting there in the living room window just last year she had shown Philomene that she could spell her name on the window pane. Of course she'd doubted her. But Claire had definitely written C-L-A-I on the frosted pane. She'd have finished too if it had not been for the Agency day maid. The maid thought mother was signaling that she wanted to be let back into the house and afraid of losing her job, she opened the door and called her to come in. She never noticed the name on the window pane and it's just as well that she didn't.

The Seymours need money and they'd have put her on Oprah or The Letterman show. It would have been disastrous for mother at her advanced age. Show biz is a young person's game! Walking on, Philomene finally recognized the one land mark she needed. Although it was not a corner property it was the only house that remotely rivaled that of Maison Anglaise and as she passed it the Viscomtesse reared her head even higher and pranced by as if she was a ballet dancer. These people were upstarts. The man who owned the house was a mere college professor and his wife didn't go to business at all. She actually WORKED around the house Philomene had been told. Moreover, they didn't own a cat. Unless one wanted to count that spindly creature who sometimes visited them from the vacant lot two blocks away. And it wouldn't be vacant very long because it was prime property and there was new construction going up there in a few weeks. She'd heard they had acquired a pet. Just a dog. His name is Rover or Dover, but who knew? She continued to the corner and crossed. She was going in the correct direction and she KNEW it. Merci bien.

At seven in the morning Monsieur Andre was tired. He had been out all night long and seated in the rear of his limousine he was on his way home when he recalled that he had forgotten the box of chocolates. He needed those chocolates to keep peace in the family. He'd bought them earlier as he knew they were his wife's favorites. He didn't like her to eat chocolates. They had marred her once beautiful figure and face he claimed. Chocolates and other rich foods. In fact, all the food that she or any normal human being could possibly consume in one 24 hour period.

She was obese and she was constantly Changing her mind about what she intended to do about it. It was exercise, it was exercise and diet. Then, she would have her stomach stapled and have liposuction.

She was always promising but she never delivered. She delivered nothing. But the pizza shop delivered and the Chinese Restaurant delivered. Even the new gourmet boutique in town delivered to her door. Whatever she needed or desired to stuff her face and pack on the pounds was delivered. It was degoutant. He didn't like bringing her rich foods but he knew it was the only way to smooth over the difficulty he was going to have in arriving home this late, ostensibly from work. She would never believe him without the excuse that he had gone to Manhattan to buy her favorite chocolates. She would forgive him his occasional infatuations. After all, she knew he loved her mostly for the huge inheritance she'd been left from her late grandfather's estate. His occasional flings were to be tolerated. But Dominique would never forgive him if he began neglecting her dietary whims. Andre smiled when he thought of his true whereabouts that night. He had spent the night wining and dining the widow Bennington and it had all been a worthwhile effort. Realizing the box of candy was not in the car he remembered he'd left the box on his desk at the shop earlier that afternoon. He directed the chauffeur to turn the car around and go back into town. Darn that Veronica Nelson, she had talked him to death about her cat and about their on again, off again affair. He'd stormed out of the shop leaving the box behind in an aborted effort to avoid another confrontation with her. Surely, she could see that he was tired of her and of the children's games she seemed to revel in playing. Well, no matter! He'd have to speak with her on a more serious note. He didn't like admitting it but he could not be with any woman longer than a few months before he grew tired of them. And he'd never leave his wife and all that money. Monsieur Andre sighed his exasperation. He would run into town and pick up the chocolates and voila, he would be on his way home again. Madame Bennington was a most exciting and intriguing personality, he smiled with much satisfaction.

Meanwhile, Philomene, tired from her long trek into town, had already arrived at the shop. It was closed as she expected and she knew that it would be a long wait until Monday morning but she could do little else but sit there with hunger pains gripping her body. She tried desperately not to focus on food. After all, mother had told her that a skipped meal now and again was good for the figure. But with her mind wandering back to the kitchen at Maison Anglaise and the specially prepared meals, the pantry shelves lined with imported gourmet canned foods bought especially for her plate of crystal; it was difficult to think of anything else. "Hi beautiful," a voice called to her seemingly from nowhere. "I'm over here, between the Land Rover and the Jeep and I'm comin' at ya babe!" Philomene lifted her head just a bit higher than usual. There was no one else within blocks of the grooming spa, so no one could be speaking to her. And certainly not using such crass language! Just then a tall black and white cat appeared on the curb in front of Monsieur Andre's shop. "An' what cha doin' up at this time of the morn, might I ask," he said. She knew he was pretending to put on airs for the fun of it and she didn't say a word. She just sat there in the doorway of the shop and stared as only she could do. But he would not be put off. "You should be at home catching up on your beauty rest, mee lovely! Now don' tell me you ain't the breakfas' in bed type 'cause I kin see you is.

Yo' precious little hands ain't never been near no kitchen befo', lessen it was to wash 'em!" He had dropped all pretense of dignity now and he continued in his street vernacular. "Don'cha know dis here 'stablishment is closed on Sundays," he inquired of her. "That's right, closed up tight as a drum all day. So ain't no sense in sittin' an' starin' in space ackin' like you don' hear what I'm sayin'. I ain't one for waitin' round wastin' up time, so let split!" When Philomene still didn't answer, he asked, "what da matter Mademoiselle, cat got yo' tongue? S'cuse me, no pun intended der."

Unable to hide her laughter at his poor attempt to make a joke she said to him in mock indignation "What do you want of me kind sir?" "Well, I won' answer dat question lessen you consent to havin' breakfas' at my abode an' at my expense," the stranger said. Although she was hungry Philomene politely declined the offer. Claire had warned her more than once about people like him and about going anywhere with strangers. Why he was lucky she was even speaking with him. "I know whatcha thinkin' mee lovely," he said quickly. "But t' prove, I ain't just givin' you da run around I will bring breakfas' to you. A kin' a sidewalk 'livery, if you will, my pet." And with that he dashed down the street and around the corner.

It took only five or six minutes and he was back carrying something hanging from his mouth. Dropping it unceremoniously at her feet he stood back and proclaimed in an attempt to imitate the voice of those old movie caricature of butlers, "breafas' is served, m'am." "That's not funny." Philomene said. Putting her head in the air. "And you should be ashamed of yourself. Your ancestors and mine were black. We came from the Middle East and we were worshiped in Egypt and." "Hold on, hold on," he said.

"I know my Black history, what do you think I am- a Martian?" "Oh, I didn't know," she said. "I can see that your coat is mostly black but I never assume anything. You know what they say about that word." "Well eat," he said. "Then, we'll talk about da drinking an' da being merry part." For the first time Philomene looked down at her feet. She had been so busy admiring his muscular and well-built frame that she hadn't noticed that lying at her feet was a baby mouse. "Oh nooo," she screamed, "What do you expect me to do with, with … that? Why, it's a mou … Mouse! A rodent. I have NEVER eaten mice before," she said in an indignant tone! "Well, dere's always a first time," he said- grinning. "Lessen, you too good to eat my food!" "Oh noo sir," she proclaimed her innocence. "I didn't mean it THAT way! It's just that, oh, you wouldn't understand and I don't have time to explain." "Try me, go 'head, I ain't got nuttin' but time, so knock yo'self out, lady."

"Oh my goodness sir! Excuse me for being rude but I have to go.

Something unexpected is happening! I'm sorry I have to be so short with you." "Sure Shorty," he said, looking down at her in mocked disdain. "But if you ever need a friend, or start thinkin' 'bout tyin' the knot, look me up. You'll fin' me right 'round dat corner behin' da bakery and near da Chinese Restaurant. But not too near, if you know what I mean," he said with a wink and a smile." "Oh, don't you start with your tasteless jokes again," she said. "I can't stand prejudiced people!" She wanted to say more on the subject but in the corner of her eye she'd caught glimpse of Monsieur Andre's limousine and he was being helped out of it as they spoke.

When Andre looked down and saw Philomene standing in the doorway of his shop he could scarcely believe his good luck. He thought that Veronica had brought the cat there as a kind of appeasement gift. One that he could use on two fronts. He would take her home to his wife along with the chocolates. She had always been fond of this cat. Then, on Monday morning he would bring her back to the shop to serve his purposes there. He reached down and picked her up in his arms. He began saying nice things to her in the French language. "OO la, la ma Petite. Qu'est gue tu faites ici ce matin? Etc. etc." Philomene wanted to die right there. She was in Paradise. She had made the right choice as she always did. And now EVERYONE would be jealous. She had saved her beloved Mistress' home and her own name for posterity. Perhaps they'd consider her for the Nobel Peace prize or even a special kind of Sainthood. Maybe they'd call it Cathood. She had certainly shown everyone that she was nobody's fool.

Holding her under one arm Andre used his key to open the door. Then he placed her in her usual place of importance- in the window with the satin cushion. "Now you stay here my love.

I'll be right back. I see you've got an early start with breakfast this morning." She wanted to answer him but she was too busy looking around the empty shop. She had never been there except as a client and with no one in the place it seemed a bit eerie to her. In only a few seconds Monsieur Andre had returned with the box of candy. He took from the rack one of the fine velvet-lined bags that he used for promotion. He placed the candy on one side of the bag and picked up the cat. He placed Philomene inside the warm and cushiony bag.

He was ready to leave when he had a thought. He needed to call Veronica. He needed to thank her. Monsieur Andre picked up the telephone and dialed her number. He let the phone ring several times and thinking it too early in the morning he was almost ready to hang up when she answered. "This is Veronica speaking. May I help you?" "Bonjour, c'est Andre." As though she didn't know his voice. "I just wanted to thank you for bringing Philomene over this morning. It was sweet of you." Veronica sat up in her bed. "Philomene! My cat," she said. "At YOUR place! What's she doing there, I certainly didn't take her there. Oh, the poor baby, I had no idea …She's so clever to be able to negotiate the traffic. It being so far away and all." Andre was as mystified as Veronica but he needed to get as much mileage out of this as possible. There was the wife to think about and his OTHER problem. He shrugged his shoulder and said to Veronica. "Well, it's too early in the morning to bring her to you and I just came into the shop to pick up some papers I'm going to need on tomorrow. Do you …. Oh? I can? Do you mean that?" His face was glowing and he began smiling. "Then it's all settled. I'll keep her here until next weekend when you return from visiting your friends in Miami. Meanwhile, I'll take her home and bring her back on Monday and then she can start her job catching a few of these mice in the shop. There are enough here to keep her busy and to make her fat but not too fat. Maybe you'll be kind enough to let her stay an extra month or two. Oh yes, I will even PAY you for her service. …Oh yes, she can catch mice. When I drove up this morning she had already caught one. In fact, she had even started eating it. Hadn't you my sweet?" He looked down at Philomene sitting at the bottom of the bag in total shock?

EAT MICE! CATCH MICE! Philomene said almost aloud. She was aghast! Is this his idea of a joke? But it can't be, she thought. She had heard her Mistress' voice at the other end of the phone. No, this was very serious. Me? A common mouse catcher? A live rat trap? That's what is to become of ME? Oh no sir, I'm nobody's pest control company. That's a job for Orin, or Dunhill Pest Exterminators. Even Rota Rooter or somebody. Not Viscomtesse Philomene of Larchmont.

I'm sorry Monsieur Andre or whatever your name is. Thanks but no thanks baby. Philly's out of here. Sayonara, Marco Polo. And with that she jumped out of the bag and ran toward the door. Luckily, Andre had left the door open just wide enough for her to squeeze through. And although he ran toward her calling after her, the cat was nowhere to be seen. Philomene ran down the street as though she didn't hear him calling her name. She had thought of stories of the Jamaican track sensation Hussein Bolt. She pretended she was racing against him at a major event in Brussels. She had not seen the race but she knew it had taken place somewhere in that beautiful city where French is spoken. It was so romantic there.

Down the street and around the corner she ran. Her mind was racing too. She thought of the only one she knew she could depend on besides her Mistress and mother. Although she had just met him and didn't even know his name or if he HAD a name. She stopped for an instant to compose herself. She began to whimper, pretending to cry. "Help meee. Help meee." It wasn't long before she was joined by her new found friend. "You rang ma'am," he asked?

"Would ya be a needin' my services?" "Oh can't you ever be serious about anything," she said.

For a second she had forgotten her dilemma. Then, collecting her thoughts she told him what she had just learned. "Well, whatcha gon do babe? Whatcha gon do," he asked? "Well," I was thinking,

Philomene said… "Thinking about what you said earlier. And it IS time for me to settle down." She paused for a moment or two.

"AND" he asked her mockingly? But Philomene WAS serious now. She ignored his playfulness, continuing, "I… I," "Go 'haid girl, spit it out. Lay your cards on da table," he said encouragingly.

"I was thinking that maybe you and I could get married and live over at my place. That's at Maison Anglaise. Of course, you wouldn't know where that is located." He interrupted her- "'cos I knows where dat is. I been 'round da block a time or two. I is an alley cat an' I know where mos' things is in dis here town," he said proudly. She ignored him. "I would have to spend most of my time in the house but if you are willing, I have a plan that I know will work." "I'm down, Ms. Brown, 'cause I wanna stay around," he answered while looking her up and down and smiling.

"Anyway, the pickins' is getting slim 'round here lately and it's time I split the scene befo' I become part of it," he said glancing cautiously in the direction of the restaurant. Again she ignored his comment and said, "I think we need to leave now because it's a long walk home and I have a few things I need to discuss with you." "It ain't such a long walk and 'sides, I'll show you a short cut Shorty." He started down the alley in what looked to be the opposite direction of Maison Anglaise but it wasn't long before she began recognizing familiar territory. Past the church they went and around the corner until soon they were walking right past the house where her mother and sister lived. When they entered the yard of Maison Anglaise Philomene stopped. Growing solemn, she explained her plan. He was to go into the garage and catch mice. As many mice as he could catch in an hour or two. Place them in a pile in the corner and wait for her to begin calling her Mistress. When Hugh Nelson came out to investigate he would find the pile of mice and he'd be so happy.

Why he would be GLAD to have an extra paw around the place. He had often talked about getting a cat just for that purpose. That was the easy part. As far as them as a couple was concerned- sure, she'd marry him but there would have to be a pre-nuptial agreement. And she did not want kids. Not yet anyway. Not until she knew for sure how her career was going. Philomene wiped her face with one paw, smoothing her hair. Really, she only wanted one or two and if he didn't understand she would just get spayed. With or without his permission! Also, she would not tolerate laziness, slovenliness or unfaithfulness on his part. She needed to be sure he could be trusted. Finally, he needed a title. Something she could pass on to her children. Whenever she had them. Just a little something they all could be PROUD of. It didn't matter if he knew his lineage or not. Everyone came from something special. She didn't expect him to have a royal bloodline like hers but she could always make one up. Claire would be glad to help her with that. After all, even royalty had been known to marry an occasional commoner.

The Duke of Windsor and Mrs. Wally Simpson came to mind immediately. She'd watched the story on PBS while lying at the foot of her Mistress bed and she had cried all the way through. Actually, she had been considering a name for him on her way home. He needed something strong and masculine as well as important sounding. "How does The Marquis Henri Louis de St. Jacques sound to you?" He looked at her with a twinkle in his eyes. He hadn't paid too much attention to her but she was quite a dish. With those slanted eyes and fluffy tail.

I can work with dis, he said to himself. Yeah, dis is gon work big time. But to Philomene he asked, "Huh?" And then he added, "that'll do, boo!"

THE END

111

An Envoy from P. O. T. S.
(Power of Thoughts Suggested)

By Maurice P. Fortune

Days later no one would remember having invited him. No one from the Board of Directors of the College had heard his name before that day. Certainly, no member of The Graduation Planning Committee or The Student Council was aware that he'd been asked to address the seniors. In fact, not a soul had noticed his name on the program ten days earlier, the day before or even the morning of the exercises. But when all were seated and the opening song was sung the name was noted in bold letters.

It was sandwiched between the invocation and the Battle Hymn of The Republic. Remarks by H.E. T. Lifan Lapent Tou, P. O.T.S. He was to make the closing remarks and then receive an Honorary PHD. Well, he must be important, they all thought. So much so that his name had been kept a secret. Secret from all but a few important people. But why had no one noticed it before the ceremonies began? What kind of magic had they used to insert it on the program at the very last minute? Would anyone ever know?

With the title His Excellency he had to be a diplomat. The only question was a diplomat from where? From which newly independent Asian or African nation did he come? There were many to choose from and everyone's head was full of questions. Yes, there were questions about Mr. Tou but they would have to wait because the program had provided no additional information. Those left in doubt had their thoughts interrupted by sporadic applause. There were quizzical glances as the name was announced and he rose from his chair just to the left of the senior class.

Methodically and gracefully he approached the podium. He was an ordinary looking fellow of medium height and build. Not more than 5'7 or 8 inches tall and 155 lbs. in weight His Excellency was of middle age. He was balding slightly, not much but in the front of his head. This gave him a distinguished look- like that of a professor of the sciences or mathematics. As he stood looking out over the audience he appeared to take longer than necessary to begin, almost as though he was examining each one of the 3,600 attendees.

Turning his attention to the seniors he smiled. That there was also a furrow on his brow was apparent only to those seated closest to him. He was a man unacquainted with smiling. It appeared that he was about to ask them something. Perhaps the answer to a test question. A question to which he was certain they were unable to answer. But just as quickly he waved them away with impatience. It was the wave of a parent annoyed by youthful arrogance and it carried the hint that their presence was not needed for this segment of the program. In unspoken words it seemed to ask them why they were there. Could they adequately explain the purpose of their presence on this day? And how they dare appear to collect pieces of paper. Paper that signified only their willingness to show up on time for classes over a period of thirty odd months in their young and foolish lives, or their willingness to spend their parents and their sponsors hard earned dollars. Sometimes, wasted money to obtain degrees that would ostensibly give them a head start on the unfortunates. They'd get better jobs and earn more money, buy bigger cars and houses and move to better and gated communities.

The suit Mr. Tou wore was single breasted. It seemed designed with the sole intent of showing off his lean and trim physique.

But it was his skin tone. His skin was very dark and a good match for the black suit and tie. So dark and even toned was his skin that it almost appeared to be make-up. The skin positively glowed and the light seemed to give his eyes more purpose. He raised a hand like a Methodist Minister about to deliver his first Sunday sermon or preach his first funeral. A preacher who, despite the occasion is so mentally and emotionally hyped that on this day the devil himself could not thwart his delivery. It was clear that The Board had chosen well. The man's presence jumped out at his audience as though he was the centerpiece of some set designer's mind. If his appearance there had been in someone's head they had succeeded beyond their most fanciful imaginations.

On stage, Mr. Tou's image captured one's attention in a way that left no escape.

All eyes watched as he placed a single sheet of paper on the stand. A quick glance showed that without uttering a sound he'd captured the attention of the entire senior class. Each appeared anxious that he or she would not be singled out for failing to bring in a required assignment. Or, that even at this late hour a hidden axe would fall and the much coveted diploma would be on some technicality withheld.

He stood there waiting for the applause to die down and when it didn't cease soon enough he cleared his throat and tapped on the microphone. But this wasn't due to impatience. He wanted their attention but he seemed prepared to wait for it and what he was waiting for was the total silence of his audience! What he had to say to them seemed of the utmost urgency and importance. And his were words that would not require applause. As the audience slowly quieted it was noted by a few that without the use of words Mr. Tou revealed that he had never in his entire life rushed the outcome of any event.

He began.

"Ladies and Gentlemen, Distinguished Guests and Members of the graduating class. This has been a glorious Day for all of you. I extend my most heartfelt congratulations to this year's seniors. Especially to the Valedictorian and to all of you receiving honorable mention for your distinguished work. I bow to each you for your efforts and for your achievements." Mr. Tou bowed slightly. "All of you deserve the full measure of fine praise and the accolades you have thus far received. I only regret that time does not allow me to mention by name those who have excelled and those awarded the highest honors. Suffice it to say that you know who you are. We all recognize your accomplishment."

His Excellency's face grew grave as he continued. "I don't wish to be the bearer of sad news but that is precisely why I have come here today. I am here to tell you that a friend of yours is dying. In fact, I've come to tell you that YOU are dying." The decibels in the almost capacity audience rose in a chorus of crescendo and gasps! He paused to allow the full measure of the statement to penetrate.

Just seconds before they had been restlessly leafing through programs trying to figure out who he was and why there were no liner notes about him.

Some had circled his name with their pens. Not with the intent of later finding who his was but with some degree of anger. How could this happen? How dare the college surprise them with an unannounced quest? Diplomat or not! They had a right to know. There were daily schedules to be met and meals to be prepared. People liked to be able to check off the names of the speakers at these events. Not as a later reminder that they'd been present but in hopes that the ritual would somehow spur the speakers to finish sooner. And that the singers and players would play their songs faster thus allowing everyone to leave on time. They'd leave the hall to flash their false smiles and extend meaningless handshakes. They could then go to their parked cars or catch their buses and trains and the world could continue its relentless rush to end one more meaningless day.

Satisfied that he had got across his point to them, Mr. Tou began again.

"I'm sorry to say that but it's true. Mankind is dying. To put it bluntly, it stands on its last leg! Like a condemned murderer who has been denied a stay by the Supreme Court of the land or the Governor of a State. Of course, I don't know how long you have to live. It could be 1,000 years or 100 years. Then again, it could be double that or it may be just months or days. But the inescapable truth is that all of you are like patients at an end of life facility. It's only a matter of time. I must stress that it is not my purpose to be negative but I am sure that some of you are aware that what I tell you is true. You have known it for years. Yes, you have recognized that these cities built of concrete, brick and mortar; these walls of glass and stone and wood cannot survive forever. Today, they rise to the sky in the four corners of the earth. They are I will admit, a sight to behold.

We believe that Earth has never before seen its kind. But are we certain of this? How do we know that there have not been Empires that ruled this planet that were more magnificent in their structures than any of the architectural wonders we see today in the metropolises of the world? Actually, we don't know! What we do know is that the Sumerians and the Egyptians, the Greeks, Romans, Africans and South Americans built their Pyramids and monuments and cities in the last 10,000 years or so. But where are these structures and monuments I ask? Many of them lay in ruins from North America to Africa and the Far East. This, I am afraid my friends is what will happen on an even greater scale to the civilizations of today.

There is greater stress on the Earth today than ever before in recent history. Whether you place the beginning of the industrial revolution in the middle of the 18th century or near the beginning of the 19th century it is clear that it ushered in a time in Earth's history that marked the decent of mankind.

The great industrial plants that spew out the poisons and the slags into the great waterways of the world have not been contained. The great glut of agricultural products will one day take its toll on more and more people as the number of humans now estimated at well over 6 billion continues to climb. And this while millions in the world go to their beds each night suffering from malnutrition and with stomachs cramped by the pangs of hunger. This does not happen solely in the so called Third World countries of the earth but also in the cities and towns of the West. Soon there will be no way to grow and manufacture enough food products to feed all of you. No way to transport so many souls on already overcrowded roads and highways, rails and ports, runways and waterways. There will be no hope for the poor and disenfranchised peoples of your world.

What will then become of you? I will not belabor that point, but surely you have known that for all its splendor and beauty mankind's inventions could not begin to rival the beauty and the simplicity of a wondrous natural world. Your computers and televisions, I-pods, CD's, DVD's and Smart phones. Your jets and high speed rail, rockets and pleasure ships all come with a heavy price. And that price is stamped in the emissions of larger and larger amounts of smog, the deeper and deeper drain of fossil fuels and other natural resources and more and more pollution of the soil, the air and the water. You have razed mountains and cleared great tracks of forest land. You have denuded jungles and killed thousands upon thousands of species of plants and wild life that were put here to help you. But in not a few cases these discoveries and accomplishments have only served to feed the egos of only a few souls.

117

What has happened when other sources of food and medicines have been discovered? I'll tell you what has happened. The older medicines have been abandoned or left to rot in warehouses and the foods have been destroyed or fed to domestic and the other precious animals of this beautiful paradise. All such a terrible, terrible waste that will take centuries to regrow or re-create. If that can be done at all. And now man finds himself in the uncomfortable position of trying to re-create Nature. My friends, my friends I remind you that these things are all inspired by the imagination and purposes of The Almighty Power. The ruler of all worlds and all galaxies. They exist only by the grace and the wonder of God. Indeed, they are nurtured by His natural forces. Certainly you know this in your heart of hearts.

This place that enjoys the rays of the sun from 93 million miles away is but one of billions of stars. I know there is much talk of billions and billions of stars in the universe and galaxies and I don't blame you if the numbers sometimes make one's head spin. On a lighter note your great astrophysicist Carl Sagan admitted before his death that he did not say this on the Johnny Carson Tonight Show." There was sporadic laughter in the audience but Mr. Tou continued. "With the additional talk of more and more possibilities and more black holes it is not only frightening to small children and fools who want to live forever but I must tell you that these are only the estimations and calculations of man. There could be fewer and there very well may be billions of times more than even the most educated can guess. One thing is certain. There is but one Universe. Let me say it again. One Universe and one God. It always has been and it always shall be. Earth, the third planet out from a small sun is a lucky place and a special place and you have been fortuitous to draw this plum. However, make no mistake: it is just one of many such fruits that orbit the great galaxies of the unknown. Well, unknown to some, anyway! And whether it is known as the green planet or the blue planet it is of no more importance than the red planet and the planets of ice are to other civilizations of Universitarians. But I don't blame you for feeling special.

As Earthlings you should be counting your blessings. The Blue Marble is renowned for its leadership in every aspect. In every sense save one. You seem to be determined to self-destruct and to annihilate one another and everything in your path- animal and vegetation included. Do you not recognize your position in this fantastic universe? Moreover, do you not know that there are as many other universes as there are planets and galaxies? It is, in a word: INFINITE. Just as the Almighty God is Infinite. This makes you no less important in the scheme of His plan. If I may borrow a word from the vocabulary of your young people, you have been chosen to represent! Yours has not always been a history of which you can be proud. This much is well documented in the libraries of the greatest cities and universities of the galaxies. But honorable or not the inescapable facts are that from a species that descended the trees to live in the savannahs of a place you call Africa you vied with others of your kind and with those slightly different. From those humble beginnings your kind and yours alone survived. You fought and maimed and in too many instances murdered your way to the top of the hill. You clawed and survived famine and drought, earthquake and meteorite, tsunami and disease.

For hundreds of thousands of years, even the most extreme elements have not defeated your quest for supremacy. Finally, you stood alone. Victorious as the most successful kind. The top dog, if you will. The one who towered, bared fangs and panted while others looked away. They'd had enough of the fight and vanquished, they were forced to interbreed and join your growing numbers!

The problem is that you still have not learned when enough is enough. Or, when it's your turn to lend your support to help other species achieve a modicum of the success that you so much coveted. Who is to say that many eons ago this beautiful planet called Earth

Maurice P. Fortune

did not require a helping hand from some other worldly places? Do you think it possible that everything you see or have known in your lifetime came about as an accident? Isn't there some possibility that a few of your resources came from somewhere in the Universe? Maybe it was water or nitrogen or an element like gold or maybe tungsten. There are so many species of trees and flowering plants and animals on Earth that there is at least a remote chance that a few were brought here when some other world died or when this very Earth was still in its infancy and struggling to gain a foothold! My dear ones, God is everywhere in the Universe. He does not need to plant every tree or shrub. He does not need to be present at the birth of every lamb or whale, every bird or honey bee, every gnat or bat. That is your concept and it may not exist anywhere except in the naïve corridors of the human mind.

Friends of the World, I can see by the time that the clock is ticking on my participation here but I am wondering if you recognize that time is also running out on yours. The question is of course, what are we all going to do about it? In a few minutes I shall end my work here. But your work must not end. It must be only the start of what each of you can do. Not only as individuals but as a chain. A chain forever linked together to bring about the changes that must occur if you are to preserve this place for posterity. I know you have it in you to do this. Just as your forbearers had it in them to arrive at this juncture. But there must be one marked difference between you and them. More of you must take the initiative to save yourselves. I implore you to do this.

His Excellency turned.to look at each of the graduating seniors. There were tears in his eyes. Deliberately he spoke his final words. "Some of what I've said may seem a bit farfetched to the innocent minds of those only concerned with the immediate. But others of you will understand that the term light years might only exist in our heads and that it is a barrier that can be overcome by simple solutions. In the very near future you will talk of inter-planetary, inter-galactic and even trans-universal travel and exchange as easily as you speak today of a trip to Times Square on New Year's Eve. And I am betting that this planet that you've inherited will be around for the celebrations. So much, so very much depends upon what you do from this day forward!" With these words Mr. Tou collected himself and headed toward the wings of the auditorium. He disappeared down the steps and into the deserted corridor behind the stage.

The head of the program committee ran after him. She believed he had been confused by the thunderous applause and the standing ovation and cheers from the graduates and the audience. There was much foot stomping and whistling. The applause continued for several minutes as she searched for her guest but at the auditorium's exit she realized she'd lost sight of him. Sadly, she turned and hurried back to the podium. It was then that she noticed the single sheet of paper he'd left behind. On it were large initials. It was writings she'd never before seen. All save one line. It was written in English characters. Written in a single line it meant nothing to her. She wondered how he could have used just these few notations as a guide for his speech but with her audience growing increasingly restless she placed the notes among her own. She drew herself closer to the mike and furiously tapped it to gain their attention she offered them an explanation.

She said there had been some miscommunication. His Excellency had left the building. But not to worry she lied, he would be sent his honorary degree that very afternoon along with the profound thanks of the entire graduating class. Her audience seemed satisfied with her explanation and they quieted.

The program continued and the ceremony ended as the graduates, their four-year degrees in hand left the auditorium in thoughtful but obvious jubilation. There was much smiling and commending one another as the newly crowned scholars still in their blue gowns and mortar-boards caps strolled through the exits and into the hallowed halls of the university. A few mentioned that they felt incomplete. Almost as though they hadn't accomplished very much. Like there was still a lot to do. Like they were running out of time. It was strange. They hadn't felt that way until His Excellency Tou or whatever his name gave his remarks.

Outside the huge crowd spilled into the lobby and onto the lawns of the campus. It was a fine day for a graduation ceremony. Yes, what a beautiful day Mother Nature had provided for their coming out party. Suddenly, two of the graduates did something that had never been done before after a graduation ceremony. It was a simple gesture. They linked arms. It was only intended to signify their determination to remain forever connected but soon more students were linking arms on the campus grounds. Soon the links had formed a chain half way down the block and around the corner. People stood in the street linking arms.

Cab drivers and delivery van drivers parked their vehicles and linked arms.

No one told them why. They had not been asked to do it. It all happened spontaneously. The chain continued from block to block. Without knowing why people all over the city were linking arms. There was no singing. No speaking. People seemed defiant and single minded. Perhaps they did know why. Maybe without being told they understood what they had to do. Somewhere in the line, maybe a dozen blocks from where it had all started a thin black man in a black suit with a white shirt and tie joined the line. Like the tens of thousands who had felt the compulsion to participate he linked his arms between those of two strangers and the chain continued. The only difference was that unlike the others that distance from the college he understood why he was joining the chain and it pleased him greatly.

He had a lot of other places to go that were in similar situations to planet Earth but none of the others so desperately needed his attention. It had been a gamble, his coming here. He'd been warned about that but it seemed that he'd won. At least he'd won here in this city. But there was still one last place to visit on Earth and he hoped he'd be as successful there. Maybe all the stories about the indifference of human beings and especially city folk was incorrect. Everything he'd ever heard or studied had been a reminder that Earth's people no longer cared about anything much anymore. Just about their own selfish gains and usually that boiled down to two things: sex and money.

But he had succeeded. He'd broken through the armor of greed and tastelessness and it was too bad he couldn't stay to see how things played out. But he would hear and read about it soon enough. Where he came from these things were a part of the entire universal tracking system. Like the slogan: give us sixty seconds and we'll give you the world. News was played over and over on the huge monitors across the outer world. And it was never as redundant as the local news played on New York City's Channel One. He had seen the calendar and read the charts and he knew he had been overly kind and politely generous when he warned of impending disaster on Earth. Things would not be coming to a head sooner or later. Sadly, it would have been more correct to say sooner. He hadn't mean to be disingenuous

.Well. His visit here was over. After more people joined the chain he quietly slipped away. His mission done he walked quickly to the nearest subway. There he took the shuttle train to Grand Central Station. It was the only place on the east coast of the United States where he could covertly disappear into the underground zone! He would able to board the monorail that would take him to his next appointment at a place the Earthlings called UCLA. It was known as just as another university.

But it was known in the Outer World as the Universal Command and Launching Area. It was closer to the old Hangers in Area 51 and where years ago a few of the old astronauts from Neutral Hameau had "Ascended." They'd been on a mission of peace when something went terribly wrong with the system and they were transported to another plateau. He wished he could have told the group gathered at the college about the Zone. The knowledge would make life so much simpler for them. He walked through the ground level of Grand Central Station passing the huge clock. He noted it read 2:30 p.m. and he smiled, remarking how out of touch it was with Zone time. Pushing his way among the hundreds of commuters and travelers he located the elevator marked with the invisible code. He alone could see it and he would need to stay on it after everyone left. He'd ride it to the very lowest level and using his remote device the elevator would descend to the 5th Unit located far below the station. It was quick and simple and from there he could board the Air Rail commuter that would take him across the continent in 13 minutes. This included a stop in Chicago. After all Los Angeles wasn't that far away. Not compared to the time it took to get around on Neutral Hameau. That's where he'd come from and it was at least 25 times the size of Earth. It was a pity that their sun was only half the diameter of Earth's sun and that it was dying quickly. Maybe there were a thousand years left before it burnt out. Then, his people would be forced to move to a new home. It was going to be a massive undertaking: moving 30 billion folks. And where would they all go? There was only one planet that could even remotely accommodate them. Even then so many would need to be euthanized. So many of his own people and nearly all of the other more backward species.

Yes, these Earth people were fortunate. Well, they'll learn. They'd better learn or they will perish. If only they'd stop killing themselves with those so-called fossil fuels.

Those oils and gases. If they'd just cease sending those ancient contraptions to pollute their solar system and the neighbors in their galaxy. They'd just announced another expedition to begin in 2018. It was ridiculous and something needed to be done to stop them before they blew themselves to smithereens. No civilization he knew had explored space using such ancient methods in more than 100,000 years. He knew that because it had been at least that long since anyone had been born or died on Neutral Hameau. Didn't Earthlings know that space has already been explored to its fullest? There is nothing left uncharted or undiscovered. Everyone else knows this. And they have all studied the Master's plan. The Plan is common knowledge and has been so for several millennium. Even elementary school kids know these very basic principles. It's taught as early as Earthlings are taught their ABC's.

He smiled when he remembered the clue he'd left behind. It was the least he could do. Besides, it would give them something to think about. He hadn't really forgotten the paper on the podium. It was his practice to make backward civilizations think. That's why he'd written in English only the letters S.T.O.P. on the sheet of paper. The rest of the information wouldn't be understood by Earthlings for a few thousand years. Or, at least until the final contact. But as for the letters S.T.O.P., he knew that someone would figure that out sooner or later. It wasn't that obvious. Of course one could look at it as a kind of double entendre but it had nothing to do with sex or of Earth's money. Not even of his own planet's position in the galaxy. To get close to the meaning one had to start backwards. The initials stood for: Power of Transcendental Suggestion. This explained in full what had happened in the college auditorium. It was an easy thing to do. Once he entered the room he merely 'suggested' that his name was on the program. Just as he'd 'suggested' to the security officers at the college that he'd been invited. And he'd suggested he had a pass to enter the subway. He didn't really have one. He had not been scheduled to speak at the university any more than their Mickey Mouse was scheduled to serve cheese to all of the attendees. But they'd never know. Not for thousands of years. Especially the way they were headed. The other thing was that he had not actually spoken. Those from Neutral Hameau had long ago lost their ability to make sounds or even to hear sound in the way humankind does. Such primitive means of communication are not needed. Not only are they a waste of time but it was conventional wisdom and proven science that using any body organ for other than their original intended purposes makes ageing inevitable. It is only through an absence of activity that organs achieve maximum longevity. All save one: The Brain. The brain must be used to its fullest capacity. Unfortunately, humans have not yet learned to do this. After all this time, they are still using but a third of theirs.

Two weeks later the Planning Committee met to discuss the graduation. All conversation was about the mysterious stranger who had made such a positive impact on the students and on many others in the city. It had been front page news and the wire services and media had a field day. The Committee wanted to know which one of its members had had the foresight to invite Mr. Tou as a keynote speaker but no one could claim that honor. Everyone wanted him to return next year and the following. Perhaps even a professorship was in order. It was necessary. It was demanded!

Just before adjournment someone mentioned she'd noticed something odd about the spelling of his name. She had made a study of anagrams and she thought she had this one figured out.

The night before she'd gone through her notes and found the single sheet of paper His Excellency had left behind on the podium. She'd been at a lost to figure out what the letters S.T.O.P. actually signify. She'd sat there with her computer, her dictionaries and her Thesaurus. She'd looked it up and googled it. She had searched Wikipedia and found nothing.

The closest she came to it was when on an impulse she'd written People of the Sun. But this was all too old. There had been so many ancient civilizations that had used this name and there was nothing ancient about His Excellency. He was more modern than anyone she had ever encountered. In fact, he was almost frighteningly futuristic. Frustrated, she left the note on the kitchen table and when her 10 year old son came in from playing baseball he sat there eating a peanut butter and jelly sandwich. He absent-mindedly used the paper to draw a picture of the Sun and two human beings walking arm in arm. She held up the paper to show the Committee. They looked at the writings and a child's drawings. They were only stick figures but under them the boy had written the word: STOP! Suddenly, she thought she understood it all. But it wasn't possible. It was unthinkable and she dared not mention it to anyone with a sane mind. Why they'd think she'd taken leave of her senses. It all sounded so strange and unconventional. Here she was, a university professor, contemplating the absurd notion that the school had been visited by someone, something from another dimension. A far out galaxy. Moreover, the last place in space! But was it possible that the mysterious man was from the last planet in the Universe! THE LAST STOP. She dared not utter it but she could not help but think it. It was the only way things made any sense. After Earth there is no place left to go. Even though the stranger had said that the Universe was INFINITE everyone knows that there is a beginning and an end to everything. He was from the beginning AND the end. There simply was no other explanation. It had to be that. Gathering her courage and bracing herself to brave the scorn and ridicule she knew would come from her peers and superiors she rose from her seat. "H. E. T. Lifan Laplent Tou is an anagram, she began softly. H. E. does not stand for His Excellency at all. Once you drop the periods between the letters it becomes the English word THE. And the other three words are anagrams as well. Lifan is simply FINAL and Laplent Is PLANET while Tou is an anagram for OUT. The Final Planet Out. THE LAST STOP in the Universe!" Sitting down again quickly she dared to brave looking at her colleagues who stared at her mockingly. She folded her hands. After a while she heard the shuffling of feet and the movement of chairs as the others rose to leave the room without a word. The stranger had been correct. Earthlings don't have a clue!

END
THE FINAL STOP

The Last Guest

"The dead be a restin' when the living be asleep!" - M. Fortune

This was it. The final curtain call. The last hurrah or whatever one calls it when the end has come.

And make no mistake about it the end had come for him on this job and maybe for working on any job. At his age he'd been lucky to find work and he had been there for more than sixteen years. He hadn't made a lot of money. In fact, even when he worked double shifts or filled in for absent or sometimes absent-minded employees his salary just managed to cover the bills. Someone was always calling him to ask if he could replace a worker who had conveniently forgotten to set the clock or to tell his wife to wake him up when he'd overslept yet another time.

He'd heard every excuse on record. The wife had left, the kids were lost, there was fire in the kitchen and granny had died. Then, granny had died again. People were so full of it and they'd tell the strongest man the weakest crap. But he lived nearby and he wasn't doing anything at home except sleeping and missing his wife. He'd never get over that part he knew. Even with the years passing so quickly since her death he still found himself stuck in that part of his life. His was the first number dialed whenever anyone was out so he didn't mind. He needed the extra cash and he was convenient and available.

Convenience had been his motivation for moving to the neighborhood nearly fourteen years ago-to save both time and the ever rising cost of traveling to and from work every day.

The work site was only a few blocks away and he could walk there and home again in minutes. Of course, the old place had changed hands twice since then and so many employees had come and gone that he'd lost count. But he had survived all of the changes. He alone had remained the one constant of the old place and it was fitting and right that he work the last shift. For him it was to be a double. He would work his regular time and after his relief arrived he would stay just in case there was trouble. In the old days this had not been necessary but since the beauty salon next door and the nail parlor had relocated two years ago there had been several attempts to break in and burglarize the mansion. Once it was reported an employee had been struck from behind and tied up while walking the grounds to investigate noises. Someone, an accomplice, had then entered the building and taken one of the last beautiful stained glass windows that adorned the fabulously designed place. It was a priceless object and irreplaceable.

Although he had never told anyone, Ralph did not believe the story. For one thing whoever did it knew exactly what he was stealing and had been able to remove the glass within ten or fifteen minutes. That was all it took for the guard to untie himself and call the police. He had always believed it was an inside job and he wasn't surprised when the man had been let go two weeks later. Apparently, someone else doubted the story.

Ralph hated missing one of his favorite days of the year. Even though it was not an official holiday Halloween was still a fun day for him. Luckily, he would not be going in to work before six in the evening. It meant he had another forty minutes to give out gifts of candy, candy apples and small packets of coins to the little ones. Each packet contained random amounts from one dollar to one dollar fifty. All save one. One of the envelopes held five or six dollars and someone's kid would be the happy receiver.

Ralph saved his coins all year for this time. He'd place the bags and envelopes into three large shopping bags and let the kids choose whichever bag they pleased. Money or food. He never told them in advance what was in the bags. It cost him about one hundred dollars to do this but it pleased him to no end to see the smiles on the faces of the little ones as they closed their eyes and dipped their tiny fingers into a bag. He would switch the bags and turn them around to avoid detection by the children and there would be a lot of screaming and yelling as each in turn tried to direct the others to the bag holding the coins. It was a lot of fun and when it was over it was over. "No more until next Halloween," he'd say to the kids good naturedly!

But they knew he was just kidding. Just as his wife had been, Mr. Mention was an easy target and whenever they or anyone else needed anything he was the first to help. They were the real thing. The real Mc Coy as it were and everyone knew it. Following his wife's death there had been talk in the neighborhood about investigating the rules and requirements for Sainthood. After all, she was a Catholic and it was said people had been nominated for less. Quietly, he had asked people to stop thinking and saying those things about her. She was nobody's Saint. In her early years she had partied and run with the best. No one questioned him on it but it was a lie. Tillie Mention had never been a party person or a loose one. Each of them had had only two affairs in their lives. They had met and married after the deaths of their respective spouses. Both had passed within a year of each other. It had not been a question of marrying for companionship. The Mentions had married for love and they both could attest to that. Tillie had been a great wife and when she died of pancreatic cancer he had wanted to follow her.

They had no children of their own but they made all the kids in the neighborhood their kids. It was she Tillie, who had begun the tradition of giving the kids gifts and on Halloween. She gave Christmas gifts as well but she told him. "You know honey, Christmas is so spiritual. After all it's the day that is celebrated as the birthday of the Savior. People should be giving gifts to him and not to one another. But Halloween is just a fun day. Let's try to make it fun for the kids."

And they did every year until her death. That was the only year he had not been able to get up enough enthusiasm to do it.

He'd tried. It was 2005 and he was beside himself with grief. He had only been able to save a few coins in the plastic jar Tillie kept under the bed before she died. But he gave them to the children along with the few dollars he had in his pocket. It had not amounted to much because there wasn't much left after funeral expenses and all. They hadn't realized that her insurance policy was a diminishing term plan. He'd had to scuffle up another two grand and if it hadn't been for the old house he would not have been able to bury her. She'd have gone to Potters field with the indigents. But the old woman who owned the house had stepped in and the funeral was held there. Back then the place was still being used as a kind of spill-over facility for holding bodies awaiting services and burial. Actually, the old woman's main funeral home was several doors away on the opposite side of the street. Eventually, he was able to give the money back. Mrs. Esther Featherson didn't want to take it but he had told her. "I pay my bills and my Tillie would not appreciate me if I let her go to her grave owing the house that put her away." So he scraped and scratched until he had the money. After her burial he'd gone without lunches and sometimes dinner but he'd survived and he believed he was all the better for the experience. It was true, Ralph Mention was no Priest but if anyone had a claim to that title it was he and maybe his late Missus too.

At five fifteen Ralph took his three bags of goodies downstairs and stood on the stoop. He wasn't there for very long before a line of small children had formed nearly halfway down the block. "Mr. Mention, Mr. Mention," they screamed with joy. But they knew the rules.

Everyone was to get something and they could not be selfish and gather around him. At least not until they had their gifts. And then they were to step aside to make space for the others. He knew from past experiences that it would all finally end in chaos with jumping and screaming but at the start of the festivities it was always an orderly process. He never let any child walk away without something in hand.

He kept extra money in his wallet just for that purpose. Sometimes they were his last few dollars.

With the gifts passed out and the bags folded neatly in his backpack alongside his lunch it was time to begin the short walk to work. He would relieve the day man and do his tour of duty.

There were thoughts of uncertainty in his mind as he set out for work. It was a happy occasion and a sad one as well. After 16 years he would leave this job and start a new chapter in his life. At sixty-eight years old he was still agile and healthy but he had nothing else to do. Certainly, he could collect social security for the rest of his days but that was barely enough money to pay the bills and eat. It was about five hundred dollars less than he was making when he worked and he'd have to do without a lot of things. He wanted to continue working if he could find something. It was more than just the matter of making a decent living. Just walking in the neighborhood and seeing the numbers of men younger than he who had decided to quit working or take an early retirement package was enough to scare anyone almost to death. Ralph didn't want to end up on the corner playing numbers and drinking or girl watching every day for the rest of his life. It was all a depressing prospect. Finally, there was the matter of the credit cards. He was $7,000 in debt and the interests and penalties were steadily changing and climbing. It was overwhelming sometimes but Ralph tried not to focus on his own troubles. There were many others who needed help more than himself so he thanked God every day for his good fortune.

Passing the barber shop he encountered a small group of older men. They needed a dollar sixty to complete the price of a bottle of alcohol. Could he help? He gave them two dollars and said, "Happy Halloween Fellas." Continuing down the street he passed the neighborhood boxer. He was no longer a fighter but he had once been good enough to get some pro fights. Drugs and insanity had now made that no longer an option and the man spent his days hanging out in the street and begging for money. Ralph gave him a dollar and the usual "Happy Halloween." Just one block now from the worksite he came face to face with a group of teenage girls. They were all wearing makeup and masks and seemed to be on their way to a Halloween Ball or party. "Mr. Mention, Mr. Mention, do you have any money to give us like you used to when we were small," they asked? He smiled and reaching in his wallet he pulled out a ten dollar bill instructing them to split the money four ways. He walked on. "Happy Halloween," they said almost in unison. "Happy Halloween girls," he shouted back as he crossed the street in front of the old house. He remembered that the ten dollars had been the money he was keeping to pay his cell phone bill. He would have to make do without a cell phone until he received his check on the following Monday and he was happy that was just three days away.

Let the kids have their fun, he said to himself. They are good kids.

He'd known them all since they were toddlers and he had watched them grow to become pretty young teems.

He was as proud as any father could be at their growth and progress and they knew it. It wasn't their fault that one or two of their parents had turned to drugs and heavy drinking. They certainly had nothing to do with a father who had spent half of their own young lives in prison.

Just before he opened the gate to enter the yard of the old house he spotted the familiar figure of Ms. Pat. She was headed in his direction and she waved at him to attract his attention. Pat was a handsome woman of about 57 years. Like him she had lost her soul mate a few years back and had remained unmarried. Not that they had that kind of attraction for one another. They would sometimes laugh and talk whenever they met. Especially when she was on her way home from work. But today she was coming from the other direction. This indicated to him that she was going to church or to visit the sick at the hospital. She was a kind woman he thought. He wouldn't mind visiting her or taking her to a movie or dinner sometime if she would allow him. Maybe things would go further from there or maybe they wouldn't. Perhaps he'd ask her soon. You never know about these things until you ask.

He smiled at her and said, "evenin' Miss Chalmers. Don't tell me you're going to a party this Halloween night." Patricia Chalmers grinned at him. It was the first time she'd had time to smile all day.

"Oh no Ralph, my partying days are long gone, I'm on my way to visit a friend at Mercy Hospital and I just remembered that I forgot to leave these things in the fridge. I was wondering if you'd like them. You've got a microwave oven in there haven't you?" Ralph nodded. It was one of the few new things in the old house. It had been left there when the secretarial office moved down the street a few years back. There was no water in the kitchen but the spacious old bathroom still had water. "Are you sure, he answered? Maybe I can just keep them for you until you return and ..."

"Heavens no, this was my dinner. It's one of those microwave dinners, a soda and cake. I won't want them later. Please take them off my hands. You'll be doing me a favor," she added. "Well, alright. If you're sure you don't mind. Anyway, I have something I'd like to speak to you about. I won't hold you up right now but if you get back early enough and you have time just open the gate and knock on the door. I might be standing outside anyway, if it's not too chilly." She smiled, indicated her acceptance of his proposition and headed across the street. She was aware that he watched her disappeared down the street and out of sight.

Patricia Chalmers didn't like Halloween. She never had. It was not the celebrating and the having fun part. She saw nothing wrong with that. People needed to relax and wind down. It wasn't even the occasional mischievous pranks that the young people and sometimes not so young people pulled.

It was the disrespect they paid to the deceased. She hated that part of Halloween. "Go, make fun of the living and leave the dead alone," she told them. "After all they've done their part on this earth." Her grandfather had once told her when she was a young girl and still afraid that he might die while she was alone with him in the house. "Chile," he'd said. "You don't have to be scared of the dead. It's the living you need to watch out for." And Poppa had been right as he usually was whenever he chose to speak. He had been a very wise old man and a credit to the human race. Patricia was devastated when he died. She had never forgotten those words. There was something else that Poppa would say now and then but she could never seem to remember it. Yes, Halloween was fine but there was nothing funny about tomb stones, skeletons, spirits or coffins.

The other reason she felt that way was that she visited people in hospitals and nursing homes who were elderly and whose sicknesses would soon take their lives from them. They were folks who had served the communities they lived in with grace and humility. Sometimes they were young people who through no fault of their own were facing an early demise. Most had contributed and now they were sickly and they couldn't be healed. They just wanted to leave this world in dignity and in peace. She talked with them, she laughed with them and sometimes she cried with then. She always cried with their loved ones after their deaths. This was to be one of those nights she would cry.

She had come home from work as was her habit and she was tired. She had only one thing in mind when she'd left work and that was to beat the rush hour traffic on the bus, grab a quick meal at the super market and get in the house before the Halloween madness started. She didn't even want to take the time to prepare a meal by thawing out something in the microwave. That was why she'd bought the TV dinner she had given to that nice man Mr. Mention. He was always looking out for her and others in the neighborhood and it was time someone did something for him. She had been sad to learn that it was his last night at the Castle. That was what everybody called the old house on the corner. Everybody called it that except Ralph Mention. He still referred to it by its old name: The Old house.

Ralph loved that place and had probably been in and out of there more often than anyone dead or alive. She knew the place well and she knew the stories that circulated about the Castle. They'd been around for years and she guessed they had come about because for a time it had been used as a Funeral Home. Well, it was all nonsense. Even she could see that the place was an architectural wonder. To begin with, it sat on a slight embankment. It was not really a hill but enough so that it gave that impression.

In her opinion this gave it the advantage of overlooking the rest of the old buildings in the area. And it held its own among the newer structures too. Yes, the Castle had an air of majesty about it that seemed to say. "I have been here longer than any of you and I will continue my long reign when you are no more than a memory."

When her bus arrived she boarded it. She paid her fare with the quarters she had taken from the jar in the kitchen. She felt a twinge of remorse for having used some of the quarters she would have distributed to the children who lived in the building. She had not been able to hand out the small bags of store bought cookies she had purchased on her way home just for Halloween. It was a habit she had acquired only two years ago after listening to Mr. Mention talk about Halloween. Well, this year the fun and games would have to wait. She hadn't planned it that way but the moment she walked in the door her phone rang twice and then stopped. It wasn't long before it was ringing again and when she picked it up she was shaken to hear the voice of a familiar staff member at one of her hospitals.

Doing volunteer work does that to one she always said. You start referring to everything as your own.

It becomes your nursing home and your hospice. Your doctors and your nurses.

She even called the patients hers.

She was no medical professional. She was not even a quasi-care giver and had never been. She was a volunteer who sat and visited the sick and terminally ill whenever she was needed.

And she would go anywhere to do it. On the telephone she listened as she was told that Mr. Browne had taken a turn for the worse and that family members and friends were being called. Someone had left a list of emergency numbers to call if the worst happened. Her name was one of those listed. It was not looking good for him and he was not expected to survive the night.

This call was different from some of the other's she often received. Very different. She knew Mr. Stephen Browne. They had worked together as teachers in the area High Schools. They had studied together in the local church Bible study group. They often shared lunches and dinners and to her he was more than a patient. He was her best friend and she felt an obligation to be there for him. Hanging up the telephone she hadn't bothered to change. She just brushed her short-cropped hair and her teeth. Then, she took out half the coins she always threw in the vase with the chipped top. She put the remaining coins in a clear food container and placed them on the outside of her door where the kids could see them and take whatever they wanted. She knew they'd all be gone when she got home and she smiled at the prospect of finding the container empty or gone. It was what she wanted and expected.

Finally, Patricia took the cookies from the shopping bag and placed the lot of them on the kitchen counter. She'd hand them out to the kids later or mix them in with the home made ones she always baked at Thanksgiving. It was then that she noticed the dinner she'd purchased at the bottom of the bag and Ralph Mention, she decided to take it to him. It was the least she could do for him. The story about forgetting to leave the things in the fridge had been a lie. Maybe a little white one but it was a lie. She was sorry she had not just told him the truth. But then, he would not have accepted the food. God will forgive me, she thought to herself. She liked Ralph and his even temper and commitment to things. They were rare qualities.

On the bus ride downtown she was thoughtful. Stephen had family but they were not close. And of the few friends he had in this world she was probably his closest. That's the way it is in this City.

It's the one thing that she didn't like about New York. People come and go and your circle of friends has to be constantly replenished. If not you end up alone. It's like putting food in your refrigerator.

If you don't use what you've got and keep buying fresh the old will rot and must be discarded. Before you know it you've got nothing but ice cubes and a pitcher of water. As a friend used to say: "It's all so depressing."

As she was getting off the bus near the nursing home she realized she might be there until very late. Who knew about these things, she asked herself? Sometimes a patient died right away and at other times they lingered through the night. It was all God's work and His decision alone as to when someone would be called Home. She wanted to be there when that time came and since the next day was Saturday and time didn't much matter. Pat Chalmers did not have to return to her substitute teaching position until Monday. It would be November 3rd and it would also be her 59th birthday.

The instant Pat entered the room on the 5th floor of Friends of Mercy Nursing Home she knew she had done the right thing by dropping everything and getting there. Mr. Browne was dying and there wasn't a family member in sight. She hadn't expected to see a wife or children as the man had never married. He was not alone in this latter category as she had no kids either. They had often talked about growing old and spending their golden years sitting on the park bench and going to the movies. They both loved New York and they'd wanted to stay there. Stephen Browne had two sisters and a brother. He also had at least four or five nieces and nephews. His brother was a very wealthy man and lived in Florida. Retired, the brother spent a lot of time traveling in South and Central America. He particularly liked Buenos Aires. In fact, he probably liked that city more than he liked his own brother. She knew this because Stephen had told her many times that he and his brother had not spoken in years. His name was Mitchell and he was older than Stephen by nearly 12 years, Stephen would be 61 on his next birthday. It was apparent that God had other plans for him and he probably would not survive more than a few more hours.

As for the sisters, she had seen them but once. When Stephen was transferred to Mercy from Brooklyn Downtown Hospital they had made the trip from Long Island to see him. He said they had only come to gloat as they were still angry about being excluded from their late father's will. Well, not entirely excluded. They had received a quarter of a million each and they had not been happy to learn that the bulk of the estate had gone to Stephen and to the grandchildren. Stephen had wanted to continue his teaching and his single way of life. He had a fine apartment in Chelsea and he loved antiques. Anything old. It was said that you could always find Stephen at every antique and art show in the City. Patricia had gone with him to two shows at the Armory on Park Avenue a couple of years ago but she hadn't gone to anymore of them. It was distressing to see such fine furniture and paintings and to be unable to afford even a small item. The sisters didn't care for the man because of money and his brother didn't care for him because he felt that teaching high school was a waste of one's life. And of course there was Stephen's 'other' career. He was a writer. A very good writer but an unpublished one. "Why are you wasting your time writing," Mitchell had asked him? "You should be doing something more 'practical 'with your life." He never told Stephen what he considered practical but Stephen supposed that by practical his brother was speaking of following in his own footsteps. He was a 'Practical' man. He had practically embezzled his brokerage firm out of millions and would have spent practically all his life in jail had he not made a deal with the authorities! Instead, he was fined and given three years in one of those country club facilities somewhere in Virginia. But he held on to the money by hiding most of it in bank accounts outside the United States and he'd survived the 'rigors' of his confinement to live a life of luxury.

When Patricia walked out of the sick room she said a small prayer and went down stairs to begin her death vigil. She thought of grabbing a magazine from the rack but she didn't feel much like leafing through pages of over-dressed and overly made-up very thin young girls. It was almost 6:30 P.M. and she hoped that it would soon be over because she didn't like to walk that dark block home after she got off the bus. It was comforting to know that Ralph Mention was on night watch at the Castle on the hill but he was inside and there was a blind spot. It came right after she passed the midway point in the block. There was the stone wall of the gardens. At that point the hill descended a bit more. It was not much but enough so that the back gate and wall formed a recessed niche large enough to house a full grown horse. The ancient iron gate was often left open until the last watchman came on at midnight. During the heyday of the Castle the gate served as an entrance to the servants' quarters and there was but one way to see into this area from the main house. This was from one of the windows in the turret. The turret was a magnificent one and it imposed its presence upon the house like an over- fed matron. Usually, when Ralph was not on duty the gate was left open all night long. Pat was always afraid that someone would be dragged into that space. If that ever happened, well, the results wouldn't be pretty because once the gate was pulled shut no one walking past in the street could see or hear anything. To cross to the other side of the street was out of the question because on that side there were just too many hidden spots.

Exhausted from a long day at school Patricia sat in the waiting room nodding. And now there was this unfortunate turn of events in her life.

She had known that her buddy Stephen wasn't doing well but he had rallied several times before. I should have guessed, she reminded herself. I should have seen this coming. But she had been in denial. But she couldn't blame herself.

On the last visit he had given her the keys to his apartment. He'd also given her an envelope. Stephen asked her to open it only in the event of his death. Now, as she kept vigil all alone in the reception room on the first floor she watched visitors come and go to see relatives and friends. It grew later until finally, there were only a few arriving and leaving.

Occasionally, she would catch a glimpse of wheelchair bound or bedridden patients as they were transported into or out of the elevators. She could hardly keep her eyes open and the monotony caused her to doze as she listened to the voices of the Medical staff as they passed or the voice of someone, somewhere paging a nurse or a doctor. The announcement would wake her from her brief slumber in the comfortable chair. There were the voices of children as they came into the reception area from the street. They'd scream, "Trick or treat, trick or treat!" She had noticed at the desk a large dish of candy and without even a glance at the kids the receptionist would point to the dish. Without missing a beat she'd continue talking on her cell phone or doing her nails. The girl was disinterested looked as if she couldn't have cared less about Halloween or the children. She also looked like she didn't care much about her job.

Settling in for his last work night at the castle Ralph Mention took off his back pack and pushed it under the desk. It wasn't a big desk and half of the bag protruded. This always made for uncomfortable sitting but he was so used to bring the bigger bag to work he had not been able to stop after Tillie died. He reminded himself that she wasn't alive to fill it with a big meal. Ralph took his foot and pushed the bag hard against the wall. He wasn't trying to hide it. No one is coming near this place tonight, he said to himself. He went into the bathroom to wash his hands, took a cup from the dispenser and ran some water. Ralph thought he heard the footsteps of the day guard and he called out his Halloween greeting but there was no answer. Sitting again at the desk he tilted the chair back as far as possible. Suddenly, from the adjoining room came a voice. "Booo! Booo!" The relief guard poked his head around the corner. He had a white towel over his head and he had cut open spaces for his eyes, nose and mouth. "Booo," he said again! Trying to make his voice sound as eerie as possible. "Boo, hoo to you too!" Ralph screamed back, mocking the voice. The towel came off and they both had a good laugh. Ralph asked him if he was ready to check the basement and the outer grounds and the guard opened his jacket to reveal the heavy night stick they all carried while on his tour. "I stay ready roll." He said with a smile. "I don't wanna be here no longer that I have to. Especially tonight." Ralph was already on his way to the basement stairs and he didn't answer. He knew that Halloween or not Kareem didn't want to be there any longer than he had to be. He was 34 years old and still chasing every skirt he could chase.

The security check took only fifteen minutes and when finished the younger man prepared himself to leave. "Booo, Booo," Kareem repeated. Ralph did not laugh and he almost pushed Kareem out the front door. "Go on. Go on home man so I can have some peace and quiet around here. You're not scaring me with that ghost junk. Do you think I am eight years old? I didn't know you were so ill!" Ralph laughed.

Soon all was quiet and Ralph reached for his cell phone to place on the desk. He recalled it was still in his bag under the table. It didn't matter. It was useless. He had used up all his minutes. He thought to take eat a little of the food Patricia had left and he reached under the table unzipping his bag. Then, noting it was only 6:45 P.M. he decided wouldn't eat lunch before ten.

On his last night on the job Ralph Mention sat at the desk. Sometimes he walked to one of the windows and looked out on the avenue. There was always stuff to see. Something was always going on in the neighborhood but for some reason on this Halloween night seemed unusually calm and quiet. And the night seemed to zip by. Soon it was 8 p.m. and then 10 o'clock. Shortly before eleven he realized that he hadn't called the office. He didn't have to punch a time clock and it was just a formality, a courtesy call and a chance to speak with someone for the first time in a few hours. Tonight Ralph would not bother to call.

"Excuse me ma'am, I'm sorry to disturb you but didn't I see you upstairs on the 5th floor a couple of hours ago?" Pat Chalmers sat upright and straightened her twisted skirt and blouse. She peered in the direction of the voice of the woman standing a few feet above her head. "Oh, I didn't mean to alarm you but I was in 560-B when you were coming out of the room next door. Do you remember? We almost bumped into one another?" Now fully awake, Patricia indicated she remembered and cleared her throat. "Oh yes, I recall." She answered. "How are you?" "Oh I'm fine," the woman said. It seemed as though she hadn't heard Patricia. "I hate to be the bearer of bad news or anything but you might want to go up there." The stranger was doing her best to avoid eye contact. "I hope nothing bad has happened to your relative." Patricia Chalmers rose to her feet and headed toward the elevator. She stopped and thanked the woman just before pushing the elevator button. Threading her way past the other occupants in the elevator she excused herself. She felt strange and empty. It was almost the same feeling she'd had when her husband passed. Heading in the direction of Stephen's room she was stopped by a voice. "Miss, Miss, you can't go in there," a nurse said, closing the door. "Are you a relative?" Pat's heart sank and for a second she could say nothing. When she finally spoke she could only say, "no, not exactly." She looked searchingly at the nurse. Hoping against hope that what she knew was true could not be. "I'm sorry to tell you this but he passed about 20 minutes ago," the nurse said. Her tone left no other questions in Patricia's mind. It's over she said to herself. It was at last over.

The nurse continued speaking and although Patricia heard every word these sounded as if they were being spoken a few hundred feet away. "We tried calling the list of names of the next of kin someone left on the contact sheet but we could only reach one person." She looked at a sheet of paper in her hand. "Are you Barbara Smothers, his sister" the nurse asked?" "No, I'm not Ms. Smothers and I'm not his sister, but my name should be on that list too, I think. I am Patricia Chalmers and I am the one who gave you the list a few weeks ago." "Of course. He Okayed it," the nurse confirmed. "Here's your name. It's at the bottom and it says you are his partner. Right?" Pat didn't want to belabor the point so she just nodded her head in agreement. "Well we will allow you to go in and you can identify the body. It's for the record, you know, someone has to. But you can only stay a few minutes, they're on their way up to take him downstairs to the morgue." It was clear that the nurse was uncomfortable dealing with death. "Are you alright Miss Chalmers? I'm so sorry about your partner. I'm glad someone is here to be with him. His sister said she couldn't make and it seems he has nobody else." No, she wasn't alright. Patricia Chalmers was hurt. As many times as she had seen this she had never been present when a family member wanted to come to a hospital or nursing home after a loved one's death. It was upsetting and she was glad she had come but it made her think of her own demise. Without children of her own she too had no one to be there when she died. She would probably die like this. Alone and unwanted in a nursing home or hospital or in her bed. She would be unloved and uncared for unless she did something about it very soon. And by soon she meant Mr. Ralph Mention. Her friend's passing had convinced her that she could wait no longer. If he didn't have the courage to ask her she sure as heck had enough for both of them.

Room 560 was quiet and the only sound was Patricia's footsteps as she approached the bed. It was quiet and yet it was almost peaceful. Stephen lay there covered in a white sheet with only his head exposed. His face no longer looked wasted and he had almost regained his color.

In fact he looked better than he had looked in a couple of years. He appeared to be just resting. She remembered what her grandfather had been fond of saying so long ago whenever someone they knew passed. "Don't you worry honey," he'd say. 'THE DEAD BE A' RESTING WHEN THE LIVING BE ASLEEP.'" Apparently, he had been right. She had been asleep when her grandpa had passed, and when her husband had died and once again she was asleep when her friend Stephen took his last breath.

Patricia stayed in the room only a few minutes. She knelt by the bed and said a prayer. She crossed herself and walked toward the door and down the almost empty hall and past three nurses seated at the station. They didn't want to look in her direction and she was grateful. They would have noticed the strain on her face and the tears on her cheeks, streaking them like raindrops on an unwashed window pane. She took the elevator, ignoring the pitying glances of the two or three people in the almost empty car. They acted as if they wanted to say something kind but couldn't find the right words. And she didn't blame them. What's to say when someone loved one has passed away. Which words are right and which would be totally inappropriate? And when do you know when you've said enough and it's time to stop the chatter that sometimes goes on and on with no other purpose than to assuage one's own ineptness or guilt. The ineptness of not being able to offer more than words. The guilt of not also being in a state of mourning or the guilt of still being alive.

Patricia suddenly remembered the line from the PBS series "I, Claudius". In the scene a recuperating Caligula is greeting Senators and is told that a very prominent Statesman had prayed for The Emperor's recovery. In fact, he was told, the man offered himself to the gods if they would but spare the life of Caligula. The Emperor Caligula approached the Senator and commended him on his prayer. The man stood there humbly accepting Caligula's praise until Caligula reminded him that they were both still very much alive. "And one of us oughtn't to be," the Emperor said. He looked at the man in a way that bespoke the man's finality.

The people leaving the nursing facility were going home yet another night. If only once more to laugh and to dance. To celebrate Halloween. But Patricia was going home to mourn yet another time in her life.

She headed toward the exit and to face the chill of the last night of October. Glancing above the head of the receptionist she noticed the time was 10:47. The girl was noisily chatting on her cell phone and she didn't seem to notice Patricia as she headed for the exit.

What a blast they'd had! In every way possible they'd had a good time. The music, the girls, the booze, the smoke and the food. Everyone had agreed to have the Halloween party at their friend's house.

It was the second year they'd done it and it seemed better this year. Of course it made a difference that Monique's new boyfriend was actually born the day before Halloween. She'd decided that it made sense to give the Halloween party for her friends and the birthday party together. One giant revelry. One big orgasmic celebration with no holds barred and no feelings spared. The day before had been a workday for most and it was not often that Halloween fell on Friday. Sometimes it happened on Sunday or Monday and that was always a downer but this year it all seemed to come together. Most of those invited arrived right after work. They'd all brought something to contribute since she'd let it be known that money was a bit tight. No one had any complaints about the food or the drinks. There had been plenty of both and the festivities continued until well after eleven and no one seemed in a hurry to leave.

Only two or three people had to end a bit early. Jerome Tillman and Charles Fillmore were among the earliest to leave. Jerome lived in Queens and he needed to get home at a reasonable hour to get up on time for his job as a department store clerk. It was a long ride and he knew it could be dangerous and threatening on this night. He didn't want to blow his job and he certainly didn't want to go back to jail. At 24, he had already spent 3 years there for being in the wrong place at the wrong time and for selling small amounts of crack cocaine. This was his 2nd chance to turn his life around and he was determined to get it right this time. But he had a problem. He was still an occasional user. Few people knew it and he meant to keep it that way. His mother and his wife could not be allowed to know this. They had stuck by him over the years and they'd be devastated to discover his lie. Jerome was married to his childhood sweetheart and they had one child.

Cha Cha, as Charles was called was another matter. At twenty three he had never been in jail. In fact. He worked as a Jr. Counselor to youngsters who had been in some minor trouble at one time or another. He worked for the Police Athletic League somewhere in the Bronx. That he had never been in trouble was a tribute to his parents. His mother was a very religious woman and his father ran a tight ship. As long as he was in their house he would have to abide by their rules and regulations. And that meant home by midnight or not home at all. Once he had defied this order and come home at three. He hadn't been allowed in the house. At another time he had come there just five minutes past midnight. He was sweating bullets as he ran up the stairs to the third floor and put his key in the door. But the night chain was already in place and he couldn't get in.

He rang and rang and when his father finally came to the door he didn't open it. He just peeped over the chain and said. "You're too late buddy, this ship has already sailed." Cha Cha had been forced to spend the night on the dock. In this case the welcome mat outside the door. He hadn't been welcomed into the house until after 7 A. M.

As the two friends said goodnight to their colleagues and headed toward the subway they were met by two strangers. They too were Halloween revelers and they were coming from an early party. It had grown too dull for them and they wanted more action. They stopped on the sidewalk and asked for a cigarette. They wanted to make a blunt. Cha Cha reached into his pants pocket and took one out of the pack as he looked the girl up and down. Taking it in her hand she looked up at him. "Watcha doin' Papi" she asked?

"You wanna come with me to a party?" He could hardly tell her the reason he couldn't go so Cha Cha figured he'd string her along for a few minutes then tell her he was occupied and go home.

It was just eleven o'clock and he didn't have a lot of time to kill. It was a ten minute ride to the next stop where he would get off the train and race the two blocks to his home.

Jerome was in no hurry. He just needed a few hours of sleep but he was still nervous about the whole idea of being on the train after midnight hour. The fourth member of the group was a tall thin man whose only mission in life seemed to be to smile at every word the girl said. She'd introduced herself as Sonja and she was 20 years old. She never said who her friend was but just looking at him Jerome could tell he was an ex-con. A jailer as they were known. He was older than the others, about twenty-seven. He had been a crack baby and like Sonja he was fired up. At first Jerome and Cha Cha thought the two others were a couple. But when she started coming on to them they realized the two were just hanging.

She offered them some smoke and they decided that they'd take her up on it. Maybe there was still time for a little play. As other thoughts ran through his mind Cha Cha envisioned himself locked out again at home but it was Halloween Night and if necessary there were several places he could go to hang out; could always go back to the party they'd just left. As for his friend, it wouldn't be the end of the world if Jerome missed a day at work. Of course, he'd miss the money in his next check but he'd get over it. After all, his boy Jerome knew how to scramble, baby. Sonja prepared the blunt and they stood in a huddle passing it around until it was only a stub in her fingers. She giggled as she smoked the last of it. She asked again if they wanted to hang out. She was going to try the house of a friend who said he might have some people over and if that proved to be slow they could always crash another place. "Anyway, the night was young," she said. "People do all kinds of freaky things in the Village on Halloween." Cha Cha and Jerome looked at each other and grinned. "Yeah," they chimed in unison. "We down!"

Arriving at the bus stop Patricia Chalmers felt a slight chill in the air and she pulled her coat closer to her throat. She was sorry she hadn't worn a heavier one but she was in such a hurry to get to the nursing home before anything happened that she had not thought of it until now. She was relieved to see that the few people ahead of her had already begun forming a line. Others huddled together as an indication that a bus had been spotted approaching a block or two away and she took her place.

There was a slight wait as the bus knelt to allow a wheel-chair user to descend. She noted that it was a young man. He already had a cigarette dangling from his lips before he wheeled himself clear of her group. With the bus was half empty she found a seat and moved next to the window. She was surprised when a woman asked her if she would mind if she took the aisle seat. "Of course not, dear," she said. "You paid your money just as I paid mine." The woman smiled and sat down. She answered, "I have a free pass. I didn't pay anything." She then said something that Patricia found odd. "Is there anything you'd like to share with me? I love to talk with people who look friendly and you look like you need a friend tonight." "I look that bad?" Patricia laughed as she said it but her heart was not into the laughter.

"Oh no, you don't look bad at all," the woman answered. "It's just that you look like you have a few things on your mind. Like you've lost your best friend." The woman continued. "I can tell that something has happened to you and I just want you to know that there are always stronger forces at work in our lives. Some people refer to it as God and that is wonderful. Others call it Spirits or Saints or The Ancestors. It's different in every country and no one is wrong. No one alive knows for certain what it is but in our most difficult times there is a force that sustains us. It lifts us up and out of our misery. I know because I have been in that situation many times in my life. For me it is my faith in God but I never have anything but respect and admiration for others who believe otherwise." Patricia listened and thanked the woman. She told her about Stephen and she said she was on her way home. She would stop at the beautiful old house on the corner and wave goodnight to her friend who was working there. It was his final night at work and she felt his pain at being out of work. She would do anything to help him. If only she had money or had been born wealthy.

The two ladies sat talking for a few more minutes and suddenly the stranger stood up. "This is my stop," she said. "Oh my gracious," Patricia replied. "I might as well get off here too. I can stop at the deli and buy something quick to eat. I'm famished! And maybe I should walk with you as far as you're going, just to be safe. I hate to be alone on Halloween, particularly this close to midnight," Patricia continued. "You never can tell what some of these people will try." The woman smiled and looked at her saying. "Oh I'm going to be just fine. Nothing ever happens to me that I can't handle." "I'm sorry, I didn't get your name," Patricia said! "I am Patricia Chalmers." "Yes, I know," said the woman. "And my name is on my visiting card I'd like you to have. Although that won't happen for a few years now." "Oh," Pat said. She did not understand but she wanted to be polite. "I'll give you a call sometime soon and maybe we can arrange for a visit or lunch." Out in the street the two women smiled and said goodnight. Just before they separated the woman handed her a card. "Please take this. If you ever feel like you need to talk please don't hesitate for a second to call. You will feel better if you do. You won't get me on the phone but there are so many others who would love to speak with you." As the stranger walked away Patricia was almost sorry to see her leave. She wondered who she was. She had never seen her but the woman said she had once lived in the area and was now on her way to visit a friend. She was also meeting with someone she didn't know and they would go to a gathering of sorts. He was someone who had special needs. Kind of like Patricia's. He needed a friend and the agency had given her the assignment. She didn't mind. She was happy to help in any way she could day or night.

Patricia was puzzled. How did the strange woman know her name before she'd even mentioned it? She let it go for the moment as she walked into the deli. Purchasing a sandwich, she asked the clerk to heat it in the microwave and then she changed her mind. "I'll heat it myself." She corrected herself: "when I get home." She knew it was after 11 P.M. She didn't know how much after eleven it was and although the streets were still crowded it felt late. This is good, she thought to herself. It is going to be fine. There are lots of people in the street and I feel safe. Paying the $4.95 for her turkey and cheese sandwich Pat left the deli.

As Patricia walked the last two blocks before she arrived at the Castle her thoughts were focused on the nice woman she had met on the bus rather than on the events at the nursing home. She had almost forgotten the sorrowful death of her friend Stephen. If only temporarily she had thrown it from her mind. Patricia focused on other things. It was a beautiful night but it was growing cooler. As she walked she relaxed. Looking up at the moon she noted to that it was waxing gibbous: moving toward a full moon. How many times had she had to repeat that to her classes? When the shadow of the moon is on the left it is waxing gibbous. When it is on the right it is moving toward a new moon and is waning gibbous. She smiled at the thought but it reminded her of Stephen again.

She approached the dimly lit Castle. The first thing one noticed about it was its beautiful turret. It was round and on each of its four floors there were bay windows. The most eye-catching windows were those at the very top. While the three lower floor had only eight, there were ten windows at the very top floor. Three of them over-looked the grounds below and it was only from these that one could see the back gate. It was also the only point inside the house where there was a clear look at the sign proclaiming the birth year of the fabulous structure: the year of our Lord 1887.

On this night Patricia Chalmers walked toward the Castle and to a date with her destiny. She glanced at the entrance to see if Ralph Mention was standing outside but he was nowhere in sight. She then looked at the window on the first floor. She should have seen him there. Since Ralph wasn't in the window she decided she wouldn't bother him tonight. I can always call. Why ring the bell? It seemed rather selfish of her to disturb him. Especially tonight. Why disturb the man tonight?

It was quiet inside the Castle. Without a telephone Ralph Mention felt almost lost. For him cell phones were a luxury. It had taken him a while to get used to them but now he was hooked. He only used his to call the office once he got to work or to call a friend on occasion but it was a handy thing to have around. Sometimes he'd have to report someone. This meant to call a parent of one of the kids he called his. If a kid was doing something wrong he wanted the parents to know right away instead of waiting until it might be too late. And sometimes he would just check to make sure they had food enough or money enough for the child to get a cool drink or something after school. Sometimes, he'd lend them money for groceries until check day or whenever they could pay it back.

They usually called as soon as they had the money to pay him but on occasion they never paid back. Ralph never asked for the money.

With Ralph the glass was always half full. He was an eternal optimist. Now it was a comfort to have a phone. Any phone. It was almost like a companion. Sometimes they talked, at other times they didn't bother to speak. It was enough just to be together. And now, with his minutes all gone he felt alone. He knew he could call the office when his replacement arrived. Tonight they were going to work the grave yard shift together and they could report in together once he got there. He wondered why it's called the grave yard shift. Working never sent anyone to an early grave. It's the lack of work that does that. Besides, there is no truth to the myth that we need to sleep at night. Sleep is sleep whenever you get it. You just needed to get enough of it. Ralph smiled. Satisfied with that thought he sat there in the chair with his arms folded behind his neck. At 11o'clock Ralph Mention closed his eyes and went to sleep. When Patricia passed the window he was still sleeping

"Let's have some fun!" Sonja said, turning to the two young men behind her. Walking ahead of Jerome and Cha Cha she was the first to see Patricia Chalmers when she paused at the corner. She was looking up at the first floor window of the castle. "Quick, Sonja said. Hide in that little spot right there."

She indicated to the two men the recessed area in front of the Iron Gate leading to the back door of the servant's entrance. Sonja slowed her own pace to match that of Patricia's. Patricia hadn't seen any sign of her friend Ralph and she figured correctly that he was napping. Poor man, she thought. I wish I could help his situation. She started down the hill to continue home: She was lost in her own thoughts and she didn't see the man and the woman until she was nearly on top of them.

155

Sonja was lighting a cigarette as she spoke. "Good evening Miss. We're Police officers and there's been a report of someone harassing people on this block. Do you mind showing me some identification?" "Why me?" "Show ID" Patricia protested! "Yes you, show us some damned papers with your picture on it or we're taking yo' ass in," the thin man said. He was tall and he looked drunk. Patricia didn't want any trouble so she said. "Well, alright but I think there are probably others committing actual crimes out here. You don't need to be wasting your time and tax payer's money by stopping me. I have never done anything wrong in my entire life." "Oh, she's a smart whore. We need to teach her a lesson. Let's show her what we do to smart asses like her," Sonja said! "Put your hands up and get up against the wall lady," Jerome said. It seemed to Patricia that he had appeared from nowhere. "Officer," she protested, but the tall man pushed her toward the unlocked gate and she was roughly shoved inside.

Patricia was trapped! And she had guessed the worse. These people were not connected with the police department. Not even remotely connected. They were a bunch of thieves. Or, maybe they were just having some Halloween fun and when they were through they would let her go. She was a teacher and she understood today's young people. She had certainly dealt with enough of them in her life.

If she didn't panic or threaten them they would soon get bored and leave her alone. She'd be none the worse for her experience. She decided to have a little fun of her own. She thought she recognized Sonja and maybe Cha Cha too. "You're not police officers at all." Patricia said. Then, looking at Sonja she asked. "Weren't you in my 11th grade science class two years ago? I remember you but I just can't think of your name." She had made a fatal error. The girl looked as if she had been struck by a thunderbolt. She HAD been in the 11th grade and she HAD taken a Biology class two years ago. In fact her teacher had been an older woman about the same height and build as Patricia Chalmers. She thought her name had been Williamson. Although she wasn't sure. She almost never attended that class. Sonja hated Biology! Could THIS be Miss Williamson. Sonja didn't say anything more because she didn't want the others to know she had been busted. Quickly, she thought of a way out.

"Stop stalling bitch." she said. Panicked by her need to shut Patricia's mouth she added, "The man asked you for identification, give me your F ...ing pocka book!" Patricia found herself being strong armed and gagged by Jerome. Her glasses fell from her face and her purse was snatched from her hand. Jerome and Sonja began searching Patricia's bag. Cha Cha was standing a short distance away. "Oh, let the woman go, he said! I'm not getting' arrested for this. I don't need this s...t. Let's get out of here!" But the others weren't through with Patricia. Jerome threw the bag to the ground in disgust. "She ain't got nothing in it," he said to Sonja. "And I ain't robbin' nobody no how." "He's right." Jerome said, looking in Cha Cha's direction. "Let's leave her be." Patricia was relieved. She thought it was over. They had tired of her and she could now go home.

With a vicious blow, Sonja slapped Patricia in the face. "You aint getting away that easy ho," Sonja said. "Gimme dem pannies! Go ahead, take them draws off bitch. Yo' ass is going home naked as a jay bird." Patricia Chalmers, at 58 years old was forced to take her under pants from her body. She was made to undress to the waist while a 20- something year old female stood giggling and smiling and three young adult males stood staring at her nakedness. It was the most humiliating thing that had ever happened to her and she began to cry. Seeing her tears the thin man with Sonja came toward her. He was making a show of unzipping his pants. "I love to make 'em cry. Ain't no shame in my game, y'all." He grabbed Patricia's underwear and made a ball. "Here, catch!" He called out to one of the other young men. Then it was Cha Cha's turn to throw the ball and soon all were throwing the panties around and screaming. "Catch, Catch it." Throwing them from one to the other they laughed and yelled "PSYCHE" then they were thrown to someone else. They were tossed over Pat's head. Then to her left and to her right. Crying and frustrated Patricia ran from one to the other chasing her underwear in a frantic attempt to retrieve her very private possession. Tiring of the Game Sonja stopped and asked her tall companion. "Didn't you say you wanted to hurt her? You know what I mean, man!" The thin man laughed. His thin chest stuck out, he began strutting like a Bantam rooster in a pen of hens. Intent on demonstrating his manhood he began to slowly unzip his trousers. Then he went further and exposed himself. "Yea lady teacher," he said. "What about dis here?" He moved toward Patricia.

Suddenly, he stopped. Looking up he seemed frozen in space, as if someone had pushed the pause button on a DVD player. All eyes followed his to the very last floor of the turret. There in the open window stood two figures. A man and woman. Later, they would say that they thought it was a couple of kids looking out the window wearing Halloween masks. But they would be wrong about that. The figures they saw were not masked. There was nothing horrific or frightening about them but there was a faint glow in the window. A glow that was not coming from the overhead chandelier. One of the two windows was slightly open and a breeze blew the curtains against the panes.

The faces were clear and their countenance was so strong that even the nearsighted Patricia Chalmers could see them clearly. And from that distance she shouldn't have been able to see faces that were more than a blur. She certainly should not have been able to make out facial features. But Patricia saw the face of her dead friend Stephen in the window. And he was standing there with the woman Patricia had met on the bus. She was not mistaken. It was the very same woman who had sat next to her on the bus. The same kindly soul who had sat talking with her and who'd given her consolation and peace of mind not even a half hour earlier. She was wearing the same clothes. A brown hat and light beige trench coat. She was shaking her head and waving her finger at the young people. She was admonishing them and shaming them with her silence as though she was communicating to them by telepathy. You've gone too far with this nonsense. Enough now or you will have to pay for your foul deeds, she seemed to say. But she didn't utter a word. She didn't have to. All of them heard her as clearly as if she had shouted it over a loudspeaker.

Inside the Castle a phone was ringing. It was ringing so persistently that it woke Ralph Mention from his nap. It took him a few seconds to collect himself and reach into his bag to pull out his cell phone. "Hello, hello," he said hoarsely into the receiver. There was no answer. Of course, there's nobody on the other end he thought. The phone is off. The bill hasn't been paid and anyway it's not ringing. There's a phone ringing somewhere else in this building. But from where? Standing, he remembered that there was a telephone. It was upstairs in the green room on the fourth floor of the turret. He had seen it just this afternoon when he and Kareem had made the evening inspection tour Kareem had been joking around with the phone. He'd gone into the Green Room just to make sure the chandelier lights were off. Kareem pretended he was calling his girlfriend to say Happy Halloween and he had asked her if he could make a 'booty call'. It was Ralph himself who turned off the lights. He had been the last one in the room.

But how could it be that the phone was ringing in that room, he asked himself. That phone was old and dusty and it had not been connected to anything in over 5 years. As a matter of fact he remembered when the office had had the thing disconnected. That too was one of the reasons he'd decided to get a cell phone of his own. Some of the employees in the building were misusing the phones and one of them had been fired for calling a telephone hot line that promoted sex. He had called the 900 number listed on a match book cover and talked for hours. It turned out that the number was actually a connection in an island in the South Pacific called Vanuatu. The bill had come to over eight hundred dollars and the front office had taken a good portion of the money from the final check of the fired employee. Ralph stood and hovered above the desk like a bird of prey. His eyes focused on the log book on the desk. There it is: 4th floor lights and a check next to the initials of both men.

Ralph had a quizzical look on his face as he walked to the window and as he looked out he saw the four young people run past the building. They turned the corner and headed toward the subway station. He wanted to be sure they hadn't broken into a car or done anything stupid so he took his keys and flashlight and walked outside and around to that side of the building.

When Patricia looked up and saw Ralph she became hysterical. "Oh, thank God you came. I have never been so glad to see anyone in my life." "Why Pat. I mean Miss Chalmers, what on earth are you doing here? Are you hurt? Ralph was frantic. Don't tell me those young punks did anything to you! I'll catch the lot of them and strangle them with my bare hands." Only half-dressed she tried to cover herself with one hand and gather her belongings with the other. She asked him for the flashlight so she could find her glasses and her purse. They were found inside the gate and lying on the ground. "You just stand right here and I'll get your things and then we can go inside and call the police." He headed for the grounds inside the gate just as two police cars turned the corner with lights flashing and sirens blaring. The cars came to a screeching halt.

Officers got out of their cars and walked back to where Patricia and Ralph stood. "Did you call us ma'am? What's the trouble here," one of them asked? He hitched up his pants as though he was demonstrating his masculinity to a group of single girls lying on a beach. "We got a call from someone who said there was trouble here. She gave this address and the name Ralph Mention! Is that you Sir?" "Are you Mr. Mention," the other officer asked? "Yes, that's my name. I'm the security guard here but I was inside the building and I didn't see anything. You'll have to talk to this lady about that. I didn't come outside until I saw three or four young people run past the window. And as far as the telephone call… I don't have any idea who called. We don't even have a telephone in that place."

There was a flash of light and one of the cops looked up toward the turret of the building. He asked, "who else is in there?" "Why nobody, officer." Ralph said. "I'm the only one on duty. I'm waiting for my relief man. He should be here at any minute." "Well, either he's already in the building or you're lying to me because somebody just turned off the light in that room up there. Did you see that Rice," he asked looking at one of the other officers? They turned to Patricia asking what had happened and if she had been violated or otherwise harmed. "No," she said! She said she was fine. Of course she was angry and embarrassed but she was otherwise unharmed thanks to certain people.

They took that to mean their timely intervention or Ralph's but she wasn't referring to that at all. Something else had happened there and she wasn't sure just what. Patricia didn't want to be thought of as a kook. If she'd said what was on her mind she'd have been carted straight away to Bellevue or to some other Psychiatric Hospital. She decided that would keep those thoughts. She had just wanted to get the night over and the entire affair behind her, but the officers had seen the light go off in the turret and they felt duty-bound to investigate further. They followed Ralph and Patricia inside the Castle doors.

The moment they walked in the door Ralph's replacement arrived. It was 12 minutes past midnight and he apologized saying he had been delayed on the train. He lived in Brooklyn and there had been the Halloween parade in the village. His train had remained stalled at 14th Street for more than 30 minutes.

"What's up Ralph buddy," he asked? "Is everything o.k. here?" Ralph was about to answer him when there was the sound of a telephone ringing in the building. It kept ringing. Indignant, one of the officers turned and looked at Ralph with suspicion. "You'd better stop lying and playing these children's games with us," he said. "I asked you who was in this building and if there was a telephone here."

"What's your problem? Now, either you tell us the truth or we'll take YOU to the precinct in handcuffs." Ralph shrugged. He didn't understand what was going on either.

Again the telephone rang. It kept ringing as the group climbed the stairs toward the sound. It was ringing when they got to the 2nd floor and it rang as they reached the 3rd floor landing. At every floor the police officers searched the empty rooms. They turned on every light and looked in every bathroom and closet just to be sure there was no one there. Still there was the sound of a telephone ringing. At last the group arrived at the door of the Green room. The light was on again and there on the floor in the otherwise empty room was the old telephone. And it was ringing! It was not a mistake.

The sound was coming from that phone. The tall officer walked over and picked up the receiver with intentions of answering it but he dropped the telephone. His hand shook noticeably.

Another officer walked over to the phone and picked up the entire apparatus. He looked under it and around the room in disbelief. The telephone was still ringing but there was no wire connection. The phone had no dial pad and the receiver had no innards. It was an empty phone. It was just the shell of an old phone and it should not have been making a sound. It was useless and yet, it was ringing. And it would not stop. Finally, Ralph walked over and asked to hold the empty receiver.

When Ralph Mention walked into the Green Room he had smelled it and he knew immediately. He'd bought the perfume for her so many times he'd lost count. In fact, there was still an unopened bottle on his dresser. He kept it there as a reminder. The scent was called "Rose of Paradise" and it had been her favorite. When the police officer placed the receiver in his hands Ralph spoke into the opening. In an almost inaudible voice he said, "Hi Till, I love you and thanks for coming."

Ralph Mention returned the telephone to the officer who looked at the empty space. He didn't understand. But Ralph Mention understood all too well and with tears streaming down his face he walked out the door and back down the stairs.

The police officers took no more notes. They said good night and offered to take Patricia home but she declined their offer. She said she had a lot of thinking to do and needed the fresh air to clear her mind.

After they'd gone she accepted Ralph's offer to walk with her. He was entitled to a few minutes of free time before starting his last shift there and he insisted on walking with her if only to keep her company.

On the way to her apartment Patricia Chalmers and Ralph Mention barely said a word. She spoke briefly about the two figures she had seen in the turret window. They had all seen it she remarked. Even the rude and disrespectful Halloween pranksters had seen it. She'd have filed a complaint for their arrest but she didn't want to sully Ralph's name. The cops seemed so intent on trying to hold him responsible for something that had happened in the street. They said goodnight at Patricia's apartment door. As soon as she got inside Patricia sat on her bed and opened the envelope her friend

Stephen Browne had left for her. Slowly she read the letter. He'd left the instructions for his cremation and the dispersal of his assets. She was to spend only what was necessary on him. No fuss, no frills. The rest of the money from the insurance policy of $250,000 was hers to do with as she pleased and to spend as she desired. He thanked her for being a friend and mentioned that she could take from his apartment whatever she wished. Especially the antiques she had always admired. There was a little money in the house, maybe $2,000 dollars and he told her where she would find it He had no bank account to speak of. He'd paid the rent through the end of the year and that was about all the cash he had. He thanked her again for being a good friend and wished her peace and happiness. "I'll be fine now, the letter read and we will meet again someday."

Dearest Stephen, she thought as she closed the letter and folded it together with the insurance policy naming her as the only beneficiary. On the line requesting that he state their association he had written: Life partner. He'd thought of everything. Patricia got up and took a bath. She felt dirty from the night's events and she was suddenly very hungry. After her bath she ate what she could of the somewhat soggy sandwich she'd purchased at the Deli it seemed hours earlier. Just as she prepared to turn off the light and go to bed she remembered the card the woman on the bus had given her with the aside that "it would not happen for a few years." She was definitely the woman whose image she had seen in the window standing there with her deceased friend Stephen.

She understood why she had seen her friend there. It was common for people to see what they want to see in times of crisis. He had appeared to her because he was on her mind. After all he had just died. But who was the mysterious woman? Moreover, what was SHE doing there at his side? Patricia Chalmers took the card from her pocket and looked at it carefully. There was a telephone number on it, just as the woman said there would be. She could call when she wanted. The number read 1-800 243-2836 and underneath in letters it spelled 2 ETERNITY!

At the bottom of the calling card was the woman's name: Near Angel, Tillie Hall Mention, a.k.a. Mrs. Ralph Mention. She sat for a long while in her chair. She had seen him pick up the phone in the Green Room and say something into the mouthpiece. She didn't know what it was he'd said but he had been much touched at that time. She could see that much by looking at his face. He was trying to hold his emotions in check but he'd not done a very good job of it. But there was so much he was dealing with. With this being his last night at work and all at the time she had thought only that it had finally gotten the best of him. Walking home with her he seemed alright again.

At last, Patricia Chalmers knew what to do. There was a lot to be done but first Mr. Mention needed help. She would speak with a friend down at the board. She owed Patricia a favor. They needed someone in one of the schools and she knew that Ralph would be just perfect for the job. He loved kids and they loved him back. In the meantime he would need help paying off those credit card bills he'd once spoken of and she knew just how to do that without his knowledge. She would think of a way to give him some much needed extra cash. He was such a proud man and he would never accept it as a handout but there were ways to accomplish such delicate matters.

As Ralph Mention made his way back to begin his last eight hour shift at the Castle he walked slowly. He climbed the hill with deliberation. "This is it, he said aloud. The last time I will would walk these grounds as an employee." But he wasn't too unhappy about it. He would make ends meet somehow. Things will work out. They always do, he consoled himself. At the back gate he stopped for a second to double check that it was closed. Then he looked up at the 4th floor of the Turret. The window was open. At first he thought he had forgotten to close it but then he remembered he'd closed it on his early rounds. She's still there. Tillie's still there in the Green Room.

On her visits to his job she had often climbed the stairs just to visit the room and to look out over the grounds below. It was a great view. She would sit there overlooking the little park or just watching the young people as they played. Tillie had come back on his last night to keep vigil with him. Unseen, she would stay until dawn. Then she would go back to her place in the unknown to await his arrival. And like the good wife she had always been Tillie Hall Mention would shut the window behind her. Tonight SHE would be THE LAST GUEST.

PRACTICALLY THE END OF STORY!

Turner Allen put his pen down and pushed the arm chair away from his desk. He looked at the time on the small alarm clock and sighed. He took a small sip of the slightly tepid tea in the little porcelain cup that had been his grandmother's before her death some seven years earlier. It was now the only reminder he had of her. He had once had so many small mementos from her small estate. When the moment passed he refocused on what he had just written. Well, I hope I've done it some justice. The old place deserves justice and honor. Of course not a word of what he had written was truth. Ralph and Tillie Mention, Patricia Chalmers, Stephen Browne and all the others existed only in his imagination.

Mercy Nursing Home had never been. Just as the four young people had never existed. The only truth to the story was the old house. He had done his best to describe a few features of the old house. At least what he could see from the outside of the building. And The Castle was the way how some of the area residents referred to it. Turner passed it nearly every day and each time he did he felt compelled to stop and look at it with admiration and hope. Admiration of its splendor and hope for its future. He was never disappointed. The iron bars on the first floor windows were a necessary evil. They were placed there no doubt to foil would -be thieves from despoiling its interiors. But even these failed to dim the lights of the Castle's grandeur. Each time he looked at it some new feature revealed itself. Always something he'd never before noticed. It was a pity that some people seemed reluctant to honor the place. He felt that this was mostly because of its brief history as a funeral establishment. That was what he'd heard about it. He had also been told that the place had been sold for three million dollars. For certain it needed some serious renovation and some modernization but the outside structure seemed sound enough and it was an historic landmark. If only it was located in a more influential part of town. Then, the price would have been affordable to only the wealthiest. Turner hoped that someone or some organization had seen its potential and purchased it. It could house diplomats or some international organization. It should have a special place in the hearts of people and it could be the uptown offices of an organization like Save the Children or The International Red Cross or even UNESCO. Who knows? Maybe someone would actually give it a name like 'HUGS'. It could stand for Haven under God's Sky. Occasionally, people come up with all kinds of unique names and ideas. A place that would feed the hungry of Africa and South America or wherever hunger exists in the world. Even right here in its own back door. An agency that promotes peace and stops wars in places like Darfur, Haiti, Afghanistan and The Congo. So many countries could be helped just by digging wells for clean and fresh water. He sighed once more. Then, smiling at the audaciousness of his wish list he glanced once more at the clock. It read 11:43 P.M. Good he thought. It is fitting that I completed my first Halloween story just before Midnight on the Eve. 'Before the clock strikes twelve and the witches stew the elves,' he often said.

Remembering the old castle he decided to leave the house and visit it at the bewitching hour. It only a minute walk and if I leave right away I'll make it before time, he thought. He pulled on his hat and coat and in a minute he had walked out the door headed for a glimpse of the beauty of the Castle at midnight. He had passed it on his way home and two strangers, seeing him looking up at the Castle had briefly spoken to him. One, an elderly woman had commented that the place was still for sale. Not that Turner had any money to purchase it. He had just smiled at her. The other stranger had been a Hispanic man. He'd simply commented to Turner that it was a nice house.

"Yes." Turner had replied. "It is beautiful." Hurriedly he walked toward it he looked up at its magnificent architecture.

He liked thinking of the place as feminine and he referred to it as she. But it could just as easily have been Male. Especially with the turret rising skyward like those huge Egyptian and Greek Phallic symbol.

Yes! That was it. It was the symbol of the reproduction of life. Not of the end of anything. It was like death: the beginning and not the end. The Alpha and the Omega. The area residents had it all wrong. It was its destiny to become for a short time a funeral establishment and now it would become something else.

He walked toward the tower looking at it. Turner was submerged in his thoughts.

Suddenly, he stopped.

He had not noticed the police car and van on the other side of the street. He had not noticed the small crowd that had gathered. He was not a curious person. He had learned from years of urban living that the safest way of surviving in the City was to walk away from crowds. Never walk toward them.

But this was different. This was close to his beloved Castle and he had to know if there was a problem

Something must have happened. Crossing to the other side he mingled with the already dissipating throng of on lookers. He had arrived too late someone said. They had just carted off to jail four young people who were involved in robbing an old lady on this very spot not even half an hour ago. The only female in the group of bandits had taken the woman's money and her gold necklace and earrings. But the entire group of thieves were apprehended by a police car and returned to the scene of the crime just minutes ago where the woman identified them. "They have some nerve these kids, robbing an old woman like that. It's good they didn't get away with it," the man said. He and Turner stood there talking. "Somebody was watching and whoever it was called the cops. That'll teach them a lesson." The man laughed with satisfaction. "That is, if they ever get out of jail. That'll learn 'em," he said as he walked away shaking his head.

For certain somebody had called the cops, Turner said to himself. They didn't know who had called. Well, maybe they didn't know. But he sure as Heavens knew who'd called. He walked back to the other side of the street. He had already noticed the windows in the turret. One of the windows was open on the 4th floor and a slight wind created the impression that someone was standing behind the curtains. The large chandelier in the room was lit, its crystals gleaming brightly. Looking at his watch Turner noted the time. It was midnight.

October 31st, 2009 - Midnight   THE END

Not Maid for Mayhem

Maurice P. Fortune

Ms. Daisey had seen something awful. Well, actually she hadn't. She just thought she had and that was even worse. It would have been better if she had seen what she thought she had seen because at least there would have been a modicum of truth to the story she was now planning to weave. And this time she would pull out all stops. Daisey would leave no stone unturned in her attempt to convince the authorities and her closest friends that she had actually witnessed every aspect of the sordid episode. So what if she added a 'detail' or two. It would only make the story more interesting and it would certainly save the television and movie screen writers a lot of time and research when her very own memoir was published. It was something she had been planning in her mind for months, maybe years. And just to be a part of a big investigation would make her the envy of everyone she knew.

Not that she fancied herself a kind of modern day Jane Marple. But she sat practically glued to the television every Sunday evening when the Agatha Christie episodes were being aired. She watched Jane's every move. She was some kind of sleuth, Jane was. And Daisey felt that given the right circumstances she could do just as well. Even though it was now a different world she lived in than the one of Jane's time. With the discovery of DNA and forensics, it kind of took the detective work out of being a detective. No, she was if anything, more of a Murder She Wrote woman. She certainly could identify with Jessica. Daisey too had been a teacher. An elementary teacher in a public school for more than 40 years and she was proud of that. That was the difference, she smiled as she thought about it. Jane was a spinster and she lived her life through other people.

But Jessica had been married and her husband had died. Daisey felt a moment of sadness overcoming her. To be honest, she had not always been alone. She was the first to let you know. Certainly, her only marriage had ended long before her husband died. But that was no fault of her own. She had done all she could with a drinking man. It wasn't that he was abusive or anything. In fact, he was a rather playful teddy-bear when he was drunk. But he was physical in another way and embarrassingly lewd. She had values after all. A man is not supposed to offer unspeakable pornographic photos for his wife's viewing pleasure. He is not supposed to insist upon her participation in these things. It was just not right and it always left her with the feeling that she had done something wrong. Of course he had laughed and told her how much she seemed to have enjoyed these sessions as she came to call them. Hump! Enjoyed them! She was practically violently ill afterwards. She had been brought up attending church regularly, even if her parents were not practicing Methodists.

Oh yes, Daisey Hutchins knew the difference between love and lust. She'd had them both. But the marriage had given her a life time of financial security and for that she was grateful. She had been genuinely heartbroken when it all came crashing to a standstill more than twenty years ago. There had been an affair or two after the marriage but she never overcame the bad taste that her marriage had left in her mouth. Then too, there was the financial considerations. She might have lost it all, including the social security if she had made the mistake of remarrying. She had made a good choice in continuing payments on his rather substantial life insurance policy and as the surviving wife she had his social security payments and her own to fall back on. She could have gone on and on with her thoughts but the sound of the doorbell took her out of her brief reverie. The package she had ordered from the on line shopping network had arrived. The new curtains for the living room had come a day or two sooner than expected. She was glad of that because she wanted to take the bus ride to Atlantic City on the coming Saturday just four days away. Not that she was planning to gamble away all of her money this trip.

The last time she went to Atlantic City she had actually lost two dollars from her own purse. The money just got away from her and it was something she would have to be more aware of in the future. After all, the cost of the ticket is thirty dollars and they give back fifteen. That is plenty to put in those durned slot machines. She placed the package containing the new curtains on the dining room table and made a mental note to telephone the superintendent of the building to ask if he could send someone over the following week to help her hang them. It was just a matter of formality as she knew that there was no one else he could send over. He would come himself as he always did. She didn't see why the building management kept up the pretense of having a full staff. Everyone knew that they used the same super to operate the four building complex. Unless you counted the crack head nephew he had hired for show. He was a buffoon that one, a real work of art. But she just needed someone to provide the brawn. She had all the brains necessary for the job. Daisey went into the kitchen to prepare a single cup of peppermint tea and as she did she stooped to pet Ms. Kitty on the top of her balding spot. She was worried about Ms. Kitty and if she didn't show some improvement soon she'd have to take her to the Vet. But she hoped not, because Vet visits had become so expensive. Of course, she'd spare no expense to have her cat healthy but she sometimes wondered where all this would end. She meant the rising costs of everything. Everything was becoming so expensive.

Daisey stood in her kitchen looking out over the same spot in the garden where she knew all the evidence lay. She smiled when she remembered that she was about to become famous. Maybe even be on TV. Well, there could be a call from a TV show host like Steve Harvey. People had appeared on his show for less. What would her many critics think now? Now that she had the goods and all of them would be forced to come to her for an accurate account of that awful day she had been eye witness to a crime. They could no longer call her by that stupid and insulting name she had heard bandied about for years. Oh yes, she had heard it. She had kept her mouth shut but she knew. Well, she wasn't keeping her mouth shut any longer. She would tell her story and they would be forced to recant their words of slander. She had heard and seen the crime as sure surely as she had been witness to her own birth, although she couldn't recall that event. What a pity. It must have been something special, she surmised. At 76 years of age she had a lot of living to do and it wasn't any fault of hers if things kept dropping into her lap. She just went about her normal affairs. She did her daily chores and her shopping and she spent a lot of time sitting in the sunshine, weather permitting or looking out across the street when she couldn't go outdoors. The doctor had given her specific orders to stay off her gimpy leg. But it gave her trouble and she was lucky that she didn't have to climb more than one flight of stairs to her apartment and that was only to enter the building. She could see everything from the safety of the peephole in her front door or through the curtains in her kitchen window. And she just happened to be in the kitchen when she witnessed what she'd witnessed. She was no Busy Body. It made her bristle whenever she thought of the name: Lady Busy! Of all things: Lady Busy!

Actually, she hadn't planned to be alone that day. She had arranged to meet Lona and go to the market for a few things. They always got together on Tuesdays and afterwards they would sit on of the benches in the middle of the cross walk. They'd chat about this or that for an hour or so and if it wasn't the best of weather the two of them would have tea and something sweet to eat. It wasn't exactly an English tea. After all they were African Americans and not British. But the tea was always welcome, or hot chocolate when the weather was cold. They never had coffee because it interfered with the mandatory afternoon naps they both needed to keep away the wrinkles in the forehead. It was just a coincidence that Lona had forgotten that she had a dental appointment that morning. She had called at the last minute and they were forced to postpone their meeting until the following afternoon. Weather permitting.

Daisey liked Lona and they clearly valued one another's friendship. It wasn't every day that two people met who were of like mind. There was every reason why they should not have been friends. Lona was a southern girl and had had several marriages. Also, Lona had spent many years working as a live-in maid for a wealthy family out in Long Island. She had finally been terminated when it was discovered that she was having an affair with the man of the house. It wasn't that she was hard to get along with. Not in the least bit. Lona was the sweetest person anyone could ever hope to meet. But she had made some bad choices in her life as far as men were concerned. Choices that Daisey herself would never, ever make. She had often told Daisey that she, Lona couldn't understand how her friend had managed to stay alone for so many years after the death of her husband. Daisey had tried to explain but she gave up when she began to understand the terrible reality about her friend. It was the one thing that Daisey's own religious upbringing would never permit. Lona needed a man. There! She had said it. She needed a man as surely as she needed a new pocket book every two weeks or one of the nice frilly blouses she liked to wear with her jeans or trade mark black pants suit.

As for herself, Ms. Daisey Hutchins needed no such animal. She was fine just as she was. She could visit her sister up in Boston twice each year, although Gloria never reciprocated.

Suddenly she stopped in her tracks. She realized that she was about to break her promise to her sister.

They had promised one another that they would never interfere in one another's private affairs. And they had made that promise after the last incident had nearly torn them apart. It had left them on non - speaking terms for more than two months. In fact, they had made the vow that they wouldn't even 'think' about one another in this way, since it always led to negativity. Whatever, Gloria did with her life was fine with Daisey. She could have one man or twenty. It was no skin off her back, Daisey thought. But someday her sister would have to make amends for having chosen as a companion a gigolo and a skirt chaser. But that was her sister's business. She was just glad that they had mended the breach between them. Gloria called her after she was released from the hospital following her hip replacement and Daisey had left her own affairs unattended. She took the bus to Boston for three days just to nurse her dear sister back to good health. She could feel good about that, Daisey could, and she had been 'there' for her kin when she was needed. That's what the Bible said one must do! And she was a stickler about what the Good Book said. After all, hadn't every word of it been handed down to Moses by God? She thought a moment about what had just come to mind and then said almost out loud. Well, maybe not every word to Moses but from what she could understand it was almost as if it had been. She'd have to check further on that since she confessed that she didn't know much about the Bible. She was however an avid reader and she was sorry she didn't have a copy of the best seller of that title "Don't Know Much about the Bible."

She had read the one on history and found it to be excellent.

As she stood there gazing into space her mind wandered back to that day when her whole world had forever changed. She had not been the same since. Even Lona could tell that there had been a serious upheaval in her best friend's life. Daisey tried hard to be the same but it was difficult. She would never be able to go back to being poor innocent Ms. Hutchins. No, not in this life. As her eyes wandered to the small alley between the buildings they came to rest upon the three or four garbage cans that stood lined against the wall in the rear of the building. They were still there. Just as they had been that day she saw the superintendent leave his ground floor apartment, walk up the three or four stairs and drop two very large bags behind the cans. The bags were heavy. Even she could tell that much.

The super was not a small man and he had had trouble hoisting them off the ground. She didn't want to speculate on what they held but it wasn't her fault if she had been given the gift of intuition. Besides, she had seen him do it hadn't she? She had seen him bring his wheelchair bound wife into the kitchen. She had seen him violently push the chair away from the window and into the opposite wall. And she was certain that she had seen the poor woman fall from the chair. She lay there helpless. Awaiting her certain fate. Certainly, she knew what was coming next and this made the crime even more horrendous and inhuman. It had taken only a minute or so as Daisey, recoiling in mocked agony, demonstrated to no one in particular just how she had seen the man raise a hammer over his head and repeatedly and mercilessly bring it down upon the head and body of the defenseless invalid who was his wife. Again and again he hammered until she lay motionless and dead. She couldn't see the woman from where she stood but she knew the invalid lay dead or dying on that cold kitchen floor. Oh yes, Daisey Hutchins was sure of that. Not wanting to see any more of the ghastly business, she had slowly closed the pretty pink and white curtains to shut out the whole sordid scene. She had also closed them to keep the killer from noticing her in the window less he, having committed one murder, might now be forced to commit another.

For a long time she had not moved. Afraid of being discovered. At one point she thought he knew she had been watching him. His eyes appeared to look in the direction of her window. It was a deer in the headlights moment and it passed quickly. She, on the other hand, was just as terrified as she slithered along the kitchen counter past the stove and the refrigerator and into the dining room. Her head nearly knocked the clock from its position on the wall. Not wanting to go near the back door, she had nonetheless got down on all fours and moved over to it just to make sure it was bolted and secured against the demon killer. Then, she crawled on her knees, out of the kitchen and all the way to the closet next to her bedroom door. She was afraid to stand. Afraid that any other movement might attract his attention. After all, if he had seen her he would be obliged to be rid of the only eye witness. Wouldn't he? Her apartment was the only one with windows on that side of the building. And she had only a few. Her kitchen window was small. It looked out on the two small gardens that separated her back yard from the rear of the building opposite it.

The superintendent, his name was Ricardo Rodriguez lived on the first floor of the building with his wife. She had been seriously injured in a car accident about 4 years earlier. She'd nearly died then. And now just a short time later she had been released from all the pressures of this world by a brutish husband. How sad! What would become of their young daughter and their two grandchildren, Daisey wondered. Daisey paused as she thought again of her own pleasant surroundings. She was grateful for the kitchen window and the garden and of course the two side windows that overlooked the cement and grass park where all the old people could sun themselves or watch the very young children play out of harm's way. They didn't have to cross the street to the bigger park on the other side unless they wanted to. Of course, she wanted to and she did cross the street very often. They played basketball over there and she LOVED basketball. But she also loved to sit unnoticed in her bedroom window and look out over the 'little' park. Or stand in the window of the bathroom and watch. It was a bit uncomfortable standing there because she had to straddle the toilet bowl to do it and sometimes the flush meter or whatever you call those things bit into her knees but you can't have everything your way in life. Sometimes you have to make sacrifices.

The bathroom window had a frosted glass pane and although she could look out others could not look in to see her standing there. She had seen many things standing there and she could write a book about the NASTY stuff she'd observed. But she wouldn't do that. No, she would never tell a soul.

She couldn't understand why people thought that no one could observe their behavior. Even from her bedroom window she could see. She kept heavy drapes at the window and her Venetian blinds drawn tight but any idiot might have guessed that every shut eye ain't closed and every closed eye ain't shut.

She would sit there in her bedroom for hours observing the comings and goings of the couples in the back alleys of the two buildings. After dark, the Super was supposed to put a chain on the gate but he often forgot and anyway it did no good. Even she could go right around the sides of the fence and step over it. People could spend the whole night doing their dirt if they wanted to. Why, she had even seen Lona's old man Tatum in a compromising position more than once. She could tell he had been drinking and he had seen her. All she had been doing was looking out the window as it was her right and privilege to do.

It was he who was out of place. He who was wrong. Why he should have been ashamed of himself. She stopped for a minute wondering how the poor girl had survived. He must have ripped her guts out. Daisey smiled knowingly to herself.

More than spying on her neighbors she had other "privileges" overlooking the two gardens and the back alleys of the two buildings. She and only she had the privilege of growing flowers in the garden and watching them grow. And Ms. Kitty could sun herself on the back steps when the weather was fine enough. Oh, it was a great bonus and she was sure the other tenants in the building were jealous but she had been there a long time. Longer than anyone else except Mr. and Mrs. Easley on the opposite side of the building and they were both in their 80's. They were also sickly and probably not long for this world poor things. And there were other privileges that living in her apartment gave her besides a bird's- eye- view of the comings and goings in the front and back. She had seen plenty from her windows in the front and from her window in her bedroom which looked directly across the street to the entrance of the park. There had been lover's trysts and quarrels and drug sales and once there had been a stabbing. She knew who was going with whom and when and sometimes she knew why. It was a good thing she was a good neighbor and not a blabbermouth. The sexual encounters she had seen and sometimes heard from her windows in the back were enough to fill several books and she didn't mean encounters always between a man and a woman. She wouldn't elaborate. In fact, Daisey prided herself that she had disclosed this kind of information to no one except her friend Lona and she knew Lona was as discreet as she. Yes, the building and the neighborhood were lucky to have her there in apartment 1-M. She was a real asset. That is why she felt it her duty to let everyone know of the murderer in their midst. Thus far she hadn't told a sole. Not even Lona. And she wouldn't tell Lona. Not even if it killed her. Thinking about it she realized that if the information was to get out it "could" get her killed. And it could get her friend killed too. He'd already killed once and he wouldn't hesitate to strike again just as he had bludgeoned his wife to her very death. Murderers are a resourceful breed, Daisey thought to herself and, they will stop at nothing to cover their deeds. However dastardly.

Suddenly, she thought of something she had overlooked. It was while she was minding her business and watering her hanging ivy plants in the kitchen that she noticed the Superintendent working in the adjoining garden the day following the murder. Although. what he was doing was covered up by the time she started her chores and got up enough courage to look out upon the scene of the crime, she was sure she had seen him bury something and she was almost certain it was the hammer. Yes, Daisey was sure that it was the murder weapon. That much had not escaped her eagle eye and she quietly filed it all away. Of course, it was not possible for a lady of her standing to straddle a fence and go peering about on another person's property but that was exactly what she was planning to do at first opportunity. She was just biding her time. And she had not remembered until just now that blood stains and other DNA cannot be erased or eliminated easily. This had come to mind because she had seen it become the downfall of many criminals who thought they could escape detection. She could not recall just which show it was. No matter.

What was important was that she had seen the man set the bags containing the grisly body parts on the cement and on a small section of the garden. There! Just next to the steps. The evidence would still be there and all she needed to do was get some gloves and a small garden spade. Like the one she used each spring to dig fresh holes to plant her tulip bulbs. She could then place the evidence in a plastic bags and voila! She'd have the evidence she needed to give the authorities when she called them to let them know that a murder had been done. But she needed to do it before it rained and rain was in the forecast over the weekend and by then she would be in Atlantic City. She needed to collect the evidence before she left and she was going to need help. Someone to be there just in case she was discovered by that awful brute. She'd have to tell the whole thing to Lona. She had no other choice. He wouldn't assault her in front of a witness. No one was that depraved and indifferent. He would not dare. First, she was going to have to invent a story to tell Lona which would explain her need to collect dirt from someone's garden. And that would be tough. But she couldn't tell her the whole truth. Not just yet. Lona was always so suspicious of her skills and it was far too premature to trust her with such a huge burden. Why she might let it slip inappropriately. Yes, Lona could get them both killed. Just the idea sent chills down her back. She, Daisey, the victim of a double homicide and she wouldn't be alive to tell the story.

She let that idea fall from her brain and picked up the telephone. There was the customary one ring and Lona answered. "Hello. Lona speaking." Why did Lona always say the same thing when she answered the phone? Always, "hello Lona speaking." Who else did she imagine one would think was speaking? It was annoying but Daisey could be depended upon to remain a true friend.

It was amazing how Lona never failed to pick up on the very first ring. Anyone who does that must have the telephone glued to a hand. They certainly could not have a life. "Hi, Lo," Daisey said.

"What's cookin' sug?" "Oh hi Dais, I was just about to call you. I just got off the phone with Cynth.

You know Cynth from 1423." Then, without giving Daisey time to respond she began to rev her engines.

Daisey knew she couldn't let Lona get started. She would not be able to get a word in edgewise, And there was no time for such idle talk. Not today. There were important things to consider.

The moment Lona entered Daisy's apartment she was ushered into the kitchen. It was their favorite spot for exchanging ideas and today would be no exception. Especially since they could see the garden from that vantage point. Soon, the little blue tea pot was signaling that the water was ready and Lona had assumed her duties of readying the sugar and milk as her friend poured the tea and placed the plate of homemade cookies on the table between them. They took their places: Lona always faced the back door and Daisey sat opposite the window. Daisey began to unravel her plot. She would feel badly later, having lied to her best friend but it couldn't be helped. She was certain Lona would have done the same thing if the shoe had been on the other foot.

"Lo," Daisey began, "I want you to do me a favor and I don't want you to ask me any questions." She continued, "if you trust me like I trust you then you'll do it." There was total silence at the table as they sat looking in each other's eyes for a second or two and then Lona replied. "Well, if you put it that way I don't have much choice do I? I mean I can't say no, can I?" She looked at Daisey searchingly. Looking for a hint of what was to come but her friend was taking her time. She is milking this moment for all she's worth, Lona though to herself. Well, go on get your rocks off Ms. Daisey. But if I don't want to do it I'm still not going to. No matter how many guilt trips you try to put me on. Of course Lona didn't say any of this out loud. Not to Daisey Hutchins. And besides, Lona's curiosity was piqued and she wanted to know. "Well, Dais," she finally said. "What do you want me to do, you know I'm your best friend." Daisey began to explain her plan. They would meet again later. At 8:30 P.M. By then all activity should have stopped in the kitchen of the Superintendent's apartment. The lights would be shut off and they could just step across the fence undetected. It would only take her a second to scoop up enough earth for DNA analysis and then they'd be back in the safety of her home. They could leave the back door open and M. Kitty could serve as a kind of watch cat. With the natural moon light, there'd certainly be enough light to guide them on their dangerous mission. Lona was so tempted to ask questions but her friend was not offering any information. She only said that she'd explain everything at the right time and Lona knew better than to insist. Anyway, it would do her no good once Daisey's mind was made up. Just before she closed the door and went back to her own apartment Lona waved her hand at Daisey and silently mouthed the words. "You're up to something Dais." She narrowed her eyes as she said it and the gesture made Daisey laugh out loud. She put her hand over her mouth when she realized what she was doing. It was done more an involuntary action than anything else but it seemed to fit the moment and she closed the door. But she didn't leave the door. Not just then. She stood there looking out the peep hole as

Mrs. Pitts, apartment 3-S came into the building. She was pushing a grocery cart and it was clear that she had been shopping at Path Mark. There had been some flyers from Path Mark placed near the mailboxes for tenants. Daisey had taken two and she had circled some items she would buy on the following morning. There was a special on Stouffer's dinners at $1.98 each and they were selling 3 pints of Hagen Dazs ice cream for $10.00. The ice cream always went fast when it was on sale and Daisey hoped that Mrs. Pitts had not taken the last of it.

It seemed as though 8:30 would never come. Daisey called her sister Gloria in Boston. She explained that she was about to do something that would make her a lot of money and gain her the respect and accolades of millions of folks. No, she could not elaborate at the moment but time would reveal all. Gloria wished her a lot of luck and God speed and they hung up, but not before promising to be in touch the following Monday. Of course, at times like this there was never anything to do. Idly, she picked up the remote control. Just but chance she stopped her search at an episode of "The New Detectives." She watched it for a few minutes before she realized she had already seen the program. Twice. Why do they keep re-running the same old thing, she thought? She tried again to find something of interest to watch but she could only find shows about cooking and what did she need that for. Why she was an excellent cook. Everybody said that. In fact, she was always being asked if she would like to cater an affair. You know, somebody's wedding or birthday party. Someone always mentioned these things to her but they never followed through. Oh well, they didn't know what they were missing.

She fell asleep and awoke to hear the telephone ringing. "Don't you ever answer the phone, Dais?" "Umm, What?" "Hello? It's me! Lona. Do you know what time it is? I thought you said we were going...."

Daisey didn't give her time to finish. "I must have fallen asleep. What Time is it?" "I'll say you fell Asleep," Lona's responded. "Its 9:03 and I have been at your door twice. I rang and rang, I thought there was something wrong." "Oh, my goodness, no! I'm fine. Come on down, I'm ready,"

Daisey said. It took another five minutes before Lona arrived. She looked at her friend with suspicion and said cynically, "I thought we were both wearing jeans and sneakers." "It's only gonna take me only a second to slip into mine. I'll be right back." She left Lona to go into her bed room to change. When she returned Lona had already found the plastic bag, gloves and tools they would need to gather the evidence. Although she had no idea it was evidence they were gathering. She smiled when she saw what Daisey was wearing. "Maybe you are taking this a bit too seriously Dais," she said. "Oh, mind your business her friend retorted." She stood there in her matching blue jeans and jacket and wearing what appeared to be a Sherlock Holmes hat. Lona hadn't seen one of those in twenty years and it made her smile again but she was careful not to let Daisey see her laughing.

In a minute they had left the apartment. Leaving the door slightly ajar and the purring Ms. Kitty standing at the top of the stairs they crept along the garden path on her side of the fence. Then, down the lane near the wooden Trellis she had purchased at a fair just last summer and over the short fence. It was meant only as a dividing line between the gardens and not as a barrier but there had been a little discussion about it at the time.

Well, she had the right to protect her small plot of tomatoes and peas and she was going to do it as long as she had breath in her body she had told them all at the time. Thinking of those times she had almost forgotten her current mission when she felt a nudge from Lona. "Is that the spot. you showed me," she asked? "Sssh, keep your voice down, don't talk. Don't even breathe. Daisy replied. I know what I'm doing." She bent over and began putting dirt in the bag.

She probed and probed but she could find no hint of an object buried in the ground. Well, that's not my job she reasoned. The authorities will find it easily enough and I have enough of the top soil to put him away for life. When it was over she motioned to Lona to remain where she was standing and then she tiptoed over to the spot where she had seen him place the bags the day following the murder. It was just under his kitchen window and next to the steps of the building's basement. As soon as she began collecting samples from the soil she saw the light go in the kitchen above her head. Daisey froze in her tracks and crouched as low as she could to the ground. She was about to motion to Lona to do the same but in an instant the light was off and they were safe. "Whew! "That was close." she mouthed to her friend who stood not fifteen feet away. As she did, she wiped her hand across her brow indicating mocked sweat but she forgot that she was holding the tiny garden rake she had brought along to cover their tracks as they exited that side of the fence. The tool fell from her hands and hit the top of the steps with a clatter. "Oh shit, I mean kittens." This time she said it out loud and then realizing her plight she gathered the dirt, put a couple of scoops in the other bag and turned to leave. Just in time to see the figure of a man approaching them from the alley. He had a baseball bat in his hand and he was carrying a flashlight. The bat was a metal one. Daisey knew this because she could see it gleaming in the slight moonlight. And she recalled the story on the news about such bats being considered dangerous and unfair because they gave players a greater advantage. This was not good. She knew it and she shuddered for just a moment. He was wearing a hoodie and Daisey couldn't make out the features of his face. There they were, she and her best friend Lona, some fifty feet from the safety of her back door which had been left open and guarded by a domesticated Siamese cat. No one on earth knew they were there in the garden except Ms. Kitty and she couldn't speak English, although Daisey was sure she could otherwise talk. And to make matters worse they were trespassing. Yes, trespassing according to her own rules; after all it was she who had insisted upon the fence.

"Is that you Ms. Daisey?" Daisey felt a cold sweat break out under her arms and on her brow. "What are you doing out here this time of the night?" It was the Super. He had seen and heard them from his kitchen window. He knew exactly who she was and why she was there. He had not sneaked around through the back alley carrying a torch and a baseball bat for nothing. He knew what she was doing and now he knew what he had to do to Daisey and to Lona. Of course, he would later say that he had no idea who they were at the time. She knew the game. She was sure of that. For the moment he was only trying to put them at ease by playing coy but she would not be fooled. She knew his type and she'd seen something very close to it just that afternoon on The New Detectives' re-run. It was terrible the things the killer had done to his victims even though he had paid for it later. It had taken them nine years to catch him but he had paid. Daisey thought quickly and decided that the best defense was a good offense. Almost unexpectedly she said. "They say if you collect different kinds of soil to put in pots you can successfully re-pot all species of African Violets.

But it is best to collect the soil at night when there is a slight moon, otherwise they won't live 'til morning.

Isn't that right Lona." "Uh huh, uh huh, that's what they said on the internet when we read it this afternoon Dais." She was about to go on and on but Daisey cut her off with a jerk of her head that said without words: "shut up broad, can't you ever shut your trap?" But the super wasn't giving them time to say anything else. He approached them and then without explanation he dropped the bat.

"Here," he said. "Let me give you a hand, I'll help you to the door. Why, you should have told me earlier.

I'd have collected the soil for you. Maybe even a little from the park across the street, they have good black earth over there." Lona nearly fainted with relief. She didn't know what all this was about but she knew there was a reason her friend had asked her along and sworn her to silence. And she also knew that Daisey did not belong on the other side of the little fence. But Daisey had other things going through her mind. Was the man just trying to get them closer together in one spot? Once, they got to the door would he force his way in and then grab a kitchen knife and make short work of them both? He had all night to bury their bodies and no one would be the wiser. He had dropped the bat as a ploy to make her let down her guard. Certainly he knew she was a clever opponent. Well, she had a plan of her own. She was still carrying the little rake in her hand and if he tried to force entry she would use it to rake out his eyes and then, pushing Lona inside, she would bolt the door and call the cops. Yes, that was what she would do. Ms. Kitty could be rescued later. After all, no one could understand her when she spoke except Daisey Hutchins.

As soon as they got to the steps of the back door the Superintendent turned to her and said. "Next time let me know the day before Ms. Daisey. I'm always around in the afternoons. Just ring my bell.

My wife will be back from Puerto Rico in a few days." Hmmp. Daisey thought.

He is even dumber that I thought he was. His wife will be home from Puerto Rico in a few days!

Who does he think he's fooling with that nonsense! Daisey Hutchins knows the truth and soon the whole world will know it too, Mr. Superintendent! She almost shoved poor Lona inside the back door. Then she parted her legs to allow a still purring Ms. Kitty to enter and with that she said goodnight to the Super. As an afterthought she added. "What's your full name so I can write it down on my calendar?" "Oh, it is Rodriguez. Ricardo Rodriguez." She pretended to digest the information but she already knew his name in full. At Christmas time the building management always sent around a flyer naming its employees. Half of the names were of people she had never seen or heard of until the holiday season.

And they expected HER to give money and presents to strangers! "You know where to find me," the super continued. "Around the corner, you know the building with the green canopy." "Ah yes," Daisey answered.

"Well goodnight." With that she slammed the door shut and bolted it. She stood there for a minute reflecting on her near death encounter. She didn't know why he had not killed them. Maybe it was too difficult a job to kill two people at once. Especially, someone as healthy and as vibrant as she.

Well, she didn't look a day over 50 and she could easily pass for 40 if she took more time to dress and wear makeup. But they say O.J. Simpson murdered two people at once. It was hard to believe but they say he was a good athlete in his time and he stayed fit so maybe it wasn't so hard to kill two if one person remained perfectly still and didn't try to run or scream or anything. "Dais, Dais!" It was the voice of Lona waking her from her cocoon. She'd completely forgotten about her. "I'm sorry Lo, I was off on a tangent. I guess I'm tired." She apologized. "Well, I'm going upstairs Dais and you can stay here and dream all you want," Lona said. "Okey dokey," her friend answered. "I'll see you tomorrow. I hope you make up your mind to go to Atlantic City with us on Saturday." "I'll see. I have to ask Tatum again. When I mentioned it the first time he said he didn't have any money and besides, it's supposed to rain all day long," Lona told her. She started to say that was what you always say and then you never go but by that time her friend was closing the front door. Daisy walked down the narrow corridor and locked it. Then she turned out the lights.

On Saturday it rained. It was not a light rain and it was enough to keep Daisey from going on the bus ride to Atlantic City. She could always go another time she thought. Besides, she liked to walk on the boardwalk and look in the windows of the shops. At this time of the year the shop keepers were just beginning to display their spring and summer wears and the smells along the boardwalk always enticed her to spend a few dollars on junk food. She knew it was not healthy for her but she didn't do it often enough to hurt and she'd just take a good enema or laxative when she got home. No, she would not go to the shore to gamble away her hard earned dollars. There was other pressing business at hand.

She had listened when the superintendent Senor Rodriguez told them that his wife would be home in a few days. Yes, she had listened and she had waited. After all, she was not one to make rash judgments or to do anything whatsoever to harm a body. But that was three days ago. Well, almost. It was Wednesday night when he made that ridiculous claim. And Daisey had given her plenty time to come home. Plenty of time. Why you can go around the world and back in that length of time.

Practically, she reasoned to herself. Maybe fate did not want her running off to amuse herself when there was a crime to report. Actually, it wouldn't have been fair if she'd decided to go and he outsmarted her. There were probably no extradition treaties between the Commonwealth of Puerto Rico and the United States of America. It is not like it is an official state or anything. Wherever that place is located in this world. She knew plenty about the Dominican Republic because it shared an Island with Haiti and that was where Toussaint l'Ouverture had overthrown the French and instituted the first Black Republic. She also had a few acquaintances from Haiti. A good friend she knew had nearly died when she returned from the Dominican Republic after undergoing a tummy tuck and liposuction there. It had been awful and only another operation here in New York had saved her life. But this was different; this was murder of a most heinous nature. And she'd have to inform the press. It would be front page news so she'd have to move to a secluded area the way celebrities do. She was one to understand the pressures of celebrity. Of course, she'd need a security force for her protection because the news reporters would hound her to death. And naturally, Lona would share top billing, well maybe not top billing but she'd certainly get honorable mention. After all, if had not been for Lona she probably would have been bludgeoned on the spot right there in the little garden beneath the trellis.

The super was a clever fellow and she could sense that he was just biding his time. Giving himself time to maneuver and maybe clear as much cash as possible. Maybe he'd already reported his wife missing and dead. Maybe he was just waiting to collect on an insurance policy. They say that those things can pay really big dividends. Once he had his finances in order he'd just skip town and then she'd be left holding the bag of dirt. With no proof. Oh yes, he'd have plenty of time to return to his country and even seek asylum. Then, she'd have to forego her plans of fame and fortune. But it was not going to happen. Today, she would tell the entire sordid tale to Ms. Lona Mc Kensie and then tomorrow they would go together, arm in arm to the nearest police precinct. That would be the 34th she believed, and she would tell how he'd beaten his wife to death with that piece of steel. What do they call it? Oh yes, a baseball bat. It was an awesome weapon. And he has the nerve to walk around at night brandishing it and carrying a flashlight. He plays mind games and torments his victims…Daisey shuddered just imagining how he must have tortured his poor invalid wife for days on end before finally murdering her most brutally.

It's a good thing she'd had enough foresight to insist upon her friend's presence that moonlit night. But even Daisey had to admit to herself that her untimely demise would have been sensational. It would have made a good story line for the dailies. She could see it: "Still Attractive Ex- Professor Killed beneath Trellis". Both Gloria and Lona would have simply died from envy. Well, there were still plenty of good headlines to come. Certainly, Oprah would call. There'd probably be a piece in Vanity Fair and of course she'd have to tell her harrowing tale in the Reader's Digest. She would comply even though it was not such a popular publication any longer. She had no idea why this was so but she guessed she was probably the only one in the entire City of New York who still looked forward to its monthly issue at the checkout counter. And with that final thought Ms. Daisey Hutchins in her apartment at 1475 Hedgeton Street on New York City's famed Sugar Hill in Harlem picked up the telephone and dialed her friend Lona McKensie of the same address but on the 3rd floor to tell her just why they would soon be moving to a more prestigious address.

Of course, they would have to take the entire ground floor just in case their expertise was required at some other location in the City. She savored the moment. She let her finger dial each digit and then let the dial spin all the way around until it came to rest. Then, she slowly dialed the next, and then the next and so on. She was hoping against hope that this time. Just this time Lona would not answer on the first ring. That she would say something different. This was after all a momentous occasion and it called for something a little special. Oh please Lona, don't ans…. "Hello!" Came her friend's voice from the other end of the phone. "Lona speaking." "Oh, shit Lo, I know who you are," Daisey replied. "Don't you ever say anything else? Oh never mind. Listen, I think you had better come for lunch today. Tea time won't do." "Oh, now Dais don't you start again," Lona said with mocked rebuke. And then she added almost in the same breath. "I'll see you in twenty minutes."

This time Lona didn't need to ring the bell. Daisey was standing in the doorway when she came down the stairs. "This had better be good Dais." Lona said looking past her to the smell of something sweet baking in the oven. She walked straight past her friend and then took her seat at the kitchen table; noting that Daisey had taken time to cover the table with a green and white table cloth. With frills of course. And she had a small candelabra with candles burning in the center of the table. Yes, her friend Daisey knew how to set the scene. She knew how to entertain, Lona surmised. Just as she started to ask the nature of the occasion the phone rang and she listened while Daisey told the caller that she was occupied. "I'll call you later and if not then we'll talk early tomorrow, okay?" This was important thought Lona. And she felt important and honored that her friend was putting everything on hold just for her.

She had pulled out all the stops, Daisey had. She had put everything on hold. Of course she could not take the phone off the hook nor unplug it. Something important might happen and she could be called at any moment. She was, after all a VIP. She had taken time to prepare Lona's favorite meal: Shrimp and mock crab leg Newburg. Well, the shrimp wasn't mock it was quite real and so was the rice and fresh spinach that went along with it. For dessert there would be Peach Melba with some of that delicious Hagen Dazs chocolate ice cream she had picked up at Path Mark's. And to top it off they could retire to the parlor after dinner. Each with a cup of hot apple toddy just for the occasion. Just this once. She would save her story until after dinner and until after the dishes had been washed and put away by Lona of course. It was the least Lona could do to reciprocate. After all. It was Lona who had been a maid. She, Daisey Hutchins had worked as a professor.

Finally, dinner and dishes were over and the two women went into the living room with their warm drinks. Sitting there on the sofa Daisey related to Lona her tale. She recounted how and when she had seen the man Rodriguez assault his poor wife. And between the questions and the gasps from her friend she wiped away a tear or two as she told of Ricardo Rodriquez taking the hammer and pounding it upon the woman's head again and again until she was certainly quite dead. How he had certainly decapitated the corpse and sent it along with the daily garbage to a landfill in Alabama or wherever it is that the City sends its garbage now. Somewhere far away. Along with the old beef and putrid chicken, the banana peels and rotted cabbage. It was probably lying there still, amid the ruins of milk cartons and newspapers, old shoes and canned tuna. It was sad. Poor,

poor woman. And no one was the wiser. But there was one person who had seen it all. She, Daisey, had been the only witness and now Lona would join her in that knowledge. All Lona had to do was keep her mouth shut, as she swore she would and on Monday she would accompany Daisey to the 34th Precinct to tell her story. That was it! And then Daisey apologized for the little ruse she'd pulled by not making Lona privy to the entire affair the night of the garden party. But she was sure that Lo could understand how even the slightest hint could have got them both killed. Dead as fish out of water. No one would have ever suspected that Rodriquez had killed three people. No one would have ever known the difference. Lona nodded, indicating that she understood and that she forgave her friend for being disingenuous on that night. Beside herself with joy she went with her friend to the kitchen. Daisey waited by the refrigerator while Lona bolted the door and made sure the little window was pulled shut. Then, she shut off the light while Daisey walked to the front parlor to check the windows. Daisey remembered afterwards that her good buddy had made a comment about not being too careful.

Then, Daisey asked Lona to do her one last service that night: just one. "Could you please double check the bathroom window too, Lo," she asked? "Sure Dais, I've got to go anyway." Daisey waited by the front door for a few minutes and when Lona emerged from the bathroom she startled her. "What you looking at?" Lona laughed! "Oh, I thought I heard something," Daisey replied. She tore her eyes away from the peep hole and opened the door to let her friend out. "See you tomorrow Lo." Daisey almost whispered it as she watched her best friend disappear up the stairs to her own apartment. She was sure Lona had company and would not be alone. That no count so - called boyfriend Tatum would be there. He liked to stretch out on the sofa with a beer cooler at his feet.

He was always drinking beer and smoking those Newport shorts. She knew Lona smoked cigarettes as well and she did not approve of it. You'd think she'd know better. With all the negative ads and such. Well, to each his own. But she wished Lona would stop pretending she was always alone and that she hadn't been touched in two years. Or was it three? She hunched her shoulders and went into her bedroom.

She was safe and secure and tomorrow was the big day. She had better stop worrying about others and get some sleep she thought. Reaching for her big pink hair curlers, her face cream, her night mask and ear plugs, Daisey Hutchins prepared for another night alone in her bed. She didn't like using all this stuff on her hair and skin but it was the only way to sleep straight through the night. She certainly did not want to be disturbed by the sound of footsteps as the other tenants came in and out of the building. They made so much noise going up the stairs. She would hear about all of the details of the trip to Atlantic City soon enough. Who won and lost and of course, who almost won. It was the same each time there was a gambling night in the neighborhood. Everybody talked about it until the next outing. And the noise they all made coming into the building! Well, it was enough to wake the dead; she wondered why the Easly's had gone on the bus ride. They were too old to go out. Even to a movie. Mrs. Easly was almost in a wheelchair and she had to be helped on and off the bus. Daisey had done it many times. Both she and Mr. Easly were old and they just slowed things down. And the Baldwin's: Ruth and Billy. They were nearly as old.

For a minute or two Daisey lay there in the dark room unable to sleep. It's too early to go to bed and she sat up and propped the spare pillow behind her. She reached for the remote control and turned on the TV, surfing the stations as she looked for something interesting. She finally settled on a basketball game. She recognized the colors of the Lakers and she put the remote down. Actually, Daisey liked the Lakers. Well, she liked Kobe. Kobe Bryant. She knew his name well and she had followed the young man's career. As a matter of fact she liked basketball. After all she was still a teacher at heart. And she would go often to the park just to watch the youngsters play. They called it "ball" and they played it well. They were so agile and strong too. They would always joke with her and give her the ball after the game to let "grannie" shoot it. She had never made a basket but she always tried just to pleasure them.

Then, one or two of them would walk with her up the short ramp and watch her as she crossed the street and entered the building. They were nice young men. Suddenly, she remembered that she had seen Lona close the back door. But had she put the bolt on? She thought she had better check to make sure so she swung her legs over the edge of the bed and slipped her feet into her slippers. She walked the length of the tight-walled hall and entered the kitchen. When she turned on the light she realized that the door was already bolted. Daisey went over to the sink and peered out at the garden as it sat silent in the night air.

She stood there for a few minutes thinking about tomorrow. Then, she took her usual seat at the empty table. Tomorrow was going to be a big day for her and for Lona. She had grown very fond of that girl. She was like the daughter Daisey had never had. She was apprehensive about letting Lona know that she had decided to leave her most of the estate in her will. In fact, she had already put certain things in motion. There were the two twenty -thousand dollars life insurance policies. She had named Lona as beneficiary over a year ago. And the only thing left to do was to sign the bill that would give Lona the bulk of her bank accounts. Admittedly, not a lot of money. Just a little over $800 thousand. Some of it left to her when her very own dear mother had died and of course that had been supplemented by the $200 -$250 thousand her Al had left when he departed this life five years ago. It was kind of him. They hadn't been together as man and wife in many years but it was clear he still loved her. Yes, Lo would have it all. Gloria didn't need any money. That was the reason mother had not left Gloria anything except a piece or two of jewelry. She had given her the big diamond and ruby brooch and a complete set of priceless emeralds, matching necklace, ear rings. Just the whole lot. But Gloria acted as though she didn't care to have even that. Her own husband had been filthy rich and was an important financier there in Boston. He had left her millions of dollars and when she died she would leave it all to charity. To the pet farm she had adopted. Not to humans. Gloria didn't particularly care for human beings. But Daisey loved others of her kind and when she died she was going to make Lona a fairly wealthy girl. She smiled when she thought of it. In the meantime there were things that she was going to do for Lorna. Just as soon as this murder mess was over she would give her one of the beautiful mink coats in her closet. And Lorna could have the sable jacket too, it was really to be worn by a younger woman and she, Daisey was past that. And just to show that she thought so much of this self-adopted daughter of hers she would give her the little strongbox she kept under the bathroom sink.

She only kept it there because she knew that Lona knew it was there and the girl sometimes "borrowed" small amounts of money. She understood. In fact, she understood more about Lona that the girl would ever know. And as far as the strongbox was concerned there could not have been more than four or five thousand dollars in it. Along with some jewelry that she had accumulated over the years.

From time to time she would make a big deal about sending Lona to the store for purchases and she'd go through the motion of going in the bathroom and then coming out and handing the girl money to use for the purchases. But most of the time she already had the money in her hand before she entered the bathroom and when she did take it from the box she always put the money back. As far as the jewels in there? Why she WANTED Lona to take her pick of them. What did she, Daisey, need with them She certainly wasn't going anywhere. Well, enough games! Just as soon as we return from the precinct on tomorrow, I am going to hand over that box to Lona she thought. It was a pity that Lona was sleeping with that pig Tatum. I can't stand him. Daisey said to herself. She sighed deeply and smiled.

Satisfied with her decision making Daisey Hutchins stood up from the kitchen table in her apartment to return to bed for a welcomed night's rest. She was startled by the sound of tapping. It wasn't coming from the back door. No, it was the little window above the sink, overlooking her lovely trellis in the garden.

Feeling safe she parted the curtains a little more and looked out. She looked out into the face of the super Rodriquez and he was smiling. Daisey froze in her tracks. What to do? It would do no good to scream. No one would hear that. Besides, the building was practically empty save a few who had not taken the ride to Atlantic City and of course her dear sweet adopted daughter Lo. But Lo was on the 3rd floor. Yes, the super was clever. He knew that most of the tenants had gone to Atlantic City. He'd chosen well his time. He knew she knew and now he'd returned to make sure he silenced her for good. Then he'd lay his trap for poor Lona.

She reached for the telephone but the sound of children's voices at the back door made her pause.

Rodriguez was saying something to her from the window. "I'm sorry to bother you Ms. Daisey but I saw your light. I just wanted to tell you that my wife came home. She gave me something for you. I hope you don't mind that I brought my grandchildren with me!" Relieved, Daisey unbolted the door. She opened it and asked him to repeat what he had said. "Oh," he said. "My wife just got back from my house in Ponce and I told her about your African Violets."

"My what?" Daisey had momentarily forgotten the lie she'd told a few days earlier when the man surprised her and Lona in the garden. "Your dirt," he said. Holding up a plastic bag containing dirt. "I told her what you told me and she said she had brought back some dirt for her window box in the front of the house; she wanted to share with you a little for your African violets pots. These are my grandchildren," he said. Rodriguez turned to point to two small children. A boy and a girl. They were about a year or so apart in age. The eldest was not more than five and they were trying to rip one another's coats off to get to the electronic toy one of them was holding. "Stop it, stop it," their grandfather shouted as he tried to separate them. Then, apologetically explaining, "they like this since they came back. I'm sorry Ms. Daisey."

Daisey mumbled a thank you to the man and something about how cute the kids were. Then, she looked up at the kitchen window. The super was pointing out the face of his wife who was sitting there in her wheelchair and waving furiously. She had seen the woman sitting in the same spot countless times and she knew her face. Daisey waved back with her heart sinking. "Oh well Ms. Daisey, I'm gonna let you go back inside. It is kinda cold out here," Rodriguez said to her. "Goodnight Ms.

Daisey." Then, to his grandchildren, "say goodnight to Ms. Daisey." But the children didn't hear him. They were half way across the garden and wrestling with one another for the toy. Daisey Hutchins didn't hear him either. In fact, she had scarcely heard a word since she looked up and saw the image of the man's wife smiling in the window. Once more she managed a wave to the woman from Ponce, Puerto Rico and then she closed the door. She didn't bolt it this time. She just closed it in resignation.

Feeling the color draining from her hands and face she turned off the light and shuffled toward the bedroom. Her mind was racing. How? How? How had she made such an awful mistake? What had she done? And to think she was going to the police. In just twelve hours she'd have been the laughing stock of the neighborhood. It was a common fact that cops can't hold water. Why they'd have told someone and someone would tell someone. Oh Heavens! She'd have been disgraced.

She'd have lived up to the name Lady Busy. And poor Lona. LONA! LONA! Oh my goodness, I've got to call that girl. Poor baby. "Move Ms. Kitty, get out of my way," she said hustling to the phone in the bedroom. But Lona's phone was busy. Daisey waited a few minutes and called again. It was still busy!

She kept trying for ten or fifteen minutes before she got up and shut off the Lakers game. They were winning but she didn't care. She was tired. All this mess would have to wait until the morning.

Lona would be disappointed about not becoming famous. But she'd get over it. After all, she would be rich and rich is just as good as famous. At least you don't have to worry about the Papparazzi at every turn.

At sicty-one years old Lona was much younger than her friend Daisey. And she was in much better shape too.

Both physically and maybe mentally. For one thing, she never, ever forgot things the way Daisey did.

Dais was always mixing up days and events. It was a wonder she didn't forget her head was attached to her neck. Then again, maybe it wasn't. Lona laughed at that thought. Even she had always considered it her responsibility to look out for Daisey. Daisey wasn't a very big person, maybe 100 lbs. soaking wet. And at 5 ft. 1 inch she barely came up to Lona's shoulders and that was with wedge heels on. Lona, was a big girl and she prided herself on that fact. She was not afraid to stand toe to toe with any woman, man or beast. Sure that stupid Super had surprised them in the garden but she, Lona was not afraid. If Daisey had told her the truth and he'd been foolish enough to start some stuff she would have thrown down and you'd better believe those apples, baby. Daisey never told her the whole truth about anything. Lona was convinced of that much. She always got things in bits and pieces and was forced to scramble to put them together. Daisey would just say, "Oh I'm sorry Lo, I always make a mess of everything don't I?" And then as if she was queen of the Universe she would ask Lona to do some menial task for her. Anything. Like she had a maid or an unpaid housekeeper. It was beginning to stick in her craw. And all because Daisey had a little bit of money in the bank.

There was one other thing that stuck in Lona's craw. She was getting the impression that there was something going on between Daisey and her boyfriend Tatum. Now that was really crossing the line. In fact it made Lona mad as hell. She opened her front door still occupied with that thought and crossed over to the living room where Tatum was stretched out on the sofa in his usual position. He was lying on his back and he had both his hands clutched behind his neck as though he was doing sit ups, which he needed to do but never even tried. He seemed unable to keep his legs on the couch and the left one was always draped across her coffee table as if his was trying to display his manhood to her. Well, she had seen it. Plenty of times and up close and personal too, so he needn't have been so bold. But every man she had ever had was like that. They wanted, no needed someone to tell them that they were the best. That their penis was the largest she had ever touched or seen, except maybe in those bizarre porno movies that men love to watch. Well, they had no idea. She had seen and touched some big ones in her day and if she lived and nothing happened she'd touch a few more. Thank you silly men very much!

Lona couldn't recall when she first got the idea. In retrospect, it was probably after dinner and before they'd had that hot toddy. The first one. Oh, she knew for a few weeks she was going to have to do something about Daisey. Her situation was growing dire and it would just be a matter of time before the woman discovered that things were missing from her strongbox. She thought Lona didn't know it was hidden in the corner of the cabinet in her bath room. Not the medicine cabinet. That was too obvious but the one beneath the sink. Right next to the Ajax and the peroxide and in the last row of the left hand corner. Oh, she knew, did Lona McKensie. Whenever Lo asked her to run an errand she would always go to the bathroom and then come out with a bill or two clutched in her tight little fingers. It was a good enough hiding place but the box was too large to be inconspicuous. Even placed inside the carton of an old bathroom light fixture. She could have chosen a hiding place in the kitchen or in an old dish carton. But no, not Ms. Daisey. She thought she could out smart everyone.

Well, she didn't out smart me, Lona smiled.

At first she only took a fifty dollar bill. She had intended to replace it the following week when her check came. Daisey wouldn't miss it. Lona was sure there had to be close to five grand in the box. And that was after Lona had taken about five hundred. Well, she just borrowed five hundred. After all, Dais had so much. But lately she had taken to removing Daisey's jewelry. Piece by piece. She'd always intended to replace it. But it made no sense to put it back one item at time, she reasoned. Making all those trips to the bathroom. Her friend would become suspicious and she didn't want that. In the beginning she had assumed that it was all costume stuff. No one could have a string of pearls that long. And there were at least 2 dozen rings and tons of watches, bracelets, earrings and brooches. No, Daisey Hutchins could not pull the wool over her eyes. She knew her jewelry and this stuff was fake. But one day she had become desperate for cash. Well, it wasn't really her fault. She had not calculated that Labor Day always fell on a Monday. She had promised her one and only child in this world that she would help him pay for new tires for his car and when he called to remind her she realized that her check would not be arrive in time. Her "day" fell on Tuesday, as Monday was Labor Day. Just on a whim she took the pearls and a ring over to Hassain's Jewels on 125th. Of course, she understood that all pawn shops were thieves at heart and she didn't expect to get a loan from them. They were not real and she just wanted to put her mind at rest about that once and for all. She took Tatum with her to stand guard, just in case. Almost at the door Lona got cold feet and poor Tatum was stuck with the task of going in to barter and or being embarrassed to no end. It had only taken a few minutes. Soon, Tatum was sauntering through the door with that smile on his face. Like he'd hit the jackpot or something.

"What did they say? What'd he say Tate, "she'd asked him? Tatum produced a ticket showing he had received over $400 for the little ring. He had not bothered with the pearls. When the man began asking him where he'd got them he knew they were valuable. Just how valuable Tatum said, he didn't know but he could tell by the clerk's demeanor that they were worth a pretty penny.

"Where did you get them anyway Lo," he asked her? "Oh, Dais wanted me to have them. She gave them to me two years ago on my birthday and she would have a hissy fit if she knew I was trying to pawn them. Give them to me," she said. Almost snatching the pearls and the money from her boyfriend, she tucked them in her purse. She took her time. She didn't want to look up at him because he could always tell when she was lying. But he said nothing more about it and the moment passed. It was too late. He already knew. Maybe he'd guessed the truth before he even asked. The man had spent almost 8 years in prison. He had settled down a little in the time they had become lovers but he still had those prison ways. Prison mentality. That's what they call it and once you have it you never lose it. After all, she knew the deal. She'd been locked up more than a few times.

In her younger days and before she'd joined Church and turned her life around with Daisey's help.

I don't care if he knows or not, dumb bastard. She'd almost said it aloud. And so what if she had. And so what if he knows. It's none of his business. They took the bus and on the way home she handed him $75. It was she knew, a kind of hush money payment but he took it and smiled. He was strangely silent the rest of the day but Lona didn't push him. She knew he'd come around by bedtime. After all, he needed his nightly medicine. His "pussy pill "as he called it and that night she had thrown it on him extra strong.

Lona sat there in the living room with Tatum while he watched yet another basketball game. It was a Lakers game or something like that. She didn't like the Lakers. In fact she didn't like any sports except maybe tennis and that was only because of Venus and Serena Williams. Well, she didn't like watching the sport so much but she LOVED their names and the outfits they wore on the tennis court. She liked the name Tiger too. As in Tiger Woods but she would never watch a golf match? It was the most boring thing she had ever seen. Looking at her man lying there half naked, she felt comfortable but anxious. She knew this game thing could go on half the night. These were the playoff games and there was always another team playing somewhere in the country, east coast or west. For a few minutes she tried distracting him.

She even offered to give him a back massage or tweeze the hair bumps on his face. But Tatum wasn't biting. He knew exactly what she was doing and he wanted to finish watching the game. It wasn't yet nine o'clock and she just wanted him knocked out so she could jump on the phone and bullshit with that dumb-assed Daisey half the night. Well, she wants it as bad as I do; although she tries to fake it off like she don't need sex. Tonight she's gotta wait for it until daddy says it o.k. He said o.k. out loud. Lona asked him what he meant by o.k. "Oh, I was just reacting to the shot that boy just made. He's a baad mother." "Don't you be cussin up in here," she admonished him. "I ain't said nothing yet," he smiled. "Wait 'til I git yo' ass in bed." "Tate," she said, feigning anger. She was enjoying every second of it. Just as he knew she was. Leaning over Tatum, Lona picked up the telephone and dialed her sister Tommie, with an 'ie' at the end. She heard his voice and she took the telephone and went into her bedroom to talk. There, they talked 'girl talk' until Tommie begged off. He had a date and it was getting late. He would call her tomorrow evening he said. And then, without saying another word he put the receiver down.

It was just after the second half of the game had started. She wasn't paying attention but she knew that by the number of empty beer cans Tate was piling up on the floor next to the sofa. She knew He'd never stop drinking and it was becoming annoying. But where could she find another man at her age. Especially one who at 50 years old that still looked that good. Although he was starting to get a little pot belly. And then there was the other thing.

Sometimes it was so good to her that ......she stopped her thought almost in midair.

She had it! She had the solution to all of her problems and no one would ever know the truth.

She knew exactly what to do. If only Tate wasn't so stupid and drunk. But she'd try to get him to help her. After all he owed it to her and she had given him money just today so he was in it as much as she. "Tate, Tate baby," she said. "Tate, are you listening to me? I need you to help me do something." "Can't you see I'm watching the game, Lo? You always do this shit to me. It never fails." "Oh Tate," she said sweetly. "I'll give you some money. Another hundred dollars." She had his undivided attention now but he wasn't going to let her off the hook that easy. "No," he said. "Two hundred or nothing." He was in a bargaining mood and he'd said it expecting her to refuse or give a counter offer but to his amazement she consented without hesitation. "You sure? Swear to it," he said, looking directly at her for the first time since earlier that day. "Okay. I swear even though I'm a Christian woman and the Bible says …..."Oh, knock it off Lona. Cut the Bible stuff. Do I get the money or not?" He had completely lost interest in the game and was already imagining himself sitting at the bar of the club on 144th Street watching the scantily dressed hostess and dancers as they served their drinks and plied their trade. "Alright, shoot," he told her. When Lona finished telling him what she wanted him to do he asked her. "That's all? That's ALL you want me to do?" He sat up on the couch and began putting on his sneakers and pulling his sweatshirt over his head. When he finished he reached for his hat and said. "Let's go Bonnie. Let's do this!" It was a reference to Bonnie and Clyde and the comment was ill-timed but Lona didn't reply. She was headed to the door with her keys in her hand.

The more she thought about the plan, the more she loved the idea. If all went well, she'd get paid and Daisey wouldn't get hurt. In fact, neither her friend nor anyone else would ever suspect the truth. The best part was that she, Lona McKensie would walk away clean as a bleached sheet on laundry day.

She walked down the stairs to the echo of Tate's footsteps. He headed for the front door. Slamming it and whistling as he walked to the corner in the uptown direction. She tiptoed down the small corridor to Daisey's apartment and quietly stuck the key in the door. Then, she turned it and pushed the door open soundlessly. But when she closed it behind herself she heard Ms. Kitty purr. Damn it Ms. Kitty, I nearly closed your tail in the door! Recovering quickly she moved silently down the hall and to the kitchen where she stood for about 5 minutes. She looked out the window and saw the figure of her boyfriend moving through the garden. For a second she watched him as he bent over and picked up something. Something big, something long. He'd found the bat, she nearly shouted with joy. The stupid super Rodriquez or whatever his name was had left it lying there when he helped Daisey into the house.

How dumb, she thought to herself. In a minute she had opened the back door and then, taking the bat she carefully laid it down lengthwise. She didn't want it to roll and she certainly didn't need to trip over the thing in the darkness. Then, while Tate stood motionless in the kitchen she went to the bath room and removed the jewels and cash from the box; placing the items carefully in the small tote bag she'd brought along. Daisey's best friend Lona left the bath room, nearly falling over Ms. Kitty and returned to the kitchen where she handed the bag to her boyfrien. It was her first mistake. She had left the empty box on the sink but she would not think of it until later and when she did she would convince herself that they would just assume that the super had somehow found the stash. But she'd also forgotten about her fingerprints which were all over the countertop. She opened the back door just far enough to let Tate out and then she closed it again. But she couldn't find Ms. Kitty. She recalled seeing her trailing Tate when he left with the tote bag in hand. Maybe, it was the smell of the bag. It was a hemp bag and it had been manufactured in the Philippines. Who knows, she thought? I'll leave the door ajar and the cat will come in when she realizes she is not going to be fed. She suddenly thought of something else that put a momentary smile on her light brown face.

Tate's getting his pussy a little bit early tonight, she grinned. Stooping, she tried to pick up the metal bat but it rolled toward the kitchen table. It came to rest with a ring against her very own chair. The one she always sat in when she faced the door. The door she had purposely left ajar for the now errant Ms. Kitty. The sound of the bat as it rang against the metal leg of the kitchen chair almost brought her to sanity and she nearly lost heart and nerve. But it was too late. She could not undo the damage she had already caused and by now Tate was back upstairs watching the football game. It would not have taken him more than a few minutes to retrace his steps and walk undetected beneath Daisey's bathroom window, down the cement steps and back into the building. He wasn't more than 5 ft. 10 but he looked taller and he was a fast walker. With the building practically empty he would not be noticed and anyone who had seen him leave would assume he had not yet returned. Oh yes, she had thought it all out very carefully in the last few hours and this was best. Best for all concerned. Now all she had to do was to stop being such a punk and do her part and she knew very well what that meant. She would have to suck it up as they say and go into Daisey's bedroom. And there she …. "Lona, Lona is that you?" It was Daisey. The damned metal bat had woke her up. What in the name of hell was she going to do now? How would she explain this one away? She didn't have an answer. Walking toward the kitchen Daisey tried again to call her friend. "Lona, Lo are you there?" Daisey noticed for the first time that the door was ajar. She almost screamed. Ms. Kitty! Kitty girl, oh my gracious what did I do? I forgot to lock the back door!" But I thought SHE did it. I thought Lona locked it. She was hysterical now. Suddenly, the light came on and she squinted as her eyes reacted to the jolt of Edison's invention. When she saw Lona standing there she screamed and then started crying.

"Oh Lona, Lona you scared me, you frightened me, what on earth are you doing here and where is Ms.Kitty? Lo, what have you done with my poor darling baby?"

But Lona wasn't listening. Oh, she heard the questions and she heard the sobbing of her friend but she had but one thought in mind. She knew what she was doing there. And she had no idea where that silly Ms. Kitty had gone. Lona knew one other important thing. She, Lona Martha McKensie was in trouble. Not just a little bit of trouble; she was in deep do- do and she was left now with but one thing to do. She had to save her ass!

And now, all of the things that she disliked most about Daisey Hutchins, Daisey Florence Hutchins came to mind. It was enough that she was being dubbed as the other half of the busy bodies, which she certainly was not. She could care less what others did with their lives. That was THEIR business. She only pretended to be interested to please her friend. And she NEEDED Daisey. Well, to a point. She needed her occasional loans and gifts of money and merchandise. Daisey liked her and trusted her and since Daisey's own sister was miles away, she depended on Lona's support. What did Lona care about what one did or who they were sleeping with and any of that gossip Daisey liked to spew? As far as support was concerned, she had Tatum or she could get somebody else. And then of course she had Tommie. That's Tommie with 'ie' and not a "y" at the end. She was Lona's own blood sister. Well, maybe he wasn't really a girl but he thought so and everyone treated him like a girl so that was close enough. And it was nearly impossible to tell the difference. If you didn't know or didn't look really, really close you could miss it. As they say, don't ask, don't tell. No, she didn't care for or need Daisey's emotional support. She needed her money.

Besides, she was tired of everyone always fawning over her friend. It was Daisey this and Daisey that.

And Daisey didn't help matters either. She was just too damned proper. She never cursed. That is, until she became angry or hurt and that was very rarely. She wanted to take tea, and she wanted to attend church every Sunday. Oh, Lona was a devout Christian, she'd told Daisey and she didn't mind going to church perhaps on Mother's Day but that was just to show off the new clothes Daisey insisted on buying for her and choosing everything including the underwear she wore. Yes, she had just about had it with Daisey and Ms. Kitty. There was one more thing that Daisey didn't know. Lona was an ex-prostitute and so all the jokes and evil words Daisey used to describe whores were really an insult to Lona's former profession. She hadn't been in the business for very long. Just 5 years or so. But in that time she had seen and known plenty. People just didn't know. They didn't have a clue about how ugly and tough that life can be. They think that all you have to do is get on your knees, or lie on your back and wait until it's over. But men want more than that. MUCH MORE! And sometimes they don't want to pay to get it. Don't get me started, she thought to herself. I could tell a tale or two.

All of these things flashed through Lona's mind as she was confronted by Daisey there in the kitchen with the silly frilly curtains at the window and the stupid green and pink table cloth still on the table. She'd wanted to explain herself. She wanted to tell Daisey that if only she had been a TRUE friend. A real friend would have understood. Of course, she never would admit that SHE, Lona had not given her friend a chance to understand. Whatever her life had been Daisey knew about none of it. She only knew what Lona had told her. That she too had once taught school and that she had ended her career as a social worker just a few months before their first meeting. It was all a lie. But nobody knew that she had actually been a maid.

In those fleeting seconds Lona worked herself up into a frenzy. She was angry, real angry at Daisey for her audacity. The audacity to have lived a successful and comfortable life while others like herself had had to struggle most of theirs. Lona's eyes were wild and full of hate and now because of Daisey she would have to commit the ultimate crime. Daisey had been foolish to tell her what she'd seen the super Rodriguez do. She must have known in her heart that people used these opportunities to their own benefits and profits. The super would pay for being dumb but Daisey was dumber. The Super might even have got away with killing his wife but now because of Ms. Busy Body Daisey, she Lona, would be forced to drop the dime on him. Daisey could see that she had to do something quickly. Something to calm her friend's nerves. But what to do? Maybe she had waited too late. Maybe she should have given Lona the minks earlier today. Or the sable jacket on yesterday. Perhaps the strongbox should have passed to her long before. What on earth had she been thinking? Well, it was too late to start making promises. Lo would forever hold it against her. And she knew a lot about this girl. She knew Lona had been a prostitute and that she served time in prison for forgery of checks. She hadn't really believed the child was once a teacher. One just had to listen to her speak to know that much! No EDUCATED human being spoke the way Lona McKensie spoke. No educated person split verbs and left prepositions dangling. Why she'd be surprised if Lo had a ninth grade education. Who was it who said, "You can fool some of the people some of the time but you can't fool all of the people all of the time!" It was Benjamin Franklin or Franklin Roosevelt. Those Franklins were always saying something. Or maybe it was just Abraham Lincoln. He was a wise one, Lincoln was.

Daisey was nervous now and afraid as Lona moved toward her with the bat raised. The same metal bat The idiot Rodrigez had left lying about in her garden. She'd seen it and she'd left it lying right there. It had his fingerprints all over it and it would have tied him to the murder of his wife.

In an instant she recalled that they might still be up. Or at least his wife. If she could just get to the door and scream. Daisey inched closer and closer to the door and somehow managed to pull it open. Not far enough to escape but wide enough to scream and be heard. She was just about to yell for help when Lona struck her with the first blow. The sound resounded throughout the kitchen rattling the pots and pans. Daisey fell clutching at the frilly table cloth. Her legs went over her head revealing the beige cotton stockings she was wearing. They were only knee length and when her short night gown rose up over her thighs revealing her cotton panties she felt a moment of embarrassment. I should have dressed for the occasion she thought.

What will they think when I'm admitted to the hospital dressed like this? Or even worse, what will the undertaker think? And then she began to cry. Crawling toward her murderess self-adopted daughter. Sobbing, with a pleading look in her eyes. Lona had never heard Daisey cry. It stopped her for an instant and she quickly recalled how it had torn at her heart strings when at her father's funeral she had heard her own grandmother's wail. But, she raised the bat again and again cracking Daisey Hutchin's skull like an overripe coconut. She had to hit her harder because of that damned night cap Daisey was wearing and the little dumb curlers that Daisey always insisted on wearing to keep her hair in place as she slept. It always reminded Lona of those pictures of rich little white ladies from the 1950's as they sunned themselves on the fine white sand beaches of Miami. She hit the woman a fourth time and when she was through she stepped over Daisey and closed the door. She tried to let Ms. Kitty back in the house but the cat wouldn't move from the back steps.

"Shit Ms. Kitty, you always in the way, why can't you keep yo' ass still," she demanded of the meowing cat? Then she closed the door, bolting it shut and making her second mistake. Walking over to the sink she wet the bottom of her shirt with hot water and wiped her fingerprints from the bat. She dropped the bat on the floor and noted that when it hit the tile floor it sounded like a grandfather's clock striking the half hour. Her evilness now complete, Lona walked to the other side where Daisey lay dead. She thought of stabbing her with the big kitchen knife Daisey was always demanding that she use when Lona carved the stuffed Cornish hens. She absolutely hated those little birds. Why there was nothing to them, with those tiny little wings and legs! If Lona was gonna eat chicken, Lona wanted chicken, not over -sized Robins! Shutting off the light, she was almost out of the kitchen when she thought it would be a smart idea to close the kitchen curtains. No one would be able to look in for a day or two and when they did they would all assume that that idiot super had killed Daisey. She'd make sure of that. Especially with his fingerprints all over the bat. That is if she hadn't wiped them off when she wiped hers. Whatever. They'd believe her story and not his. Oh sure, she had a record a foot long but it wasn't for murder and hard stuff. When she told them what Daisey had seen Mr. Dumb butt would be tried and convicted of murder most foul. Oh yes, she had it all planned out in her head. After all he could not produce a dead wife and they could always find HER remains at a landfill somewhere. The police knew what they were doing. She too watched "New Detectives" sometimes. She walked over to the window and closed the frilly curtains, noticing that there was a light on in the apartment across the two gardens. But as she was closing the curtains the light suddenly went out.

It was not unusual. She was not alarmed. Someone had probably gone into the kitchen for a glass of water or something cool to drink. No one could possibly know what had happened to Daisey and besides, the super was alone now, that he'd killed his wife. She was certain it was not yet 10 p.m. and all was very quiet now. Quickly, she collected herself and walked back into Daisey's bedroom. From her purse she took the American Express credit card and her I.D. There was a Rolex watch in the top drawer and Lona took that as well. She took a pair of socks from the floor, wrapped them around her right hand and began opening the drawers and closets and pulling out as much stuff as she could. With her right foot she kicked the contents of the drawers all over the bedroom floor. I've got to make this look good, she thought. Finally, she was done. The table light was on and she left it that way. It gave the room a peaceful glow. Just like in the movies. She thought she'd have been great in movies but she was definitely no Kathy Bates. Oh no, the character she played was a real evil bitch and she was crazy too. With that thought in her mind she almost laughed. Giving the blinds an extra tug Lona clicked off the remote. Almost triumphantly she lifted her head in the air and sucked in more air as she walked toward the front door. Just before Lona left the apartment the telephone rang. She stood there at the peep hole making sure no one was in the hall and counted the rings of the telephone. Eight times before it stopped. When it stopped Lona stepped out the door and used her key to lock Daisey's door. Slowly, she climbed the stairs to her own apartment, her mind racing. What was she going to say to Tate? He would know the truth when he found out Daisey was dead. And look at her! She sure she looked a wreck. Anyone could tell SOMETHING had happened to her. And it had. She was now a murderess. But no one would ever know! It would remain forever her secret. One she would take with her to her grave.

The first thing Lona noticed when she entered her apartment was that there was no sound. Nothing.

Tatum must have fallen asleep watching the game she thought. She passed the living room and looked in. She looked in the 2 bedrooms and bathroom. She checked the kitchen, calling Tatum's name as she entered and exited each room. Oh well, he must have been delayed. Or maybe he got tired waiting and stepped out to the bar for a few minutes. Tatum might have gone for more beer she reasoned but a quick check of the cooler near the couch dispelled that notion. It was just as well that he wasn't there. She wouldn't have to explain anything. It would give her a few minutes to refresh herself. She went into the bathroom and began running water to take a bath. She sat there in the tub for a long time. Trying to wash away the knowledge of the crime she had just committed and the smell of her friend's blood.

Across the garden in Superintendent Rodriguez's apartment Maria Acevedo was restless. It had been a long day for her and her internal clock had not yet wound down. Maria had had to pull and tussle with her daughter's children through three airports on her way back from San Juan. They were a handful those two. But she was glad to help out. Her daughter Felicia had needed a rest and Maria agreed to take the kids with her when she went home to her country. Anyway, the kids needed to be reminded of their true heritage now and again. Like most of today's youngsters, they could hardly speak Spanish and when they learned they did so badly. It was a kind of mixture of Spanish and English and it was heavily influenced by the people they lived around. And that mostly meant black Americans. She wasn't prejudiced or anything like that. No, for goodness sake. No! Cross her heart she wasn't biased. Why her very own Ricardo was black. She had a very fair completion but her Ricky was a Negro. She liked to call him Papi Chocolate but he didn't seem to like the name too much. They made a nice couple she thought. She was weak and now a bit frail but he was a tall and very muscular. And he was very, very black. In fact, most who met him for the first time assumed he WAS a black American and a football player too. She was so proud of him. It wasn't his fault that he had been driving when the accident happened. It was the second day after they bought the new Explorer van. They had gone out together to do a little shopping.

She had almost insisted on stopping to pick up her daughter and the newborns but Ricky said it was too late and it would be against the law to have the babies in the car without the benefit of car seats for both kids. "Well, you'd better get some seats dear because I need those kids with me as much as possible. Maria, she don't know nothing' about raisin' kids you know, she still a baby herself. Almost!" They were almost at home when the old man, alone in a little car smacked right into them. He ran a light or something and just barreled into the passenger side of their brand new van. Afterwards, Maria had been glad it had happened on her side of the car, thank God and all the Saints. She didn't know what she'd have done if something had happened to her Ricardo. And the old man in his car had not died. He was badly shaken and had to spend a week in the hospital but he was o.k. As for herself, she was blessed. Blessed that her grandchildren had not been riding with them, thanks to her husband. Her own pain didn't matter. Maria Acevedo was a trooper. She could handle the pain and the 2 months in the hospital. And when she came home... Why Ricky had treated her like a queen, with fresh flowers every two or three days and her meals in bed. He washed her and changed her dressings. Oh, he was special that man. She had finally put a stop to the pampering. One day she told him. "Listen Papi, I got to do this myself. I love you and I take care of you house and you. It's not the other way 'round." Oh Ricky, he protests too much but I don't stop. Every day I beg and beg he stop until one day I say, "Ricky I need something to drink, Papi and you know what Ricky say? He say get it yourself, you can move, there's nothing wrong with you. All you have to do is roll your chair in the kitchen and get it." And I did. From that day he let me do everything. He so smart, my Ricky.

Sitting there in the kitchen she was thinking all of this as she looked out across the peaceful scene that was her own garden, her very own! She had forgotten why she came into the kitchen. Sometimes, she just liked to roll her wheel chair into another room and think. Especially when he was asleep. And tonight, with Felicia there to mind the kids she could finally relax a little. She would let Ricky sleep. He needed his rest with all that running between buildings. It wasn't fair. The management knew they had a good thing with Ricky and they took advantage of it. And just because they had helped him get that old boiler license or whatever it was you needed. Number 4 or number 6. Whatever number it was they knew he could not have passed the test either in Spanish or in English. But he was so handy. Why look how he made everything easy for me in my kitchen. Ricardo cut the legs off everything he could to make things easy for me. He'd made a special table to prepare the food and salads. Then, he made low cabinets and shelves for the dishes and pots and pans. He was resourceful and he had even cut the legs off the chopping block I used to cut up meats, and chickens and fish. She always liked doing these things herself. Maria bought her food in bulk. Her rice in sacks. Her meat at the wholesale butchery. Her fish, un-cleaned at the fish market and she cleaned it herself, thank you. She went to the live poultry market when she bought her chickens. Shaking her head as if she was hearing a slow salsa beat she recalled the last time she had been in the kitchen. It was the evening before she took the kids to Ponce. She hadn't been tired but Papi wouldn't listen to her. He wanted her to rest that night and he insisted on doing the cooking himself.

But first he had to go over to that building number 1459. The lights had gone out in the lobby and people were complaining. People were always complaining. Most times for no good reason. When he returned he found her in the kitchen starting the supper. He was furious! "I ask you not to do this, baby. I ask you to rest," he'd shouted. He was so loud, she had been afraid he'd disturb the neighbors. The tenants in these buildings don't think the super has any rights at all. They just think we're there to serve them. They will call any time of the day or night if you let them. And just because they think you live free. Well, I got something to tell them. It's not

FREE baby! Anyway, Ricky comes in, sees me and pushes me away from my chopping block. He so strong my Ricky, he doesn't even know his own strength. Anyway, the wheel chair was not locked and it rolled back very hard and hit the stove on the other side of the room. I was so mad that I threw my pillow at him. It didn't hit him but it fell on the floor near the dishwasher. The one I never use. Then, Ricky grabbed the meat mallet from me. The one I use to make the meat soft. I think they call it a tenderizer in English and it does a good job. He got down on his knees next to the window and he started hitting those steaks like he was hammering pipes or something. I thought he would never stop but I didn't say anything else. I was already at the stove and I just started preparing the rice. I hate Ricky's rice. When he fixes it he put too much water in it and it come out too big and too wet.

Maria was suddenly very sleepy and she moved the chair across the room and shut off the light.

She was heading for the bedroom when she recalled why it was she'd come to the kitchen. She wanted a cold Corona. She knew her husband would wake up and want one in a little while and she would save him the trouble of going to the kitchen. She had the beer in her lap when she noticed that there was a flash of light across the gardens. She stopped for a moment and what she saw made her blood run cold! That woman Daisey's door was open just a little and she could see the shadows of two women. One was Daisey and the other was standing in front of her holding something. It looked just like that bat she had told Ricky to get rid of. "Ricky, she had said, that thing is dangerous and you know how the kids play rough when they are over here. It wouldn't take very much for the little man to hit his sister with it and then we'd get in big trouble." Ricky has listened to her and he had taken it out of the house.

Of course, he didn't know that she'd seen it earlier in the evening when he took that dirt to Ms. Daisey across the garden. She'd wondered why it was lying there on her side of the garden. But she hadn't questioned him about it right then but she intended to ask him. She didn't particularly care for Daisey. She was too, how do you say it? Full of herself. With her airs and pretense and all. She had thrown the tomatoes Daisey gave her last summer in the garbage. She later regretted parting with them because they were beautiful and Maria had had to buy some because there were none in the house. And with tomatoes being so expensive lately, why …. She grabbed her throat when she saw the figure strike the first blow. She watched Daisey fall. And then there was another blow and then two more strikes. Maria could hardly contain herself but she had to. Her Ricky was asleep and she didn't want to wake him. Oh no. She would never disturb her sweet husband. He worked soo hard. Looking back across the yard Maria watched as the other woman peeked her head outside as if she was searching for something and then closed the door. Later, Maria would remember that Daisey had a cat. Maria couldn't stand them. She preferred dogs. She had had a dog when they first took this job but the tenants had complained. It broke her heart to part with dear Tito and he had not survived long living in Felicia's house. It was no wonder. Her daughter was too dirty and Tito wasn't used to dirt. He had probably caught a germ or just died from being heart broken. It had been a real tragedy.

But tonight had all been like a cartoon. A very scary Halloween cartoon. With the shadows of the two actors being projected like silhouettes on the wall. Sadly this was no cartoon. It wasn't funny. It was all too real. She had just witnessed a murder. She continued looking across the garden. Her eyes glues now to the figure of the woman as she stood wiping something just in front of the kitchen window. Maria moved her wheelchair to the left, making sure she was completely hidden from view. And over in Daisey's apartment Lona finished wiping her prints from the bat and cut off the light. Then, thinking it smart to close the frilly curtains, she went back and took care of that, glancing up at the super's window as she did so. It was then that Maria recognized the killer. It was that OTHER lady, the one who lived in the same building. She had watched her in the doorway when Daisey had brought over the tomatoes last summer and handed the basket to her dear Ricky. She NEVER like her. Mona, or whatever her name was. And she didn't trust her around Papi. After all he IS a man. Maria thought she'd been spotted and her head instinctively recoiled. But across the garden the light went out again as Lona headed for the bedroom, leaving Daisey lying dead on the floor. So she thought.

All was still. With no movement in the apartment across the yard Maria slowly wheeled herself out of the kitchen. She steadied herself when she heard the sound of the TV. It meant that her dear Ricky was awake. Papi Chocolate as she called him. It was then that she realized the beer in her lap had become warm. Oh no, that would never do Papi didn't like warm beer and he might get mad at her. Might even scream at her. She had stayed too long in the kitchen. Well, she'd take it back and get a cold one. Just to keep him happy.

It took her a few minutes to wheel herself backwards and into the kitchen and when she passed the window she saw the light go on again in Daisey's apartment across the garden. It scared Maria because though she was at home, she was afraid of what she might see. Afraid that that evil -spirited woman who had done those terrible things to Ms. Daisey might somehow take wings and fly up to Maria's own apartment to continue her murderous rage. Even while her Papi lay defenseless in his bed!

She sat there on the side of the window trying to stay out of view when she saw the head of Daisey Hutchins peer through the door and call her cat. Maria only caught a quick glimpse but it was enough to confirm to her that the woman was still alive. At least barely alive. She drew in a quick breath and crossed herself right there in the kitchen. Then, she saw Daisey's door close and in a minute the light was off. Maria said a short prayer and crossed herself a second time. Taking the ice cold beer from the refrigerator she wheeled her chair into the bedroom where her husband lay talking back to the television. "Where you been," he asked without turning his head to look at her directly. She was relieved. She didn't want him to notice anything peculiar about her and she softly placed the beer in his hand. He took it without complaint.

"Where you been," he asked her once more? "Oh," she said, "I just got myself some water in the kitchen." She responded without looking in him. "That was a long drink," he answered, smiling. Her Ricky had such a sweet smile. How could she spoil anything for him? This was not the best job in the world but where would he find another to support his family and pay the bills? And the rent was included and of course he could make money on the side and there were the TIPS. Particularly at Christmas time. No, she would keep this to herself and not tell him or anyone else. The tenants might think HE had something to do with it. If only she could work. If only she hadn't had that damn accident. Well, maybe Ms. Daisey could help her. After all, she was getting stronger every day and she could sit in her wheelchair and do the dishes and the wash and even help out in the garden. Ricky said Ms. Daisey had a lot of money. Everyone knew that. She would tell her Ricky to ask the old woman if she needed anybody. Yes, that's what she would do. She'd ask Papi. Papi take care of everything.

The moment Tatum got the strongbox in his hand he knew what he was going to do. He walked back down the short cement walk and climbed over the fence. He could have used the other side like Lona had told him to do but there was too much light over there. Also, the gate was closed and he couldn't tell if it was locked or not. Sometimes they locked the little sitting area just to keep people from coming in to use the side of the building and the dark alley as a kind of outdoor motel. He'd used it himself more than once and Lona would kill him if she had any idea with whom. Then, there was the time that he wanted to use it but it was locked. He was pissed about missing out on a good piece of ass but he had no money and the poor- behind bitch didn't have any either so they both went home "empty handed."

But that was then and this was now. If he'd had the strongbox in his hands then as he now did he wouldn't have had to worry about a place to get off. He could have gone right over to that hotel on 135th. Now, upstairs in Lona's place he grabbed his wallet from his jacket and changed into a heavier one. He didn't want to put on a coat just in case he ran into her when he was on his way out. If he did he'd just say he was going to the store or something and that he'd left the shopping bag on the table. By the time she discovered it contained only crumpled paper he would be long gone. And he was not coming back. He had no way to know for certain what Lona was planning to do to the old broad but he had an idea. There was a much easier way to get her money and he had discussed it with Lona many times but she wouldn't play ball. On his own he had made several sexual overtures toward Daisey. But she wouldn't bite. Even though she had not had a man in a hundred years she was playing hard to get. But he felt that given time he could get the sex and the money too. He was thinking about "flashing" on her in the near future and if only that moron Lona had not come up with this hair brain scheme of her own. Didn't she think that Daisey would eventually find out that she was stealing? Then, what would Lona do? Lie of course! That's all she ever did. Try to lie her way out of everything. Lona would lie for almost any reason. And she wasn't even good at it. If you're gonna tell a lie then tell a good one. That's what his mother had always said to him.

Don't be a DUMB mother fucker! Tatum managed to creep down the stairs. He was glad he had taken the time to put on the new Jordan's he'd just bought. They had cost a pretty penny and he was hoping to get the money back when he made that hard bargain with Lona. Well, she could keep the $200 bucks. He'd had enough.

GOTCHA! Got you Lone! He knew Lona would come looking for him but he was not going near his old haunts. Not is a million years. He wasn't even staying in Harlem period. Not even close!

Tatum made the two blocks to the subway in a near sprint. He used his weekly pass and walked down the stairs, not stopping until he got to the other end of the platform. He was nervous and he paced back and forth along the yellow line they painted on the cement floor. As if that would somehow keep people from ignoring the warning signs and stop rushing the train doors. Especially during the business hour rush.

By the time the train rolled into the station he was almost a wreck but he knew he had to get a hold of himself. Cops sometimes stop you when you appear nervous or agitated. They do it just to fuck with you!

Ever since the September 11th bombings. He'd be dead in the water. He grinned when he thought of the $4,500 hundred dollars he had in there. And the jewels. He'd scored big! And that old bitch Lona could get mad all she wants. "I'm out!"

It was a busy night and the midtown area was packed. Tatum had changed trains at 125th Street and he'd taken the express all the way to 42nd Street. From there he started walking. He wanted to stop for a sandwich but changed his mind when he realized he didn't have any money other that the stash in his back pack and he wasn't going to touch that. Not until he made up his mind exactly what he wanted to do. He passed by several obvious prostitutes on the stroll and made his way down Eighth Avenue until he reached a bar. It was about 38th Street and it seemed like a nice place to have a drink. Just a rum and soda to steady his nerves and a bathroom to go in so that he could take out a few dollars in secrecy.

He walked in the place to the sound of Beyoncé singing, "All You Single Ladies." Walking to the bar he ordered his drink and asked to be buzzed into the bathroom. Except he used the word restroom. He was, after all, not uptown. When he came out he found his place at the long bar and got his drink and paid with one of the five twenty dollar bills he'd taken from the wad of bills in his back pack. Quickly he downed the drink. He ordered another and sat on the stool between a group of three and a couple of guys talking loud about nothing. Tatum's mind began to drift back uptown. Lona would be back upstairs in her apartment looking for him by now. In fact, she would be expecting him to walk back in the door with that teasing look on his face. He was just fooling her. He had not really gone anywhere with the money. Just to the local bar with the strippers or whatever you call those girls. She would never guess the truth. But Tatum was tired of loose women. Especially of street hos. They took your money for short time sex and went on their merry way. Leaving you to wonder if you were dead from AIDs contamination or Hepatitis C or some shit like that. He could use a condom he supposed but he was too large for most condoms. Even for the super-size one, they were too tight on him and anyway, condoms didn't give you the same feeling. Especially wearing one when you wanted some "skull." Well, forget it. They could keep that shit. As he sat looking around the bar he suddenly realized there were no women in the place. The patrons were mostly white or Hispanic with about 3 Black people there, including himself. Hey, he didn't give a fuck. People could do whatever they liked. He just liked to have a good time and hear good music and as long as no one fucked with him they were Kool and the Gang. He knew what he wanted and they knew what they wanted. They didn't have to explain. After all, he was nobody's homosexual. No one was going up in him. But he might sneak a little skull now and then from another man and he had been known to "bust buns." Especially when he was incarcerated. After all, a man's gotta do what a man's gotta do.

A Black couple came in. A man and woman. They looked like tourists and Tatum remembered that he was on the strip and in the middle of the bus station and the train terminals. The couple didn't come to the bar. They took seats at one of the booths on the side and the man walked up to the far side of the bar and ordered drinks. Tatum looked closely at the female. At first he thought it was Lona but she was about ten years younger than his woman.

She made him think again of Lona. He liked the bitch. Faults and all. So what he wasn't 'in love' with her but she had her good points. And good sex too. Most of all she could "take him" and he knew that was a tall order. He could ride Lona for a few hours or all night long and she never complained.

At least not until she got mad at him. But even then she kept coming back for more. As a matter of fact, for an old broad she looked good. Not all fat and flabby and shit. Yeah, Lona had it goin' on, bro. Hell yeah!

He liked older women. He had told Lona as much. That was why he wanted to knock the boots off that bitch Ms. Daisey. Sometimes Lona teased him saying Daisey was too old and old enough to be his grandmother. But Lona didn't know. Grandmother or not he'd have screwed her. And for money!! Shit! Why for money he'd nail Lona's great grandma! No shit! There's no shame in my game, he smiled. He turned to his left to pick up his drink and one of the white men was looking at him smiling.

He thought Tatum was smiling at him and Tatum quickly turned away, not wanting to seem friendly or like he was on the make. But the man wouldn't let up and Tatum was in no mood for conversation.

He didn't even want to pretend by being polite. It was only by chance that he had wandered into this establishment and he had nothing in the world against people who did their own thing but there is a kind of unwritten law that goes something like, you do your thing and I'll do mine. But this clown had crossed the line. Tatum asked the bartender for his check. He paid the bill and walked out onto the Avenue again. He crossed the street and went into Kentucky Fried Chicken where he ordered a happy meal. Sitting at the smallish table for a long time he looked out the window at the people passing by in the street. By the time it came to him in full measure he was already walking toward the door. Where the fuck would you go? He said to himself. What you gonna do when this little bit of change runs out? Then too, he was still on parole and leaving the state to go down south to his estranged wife in Jacksonville, Florida was out of the question. He would not only be arrested for parole violation but he would end up killing that whore. No, he was going back uptown to Lona. That is if the bitch hadn't really done something stupid. They could always give the money and jewelry back to that broad Daisey and be done with her. He and Lona had never had a real fight and then there was that big ass of hers. And if there was anything Tatum Montgomery loved it was a big round ass!

Daisey's head hurt something fierce. She stood there in the bath room holding on to the sink for dear life but Daisey couldn't look at herself. It wasn't that she was bleeding so much. But she just might be bleeding internally. People often bled to death internally after a head injury or some trauma and her face and eyes were swollen almost beyond recognition. As she lay there after Lona attacked her with that vicious weapon she had thought about giving up. Just quitting. She had had such bad luck with close friends and people in general. They were always mistaking her kindness for weakness. Well, she wasn't weak.

In fact, she had the strength of a bull she reasoned and now she would show them. She would survive this brutal and savage beating and she would show Lona what she was made of. Ms. Hutchins would show her true colors. And the girl was not going to like it very much. But first she had to have a convincing story to tell. She couldn't let the police into her apartment because if they saw the condition it was in they would never believe her. Besides, it was Lona and only Lona was going to clean up the mess she'd made. No, she would need strength. The strength to go out of the house. At least into the little vestibule or onto the stoop. It would take all she had but she knew she had to do it. And she had to do it soon.

Using the kitchen chairs for support she struggled to her feet. She was breathing hard but she rested her head and arms on the table for a minute. Then, she called to Ms. Kitty but the cat didn't answer. I can't leave my baby outside all night. Suppose I have to stay in the hospital for a few days, she thought. Holding on to the kitchen counters she navigated around and grasped the back door knob in her right hand. She used all her strength to pull the door open and pushed her head through the opening. Not a lot of space but enough to call. "Ms. Kitty, Ms. Kitty," she called feebly. She felt the cat slither around her feet and begin purring, from inside the kitchen. "Oh, damn it cat," she cried out! She was about to close the door when she thought she saw a light go on in the Super's apartment. But just as quickly the light went off again. In the faint moonlight Daisey could still see the shadow of a woman sitting there in a chair. Someone who was trying now to hide her face. Daisey was sure it was that woman Maria. But how long had she been there and just what had she seen? Well, I'll have to take my chances, I'm sure it'll be alright she said to herself as she now used whatever strength she had left to close the back door. She tried for a few minutes but she didn't have enough force to put the bolt on. Giving up she walked unsteadily toward her bathroom, almost collapsing when she reached the sink. When she turned on the light she nearly fainted. Her face was a swollen mass of nothingness.

She had always bruised easily and now the right side of her face was nearly twice the size. And her eyes.

Her eyes were almost swollen shut. "That Bitch," she said aloud! Look what she did to me. And I have tried to be so NICE to her. Well, no more. Now she will see the other side of Daisey Hutchins.

Oh, yes she will. She's going to wish she'd never laid eyes on me in her entire life! Noticing the l carton on top of the sink the old woman bent over and pulled open the doors of the storage space beneath the sink. She already knew what she would find and Lona had not disappointed her. She wasn't expecting to find the strongbox in the cabinet. Daisey smiled. It was just what she'd hoped to find. People are so predictable she thought. They're all the same. She turned off the light and walked the few feet into her bedroom. She knew she had to hurry but she could not just go out in the street. Not dressed as she was. No, that would never do. Why, who would ever believe you Daisey, she scolded herself? She waded her way through the mess on the floor until she found what she was looking for. Nothing fancy. But enough to convince whomever found her that she was just looking for her cat when it happened.

She managed to dress herself and slip on her flat shoes. Then, she struggled into her coat and started to put a hat on her head but the curlers in her hair were too big and the hat would not fit. Daisey let it alone and searched the room for her purse. When she finally found it she checked for her keys to lock the door. Now, struggling to stay conscious she started toward the front door. She was so tempted to just lie there on the bed. She was so very tired. More tired than she had ever been but she wouldn't give up. No, Daisey Hutchins wouldn't give in to the demons of the world. She shuffled to the front door and tried to open it but it was double locked. Oh, she thinks she's clever that one does. Well, I'll show her what brains really are, I will! She was having trouble getting past Ms. Kitty.

"Oh move Ms. Kitty, mommy is alright, sweetie. We are going to be just fine."

With that the cat allowed her to pass into the hallway and although she tried to close the door. Miss Kitty wasn't having any of it. She would not let Daisey out of her sight and the woman had no strength to force the animal back into the apartment.

Slowly, painstakingly Daisey shuffled her way to the front entrance of the building. With every muscle and sinew of her body she walked, limped and half - dragged herself until she was inside the vestibule. She tried desperately to make it to the sidewalk but she just didn't have anything left to get there. She sat down and rested her head on her pocket book.

It had been a great day in Atlantic City for the little group descending the bus at the corner of Hedgeton and headed down the block to number 1475 and beyond. That was the thing about bus trips everyone complained of: no matter what the time of day or night the driver never let you off in front of your respective building. And he expected a tip from everyone. Regardless of whether they had been lucky or not. None of the drivers ever considered that. And if someone hit a jackpot they always seemed to know about it before the bus got on the highway for the return trip to Manhattan. "I know I've got some money in my pocket this morning," the driver would call into the microphone. Well, there would be nothing extra tonight. No one in the group had been so lucky. They all gave him five dollars and got off the bus at their stops. Saying good night as they disembarked the group, now on foot, they would first drop off the Torres' and the Jamison's at 1501 and then continue on to drop off the old Easley's and Thomas' and the new people from 1475. Cynthia and two others would continue on to number 1423 and she would call everyone when they were safely at home. Those from 1475 would have been larger if Lona and the other busy-body Daisey had not changed their minds about taking the ride. They were sometimes a pain but they kept everybody laughing. There was a sudden scream from old Mrs. Easley. "Lawdy, Lawdy. It's Daisey Hutchins!

Somebody done kilt her. Lawd, somebody done struck the po' chile daid," the woman mumbled almost incoherently. She said to her husband.,"see Ralph, that's why I didn't wanna stay up here in New Yawk no mo. If I gotta go let me go down Sous!" But Ralph was made of cooler stuff and he had already bent over Daisey and determined that although she appeared unconscious she was not dead. Half bent, he straightened his back enough to bark out, "call 911, and tell them to send an ambulance right away!"

Amid their cries and their groans and their condemnations of New York City and perhaps of their entrapment in the biggest city in the world someone had the presence of mind to do as Ralph instructed. Someone called the police and reported the crime. No one was counting the minutes but that was all it took for two police cars to arrive at the scene. The ambulance came just minutes later.

Walking around the corner just in time to see the ambulance arrive and the flashing lights of the two police cars strolled Tatum Montgomery. The police cars were parked as if they were trying to avoid each other in a head- on collision. He was apprehensive. He had no idea what had occurred but he convinced himself that since he had done no wrong, he had nothing to fear. Maybe someone had got sick. Why else would an ambulance be called? He was certain about himself but what, if anything had Lona done? Lona had taken the metal bat from his hands at the back door. He had no idea what she intended to do with it. She was Ms. Daisey's best friend and for all he knew the two women could have been trying to kill a rat in the house or a rabbit. After all, the back door was always left open to let that stupid cat in and out. As for the cash and jewels? Hadn't Lona told him that Daisey GAVE her those pearls? And that was days ago.

He didn't remember when but the pawn ticket for the diamond ring had the date on it and the pawn broker could verify that he was not alone when he entered the store. Maybe, they even had a video tape to show his and Lona's face. This was, the computer age and as they say, the camera never lies. But just to be sure, he cautiously mixed himself in with the crowd. It was growing larger with each passing second. People were gathering on the sidewalk and street outside 1475 Hedgeton. Tatum didn't want to be seen or overheard asking too many dumb questions but he knew he needed to talk with someone. To hear what the news was and maybe to find out if he was implicated in some crime. Nonchalantly, he asked a stranger what had happened and he was told that they had found the old woman almost dead. She was lying there in the vestibule of the building when a group returned from Atlantic City. "Cynthia from 1423, you know Cynthia, the skinny bitch who used to go with the barber over on St. Nick. Anyway, she used her cell phone to call for help but by the time they got there the woman had regained consciousness. She managed to tell the cops that she had gone out to look for her cat. See the cat with that woman over there? The one with the white sweat shirt and pants on?" "Well," the stranger continued, on her way in the door somebody sneaked up behind her and started hitting her on the head with a two by four or something. She didn't see exactly what it was he was using and she never saw his face. When she screamed, he ran. He didn't even take her pocket book. Ain't that some stupid shit! Ain't that the dumbest bastard you ever heard? If you gonna do something, if you got balls enough to hit someone in the head with a big- ass two by four then you should at least take the money before you run. I never heard of anything so ass backward in my life. Going out the back door, that's what I call it." He continued almost without taking a breath. "It had to be a po behind. Only a po dumb ass would do something like that. What you gonna git from an old broad with a cat? At least be smart enough to rob a bank. I would. Yeah man, go down town and rob a bank, that where the money is. What you say brother? Ain't that where the money is?" But Tatum had heard enough. He didn't know what to believe. All he knew was that he had to get to Lona. And fast! She was standing there in HIS white sweat suit holding Daisey's cat and acting like she didn't have a care in the world. He negotiated his way through the crowd and by the time he got to Lona he had used the words -excuse me - a dozen times. He had to know the truth. He HAD to know!

When Lona looked up and saw Tatum her heart started beating faster. They needed to talk and they needed to talk now. He didn't know any of the details but if they asked him he HAD to say he'd been at a bar all night and that he knew nothing. He was just coming home. How could he know what happened? He had never been anywhere near Daisey Hutchins and that was that? She would. take care of the rest. If Tatum loved her he'd do this for her. Her LIFE depended on his help. "Please Tate, please just do as I say," Lona whispered. As she said it she could almost feel the questions he had. She could see them in his eyes. They hung like weights on her shoulder but she would only say to trust her. Please, just trust her! The moment Lona said that, Tatum's head began to spin. He didn't know what had actually happened but somebody was lying and he was certain that it was Lona who was responsible for Daisey's current condition. If he played his cards right he would still come out the winner. Sure, he would keep quiet as long as Lona kept her mouth shut. And he knew she would, knew she MUST. Meanwhile, Tatum would keep the money and the jewelry. He would give her very little. The same way she had given him just $75 dollars to buy a pair of Jordan's. Did she think he was an old man? No, he was still young and vibrant and he could still pull any bitch he wanted to. He could even pull some 'stool' now and then. He just wasn't in the mood for buns tonight when that dude had tried to pick him up in the bar. But there'd be other days. Look out! He, Tatum Montgomery was back in control, whore! He was wearing the pants again and he didn't mean knee pants. The only other person he had to worry about was that old broad Daisey. He needed to find out what her motive was in not telling the cops the truth. What did Daisey want from Lona in return for her silence?

He could never have guessed Daisey's true intentions. In fact, Daisey didn't even know what they were. Well, she had some ideas of course but they were still in the formative stages. She needed a little more time to see how she could get the most out of the situation. There were still a few stones left to be turned over in her mind. And one very important unanswered question. Why, why had Lona attacked her? If it was for money, why hadn't the girl just asked for it? She must have known I would have given her anything she needed. Daisey pondered the question as she lay on the gurney. To begin with, Daisey had not been unconscious when Ralph Easley "found" her lying there bleeding. She was only pretending to be. Just until the cops came so she could tell her story. It was the same story Lona had whispered to Tatum but there were a few details she had added. She had mentioned that she had not been at home in her own apartment in a few hours. She had had tea upstairs in Lona's apartment. A kind of make up for making the poor dear 'miss' the bus ride. She had reneged on her promise to take her adopted daughter on the trip but she would make it up to her soon. Daisey didn't say how she intended to make it up to Lona. She told the police that Lona had a set of keys to her apartment and would feed Ms Kitty as she always did when Daisy was away. She would collect the mail and bring it to her in the hospital if she had to stay there more than a few days. And, she was sure the girl would ride with her to the hospital to help her get settled, just in case she needed surgery or did not survive this terrible turn of events. But Daisey knew that she would survive. In fact she was certain of it. And the ambulance attendant had said as much when he first looked at her. It was those damned hair rollers that saved her life. They, and not the two by four had caused all the bleeding. After all, they were held in place by bobby pins and they had punctured her skull with each blow. But the curlers were made of a soft rubber or plastic they had softened the blows. The injuries looked much worse than they actually were and after a night or two or rest in the hospital she'd be home. Not exactly fine but none the worst for it all. Daisey had thought of everything. It was all a lie but it saved Lona from jail and Tatum from jail too.

Most of this was all terrible news to Lona. She had thought the woman dead. Wanted the woman dead. Needed the woman dead and here she was talking and very much alive. And Daisey was now asking her, Lona, to ride in the ambulance. In fact she was insisting on it. How could she refuse to go? Lona knew she couldn't refuse and the knowledge made her feel worse than Daisey must have felt at that very moment. Lona excused herself and handed Ms. Kitty to Tatum to take care of until she returned from Harlem Hospital. She didn't like hospitals and she knew Tatum didn't like cats but she had to go along. Besides, she had to know. Why had Daisey protected her and why had she told the police this bald -faced lie?

The lady EMS attendant held Daisey's hand and got into the truck first to prepare the IV they were going to administer to her in route to the hospital. Then, she prepared to take the old lady's blood pressure and temperature. She asked Daisey a few questions and wrote the answers down using the clip board as a table. She was relieved that the crowd was thinning as she was sick of the oohs and aahs and the shaking of heads and fists. These were her people and she knew that underneath all that fuss they would not bust a grape if the attacker had revealed himself right there. If the story the old lady told was the truth! Personally, she doubted the validity of the story because it certainly did not look to her eyes like wounds from a two - by -four. This looked like something else. She wasn't sure what it was but a two - by - four would have killed the woman. Whatever it was, the woman was lucky to survive it. Sure, it was a terrible thing that it happened but she had seen worse. A whole lot worse and the woman would be fine after a night or two in the hospital. She had told the police what she felt in her heart but they didn't appear to be interested in pursuing it further so she just let the matter drop.

At long last they had Daisey aboard the ambulance and were almost ready to close the door when she whispered, "Wait." She tried sitting but it was impossible with the restraining straps tied tightly around her. She beckoned for someone standing just outside the door to approach the vehicle and extended her long thin fingers. They were cold to the touch and the super Rodriguez almost withdrew his hand. She wasn't such a bad old coot, he thought as he wished her well.

He promised to keep an eye on things while she was in the hospital. And that went for his Maria as well. Oh, she was in her wheelchair but she was getting around better and better. As a matter of fact she was right there.

He moved a bit to let his wife approach the ambulance. Maria stuck out her small hand and grasped Daisey's fingers. It was the first time they had ever met up close and they eyed one another suspiciously. Daisey because she was curious and Maria because she knew that she had to protect the lie that the old woman had told the police. After all, she loved Ricardo. He was such a good man. Poor Papi Chocolate. Then, the woman in the wheelchair said something that only Daisey could understand. "Don't you worry Ms. Daisey, I keep a eye on your flower garden while you in the hospital. I see EVERYTHING!

I watch everything tonight from my window while my Ricky, he sleeping." It didn't mean very much to anybody else who heard Maria. Nobody paid attention. Nobody except Daisey Hutchins. Maria might as well had said to her by public broadcast that she had seen the whole attack. And she knew who had attacked her. But Daisey was confident that Maria would never say a word. She knew of Maria's love for her man.

And she could help things along. Daisey could be very generous when she needed to be. Maria would be her back up. Her ace in the hole. If ever Lona tried to get out of hand she'd remind her that there had been a witness. It was all Daisey needed to hear to put her plans into action.

The moment the attendant wheeled Daisey into her room on 12 south and closed the door Lona knew she was in trouble. For one thing Daisey had lied to the police and secondly she was being too nice. Lona was about to find out why. "Lo dear," Daisey called feebly. "I don't want to keep you here unnecessarily sweetie.

Why don't you run along home now and take care of Ms. Kitty for me? Then, tomorrow morning you can begin cleaning up that mess you made in my bedroom. All those clothes will need to be washed and ironed and the ones in the closet taken to the dry cleaners. You may as well clean up the kitchen and the rest of the rooms too. Maybe you should do it all tonight just in case the cops want to have a look inside the apartment. And Lo, Lo, would you mind just this once going shopping for me? I'm sure you have enough money SAVED. Buy as much as you can because we're going to have plenty of afternoon teas and dinners when I come home. Make sure you buy enough for that nice young man of yours. What's his name? Tatum? It's such a nice name and he's such a STRONG young man. WE need a strong man in our lives don't we, Lo? The three of us will be spending a lot of time together when I come home. A lot of time! It'll almost be like a ménage a trios. Won't it baby girl?" She managed a weak grin when she said that. Then, she added: "I'm sure you won't mind too much if he kind of does things for me around the house. He needs a job. Young men like him need to be kept busy. Just so they don't get into trouble. Besides, it'll be good to have on his record in case he does get in trouble. Ah yes, he's still on parole. Isn't he dear?" Daisey closed her eyes indicating that Lona could leave.

But she was not asleep. Despite her injuries, Daisey couldn't fall asleep. She had so many plans for the future. Why should she spend the rest of her life alone in that apartment or up in cold old Boston with her sister Gloria?

She had always wanted a personal maid. Well, she now had one for life for only the cost of $4500 and some jewelry. She had so much more money in the bank and many times as many jewels in her safe deposit boxes. Maybe she'd take some out and give them to that nice super's wife in the wheelchair. It had been kind of her to come all the way around the block to see me. Daisey was thinking fast now. I've got all the money I need just from the pension and other checks I receive each month. I'll help some of the boys in the park who let me play basketball with them. And then there's the Church. I can leave them the insurance policies when I die. One to the church and the other to the Super's grandkids. They are cute. And then there's that Tatum. Oh yes, Lona's sweet Tatum. "I know what he wants. I may be old but I'm not THAT old. I know exactly what he wants and I'm going to give it to him. Right in front of Lona's face if I have to. After all, I wasn't always a Professor.

Oh no. I came up the hard way. I came up in the streets and I had to make my money the best way I could. It wasn't always easy either. Lona isn't the only one who knows something about the world's oldest profession. I can't help it if she didn't take advantage of her opportunities. I used my money to get my degrees and I became an upstanding member of the community. I don't regret it either. People are right to call me "busy body." In my life I've been very, very busy. Just then the nurse poked her head in the door to check on Daisey. "Ms. Hutchins, Ms. Hutchins," she called! Daisey Hutchins didn't hear the nurse calling. She was in dream land. Dreaming of a busy tomorrow.

THE END

The Humannequins

A story by
Maurice P. Fortune

It didn't matter if they were male or female. Most people stopped in their tracks whenever they saw her.

And that could mean once or twice a day for some folks. She was in a word gorgeous! Or drop dead gorgeous if you wanted to sound American. Which was another thing. Nobody knew exactly where she was from or her actual nationality. She had it all going on and she could have been anything. She had so many fine features. The high cheek bones of an indigenous North American; the long thin neck of an oriental. The lengthy hair could have come from her heritage on any of the world's seven continents as could her fine chiseled facial features. Perhaps they resembled most those of someone born in East Africa. Perhaps her only give-away was her skin color. Although it was as Black as Ebony wood, her eyes were like those of someone from the Solomon Islands. They were the color of violets.

Her body was as gracefully formed as any dancer. In fact, she was often mistaken for a dancer or a model. Well, she was a model in a way but she could do many other things. That was the trouble with society. Once they've put you in a certain category their brains seem to lock, she told anyone who would listen. You're signed, sealed and delivered and you can never escape. They slap a label on your forehead and glue it. That's why she had even stopped looking for any other kind of work at the Workforce Office. They encourage you to get a job. Any kind of job. "It's the only way to be fully independent," the counselors crowed. Of course they never seemed to have any kind of openings in 'your' field. But woe unto anyone who tried to change professions. You were admonished with the words, "you can't get a job in a field in which you have had no training or degree! You can't just come in here and say you want to be a waitress or a receptionist. Those are closed fields. You have to stay in your own category. You have to have a degree to be this or that. Now maybe we can find something for you like spitting peas into a Pepsi Cola bottle. Or picking up dog litter from the parks!"

It was frustrating but what could she do? Just to make herself more useful she had accepted the job as hostess in the hotel restaurant and bar. It was an upscale hotel just down the street and within walking distance of her home and her daytime job. It was only three minutes away but it gave her a little time to breathe fresh air. Working a part-time and a full time job was exhilarating. It gave her a feeling of importance and though her name was really Suzette Spruil she had taken the name of one of her ancestors. Mlle Manes. Sylvie Manes. Most people didn't have any idea that the meaning of manes is 'honored ghost' and she loved to see their faces when she explained it. They were horrified to discover that they were themselves but ghosts.

Whenever anyone found out she was moonlighting they were genuinely happy for her. "How do you do it? Where do you get the energy? Don't you ever rest." they would ask? Most said she'd been lucky since she worked and lived practically in the same place. Sadly, it had not lasted long. She'd been foolish to expect it to work. Someone had noticed that there was something different about the window and she'd had a tough time explaining that she'd only exchanged lunch times with a colleague. She had felt ill after the meal and had taken a nap for an hour or so. It was a close call. There had been many who were severely reprimanded for far less. She'd decided it was best to give up her part-time job. But they were all lucky to be working in the store. Most times they could get away from the windows and nothing would be said about it.

It was an easy job being a mannequin. Except on the days that they changed the clothes or rearranged the scenery in the windows. On those days she had to be on the floor a full hour before her dresser arrived. On the floor and in her place in the window. That was the rule and no exceptions were permitted. After all she was often told that she was one of the city's elite: a top shelf mannequin! Some top shelf she'd answer. She didn't make any more money than the others! But to be fair it was kind of nice to be so well-known and coveted by all of the big stores in town.

"I'm not a runway model or anything like that," she would tell folks. Sylvie was a real mannequin. If you preferred to be crass, you could simply call her a dummy. "I'm not going to get all bent out of shape about it," she would say. "I'm a big girl and I can take it." They always found it funny and dismissed her with a wave of the hand. "Well, think what you will," she'd say. "As long as I know who I am and how I came to be it is no skin off my chin." There was only one person on this earth who knew how to treat her Mlle. Manes always claimed. And for that she loved him dearly. To be honest, she was IN love with him, although he had no idea. This was not the only problem with their relationship. She had heard through the grapevine that he was being fired in just two days. And the reason he was being fired had everything to do with her.

She was not stunned by the news. She had expected it. Dressers were paid on commission. The more clothes their displays sold the more revenue both the dresser and the store made. And in a tight economy with sales lagging there was fierce competition between the workers to come up with the best idea for their windows. It was a kind of piece work job as far as she was concerned and a bit of a rat race. You sell 100 bathing suits in the summer and 200 coats in the winter. By then it's spring and you start all over again and between seasons are dresses and pants, handbags and shoes, hats and oh! It could all sometimes be so trying for them both. She could understand why he went to his apartment exhausted at night. But she, Mlle Manes could tell him how to sell her and how to make money from the seasonal collections. If only she could. If only he wasn't human but a dummy like her. A Humannequin!

She had always feared this would happen. How many times had she been warned by others to stay distant? To mind her business and find a nice boy there in the store. "There are three other handsome black guys working here. Each of them would be honored to have you as a girlfriend. You don't have to go around acting like a fool, mooning over someone you know can never belong to you. You're a mannequin. Be proud of yourself. We don't understand girls like you who try to date outside their own kind." "You're an attractive girl," they said. "The store paid a lot of money to have you here. As a matter of fact you are the most expensive mannequin in the place. You are also the only black female the store has on its main floor and. don't think that's an accident. If you think they're going to take you out of circulation and lose their investment you're crazy! Don't you realize that HE will be let go? And on top of all that, he can't dress you. Why you know very well that your lines are lagging in sales. You'll see. They'll find someone who can. Maybe that nice girl Teri Palmers who filled in for Tyvan two weeks ago when he had to pass a driver's test. Or, so HE said! You just wait and see," she'd been warned by so many. "His backside will be toast and you'll be shamed and blaming yourself all the way to the makeup salon upstairs."

Sylvie didn't want that to happen. She would find some way to get a message to him. To tell him how to turn this whole sordid business into a giant coup for both of them. Then, maybe those idiots would leave them alone. But she didn't have much time left. It was already Thursday and rumor had it that if her line of clothing did not pick up by week's end Belson would be given no more chances in the store. Sylvie knew exactly what that meant. When business closed on Sunday evening the shades to all of the windows would be drawn. Then, on Sunday night the scenery would be changed and the mannequins would be dressed in the newest summer fashions. The outfits would be revealed only when the store opened on Monday morning to the stares of the morning rush hour pedestrians. It was fully expected that within a four week period one or two per cent of them would return to purchase what they had seen in the window. She'd heard from the retired mannequins that that was the way it had always been in this dog-eat-dog business.

"Day dreaming again about that Belson character, Sylvie?" Suddenly her thoughts were pierced by the voice of Barlie. She was the girl in the window on her left and she was always meddling in someone's private affairs. "What if I was? It's of no account to you or anyone else," Sylvie shot back. "Well, go ahead and make a complete donkey of yourself if you wish dear child. I couldn't care less," Barlie added. "Anyway, I made almost $600 today. And that's just in credit card purchases. How much have you contributed to the store's coffers," she asked? "I don't know how much I've made, Sylvie replied hesitantly. It's hard to keep up with the figures and anyway, sometimes it can all be so misleading. People can see me in the window and like what I have on but when they come inside the store they change their minds. Maybe they don't want to be seen wearing the outfit they saw on a Black girl. I don't know what it is." "There you go playing the race card again," Barlie said. "When are your people going to arrive in the 21st Century, honey? Slavery's so over. People don't discriminate on the basis of color anymore. Don't you realize there are laws against these thing," the girl demanded. Keeping her head perfectly still but looking through the plate glass window at the reflected image of her nemesis, Sylvie looked into Barlie's eyes. "You are hopelessly in denial sweetheart and it's clear that you haven't a clue about race relations in this country or in this store; you need to shut up and just keep your head in the sand." As usual Barlie was determined to have the last word. "There's one thing I know for sure. There's a woman standing outside your window and she's looking you up and down. So you need to be smiling and trying to show yourself to your best advantage and not be worrying over some loser. She's a Black woman and she looks like she could use some fixing up." "Sure you're right, Ms. Rush Limbaugh," Sylvie answered with impatience. "And now, if you don't mind I'd like to continue picking cotton, Miss Massa please!" And with that, Sylvie turned her attention to the woman outside her window. Obviously just a tourist, the woman was taking Sylvie's picture. She didn't come into the store.

It was Friday and although there were a few buys on her outfit her sales were still considered poor.

The other girls were simply outselling her two to one. People came over to her window from inside the store. "She is so beautiful," they'd say. "She's a real doll. And look how they've got her posing. Why you'd think she was alive and just walking down a crowded street as though she didn't have a care in the world."

But they were wrong. So, wrong on that score, Sylvie would say. She did have a care in the world and his name was Tyvan Belson. She knew he lived somewhere in Brooklyn. It sometimes took him 50 minutes or more to take a bus and walk to the train. Then he'd wait another 35 minutes for the train to arrive at the station and he'd still have to walk four blocks to this store. Provided there were no delays like robberies or suicides, lazy train operators or snow and rain storms it could take almost 2 hours each way. But he needed the job. Not simply because he needed the money but because he actually liked the job. He loved dressing the mannequins and assisting with the planning and sometimes the arranging of the background scenery. Someday he hoped to do the same with humans on a television or movie set.

It was all so exciting to Sylvie. Her man a big time movie set designer. Maybe, someday he would even win an Oscar. Wouldn't that be superb? But he couldn't do it if he was going to be bounced around like a rubber ball from store to store. It was hard enough for black men to make it in Hollywood or anywhere else. Sure, many others had made it really big. There had been many gigantic success stories but there was still a long way to go. Everyone knew and said that.

Well, she was no Betty Cruz but Janet Gayle had stood by her man and she, Silvie Manes was going to do no less. Even if he didn't yet know he was her man. She didn't care a whit about what that Barlie Thompson or anyone else said. At least she had one friend in the store who was not always trying to tell her what to do and what not to do. It was a pity that she worked the window on the other side of the building. They had to wait until after the store closed before they could talk. Sometimes they'd go upstairs to the cafeteria for a light dinner.

They could only have 310 calories a day. Anything more was prohibited but it was more than enough for Sylvie. Her friend Zaza often said she still felt hungry. She was always delighted that Sylvie saved her a bit from her own plate and she would thank her profusely. "Syl I don't know how I'd make it in this place without you. They hate me here and they keep us on this starvation diet when they know full well we are hungry. These people are sooo jealous of you. You don't know girl. You have everything going on and they have to starve themselves and spend half the night in the tanning salon in the basement and at the hair salon on seven while you just stand there and look beautiful. How do you do it," Zaza would ask? "Do what? What am I doing? I just do what I do and they should too. Use it or lose it. That's what I say." Yes, she had an honest to goodness friend in Zaza and she couldn't have been happier about it. She determined to discuss her plan with her friend that evening.

Over dinner that evening Sylvie told her friend Zaza what she was thinking. Zaza let her finish and then looked at her and said, shaking her head slowly. "Have you taken complete leave of your senses Miss Manes? What are you trying to do, get me fired? Sure, you'll only be reprimanded. But if Management finds out I had anything to do with this harebrained scheme it'll be curtains for me. And I don't mean the kind that they're going to draw around us when they change scenery and clothes. Why I'll be out of that window so fast it'll make this red hair stand up like barbed wire. I mean I will sit upside down in the storage room FOREVER. Or, until someone dismantles me and uses me as spare parts the way they do junk cars. "Oh, they won't find out," Sylvie told her. "Don't you give me more credit than that? And besides, if they did I would never let them do THAT to you. I would tell them that I forced you to help me." "Oh Syl, my love." Zaza said, looking at her over three ounces of unsweetened iced tea. "You STILL don't get it, do you? You are the only thing your side of the store has going on. YOU ARE the star sweetie. The main attraction. I don't know why your line is not selling but believe me. It has nothing to do with you and they will NEVER put you in the storage room. It's ME who will be the sacrificial lamb. I want to see you happy and I don't care if that means loving Roger Rabbit but you'd better think honey. Think!" Zaza paused and asked if she could have the other two ounces of Sylvie's tea.

Finally, it was Saturday. The last full day the current line would be on display to the public. The weekend was coming and it would be the final time Sylvie would have to do anything to save Tyvan's job. If she ever hoped to have a real romance with him she couldn't let him leave Boonton's. Even the one-sided romance she was having was acceptable to her but it was now time to do something. The time for action had arrived. All words had been exhausted and all opposing ideas discarded. If Tyvan was fired then nothing else would mater to Sylvie. As soon as the store opened that morning she knew it would be another disappointing sales day for her. For one thing it was raining. This was always bad for business. All she had to do was look at the faces of those passing by beneath her. Humans seemed to be more alone and vulnerable under umbrellas. Almost as if they were larvae in cocoons just waiting to develop. But this never happened until the sun came out again. In the meantime most stores sold necessary items. Food was a big seller and so were boots, rain hats and the omnipresent water-repellent parasol. Rainy days seemed to go by dreadfully slower than most. Even slower than snowy days. And humans seemed happier when it snowed. Maybe it was because they were anticipating a day off from work and another opportunity to shop or browse the stores and sit drinking coffee in Dunkin' Donuts or Starbuck's. Looking out on the wet and windswept streets, Sylvie Manes was close to regretting all the attention she drew. Unlike the other mannequins it left her fewer and fewer opportunities to relax. To let her guard down and just be ordinary. And there was her nemesis: Ms. Barlie Thompson who stood at her left gloating as every attempt to sell her clothing failed.

"Oh, they absolutely love you," Barile would say. They love you so much honey, they would rather stand outside in the rain and look at you than come in and purchase what you're wearing. You're a mannequin dear. A mannequin in a department store that sells clothing among other things. You're not the Mona Lisa." Every time she heard Barlie say this it made her blood boil but as much as she hated to admit it she knew the girl was right. She hadn't had a single sale until three that afternoon. Even then, the woman had to be convinced that she could wear the outfit without looking ridiculous. She didn't want to look like two hundred pounds of potatoes stuffed in a bag meant for only one hundred pounds. "Are you 'sure' I can wear this, she had asked the sales girl? I'm not too old for it am I." It was like this all the time, Sylvie recalled. People are so self-conscious and insecure. They need to be reassured and indulged at every twist and turn.

She wondered how they managed to get out of the house in the morning and back home at night. She didn't want to blame the sales girls. They tried their best to push her line but none of them made very good representatives. They were too chatty and they never seemed to be able to answer a single question the customers asked unless they consulted with another sales person or called upstairs. "Excuse me but I have to ask the Manager and he's up on nine. He'll be down in a second or two if you can wait," they'd say! What did upstairs know about what was going on nine stories below them? All of this was frustrating to Sylvie whose back was turned to the conversations and could only catch sight of the scene behind her in the reflection of the window. Unfortunately, this was possible only at certain times of the day. After her first sale there had been only two others and mercifully, it was announced over the loudspeakers that the store would be closing in fifteen minutes. Sylvie knew that the day would count as one more nail in Tyvan's coffin. She had sold but three pieces at the marked down price of $88.59 each. It all amounted to a measly $265.77 for an entire Saturday's work. It was embarrassing and this did nothing to help Linda Fordham, the floor manager become employee of the month, Sylvie noted. Just thinking about it made her unhappy because Linda was one of the nicer and more dedicated girls. Well, on Monday these old rags will be marked down to $29.95. More than a third off the already reduced price. She looked down at the pants set she was wearing! It was brown and there was a huge belt around her waist as though she was being served like a trussed up bird at a Thanksgiving or Christmas party. It was no wonder she hadn't sold.

With the store closed and the contents of the registers counted and collected the stage was set for the highlight of Sylvie's day. At exactly 9:31 P.M. the man of her dreams would step off the elevator tpMaurice P. Fortune*

in the rear of the store and head in her direction. He would check the display to make sure no one had disturbed his set. He'd look up at her and say. "Nice try babe. Don't worry, well do better tomorrow." Then, he'd turn around and head for the employee exit to her left. There he'd punch the time clock and leave the store until the next day. He had no idea he'd leave her to deal with Barlie's snide remarks and mocking laughter. "Nice try Babe. Does he actually believe you understand what he's saying," she would taunt. "Does he not realize you're a dummy?" And then she'd laugh in that low pitched cackling voice that only she and witches possess. But Sylvie would scarcely hear her. She would be immersed in her thoughts. Thoughts of her romance with Tyvan and of marriage and of a house with a fireplace and kids and a little car.

The moment security set the alarm, shut off the main lights in the store and walked out the doors pandemonium erupted. It was like that in every store in every neighborhood and borough in the city. It was probably all over the country and maybe throughout the world. At least that was what she had been told. Sylvie stepped down from her window and stretched her legs. One night each month, before the scenery was changed the mannequins would be allowed to take a long break. It wasn't really a full 24 hours but it was close enough and they were all grateful for the opportunity. At other times, you could get someone from the storage room upstairs to fill in for you for a few hours. But it was a dangerous thing for her to do. She was the only black female mannequin on the first floor. Suppose one of the daytime employees had to pass that way for some reason and noticed that there was a white girl in her window? There could be trouble. She could be harshly disciplined.

She recalled how close she'd come to disaster the last time it had happened. She'd been moonlighting at the hotel bar and grill. Even then most nights she would make time for a quick lunch break with Zaza. Usually the breaks lasted longer than either of them planned and it was always costly. The supervisor who agreed to it

246

would ask to be compensated. He'd had the hutzpah to inform them that if they were discovered he would deny all knowledge of their disobedience. For the white girls things were not nearly as hairy. They all looked alike.

It was only occasionally that the shades were completely drawn to the stares of pedestrians that they could relax and take the full and much deserved break. But, this night there would be no break for Sylvie and she hurried to the far side of the store. Her eyes desperately searching for her friend. When she finally found Zaza she was relieved. "Girl, you had me worried to death. Where the heck have you been?" "In the bath room, Ms. Jane Marple," Zaza answered. "They should have hired you for that role!" "Why?" "Oh, never mind the why," Sylvie said. "Let's have a hot chocolate and I'll explain. I'm thirsty." "I am too, Zaza and you are going to have to feed me more than hot chocolate my love." "As if I didn't know that already," said Sylvie. "Now stop talking and let's boogie!"

The two mannequins almost ran up the escalator. They chatted non-stop and when they reached the lunch room they took seats at a corner table. Sylvie waited patiently until the orders were brought to them. The chocolate for her and a milk shake and BLT for her friend. After the waiter left she leaned over and whispered her plan. "I haven't got much time so I'm going to have to leave you. I'm going to that place called, "Ye Olde English Pub" on 28th between Seventh and 8th." "YOU WHAT," Zaza shouted? There was a hush in the dining room as heads turned to look at the pair. "Zaza please keep your voice down." Sylvie smiled as she said this. "Keep my voice down when the only friend I have has just confessed to me that she's now become an alcoholic. And just because she's pining over someone she knew she couldn't have to begin with?" Zaza finally stopped long enough for Sylvie to say a few words. "I'm not pining and I'm definitely not alcoholic." "So tell me why you are going to a bar unescorted, Ms. Thing," Zaza asked indignantly! "Well, I'm going to see if I can find." Zaza didn't let her finish: "Tyvan! I knew it had something to do with him." "Zaza pullese," Sylvie pleaded. Would you let me finish without interrupting every three words?" "Okay lady, but this had better be good. Go ahead. I'm waiting," Zaza said. She folded her arms across her chest like a school teacher. She had a smirk on her face and her lips were pushed out like she'd just returned from having them puffed up with collagen.

Finally, Sylvie sighed and began to explain her plan. She had heard that there was a party going on at the bar. They would celebrate the graduation of one of the Assistant Managers in the store.

At the last moment, someone asked Tyvan if he'd been invited. He'd answered no but that he'd like to stop over. He felt that it would be a nice gesture if he stayed just long enough to buy a round of drinks for everyone. Especially since they were leaving from work and going directly there. It was only a simple gathering with a little food and drinks. No one expected to be there more than a couple of hours and certainly not past one A.M. "And just what has that got to do with you, Missy,"

Zaza asked. "Hold on, I'm coming to that part," Sylvie continued. I'm going to disguise myself with the help of my friend upstairs in Makeup. "Then, I'll put on one of the outfits I've been working on. You know the one I made from watching that group of African tourists last month. They stood in my window observing me for almost a half hour and a few of them came back the next day. "They bought nothing but while they were looking at me, I was looking at what THEY were wearing and I had an idea. We had something very similar upstairs from the fall collection two seasons ago. It wasn't an original African print but it was pretty close. Well, all I had to do was make a few simple alterations, add some accessories and BINGO! I had my own exotic creation. I had one of the girls who works in the fitting room help me. She is so helpful and it's a pity she has no legs because her face is stunning. I often tell her she could be a window mannequin if someone would just take the time to help her. She would look fabulous in evening attire or a wedding dress. Nobody has to know what's under all that fabric. A little nip here and a tuck there. And the woman knows everything there IS to know about clothes. Anyway, we did the alterations and she instructed me on the dos and don'ts of the trade. I tested it that very evening. I didn't tell you and I'm sorry but I had Security let me out of here about 11 P.M. You know, right after the theatres let out. I walked down Broadway among that crowd. Child, you should have seen the eyes. The way those people were looking at me you'd have thought that I WAS the star of one of the plays. I knew right then that the outfit was a winner." When she said this Zaza cut into the conversation. "Sweetheart, don't you get it yet? You ARE the winner. They were looking at YOU, not the outfit." "Oh no, that's where you're wrong. I had taken the precaution of covering my face with a scarf and a veil. Kind of like Muslim women do with those burkas. Aren't they beautiful? No, Za, they could not see my face and besides, I was wearing dark glasses. So you see. It HAD to have been the outfit I wore!" "Whatever you say, Syl." Zaza looked forlorn. It was hopeless to try talking Sylvie out of something once she'd decided on it. She would have to give in and help the girl, she decided. "Okay Syl," she said. "What do you want me to do?" Sylvie was already standing and she said. "Let's go! We don't have much time."

She was dressed and on the street within twenty - five minutes. Dressed exactly the way she'd looked on the night she had first worn the outfit in the theatre district. Sylvie was stunning. And the night was cooperating. She'd been afraid of that. But the afternoon sun and the warm weather had made wearing a coat unnecessary. Even a light one would have been too much for this night she decided. At 78 degrees it was a beautiful night and it was windless. Forgotten was the rain of earlier in the day. It had spoiled her sales on this final Saturday of the month but she was determined to get her revenge. She had to help Tyvan to move her clothing line. The only thing she was a bit apprehensive about was the fact that she had worn heels.

Not high heels but a cute pair of two inch ones with just the toe showing. It was different from what she'd seen the African women wearing but this year's sandals were still in the warehouse. Still, her choice was a wise one. The bar would be dimly lit and she hoped he would not notice that the shoes and bag she'd chosen were from something he had dressed her in months before. At 5'10" the shoes made her appear a bit taller than she'd preferred to look but what else could she do? She hoped Tyvan would not recognize the accessories but then again it was not a big deal. Bloomingdale's had the same bag and shoes. They were items that could have been purchased anywhere in the city.

Turning the corner on 28th she headed in the direction of the English Pub.

Having decided to walk on the opposite side of the street before crossing in the middle she passed several small boutiques on her way. She hadn't been down this street in six months and it was heartbreaking to see mannequins in the window wearing the same clothes. And someone had pushed them into a corner where they stood leaning to the side in an absolutely horrible display scene. In one window there was a sign that read: going out 'for' business! It was the same sign that had been there six months ago and Sylvie knew it was all a ruse. Just another way to avoid the law which mandates that going out of business signs must be complied with in a reasonable period of time. Whatever the shop keeper's intentions was all fine but at least he could have taken the girls out of the window. Give them a chance to rest for a while and to take a bath. She crossed to the opposite side of the street. As she was prepared to open the pub's door a man from inside the bar flung it door open and said to her, "Why, welcome beautiful, I am your official host tonight." Sylvie sucked in her breath. She gathered her courage and spoke up. "Well, if you are then I'm in the wrong place or I am too early or too late. Where's the party that was supposed to be held here tonight?" "Party? There's no party of any kind or any description going on inside this establishment tonight but if you want a party to WE can sure start one," the self-appointed doorman stammered.! Sylvie detected the strong smell of alcohol on the man's breath and she realized that he was only a half-drunk patron of the place. Brushing past him she walked the few short feet to the rather long bar. Leaning against it with her elbows she spoke to the bartender. "Excuse me Sir, I heard there was a party here tonight. It is to honor a recent graduate. Am I too late?" "No," the man answered. There WAS supposed to be a party here tonight. But they cancelled. They said the place is too small for the more than 200 guests who responded to the invitations. They cancelled two nights ago." "Two nights ago," she repeated? It had been just about that time that she'd overheard Tyvan saying he'd was planning to attend. Obviously, she had missed something. But what was she to do. In a panic she managed to ask the bartender, "Do you have any idea where the party is being held?" He looked at her and said almost pityingly, "I'm so sorry ma'am. I wish I could help."

It was over. She'd been defeated before she even had time to begin the fight, She had done all she could to help Tyvan and now she'd have to make the supreme sacrifice. There was one more coup de grace left and to do it she was going to need courage and nerves of steel. She looked up at the bartender and said. "I'll have a bloody Mary on the rocks." "Sure Miss, he said! Coming right up." She took the drink and paid for it. Sylvie walked to the table nearest the door so she could look out the window. Maybe she would get lucky and spy a face she knew. Maybe they would know where the party was being held. As she sank down in the chair she felt as exhausted as a rag doll. She needed to think. There was still a little time left on the clock. She knew what to do to assure herself a victory but she needed help to pull it off and that meant help in the person of Zaza and a few of the girls upstairs. She could count on the girls. She knew that much. But Zaza was going to be bit of a problem. Zaza was going to be pissed. And rightfully so Sylvie knew. After all she had stuck her neck in the noose already and Sylvie now felt as if she was putting on her friend a bit unfairly. But she had to move forward. After all what are friends for if not to help one another? Besides, she was now in too deep.

Looking around her she noticed that the bar was nearly empty. Except for the one half-drunk man and another sitting and talking with the bartender. The men were glancing in her direction and they were smiling. They seemed friendly enough and she smiled back at them. Just then she noticed that there was a man outside the window. He too was smiling at her and when he walked to the door he hesitated. He seemed to be having trouble opening the door. Sylvie got up from her chair and opened the door for him. "It took you long enough to notice me, Cutie." he said. "I was standing there for hours. Don't let me have to report you to your boss," he laughed. She was just about to answer that she didn't work there when two more men walked in and asked if they could sit at a table. She ushered them into the place and to be kind she escorted them to a table in the middle of the bar. Two can play this game, she thought to herself. I've done this in better places!

The two patrons announced that they wanted two glassed of beer and two drinks of vodka with nothing but water. One of them wanted to use the rest room and she looked to the rear of the bar where she saw the sign indicating a Men's Room. She pointed to it and then turned and walked to the bar where she gave the bartender their orders. She did this just as a couple walked in. Without hesitation Sylvie went over to them and asked if they wanted a table or if they'd like to sit on the bar stools. "We can start at the bar," the man offered. "But you never know where we'll end up." The man winked at Sylvie. She heard the woman say to her companion in a joking way: "She is drop dead gorgeous and I am so jealous!"

The bartender had been enjoying the little game from a distance but now he called her over and said to her in a very serious tone. "I am only part owner of this place but if you want to work here I'd be happy to have you as hostess." "Oh thanks, but no thanks," Silvie said. I can't work here but I tell you what I'll do. I will stay for a few minutes. Just until the place fills up and then I must leave. But it is kind of you to ask." "No," he interrupted her. "It is kind of you to stay. This place hasn't had this many customers at one time since we took over as owners. Unless there is a game or something on television." "Excuse me there's another couple waiting to be seated," she whispered to him.

For an hour or more Sylvie continued opening the door and seating people. She took orders and delivered them to the tables. And all the while the patrons gawked at her. They admired her outfit and commented that she was one of the most beautiful women they'd ever seen. Sylvie was used to the attention and she turned on her charm even more. There was no more room in the place. There was a full capacity crowd in the bar and all the tables were full. The music and laughter were infectious. People had to be turned away at the door and no one seemed anxious to leave.

"I'm sorry," Sylvie said to the bartender. "But really I really must go now." He tried to convince her to stay. He tried offering her money. He said he would speak with his partner and see if she could work there on commission. But Sylvie refused. Saying goodnight to everyone in a loud voice she walked to the front of the bar and slipped into the warm night. It had been a fun time and now she had to hurry back to her real job in her world. Almost as an afterthought she decided to walk to the end of the block and then around the corner before going back to the store. It was a circuitous route but it was a lot safer. It was late now. Nearly midnight, and she knew it was just about the hour when the real danger started in Midtown. How many times had she watched from the window as someone was robbed or beaten? It was common to see a crime being committed right under her nose. Several times it had been her own Supervisor who'd called the police. Even during the daylight hours it could be a war zone out there. It was her understanding that a murder had been committed on the other side of the building. Right under the watchful gaze of the mannequins in windows 8 and 10. One of the girls had to be taken down and resuscitated when she'd fainted and nearly broken her neck in the fall. And the shades were drawn for four hours while the entire set was redone before the morning customers arrived. It was a traumatic time for everyone at Boontons and the mannequin had never fully recovered. It was good that the city was now promoting the new slogan, "if you see something, say something." It was nearly an oxymoron. Well almost. Yes, she'd seen plenty Mr. Mayor!

As Sylvie hurried down the block toward Boontons Department Store she noticed that there was a sale being held at the specialty men's store on the same side of the street. She thought of Tyvan and her instinct drew her toward the window display. They are nice suits she said to herself. She loved seeing men in dress suits and ties. It was so distinguishing, she thought to herself. She looked at the little effort that had gone into the backdrop scenery. It wasn't much at all and it made her appreciate Boontons even more. Sylvie went from window to window. She gazed only briefly at the male mannequins before moving on to admire the next and latest men's styles. She thought of shopping for her man and she was lost in that thought. Suddenly, she became aware that a crowd was gathering. But their attention was not focused on the suited models in the window. They were staring at her as though she had dropped out of the sky. Embarrassed, she hurried on to her own destination. It was always that way whenever she went anywhere. Whenever she went out she could never stay long. It was awkward and distressing but she loved the attention.

At last, Sylvie stood in front of the employee entrance. She kept her finger on night bell until the night watchman opened the door.

When she entered the security area she smiled and gave him a quick peck on the cheek. He was a jovial type and she allowed herself to be scanned to make certain she was not bringing in contraband like extra food, alcohol, drugs and firearms. Finally, she was allowed into the main door and into her home. With her it was a pointless procedure but mannequins had been known to bring all kinds of things into the store. Especially drugs. In that regard they were no different from real flesh and blood human beings.

Surprisingly, when Sylvie told Zaza of her night and of her plans the girl did not flip out. She did not lose her mind. In fact, Zaza said the whole thing sounded exciting. "Even if we get caught and I'm thrown into that dungeon upstairs it's worth it. We NEED some excitement around here. I realized that just in the short time you were out of the store." The two mannequins went to the lounge and sat planning the next phase of their caper. "Finally, there will be some life around this place!" Zaza announced! Her adrenaline was off the charts. The next morning the whistle blew at 6:30 a.m. This gave the mannequins plenty of time to rinse the sleep from their eyes and take their places. At 7 o'clock the final signal was announced over loud speaker: "ALL MANNEQUINS QUIET AND DEDICATED." There was total silence as the human employees came through the door. Although it was Sunday morning they were arriving eager to begin the task of dressing the mannequins and changing the window scenes. It was a holiday of sorts for them as well and it was one of the few times they were not obliged to wear uniforms or punch time clocks. The store paid them for double time. Once the work was completed they could go home to enjoy the rest of the day at leisure. The shades would remain drawn to the public until the following morning when the store would reveal its new line of clothes. This protected the store from being copied by its competitors. That had been known to happen in some of the outer boroughs. It was a disgusting practice. But Sylvie understood the motive. It was important in this business to be first in everything.

For Sylvie Manes, this Sunday was going to be special. She could not wait for him to walk through the door when he would take a look at her before going to his locker. There, he'd change his clothes. He'd put on the familiar blue jacket that resembled a frock coat except that it was shorter.

He would gather his tools and her clothing, place them on a cart and bring them down on the elevator to her window. If she needed makeup, and she rarely did, it would be done right there in the window while he watched with a meticulous eye. "No, not that much. Yes, that's the ticket," he'd say to the makeup girl. "She doesn't need to be over -made." And then, Tyvan Belson would take his strong tan hands and lift her from her place. He would strip her bare and slowly he'd wipe her body as if he was cleaning a precious jewel like the ones upstairs in the store's jewelry department.

She would feel his strong embrace lifting her against his own muscled body as he placed her on the stand.

And finally, almost regretfully, he'd dress her in the new line of clothing he had chosen. Her body would be rigid on the outside so that he could perform his job but inside. Inside, she would be as dead and as limp as a dish rag. She would be like putty in his hands. Yes, Sylvie Manes would be in her zone.

She stood there waiting and waiting for Tyvan. But by 8 a.m. he still had not come through the door. At 9 a.m. his replacement arrived. It was the nice girl Teri whose job it was to fill in for absent employees. She was only a part -time worker but there was much talk of putting her on permanently in place of Tyvan. She walked over to Sylvie and looked up at her. "Let's roll baby girl," she said. "Daddy's not in coming today. He called in sick." Sylvie was sick too. She could have fainted dead away. She nearly collapsed from disappointment! He's not coming to work today, she thought. For a moment her brain was closed to all sound and reason. But she knew she had to think. Quickly, she pulled herself together. Her mind was oblivious to Barlie's snickering and ridicule. The girl had no idea what Sylvie was planning and she could not know that Sylvie was not only upset because the object of her affection was ill but because she had other more important things in store for him today. Never mind, she told herself. Barlie will find out in due time. Just as everyone else around here will.

Sylvie stood still as the girl dressed her. Teri was not experienced enough to assist in the scenery change and things didn't take long to complete. Soon, Sylvie was dressed and back in the window while the finishing touches were being made to the park bench she was to lean against to give a hint of leisure to the scene. It was a good attempt she thought but it was a disastrous choice. Teri Palmers stood there admiring her accomplishment and she assured everyone who would listen that this time window number five was a winner. They'd sell out before the end of the month and she would be back there working her magic with a new change before they could say 'zoot suit'. In Teri's opinion it was a foregone conclusion: Tyvan was out and she was in. That's the way of the world, she told people. Sylvie looked at herself dressed in the dreaded black pants suit with a disinterested blouse. Red shoes and a small bag completed the ensemble. Proudly, Teri Palmer had slung the matching jacket over the mannequin's left shoulder. Sylvie felt the urge to vomit. What on earth was the child thinking, she wondered? Here I stand dressed in this god-awful outfit. Why, she might as well have put me in a safari suit with boots and a spear. Who does she think is going to buy this ill-conceived men's pajama get up? Well, enjoy yourself sweet cakes because the moment this joint is closed for the day and all you humans have flown the coup, Sylvie Manes will take control of her own destiny. Thank you very much!

By six p.m. with all employees having left the store, Security activated the store's alarm system and closed all exits and entrances. The usual bedlam erupted. The mannequins, now dressed in their new fashion attire, took turns parading on one of the sales counters as though it was a catwalk.

Some outfits were applauded, while others were simply ridiculed. Sylvie took time to go to the opposite side of the store to help Zaza make adjustments to her clothes. She was kind of small and her clothes always needed alterations. Most times Sylvie did the job for her friend. It gave them one more opportunity to dish the dirt and toss around what had happened during the week. There was always a mini - scandal brewing somewhere in the store and the two friends liked to choose which girl they thought would be the latest to have her heart broken by one of the male mannequins. There was also another reason she liked to go to the front on these occasions. It was to console Rosita. She was the Hispanic girl who worked window number seven. It was next to the last window on that side and for some reason her dressers could never get it quite right with her. Sometimes Rosita would cry when she saw how she was dressed and Sylvie wanted to be there for her. But this time, by some miracle they had managed to pull things together. Rosita was thrilled to death about the clothes she was wearing. And she did look stunning in her short dress of yellow damask. She reminded everyone who saw her of a modern day Carmen from Bizet's opera. They had it just right and when Sylvie complimented her on her look she added that she thought Rosita would sell a ton of dresses. It was the thing most of the girls wanted to hear so it was almost routine but in Rosita's case Sylvie was not exaggerating. Satisfied, Sylvie waited for Zaza to finish showing off her apparel and they walked toward the elevator together. It was time to put her plan into action but there was not much time for refreshments. She had time for a soda but true to form Zaza had time to eat a full meal. "It's a good thing management has strict caloric rules," she told Zaza. "You're practically insufferable. You eat like every meal is your last." "Well, it very well may be my last meal," Zaza replied. She looked at her friend in mocked disdain. "Who knows what will be served in the tombs upstairs. That's where

I'll be languishing tomorrow after I've helped you with your suicide scheme."

The two friends arrived in the lounge and gathered together their small circle of supporters.

Sylvie announced her plan. "If anyone wants to leave I will understand and I promise never to hold it against you," she told them. She waited for the room to empty but nobody left. "Good," Sylvie said. "Now let's get to work." The two men in the group began the job of putting together the night sky that would be used as a backdrop. They decided to use the same park bench that was already in the window so they needed only a lamp post and a small dog on a chain. Both were borrowed from the stock room on the 4th floor's toy department. Then, the little band went upstairs to the merchandise room. It was being used for the storage of some old and new lines. Eventually, the clothes on the racks and in the boxes would be sent abroad to be sold in other nations while others would be discarded or left to lie unused in the warehouse. They could stay there for years and years. Sadly, only a tiny fraction would be donated or given to charitable organizations for distribution to the poor. Management felt it was better to let the goods rot than to give the stuff away. Let them eat cake, was the prevailing attitude in the entire industry. Or in this case, let them wear rags.

It didn't take long and under Sylvie's leadership they found what they needed. It was evening attire from two seasons before. It had nearly the same design Sylvie had worn on her night to the pub in search of Tyvan. Sylvie thought it too risky to use the original outfit. The city is big, but it's not THAT big, she told Zaza. The gowns were simple and light weight but there were only three patterns to choose from: black, white and red. With a few simple alterations they could be converted into nearly the identical attire Sylvie was hoping for to make it all a success. In addition to her own outfit Sylvie knew they needed many others to sell. They counted the boxes. There were 200 pieces. There was no way they could complete 200 alterations by 6 o'clock in the morning. Sylvie settled on just seventy-five. They would assemble twenty -five pieces in each color and let that be enough for the week. If they needed more they could always add them later.

With everyone on the same page they numbered the boxes and took them to the alteration room. They were surprised to see that there were more mannequins arriving each minute. They asked what they could do to help. The word had spread and everyone wanted to be a part of the exciting adventure. No one really knew why they were helping but they had thrown caution to the wind. And soon, there were so many mannequins wanting to help that Sylvie had to refuse them. Some were reluctant to leave and would do so only after they were given rain checks for the next project. That is, if this one was a success and they all had jobs for the next project.

At 3:30 A. M. everyone took a coffee break. Zaza didn't disappoint: she wanted two cups before everyone went back to work. It was an exciting time and all were making jokes and smiling but they talked low. Sylvie had to remind them to keep their voices down. They didn't want to be discovered by Ms. Meanie. She was the night supervisor and she always kept her door closed as she 'worked' in her office on the tenth floor. Of course, everyone knew that if they pushed the door open they would find her lying on the couch asleep. She didn't care what the mannequins did as long as they didn't trouble her or burn down the store. That was Meanie's motto: Do it. But do it quietly. At 5 a.m. with everything going well, Sylvie asked if the window set was in place. There was electricity in the air and everyone was behaving as though it was opening night on Broadway or the first baseball game of the year. Finally, Sylvie was informed that all was ready. She went into the change room and slipped into her gown. It only took a few minutes and with Zaza's help and the girls from make -up and hair she was all set.

At last someone gave the signal that there was no time remaining. Everyone raced to the elevators and escalators. They hurried to take their places for the start of the new season. Sylvie was the last to step off the elevator. And as she did the entire mannequin staff began applauding. All accept one. Barlie Thompson took only a cursory glance before turning away in a storm. Everyone said they had never before seen anyone so beautiful and regal. There was such smiling and the shaking of hands. They congratulated one another on their success. It was a scene never before witnessed in Boonton's. The guys from window 12 through 16 began whistling. It didn't take long before word of Sylviess's coup had spread throughout the building. Sadly, the mannequins on the upper floors could not leave their stations. It was almost time for the human day staff and customers to walk through the doors. Most of the mannequins would have to see Sylvie when the work day was over. The wait would be difficult:

"All MANNEQUINS QUIET AND DEDICATED!" It was the final warning. The announcement was made over the loud speaker and it signaled to all that the 'days' were on their way into the store and in her office on the tenth floor Mrs. Meanie was aroused from her sleep. Her name was not Meanie, although her attitude made the moniker suitable. And who could blame her? She had to be stern, she told the few who knew what she was up against. She'd had to fight for the respect she received and she meant to keep that respect. There was no other way to keep control. She knew the Association would not support her if she was weak and mixed with her charges. Boonton's had hired the Association to manage the store day and night. All was supposed to be quiet in the building. She'd been told by the Association to just shut her mouth. After all, mannequins don't talk. Mannequins remain in whatever position they are placed and they stay there until someone moves them to another place. This was the feeling of Management but she knew better. She knew and she understood so she left them in their ignorance. They would not have understood even if she had tried to explain. This store was only one of a worldwide chain, and only those in her position knew what was going on with mannequins the world over. If it became public knowledge there would be an uproar and a back- lash from the public in every country on every continent and no mall or shopping mart would survive the fall out. Meanie understood that if the truth was let out the stores would have to place only faceless and headless mannequins in their windows. Eventually, there would be half bodies and only body parts on the stands displaying the latest fashions. She would mind her own business and let sleeping dogs lie. If there was a revolution in the fashion industry Ms. Meanie would have nothing to do with it. She would not cut off her nose to spite her face. She was happy to support the models and she did not believe it was tantamount to "slavery." Oh, she knew what would be said in the press: These mannequins work around the clock without rest or adequate compensation. It's criminal!

Mrs. Meanie wiped the sleep from her eyes and straightened her dress. Then, she slipped on her loafers and prepared herself to inspect the newly attired mannequins. They didn't know that she felt for them. She really did. She "knew" what they were up against and she cut them as much slack as the manual allowed. That is why she never made inspections at night or tried to control them after store hours. She just let them "be."

A last, the long wait was over and the day staff began filing into the store. In her window Sylvie ignored the stares and darts thrown at her by the envious Barlie Thompson. She noticed how quiet the place had become and she didn't see him come in the door and walk over to her. But suddenly, he was there.

Tyvan Belson himself. She could have jumped down from her position on the platform and kissed him right there in front of everyone in the world. She strained to control her emotions. As soon as he got within ear-shot she spoke through clenched teeth.

"Tell them you did it! Tell them you didn't like the outfit they had me wearing and you changed it the moment you walked in. Tell them you came early. Night security will back you up. I've already arranged that and I had him punch your time card thirty minutes early. Sylvie didn't say she'd had to pay the night watchman to do it. "Please Tyvan, do this for us both, just this one time. Say you had already chosen this outfit and that's why you didn't come to work yesterday." Tyvan looked up at her. He was unsure how he should respond to the mannequin. She was talking to him as though she was human! But Sylvie continued. "I KNOW Tyvan, I really KNOW and I understand. I saw you in the display window at 'Handsome Studs' down the street last Saturday night. You were wearing the dark blue suit with…oh I don't have time to explain now. I want to help you save your job although I have to be honest and say that it was not entirely an unselfish act on my part but we haven't got time to talk about that now. Please do as I ask and tell them you changed the set and my outfit. Please!" So far he hadn't had time to respond and just as he was going to say something they both noticed that the shades had automatically gone up on all the windows.

It was 8:20 in the morning and already there was a crowd forming at window number 5. Beneath a night sky Sylvie stood near a park bench. She had her cute little dog on a chain. From the outside, the scene was breathtakingly real. Sylvie looked resplendent. The tag on the floor announced the entire ensemble for just $179. She was the Queen of Sheba. She was Cleopatra of the Nile, a modern day Nefertiti Merytmut of the 18th Dynasty and Helen of Troy all contained in a single package. Mlle Sylvie Manes was as beautiful as any of them had been in their day.

All of the employees on the day shift began finding excuses to come over and shake Tyvan's hand. "I knew you had it in you, they said. This time you've outdone us all," they said. A few put their hands together to mimic applause. Some gave him high and low fives. Sylvie overheard him tell a small group of those working that he had decided that what she was wearing wasn't doing her justice. That's why he had made the quick change. It was no slight on the work of Teri Palmers. He had liked her work and maybe they could use the outfit on another girl. "It's just that with the graduation and Prom seasons already here I thought that this romantic touch would draw sales a lot faster," he said. Sylvie was proud. Oh, he was a clever one, her Tyvan. He knew just how to play the game.

But so did Barlie Thompson. She had been watching the entire scene as it being was out. She was also watching the crowded sidewalk beneath the window. No one noticed the shorts set she was wearing. Barlie always prided herself on her legs and she was happy when her dresser had pulled the outfit from the box. This was to be a scene showing two women in a park. She in a shorts set and Sylvie in a pants suit. And now, those crazies had spoiled the whole thing by making this contrast. Sure, they were both still in the Park but she was in a day scene and Sylvie was queen of the night. It was not fair. And it was even less so when the lines began forming inside the store to purchase Sylvie's expensive attire rather than her own moderately priced outfit of $59.99. Well, she wasn't going to take this lying down. Not Barlie Thompkins. Not on anyone's life. As soon as the day was over she would go straight to Supervisor 'Meanie' and tell her story. And when she did heads would roll. She could promise them that much. She'd show them who to play with. She was no fool. Barlie smiled for a lone customer outside her window. The man turned away to continue smoking his cigarette.

By three in the afternoon there were only twenty-six of the original seventy-five pieces left unsold.

When the bell sounded announcing the closing of the store Tyvan was frantic. There were only three left in the boxes and he didn't want to tell his boss that they had sold out.

When he gave the news to Sylvie she said only. "Don't worry, we've got about 125 pieces upstairs and 60 of them will be ready by opening tomorrow morning. She didn't want to overstate her case because she knew it had been a long night and day for everyone concerned. Tyvan looked at her and said.

"You're something special! We need to talk!" TALK, Sylvie almost screamed! I can't talk!

I can hardly stand or walk, Sir! YOU just looked at me and spoke to me." But to Tyvan she said not a word. She listened. And as she did she heard the final tally of the day on her wear. She quickly did the math in her head. There had been 72 outfits sold and the store had made $1,288.80 on attire that had been out of circulation for more than two seasons. Attire that was ready to be sent back to the manufacturer, discarded or whatever it is that they did with the unsold clothes. Everyone was ecstatic and Tyvan was been heralded like a returning war hero. He would be named "dresser of the month" if not of the year and she had helped him do it. If mannequins could die she would have died on the spot.

But there were ominous winds blowing in the mini- person of Barlie Thompson and the minute the store closed and the human employees left for the night her replacement arrived. Barlie left her position in the window.

Sylvie knew where she was headed but there was nothing she could do to stop her. This was Monday and she was on night duty like everyone else. It would be difficult enough to get word to the girls in the storage room upstairs that more outfits were needed. They needed to complete at least 60 additional gowns tonight and another 65 in the next few days. But they were all ecstatic about what they'd done and she was sure it could be accomplished on time. As Sylvie watched Barlie disappear behind her, evil and negative thoughts filled her head.

Sylvie tried to stop thinking bad things and it took most of her concentration to do it. Barlie was headed to the tenth floor to tell Meanie the whole saga. Everyone who supported her efforts would be ruined or in trouble. The Association might replace the whole lot of them and she alone would be responsible for their dismissal. It was written in the manual the Association gave her when she first arrived at the store: Mannequins were not to have a hand in choosing any attire. It was meant to avoid confusion and conflicts of interests. This wasn't the best place in the world to work but there were worse places. Like the store over on 29th where she'd seen mannequins left in the same window positions for months.

Sylvie wanted to stop Barlie in any way she could but she realized she was powerless. She could not leave her position. There were people outside the window looking at her, staring at her face and her attire. She couldn't just walk off. There wasn't a girl in the store or in the storage room who could replace her. Especially with what she was wearing. They couldn't just put a girl wearing a pair of slacks and a halter standing in a park under a starry sky. What kind of message would that send to young people? No, she was going to have to suck it up and wait with fingers and toes crossed. She'd have to grin and bear it and hope for a positive outcome. Maybe Barlie would get stuck in the elevator for a week or forever. Or, maybe she would have an apoplectic fit or suddenly get amnesia. Or, even lose her ability to speak. Sylvie admonished herself for her bad thoughts.

The moment the supervisor Meanie heard the knock on her door she knew it was trouble coming to call. Her mannequins tried to avoid her as much as they possibly could. Avoid her like she had the plague or some airborne disease. She preferred it that way. She could get a lot accomplished as long as she wasn't disturbed every few minutes. And there was so much to do lately. So many problems, people and mannequins to handle. It was that way everywhere now. Human resources and The Association was sending in so many applicants now days. And everyone was always complaining about someone or something.

"Enter Barlie," she called, as she heard the knock on the door. I've been expecting you! "You have? You've been expecting me," an incredulous Barlie Thompson asked? "Yes, YOU! I have been expecting YOU! Is that plain enough? I didn't stutter!" She answered Barlie while looking her squarely in the face. Barlie knew the woman had a reputation for being mean and somewhat disagreeable but she had not expected this. She tried to collect herself as much as possible but Meanie was continuing the pressure. "Well, have a seat child and speak your mind. Don't just stand there like a dummy." She smiled when she said that. "You're a Humannequin and you have a mind or at least you're supposed to have one. So let me hear what's on it." "I, I didn't want to bother you but … Barlie began." "Then why are you here Miss? If you didn't want to bother me, why are you here?"

Ms. Meanie was relentless and Barlie almost got up and walked out the door but she remembered her true purpose. She remembered the clicking of the cash registers and all the sales Sylvie had produced in one day while she, Barlie Thompson was forced into ignominy and reduced to selling a paltry two outfit. The thought gave her courage. She continued, her voice growing louder. "It's about Mlle. Sylvie. You know, the Black girl who I have to share my window with? Well, she is having an affair with her dresser. I think his name Is Tyvan. Yes, that's it, Tyvan Belson. He works the day shift. Well, what I'm saying is that she WANTS to have an affair with him, although I think HE just found out about it. But anyway, he was going to lose his job due to lack of sales on his line. I'm not surprised because she's not that pretty.

She's not all people make her up to be. Oh no, she's not all THAT!" "Go on and finish," Meanie said impatiently! "I'm sorry," Barlie replied. It surprised her that there was a definite mocking tone in Meanie's voice.

She stuttered as she went on with her description of the plan that she was certain had saved Tyvan's job. She included the names of everyone involved and ended by saying. "I don't want to be a rat or anything. I really don't but right is right and I could have sold the same apparel if I'd have been dressed in it. Of course, there are certain things about it I would not wear. Like the sandals and those hoop earrings. Not that I have anything against the African-American and Latino girls who wear them but I prefer..."

"That's quite enough Barlie, Meanie burst in. "I've heard more than ENOUGH," she said emphatically. Barlie noticed that the woman was reaching for a button on the wall above her desk. It was marked Security and Emergency. She had done it, she thought! She had won! In a few minutes Sylvie would be gone and she, Barlie would take her rightful place of honor. Mrs. Meanie would have her dressed in the same outfit Sylvie was selling and that would be that. Of course, she'd have to insist on just a few changes. Like the shoes and stuff or maybe she should keep everything just the way it is after all they say if it ain't broke don't fix it.

Barlie's mind was afire with her thoughts. Maybe that Zaza will be replaced and a few of the other girls she didn't particularly care for. Now that she was in the good graces of Meanie she could insist on it. After all the woman owed her a favor. And management did too. She had demonstrated to them her loyalty. It was the least they could do for her. And just for starters she would never again in life have to look in the face of that brute Tyvan Belson. He'd ignored Barlie Thompson for the last time!

Turning her swivel chair all the way around to face Barlie, Meanie began to speak in a more authoritative voice. "I'm sorry it's come to this. But while security is on its way to detain you, I have something to say."

"DETAIN ME, SECURITY? I'M BEING ARRESTED? WHAT DID I DO Meanie? I'm sorry I didn't mean to call you that but you don't understand." The woman cut her off in mid-sentence. "It's quite alright dear," she said. I know what they call me around here and I'm used to it. In fact, it doesn't bother me the least bit. Most of the mannequins are misinformed just like you are and it's a pity."

"My dear," she said in a calm voice. "It is YOU who do not understand. Didn't anyone explain things to you when you arrived here? Did you ever read the manual that makes it all crystal clear? We are all HUMANNEQUINS! The fashion world is almost 50 per cent Humanequinn, at last census."

"There are different stages of our being. For example, I am Stage One. I have lived as a human and died. I have passed through all four stages to reach Supreme. It's the top level. I can go no further. Nor do I want to for then I would perish forever from the Universe.

People like Tyvan Belson and some others of the day staff are Stage Two. Especially managers and security. We all may live as humans as long as we go to a refueling station somewhere in the world at least once every six months. It's sort of like humans who must report every few days to be dialyzed at a licensed health care facility. Well, sort of like that. We must remain there for 24 hours until we are fully re-acclimated. You are still at Stage Three like all of the others here who work at night. There's a stage of suspended animation but I don't have to tell you what that is since it's where you will be spending the next year of your progress. We have no recollection of that period in our existence but we all come from that Stage and you are going back to it until you get some sense into your head. Just be happy that I am not charging you with a Class- A crime. It is punishable by disassemble and mutilation." With Meanie's last words Barlie began whimpering. But the woman would not relent. She had made her decision. "Oh stop the nonsense, girl. I told you that you don't understand anything. We both know it's all an act. You are certainly not fooling me because I know that Humannequins can't cry. That is an acquired trait that you've picked up since you've been working with the customers and human staff here at Boontons," she admonished. Unmoved by the girl's performance she continued.

"We were not always Humannequins young lady. We too were once but HUMANS. We were 'selected' for this experiment. Yes, our group we forewent our original classification and became mannequins to travel to Earth. And it's a good thing we were chosen. We now know that all the other experiments completely failed. We alone survived the experiment. Of course you know that not long after we left our Herta 236-A imploded and is now no more. As for your false tears child: we came here from a place in the Universe where there was almost no such thing as potable water and we certainly didn't WASTE the little we had on emotions."

"But, I thought, I thought," Barlie interjected, "that you'd have some consideration for ME." "You are referring to your color aren't you," Meanie asked with a smirk on her face? "Well, I wouldn't put it exactly that way," replied Barlie. "How else am I to put it," Meanie asked sternly? That's another thing you've yet to learn. There is no such thing as yellow, black, white, or brown people. That is HUMAN terminology. It's referred to as: LHCM or Latent Human Conditioning Mechanism! We all can choose to learn of it if we wish. Even mimic it. But most intelligent Humannequins opt not to be bothered with that nonsense! It is grouped with a whole class of prejudices and put downs that are meant solely to divide and conquer. Humannequins have no need to divide or conquer. That is precisely what destroyed the planet we occupied for several million years in human count. We were greedy. I remind you that we originally came here for Instruction and Resolution. That is what IR means, if you'd ever read your manual. In case you never noticed, somewhere between the pages of the latest fashions and the cutest hunks there exists important information. It started out as a book of rules and regulations. But that was before the new crop of young editors took control. It will also inform you that we have reached the end of our rope so to speak. This is it for us and we have nowhere else to go. If Earth dies, we do as well! Unless somewhere, one of our kind comes up with a new theory or plan to get us to one of those planets farther out in space.

Almost exhausted, Meanie sank back into her chair. She sighed and looked at Barlie with a sense of resignation and dropping her voice she began slowly. "Once you are released from your temporary purgatory you really must read dear. And try to attend the free seminars that are given on the weekends and holidays. You find time to do everything else I've heard. Like flirt with the young man who works in the sports department on the 6th floor. Sometimes they use him downstairs on three to display the latest jockey and boxer shorts. Don't they dear? I hear he's a real show stopper. Yes, Barlie, you really must apply yourself more. Otherwise you're destined to spend an eternity in that storage room along with the heads, body parts and bits and pieces of mannequins you see there.

I'm sorry but that's what will become of you. And unless you learn something in the next twelve months you will never be more than just a mannequin. Right now you are very fortunate that I don't have you standing in a window somewhere minus your head or facial features, bald and indistinguishable from half a dozen others like yourself. I suppose you're daft enough to believe it's the current trend. No, dearie! They are misguided young souls like you who've run afoul of the system. Of course, some are there because the smaller stores cannot afford the cost of true Hummanequins like the really big chains."

"Apparently you've had your head in the sand on those nightly excursions you take with your best friend Ruthie. Haven't you noticed the increasing number of headless and faceless mannequins in the store windows? Do you think it's an accident or that someone forgot to replace their heads or give them their facial features? Some managers try to cheer them up with sunglasses, hats and winter scarves but it all looks fairly ridiculous on shining bald heads. Don't you think so dear? Yes child, they are there under punishment. They are there to pay penitence! Remember that while you're lying there in a heap trying to figure out what hit you."

The woman heard Security at the door but she hesitated a few seconds before admitting them.

This gave Barlie hope. But it proved to be false hope. Behind her desk Meanie pushed the swivel chair forward. Placing her hands on the desk the woman leaned closer to Barlie and said, "One other thing Ms. Thompson. Do you think I don't know of the rumors circulating around here? There is nothing at Boonton's that I am unaware of. That is why they call me the manager, sweetie! And just for the record. My name is not Meanie. I am Mrs. Virginia Harrison Belson. Tyvan Belson was not going to be fired. You see, Tyvan Belson is my son!"

FIN

Riddles and Time

Maurice P. Fortune

He had heard it many times though he could never remember exactly how he'd come to memorize the words. It didn't matter, the words were chiseled into his brain like the refrain of a good song: "whatever you do, don't be late." Twenty Fourteen knew them as well as he knew his name. He had spoken to many souls who were hopeful of someday making the journey. He wondered if they had any idea how utterly distasteful it all would become in the end. If they had they might very well change their minds. There were so many future hopefuls ready to volunteer for the journey. He was different on that score. He hadn't chosen to do this. In fact he didn't know or remember why his name had come up. He didn't recall just when he'd been chosen. But he had accepted the assignment. One doesn't refuse special appointments. At least not if you are in your right mind he was warned. As much as he wished he could remember, that part appeared to be forever lost to him. All he could recall was someone, a voice telling him it was time to leave. Time to begin. It was a warning he'd lived in fear of hearing. Sometimes he wondered what would happen if he was late. What would they do if he didn't show up at the chosen place? What would happen if he was delayed? If there was an accident!

Don't be late on the last night. You need to be there at least one minute before midnight just to register in the Book of Time. He'd been warned that his signature was not just necessary, it was demanded. Despite all the new technologies and advancements only his handwritten signature was acceptable. And it was unacceptable to use a stamp or to have someone sign the book in your place. The procedure was clear. Be there in time and relax until the final signal is given. Until one slipped through the revolving shield into the next phase. No one ever said just what that actually meant. He suspected they were empty words and he found them amusing. He repeated them. "Relax until the final signal is given. Slip through the revolving shield." How poetic, thought 2014. He wondered who the nut who thought this up was. Yeah, it was funny he thought but it sure scared the hell out of folks and he wasn't one who was willing to put the words to a test.

He sat in the rear of the bus. Glancing nervously at his watch he peered through the window at the scene. The bus seemed hopelessly stalled and it seemed to be going nowhere in the traffic. He smiled to himself as he listened to the din of horns blowing. Amused by cab drivers, their heads hanging through the open windows of their cars with impatience, their brows dripped with the perspiration of anxiety and frustration. Powerless, they were desperate to get through the traffic. Anxious, there was urgency in their desire to drop off their current fares and find new ones in a search to line their already fat pockets with what they considered the necessary fuel of life on earth: U.S. dollars.

For the first time since boarding he looked around him. He had taken a seat at the very rear not by chance but because the rear seat was the only one available. The bus itself was small and he made a quick count. There were twelve seats in front of him. His was the thirteenth. Baker's dozen, he thought. To be truthful he was almost happy to be aboard. Happy to be away from the peering faces of the crowds. Crowds that sometimes stared at him in disbelief. Occasionally, an insensitive adult or an undisciplined child would make a callous remark. He really could not blame them because he often forgot. He would appear in cold weather wearing only a tee-shirt. Or, in the heat of summer with a wool coat over his shoulders. It was not easy to always remember the seasons. Often he was called with only a second's notice. Called to all parts of the globe to record events. He was the ultimate eyewitness news reporter. But he dressed in certain clothing to stop the stares and taunts of people he'd meet. Still, a sensitive soul he never got used to the meanest of humans. It sometimes hurt. He knew that he would never become numb to the ugly words some people used to describe his lack of fashion. "Look mama," a child would say. "You made me put on a coat and scarf when that man is wearing just a tee shirt. Isn't he cold?" He adored kids but sometimes they could say hurtful things. But as hurtful as the words were at least they won't physically attack you just because you are different. The same could never be said about adults.

With this thought in mind he took an even closer look at his riding companions. He could not see the faces of any of the passengers. Only the backs of their heads were visible. They appeared elderly. All were wearing the same uniforms of white robes. There was a red band on each shoulder. He knew he had seen this before. But where? Who are these folks and what kind of bus am I riding in? And what is the strange writing on the rear of each of the seats? What did that actually mean? In all his travels he'd never seen it. It was clearly a language but from where? Perhaps he'd boarded a senior citizen's bus in error? But that was impossible. The driver would not have let him aboard. Besides he appeared to be waiting for him. And what about the seating arrangement? Clearly the bus could only accommodate 13 passengers. He contemplated going to the front of the bus to be sure he'd boarded correctly but at that very moment the traffic cleared and the bus lurched forward. Leaning a bit he tried to see the driver but he could not see anyone in the seat. Perhaps the driver was too short to be seen from the rear of the bus. He had definitely been seated there when he boarded. Admittedly, his eyes had been growing dimmer the last few weeks. He hadn't bothered to try to see a doctor because he knew what he would be told. He knew the answer.

The bus came to a stop! The door opened only halfway but no one got on or off. Then, just as quickly it started again. All passengers sat staring in silence, without moving or even flinching. They seemed resigned to whatever fate awaited them. Maybe they were all going to the same destination 2014 thought. Maybe it didn't matter what anyone said or did at this point.

He closed his eyes reflecting on events of the past twelve month. It was December 31st and it seemed like time had flown by. Of course he'd always known he had only one year to complete the job. He'd begun the journey on January 1st. It seemed so long ago since that first day. So long since he'd taken those first unsteady steps. But the quiet of January 1st didn't last very long. It was all brutally interrupted by the giant snow storm that came out of nowhere on the 3rd. Fifteen inches of snow in New York City. And in upstate New York and Seattle Washington more than three feet had fallen and as if that wasn't enough more than two feet fell three days later. It was all very unpleasant but it certainly dulled in comparison to what was going on in some of the other places in the world where he was called. Almost in answer to the snows in the U.S., on January 3rd a total of 14 people were killed when a building collapsed in Goa, India. On the 9th of January there was a Taliban suicide car bombing in Pakistan. Fourteen people and several injuries occurred at an illegal gambling hall in Kali City, China on January 13th. The credit cards of 20 million Koreans were hijacked on the 20th and it seemed the only good news was that water vapor was said to be found on the dwarf planet Ceres on January 22nd. This was something he already knew.

The world would take a deep breath at the end of January. A much needed rest from all the bad news of the numbers of people killed around the globe from seemingly senseless acts. But it would be at best a brief respite. February seemed to gain impetus from the calamities of January and on the very 1st day of the month there was the eruption of Mount Sinaburg in Indonesia. Again 14 people lost their lives. To make matters worse it was announced that the Syrian civil war had displaced 4 million souls and the death toll there had reached 130 million. At lease the earthquake was an act of nature. Sadly, the same could not be claimed by the militarists and the terrorists.

By comparison, if there was any, it seemed almost comical relief that on February 2nd the Seattle Seahawks defeated the Denver Broncos in the most heavily watched bowl game in the history of U.S. football. Did anyone in Syria truly care? Or that not to be undone by the Super Bowl game in the U.S., Scotland legalized same-sex marriages on the 4th of February?

So this was what loneliness feels like, he thought. Of all the human emotions he'd been given as gifts this was the worst. It was so unlike happiness. That one was a pleasure. Happiness was watching a newborn smile. Now that was a wonder! Or, seeing the eyes of someone young or old open an unexpected gift. And it was much different from sadness. He'd known plenty of that too with all the funerals and hospitals he'd visited over the last year. How sad! And loneliness was different from pleasure or ecstasy. As quiet as it was being kept he'd experienced plenty of that over the past twelve months. He hoped that in the end it would not be held against him. There was also solitude. Solitude is not to be confused with loneliness. Solitude is rowing a boat on Lake Kivu in the Democratic Republic of the Congo. Or, walking by one's self somewhere on a beach in the South Pacific or on an uninhabited Andaman Island. And finally, there was joy. To 2014 joy was the emotion he felt when he walked into the most expensive hotel in town. He would look through the computer as the desk clerk was busy checking in another visitor. Without assistance he'd book, pay for and be given a key to an unoccupied room with all the amenities. Of course, he wouldn't sleep. In fact he couldn't sleep because he was never tired. He didn't have time to feel tired. That was one of the emotions he lacked. He didn't feel tiredness and he did not feel love. He wished he could feel love but the closest thing to love that he could experience was admiration.

Twenty-fourteen stared through the frost covered window at the hordes of people. They all walked aimlessly. That was always the way it was with huge crowds. No one seemed to have any real purpose in mind unless it was a rush hour. He was lost in thoughts of the past year. And he wondered about the identity of the other twelve passengers. Why were they there? They seemed nailed to their seats and there was almost no movement of heads or bodies.

At least he knew why he was there. The instructions had been clear: Appear before 11 p.m. on December 31st, at 86th and Broadway. Take the small yellow bus. The word END will indicate its destination. Exit at 34th and Seventh just across from Macy's. You will next board an identical bus which you must take two blocks east to 5th Avenue and the Empire State Building. Do not walk or hail a taxi. Walk-ins are not allowed through the check-in gate. Disembark inside the drop-off center. From there you will take the first of two elevators. It will only rise to the 60th floor. You will then need to take a smaller elevator car. Get off on the 83rd floor and enter Suite 8369. An usher has been assigned to greet you. DO NOT BE LATE!

There it was again, the warning not to arrive late. Well, what if he did? Would the world come to an end? There have been those who've prophesized the end of times for as long as there have been humans. There have always been naysayers and doomsday preachers. So far the prophesies about the end of times hadn't amounted to more than a lot of posturing, excuses or changed dates. He wasn't planning to put them to a test but he didn't think it funny or fair that he was warned every five minutes!

The bus slowed to a stop. It had turned east at 72nd Street and was stalled in traffic yet another time. They write these instructions without knowing what they are talking about, he muttered in exasperation! This is New Year's Eve. Everyone knows you can't take a bus down Broadway on New Year's Eve. The place is packed with millions. There are tourists and New Yorkers alike. A more sensible route would have been Lexington or Second Avenue, then across 34th Street to Fifth. He relaxed as the traffic jam broke. He looked again at his watch as the bus sped through the park and slid through the underpass to turn down 5th Avenue. This is going to be close, he thought.

He began to regret his decision to end his tour of duty in the Big Apple. No doubt he'd always found the city exciting. There was so much to see and do. Everything seemed especially interesting: the people, the food, its places and especially the shows. It was all so different from other parts of the globe. Different but not necessarily better. He'd fallen in love with so many remote places of the world. He smiled as he thought of May 21st. He had been present when Jose Mario Vaz was elected president of Guinea-Bissau. Yes, he'd fallen in love with that country and its people. They were so warm and open. The celebrations went on for days at an end and the food and dancing were superb. But just as suddenly, on May 24th, there was a coup. Yingluck Shinawatra, former Prime Minister of Thailand was detained by the Army. There were presidential elections in the Ukraine, Lithuania and India and although each was just one day apart, 2014 was expected to be present at each of them. It meant a lot of time packing bags and unpacking them as he tried to find suitable attire not to appear out of place in each country. Sometimes he'd been forced to appear wearing the same travel-ironed clothes. There was always much gourmandizing followed by large doses of Pepto-Bismol, This was especially true after President Abdel Fattah el-Sisi was elected President of Egypt. Now truly that was something special to see. There was so much history involved with the pyramids as backdrop. The joy of that moment nearly wiped away the mine explosion of May 10th when 238 miners lost their lives in a fire in Soma Mine, Turkey. He had wanted to be present when the Santa Maria, flagship of Christopher Columbus was discovered north of the coast of Haiti but it simply was not possible to be there when news of the miners leaked.

As the bus passed 45th and 5th Avenue it became possible to catch fleeting glimpses of the Empire State Building. But even as far over as Fifth Avenue the streets were packed with people. Most were trying to get as close to Times Square as they could. They had come to the City just to see the spectacle of the ball drop. He thought a minute of how someone had described the ball drop: "It was all over so fast I scarcely had time to look away." Looking up at the empty office buildings in the distance he wondered why there was so much office space in the city and why such space, all of it just glass lights and concrete, was so expensive. Space that people occupy for just eight hours a day- five days a week. It seemed like such a waste when it was common knowledge world-wide that New York City was suffering from a severe housing shortage for middle and most low income people. So much money poured into office and warehouse spaces that have not been occupied for years and probably never would be occupied; so many suffering in the horrific hovels that have become known as homeless shelters. Some kind of "shelters" they are when most homeless people will openly avow that they'd rather sleep on the subways and in the train stations than risk their lives in a shelter. But that is another story. Perhaps, it will be something that 2015 or another number will be able to fix.

The bus continued just three blocks before coming to another halt on 42nd Street. He looked out the window and took in the scene. The driver of a large bus had anticipated the passage of a car on his left but the driver of that car hesitated and kept the bus in its lane. The result was a near pile up of all the cars behind the bus. With everyone cursing and blowing horns and threatening one another there was almost a mini-riot. Minutes from the festivities no one wanted to be outside of their automobiles exchanging insurance information or awaiting an ambulance to be carted off to the nearest hospital emergency room, Twenty-fourteen was certain he'd arrive late. It was exasperating to be caught in traffic and unable to get out and walk. Again it crossed his mind that as great as New York was perhaps one of the other 'end' places might have been a far better choice. The instructions had given him other choices: Johannesburg, London, Manila, Cairo, and Singapore. He admitted he'd been short-sighted and selfish. He hadn't had much time to see anything or do anything since his return to the Big Apple. And anyhow, it seemed a cruel fate that he'd miss the ball drop. Of course it wasn't the same since the passing of Dick Clark but he'd heard the old-timers say the same thing after Guy Lombardo moved on. Time comes and time goes he said to himself. It all seemed so long ago.

There had been so much to do. He wondered if he was being graded on his choice of the places and events he'd chosen to be present at in the last twelve months. There was no way to know in advance how the system worked or if points were awarded or even if there were penalties. Would it have been wiser to attend to other calamities in the world? The huge concerts and sporting events? Or, the political elections? Maybe it would have made more sense to have traveled to fewer places but the rules made it clear that nothing was to be spared or ignored. He'd tried to mix things up and to be flexible, going to several different places on the same day and at distant and faraway lands. There were so many things that did not make it to the six o'clock news, or the ten o'clock news or even the Daily News. In fact, most so-called news would never get reported at all. He'd seen the reality of that. There was no way to record the shooting of a kid in Harlem. Mercifully, he hadn't died of his wounds. At least not physically. And how does one record myriad cases of drug over-doses, rapes, domestic abuse and the like. Most crimes and events never get reported. But the reality of it all is that they "happened" and it makes little or no difference if it occurred in Staten Island or in the Philippine Islands.

Yes, he had experienced plenty this year: The year had not been eventful to say the least and he hoped that the 'powers that be' would take everything into consideration. The date August 8th stuck out in his mind. Looking back he realized this was the day the Ebola outbreak in West Africa had been categorized by the World Health Organization as a major concern. He wondered what had taken them so long to "categorize" since the known death toll had surpassed 500 on July 14th. Perhaps they had all attended the Independence Day celebrations in France. Or, maybe they were still reeling from the news that on the very day Sahar Assad was sworn in for a third term as President of Syria, amid air strikes by Israel the death toll in the Gaza had topped 200. On the 18th of July the Israeli Defense Force (IDF) had called up 18,000 additional troops in the Gaza campaign. Three weeks of attacks and counter attacks followed with bombings and counter bombings as each side sought to wipe each other from the face of the earth. It was sad and it was war at its most senseless. Well, lately planet Earth seemed devoid of its senses more often than not.

His attention was momentarily attracted to the writing on the back of the robe worn by the figure seated in front of him. It seemed to be a combination of letters and numbers but none he had ever before seen, at least not in the order they appeared. As he searched his mind he realized the bus had come to a stop. In the distance 2014 caught a glimpse of a familiar sight. Its neon sign blinked- Rick's Cabaret and Steak House. He'd been there many times and he reflected on the tasty entrees served there. Not to mention the shows that were held just next door. Yes, he was going to miss New York City. The doors opened to a figure dressed in hooded black. The figure boarded the bus and stood facing everyone. "Good evening everyone," the voice said in a low and rather musical tone. "Ahem!" The figure, cleared his throat and began again. "I suppose by now you have guessed we're going to be a bit late tonight. Just a tad late: about 2 seconds. I don't suppose it really matters." He laughed and continued, "To coin a phrase –it's not earth shattering!" He seemed to get a great deal of pleasure saying this- like he had invented the phrase and 2014 smiled wryly while thinking: what an acre of corn this guy is. But the hooded figure wasn't through. "This has never before happened in the history of time," He hastily added. "And some of us have been counting for a very, very long time. Long before many of you were born and given names. This is not a threat but I just want you to be aware that there may be some consequence to pay. I can't be certain but I feel it's important to think outside the box and to be prepared for the worse. "Not for all of you," he added. "But for one of you in particular." When this last bit was said 2014 felt a chill creep through him. He thought he knew who that particular person was. Counting the driver there were only thirteen souls on the bus.

He raised his hand to speak but it was ignored. The voice continued. "When you leave the bus please hand the sheet of paper I give you to whomever is in line behind you. Your names are on the documents. Continue doing this until the last one leaving the bus has all the documents. He will know what to do with them." Handing each rider a sheet of paper the figure got off the bus and disappeared into the night. The bus continued. It stopped for a security scan and then moved slowly down the ramp before coming to a complete stop at the loading zone beneath the Empire State Building. There were no other vehicles in sight.

As the other twelve passengers began leaving the bus 2014 tried once more to catch a glimpse of the driver but he realized that there had been none aboard. Making his way past the seat where the driver should have been he was handed a document. He was the final passenger on the bus and it was an odd feeling. He had always believed that it was his personal mission and that he'd journeyed alone to this place to record the events of the last year for posterity. Who could do it better than he? He had been reassured on that point. He had been informed that he was hand-picked to attend every major event of the year. He knew them all by heart. What someone had scribbled on a piece of paper meant absolutely nothing.

He knew the count. He had been THERE The 430 major events someone had counted had probably been compiled by some clerk or secretary polishing her nails and musing about the night before in the arms of her lover. She didn't know diddly about events. Only the events in her life were important: an upcoming baby shower, some selfies she'd taken two weeks ago on a trip to Jamaica. Her sister-in-law's engagement party last summer.

Four hundred thirty events! It was laughable. There was no way to count every major event of the past year. This would be impossible to do. And to even suggest that anyone could possibly decide what was a major event was even more ridiculous. Major to whom, he had asked himself when he was given the final count? But keeping the tally was the responsibility of others. His was to be present at as many events as possible and record first- hand the thoughts of those most affected. He guessed he would be graded on that score and that score alone. As the others were leaving the bus he had tried to look each in the face. Everyone passed him with hardly a glance in his direction. There were no smiles. But even without knowing their identities he could have made an intelligent guess.

January's face wore the deep lines of winter. It could not hide the cold eyes or the grim mouth that seemed set in the face like the block of concrete or the cornerstone of an old building. April's face was stained and wet with the tears of despair from the chill of a damp spring but its mouth bore the hopeful sign of a new life. Warm and hopeful of events yet to come. But April was also remorseful. Remorseful of the ferry boat that sank in South Korea carrying 304 people to their deaths. Most of the dead were students. And on the 18th of April seventeen Nepalese climbers were killed in an avalanche on Mount Everest. Still, the hope of April came with the announcement on the 12th that a new drug had been approved that could successfully treat hepatitis C. But finally, on April 23rd there was the disaster in the Democratic Republic of the Congo: there, a train wrecked killing 60 and injuring 80. It was almost an afterthought that only three major events occurred before the month closed. They were not considered serious.

There was no way to deny it. No matter what anyone claimed the record showed that this had been a most murderous year. Of course there had been many worse years on record. Even ignoring the accomplishments and troubles of other species and civilizations that had been replaced or annihilated by modern man there was hard evidence that humans had literally clawed their way to the top. And since their ascent there had always been conflicts and wars between groups of peoples and nations. There were always ways that mankind found to kill and maim one another. There was the constant modernizing of weapons of war and mass destruction. This had been the bane of humanization. Despite all the talk of cooperation between peoples of different backgrounds and cultures the bottom line was that man was probably his own worst enemy. No one even considered that man will also be replaced someday. No king reigns forever.

But 2014 also knew there were great times too. Times of prosperity and progress. Times of love and compassion. Times of invention and development. That this was the route taken by man to become man. The questions were: Where would it all end? What did it all mean? What is the secret of life on earth? It seemed almost insignificant that science finally solved one important riddle: Was King Tutankhamen killed when his chariot overturned? It appeared to the current thought of science that this would have been impossible with his misshapen body and his horribly disfigured club foot. Of course everyone knows this belief could change in a year or so.

As each of the months passed their reports to the one behind it 2014 reflected on what all of this might mean for him. How would his year compare to those of past years? How far back would the General Audit Office go? What was their rule of thumb and most importantly, would the final tallies be enough to move him to the next level? Something kept prodding him to remember. Remembering again some of scary events about the closing year of

2014 made him shudder. Globally, it was the hottest year on record. The Western United States of America, Europe and even parts of China and Alaska recorded droughts and unbearably humid weather. Not to be undone, even the winters of the northeast had record cold and snowy weather. Everyone was asking the same question. Is this the start of global warming and the end of times? It was a scary thought and 2014 had almost wept as September walked past. He recalled that even the archaeological find of the remains of a Viking fortress from 900 CE, or the 3rd straight U.S. Open win for Serena Williams could not erase the 400 deaths in Pakistan and India that Monsoon flooding caused on September 4th. Nor the riots that occurred in Guinea on August 29th which followed untrue rumors that health care workers were deliberately spreading the Ebola virus. Of course on the 5th day of September the world was shocked by the news that the count of mortalities in Africa from Ebola had reached 2,100 souls with more than 4,000 infected. It was also stated that no one actually knew the true number.

He suddenly felt tired, very tired and very old. He hadn't felt this way earlier. As the last of the months passed a few looked him in the eye: October, November, He tried to understand the message he was certain each was trying to convey. What was the message in their eyes? Was there a glimmer of hope? A faint glow from somewhere within. Each seemed worn out and embarrassed. Yes, he thought. Embarrassment was the right word. Almost ashamed. Well, no matter how tough the auditors were they could hardly blame anyone for the way things had turned out this year. It was nobody's fault that Ebola became a nightmare. No one could have known that there would be such a fracas made over President Obama's health plan. Who might have guessed the death of a man selling "loosies" in Staten Island, New York? Or how serious things would become down in Missouri when a young black man was shot to death by a police officer?

He thought it important that Asteroid 2014 R.C. came within 25,000 miles of the earth. Now that was close! But he didn't think people knew how close and serious this event actually was. It was understandable because few people really have any concept of space and time. Most are just concerned with the small world they live in. As far as he knew it had always been this way. Just live, love and die. He'd tried even harder to look into the face of the shadowy figure of the last month as it passed to him its report. It was December. It seemed drained and absent of even a ray of hope. December with it festivities and celebrations of Christmas, Chanukah and Kwanza. Festivals of lights and beautiful music. Shopping and gift exchanging and unreasonable expectations for the on-coming year.

The approaching holiday seasons had not been enough to lift its spirits. December looked as if it was seeking from 2014 a sign or at the very least some acknowledgement of support. Or, maybe forgiveness was closer to the truth and confirmation that it was the last month of the year. And December knew that 2014 knew them all. He knew who they were. The only trouble was that he did not know who he was or why he'd been chosen on this last night of the year. Why was it he who was chosen to collect the final tally? He knew who they were and he supposed that the writing on the white robes was further indication of that identity: They were the months of the year and the numbers represented the tragedies that had happened on each of their watches. It was plain even if it wasn't very pretty or reassuring. 2014 was faced with the unpleasant task of turning in their score cards and balancing the budget if that was even possible to do. It was an awful task and he wondered what the auditors would think. Would they make unkind comments? Would there be penalties to pay? And just how many years would he compete against. How far back would they go?

The on- coming year! The on-coming year! ....The words jolted him from his reverie and he quickly descended the steps of the bus. He was careful to close the door behind him. He closed the door on the silence and the emptiness of the bus and as he did so he realized someone was calling him. He turned in the direction of the voice which belonged to the figure in black: the same figure who had boarded the bus earlier and then disappeared into the crowd after warning them they would arrive 2 minutes late.

"Hurry, hurry 2014 you can still make it! My watch was a little off but we don't have very much time to spare." Crossing the wide corridor he was ushered into the thickly carpeted elevator. "Never mind what your instructions were. We haven't time to take two elevators. We are going express. This thing hasn't been used in years but barring a catastrophe we should be alright." The doors slammed on the car marked 'private and out of service'. As they ascended toward what felt like the top of the world. 2014 swallowed hard to avoid the pressure in his ears. The doors opened and as they stepped off the car the robed figure took the documents and pushed a log book and a pen in his direction. He said, "sign-in here." He next pointed to the room on the left before leaving 2014.

Twenty fourteen turned the knob of the oaken doors and walked into room 8368. There was total darkness. But he finally made out the image of a huge table in the center of the room. He counted twelve hooded figures seated at the table. Their eyes resembled small lighted globes and there was a tint of blue in them. He thought he recognized the figures from the bus. Just behind the large table was a stage and on that was placed a silver-colored chair. A light hung above it. The light was soft and it had the same tinge of blue as the eyes of the twelve hooded figures. On each side of the larger chair were two smaller ones. There were no lights above these and sitting in each was a hooded figure wearing a black robe. Their eyes were the same as the other occupants in the room except for the glow. It somehow appeared brighter.

Twenty-fourteen stood still for a long second. From a wing to the right of the stage there appeared another figure. It was that of a beautiful woman. Her full-flowing gown shimmered with gold. Her hair, cut short was pulled back from her face and it reflected the glow of the spotlight as she walked. Descending the four steps she approached him. It was a radiant face and she didn't need to smile. It didn't matter. Either way she was the most beautiful creature he had ever seen. Twenty-fourteen had seen many beautiful faces. She bowed slightly as they met and she took him by the hand. Lamb to slaughter. The thought came to him but he knew he was powerless to avoid the inevitable. He felt more tired than he'd ever been. He was exhausted. He could hardly move his feet and he felt years older than his age. Almost through habit he walked methodically until he was at last seated in the silver-toned chair. The countdown had already begun and he could faintly hear the voice of the beautiful creature as she counted aloud: Five, four. Twenty fourteen had been exhausted before sitting beneath the light.

But now, suddenly, he began to feel something else. He felt almost new. Almost as good as he'd felt before his journey began. As good as January of last year, the year before and maybe a hundred years ago. Or, maybe it was a thousand years ago. Yes, that was it. He felt like 1066, or 25 B.C. Maybe 1917 during the 1st WW, 1941 and WW2, the American revolution of 1776, the revolution in France in 1792, the 1865 Emancipation Proclamation, Columbus in 1492, 2001, the sexual revolution of the 1960s the time of Christ, Mohammed, the time of Guatama Buddha. 2014 felt like he had felt in the warmth of his mother's womb. But when was that? And who was his mother? In fact, who were his parents? Did he have parents? No one had ever told him anything about his family or where they had come from. It wasn't fair! As long as he could remember he had been just a number. He felt sorry for himself. He felt as if he knew the answer to the riddle but he wasn't sure, He HAD to be sure. 2014 felt that tonight, on this night before he died he had to know the answer! THREE, TWO, he heard the counting in his head. ONE! The lights went out!

Slowly, 2015 appeared. He was not dead! 2014, was not deceased. He was re-born. He had become a new spirit. Just like he suspected. Or, maybe he had not expected any such thing. Maybe he was lying to himself and didn't really know what to expect. In fact, he still did not know. He suddenly heard the sound of babies crying and his attention was drawn to the table where twelve ladies sat dressed in white robes. Each held an infant to her breast. In that instant, no one needed to tell him what had happened to the 12 months of the prior year. Two thousand fourteen had died, to be replaced with the suckling babies of Twenty-fifteen: the new twelve months of the year.

The beautiful lady approached him. Looking at him she began speaking: "You are forever known as TIME. Your mission is to go out into the world and seek answers. Follow the months, survey the seasons and count the hours, days, weeks and months. I *want you to enjoy yourself. I want you to have fun at their expense.* But never interfere. For if you interfere even once, it will mean the end of mankind. The end of the world as they know it. Never confuse the end of mankind with the end of times. There has been so much talk about this that I feel it important to set the record straight. There is no end to time. Time is infinite. It goes on and on just as it has since the beginning and only one and a few know the answer to the riddle. Time has always been and time shall always be. Time is synonymous with Universe. There is no ending, and there is no beginning. It is never redundant!

She paused..." but that is a subject for another occasion and you must forgive me if I am passionate about it. It is just that I regret mankind's audacious and uneducated predictions. Whoever said silence is golden should be rewarded. Just remember, I have given you this mission and this insight into the secrets of the Universe. But you must never abuse your privilege. There is no accounting at the end of the year. Mankind's woes and troubles mean next to nothing in the larger scheme of things. Their existence is but one among many. The troubles you have witnessed, you have seen many, many times before. The murders and the killings, the wars and the conflicts are all part and parcel of the retribution. Man was created to self-destruct.

As difficult as it was to keep his eyes from her beautiful figure, and it was difficult, he was mesmerized by her words. The words were full of meaning. Why had he not known these things before? What kind of idiot was he? He had been all over the world. He'd lived out of suitcases, recorded events, jotted down this and that but the truths had never occurred to him. He heard her words in his head: "That it has taken this long is nothing short of a miracle. No one knows when man will self-destruct but it will happen sooner rather than later. Only the great Council knows this. We all know who and what sits at the head of that table. Ours is to do and not to question. For it we knew the answers we could not face the future. This is a fact that mankind must never know. At least not now, and perhaps not for some time to come.

You will now be known as 2015," she continued. "This is not your name. You are TIME! But always remember, there is really no such thing as time. Time exists only in the reality of man's imagination. It is something man invented because of his need to control his destiny. It is something he can never accomplish. Clocks, time capsules, ball droppings, watches, hours, days, weeks and months, even years. These things don't actually exist. Time goes on forever. It has done so since the beginning and it shall exist forever. On our level, on your level you have witnessed everything many, many times before. Mankind has this need." She paused again... "This need to destroy everything in its path. There is always talk of conservation of environment. Save the earth they say. And then they leave the wreckage of their explorations in space. They leave their garbage to travel in space just as they leave it to pollute the earth. Nuclear waste they call it or non-biodegradable trash like Styrofoam and plastics." She stopped talking and looked at the others. She started to speak but then changing her mind she said softly, "we shall speak again. Later, I have much to say to you." Turning once to look at 2015 she said, "When you leave this chair of knowledge you will not remember what I have told you. But remember this: December 31st, 2015. Be here before their clock strikes twelve. And no more repetitions of tonight. One last thing. It is now January 1st, 2015 by THEIR calendar. Not by yours. NOTHING HAS CHANGED because a bell has sounded and the hands on a clock have moved. Nothing has changed because a ball has dropped and there was a show at what they say is the crossroads of the world. What do they know of crossroads?

Remember my son, Time cannot be stopped. Time cannot change. Seasons can change, time does not. Time is synonymous with Universe. But that is a subject for another occasion and believe me, there will be many others. You are still young and eager and you have much to learn. Whoever said 'silence is golden' should be rewarded. Maybe I'll see to that. Go now, quickly! Don't look over your shoulder, TIME never looks back! Next year now, she said. Farewell! Don't be late whatever you do!

She was finished with her words and 2015 watched her walk away. His mind drifted briefly and expectantly to the future. What kind of year would this one bring? Would this be the year that they make contact with other worlds. And if that happens, what would become of Time a.k.a. 2015? Or, maybe this would be the year when there were no wars or conflicts as it has become fashionable to say. Conflicts, wars, skirmishes, whatever the vernacular the bottom line is that people die. Children and the aged, the infirmed are displaced, raped and abused. No one is denying that there must to be sickness and death. These things are natural processes. It just has to be this way. The old become the new and sometimes the new become the newer.

"Sir, sir, a voice on an overhead speaker gently prodded. "You must leave now, you cannot delay. Too, much depends upon you being THERE!" The voice reminded him that when he left the chair and the light his mind would remember nothing. Just before he rose he took one long last look at the disappearing figure of the beauty in the shimmering dress. He hadn't noticed sooner but she had a rather large identity tag around her neck. It was suspended on a silver chain hanging from her neck and it was visible only from the rear. It read: PERPETUITY. She had called him her son?

TIME did not understand its meaning and he rose quickly. He walked quickly through the exit doors and to the elevator that would take him back to the loading zone in the basement of the building.

He half expected to find a bus waiting. But where would it take him? He thought of the crying babies he'd left in the upstairs room and he recalled that one of the mothers was missing- January! January had already begun its mission. Well, good luck January.

Twenty-fifteen was in no hurry and just for a moment Time stood still.

FIN

Two Undocumented

By M. P. Fortune

George was glad to be on his way to work. As usual he'd woke up late and had only enough time to prepare himself a sandwich for lunch. But it was okay because since he began working nights he didn't like eating heavy meals. It only made him feel tired and sleepy and when he felt sluggish it took him longer to complete his work. Tonight, once the early workers finished the shift he'd be alone in the building. He didn't like it but it happened each month. The night cleaning crew took turns staying until the morning man came on duty at 6:30 A.M. The college big wigs felt it was safer than leaving the building completely unmanned for five or six hours. They were too cheap to pay a security company to do the job and they had tied the job in with the cleaning contract they'd let out to an independent company. They killed two birds with a single stone. It was a clever ploy. Also a dishonest one. They didn't pay the company any extra money for its services.

But that was his bosses cross to bear. He was paid to be there for a full eight hours and as long as he got his money for any overtime hours he didn't care what the contract arrangements were. Besides, the extra bucks for Monday to Friday night - Saturday morning were a welcome bonus. It was his week to pull the shift and he knew he had to remain alert. Already twice during the week he had not been at the front desk to let the relief man in the building. Mr. Bishop hadn't said anything about it but George could tell that he hadn't been exactly thrilled about standing outside and ringing the bell. It was a helpless feeling- looking through the plate glass windows and doors that were part of the entrance. It was all anyone could do to arouse a sleeping worker or one who was not at the front desk. There were food deliveries to the cafeteria which had to be made at that early hour of the day. These included breads and sweet rolls, milk and newspapers that couldn't be left outside to natural and sometimes unnatural elements. In the past perishable items had been torn apart and eaten by the areas rats or contaminated by the dogs of thoughtless residents of the multiple dwellings along the street. George had never been able to figure out why people found it more convenient to let their dogs do their business directly beneath the college canopy. The only thing he could think of was that the recessed area was good shelter for anyone trying to escape a rain shower or the extremes of winter weather. But this was a poor excuse for allowing pets to do their business in the area. After all it was the main entrance and one would think that it would be respected as such. But rain or shine, night or day, some idiot walking a pet would let the animal pee or do worse in the doorway. It was disgusting and dealing with the heavily ammoniated smell took precious minutes away from the day staff and the evening cleaning crews.

As he came upstairs in the station and out of the madness of the Number 2 Train he thought about how lucky he was to have a night job. It was sheer luck that he had been hired. He could only call it luck because cleaning was a job he had never in his life dreamt of doing. At least not on a professional level. He didn't like to clean at home. He'd told this to his uncle who had suggested he apply for the work. He was nervous about the entire thing for a number of good reasons. What if he was asked to show his green card or his application for citizenship? He had neither. He had nothing to show except a social security card and even the most ill-informed knew how easy it was to obtain one. Government Agencies in the U.S. handed those out almost as quickly as tax forms in March and April. The Saints must have been watching over him on this occasion because he'd been hired on the spot. And at a very good salary too. Experience or not he was expected to do a good job.

There were watchful eyes at every turn in the persons of a very critical supervisor. It had been tough at first. He had to be shown how to do everything. A very understanding boss had allowed him plenty of time to get the necessary on the job training. The man was kind, patient and although he was a Black American he spoke very good French. Why the man even spoke with a French accent and no one would have ever thought he was anything except foreign-born. George had been surprised and happy when he'd learned this and even more pleased about the prospects of working for someone who understood his English language deficiencies. It had not been easy for him since arriving in The U.S. and working nights was a great improvement over the torture he had to endure everyday on his daytime job. Still, as much as he liked it he knew it alone could not pay the bills and leave enough to send money back home.

Seeing it was not quite 11 P.M. he ducked into the deli, purchasing a large bottle of soda and picking up a newspaper. He couldn't read much English. He used the newspapers to practice the little he knew. He was making progress and he intended to go to school as soon as he could find the time. He could no longer use money as an excuse because with the addition of the night job he was making enough pf that. Besides, he had found out that going to school to learn English had become a very inexpensive way to get ahead. His boss had told him that. He'd also told him that you just had to pick the right school and stay with it. George knew several people from his country who had stuck with it and were now working on getting their green cards. He didn't need a green card to work on his day job. In fact, it was discouraged. He'd been told that by several workers on the job. "If you apply for it don't let anyone here know about it because you will be sent packing as soon as two days ago." It was no more than a sweat shop and it paid less than minimum wage. It was illegal to do this. But then he was illegal. And as far as the night job was concerned, he didn't need a green card to do that either. At least not right away. The boss had told him several times that for the moment he was willing to look the other way but he needed to do something about getting legal. "George, I can't continue to let you work here with only a social security card, he'd said. They'll give one of those to a horse and it doesn't even need to apply for it, the boss told him. "I'll give you just one year to start getting your papers in order and then I can help you no longer. I can't let you get my business in trouble." One year seemed like an eternity at the time but the months were going by so quickly and George still had not been able to do anything about the problem. He was preoccupied with that thought as he opened the glass doors to the college and walked into the lobby. Signing in at the front desk he spoke with the Security Officer. It was mostly to reassure him that there would be someone there to take his place when his tour ended at midnight. It was the same every night. The man asked the same stupid questions and George wondered if he ever thought of anything besides eating, reading the newspaper, doing the crossword puzzles and going home.

As they stood there chatting Byron Staples, the night supervisor exited the elevator and gave him the eagle eye. Asking George how long he'd been in the building. George pointed to the sign-in ledger.

His signature was just above the supervisor's signature. The man had signed in only ten minutes earlier. It showed that George was on time and even a little early. He knew the man was being a smart ass. Staples seemed to revel in his own ignorance. Once he'd been overheard complaining about his boss and the fact that the man hired foreigners or people who were not his own countrymen. George smiled at him and said, "Good evening Sir."

He said good evening to two fellow employees who were heading for the back door to put out the trash and the garbage from the floors they had cleaned. The security code was disabled from the front desk. The alarm would remain off until after the area was cleaned and most of the boxes were neatly stacked inside the building to await their day for cartage. This happened only twice a week. On Mondays and Thursdays. The last man to set out the garbage needed to re-sweep and mop the area. He was also required to reset the security code and lock the door. In this case, it would be George who would perform this last task. As the late night man for the week, if there was anything missing or awry he and he alone would be responsible. As bad as that was he didn't relish the idea of putting out garbage when he was alone in the building. It was dangerous. "What happens if someone is hiding behind a parked car and sneaks up on you," he had asked the boss?

"That has never happened in all the time I've had this contract," he had been told. George just let it go but he was still nervous about that part of the job and he tried to get to work in time to collect the garbage from his floors and set it out in the street before everyone left for the night.

He took the elevator to the second floor and began his work. Classrooms for the youngest was his area of responsibility and he guarded it with jealous if not zealous passion. He had been given these rooms to clean because it was the easiest job in the building. That and the eighth floor. It was just as well because he couldn't handle more responsibility. In fact, it was all he could do to keep complaints at a minimum. Even though the rooms took no more than two hours for a good cleaner to complete George usually spent at least three and a half hours there. The eighth floor should have been cleaned in forty-five minutes but it took him nearly two hours to it. He was slow and he wasn't very thorough but he was dependable and the boss knew that just getting someone to show up for work every night was a rarity in the cleaning industry.

It had not always been that way but any American born here at least two generations ago didn't seem interested in these jobs. Particularly in the big cities and New York City was as big as they get. It didn't take George very long to learn this or to understand that except for the little problem of the Green card he had it made. Some of the other employees were more than a little pissed off about the impression it gave that he was being favored with overtime hours but the way the boss explained it made sense to George. Even though the schedule was rotated most of the others did not like working on Friday nights. Someone had to be in the building until the morning man arrived and with George taking 6 hours or longer to do his work this meant that he should have been able to finish with an hour to spare. Sometimes, the others shared late night responsibilities just to keep one another company but George always found himself working alone.

Once the building emptied it was a scary place to be. George liked to pair with the other foreigner on the job. He was from Senegal and he was a much faster worker than George. It puzzled George that he seemed able to complete his duties with plenty time to rest or to take a long nap before the front desk person arrived in the morning. Like George he had little conversation with the American workers. The two of them tried to get together as often as possible it only to chat in French for a few minutes. This was not very often because the supervisor was always on his back about forgetting to do this or that task. Of course the earlier they finished working the more time the two would have together. "I have no problem with that," his boss had told him more than once. "If you can go into an area, blow hard and make everything clean and fall into place then the more power to you. The only thing I ask is that you blow out the candles too."

By 'candles' he was referring to the electricity. The school was very sensitive about lights being left on all night in the building. Well, tonight I'm going to be here alone so I'll get the garbage out of the building and then take my own time doing the work, George thought. He was tired and relieved that it was Friday night. Most of all he didn't need the supervisor complaining about him. It was annoying and George wondered how long the boss would tolerate it.

Just before he left in the morning he would pick up his check from the box at the front desk where the boss always left checks on pay nights. It was standard practice. The boss arrived around one a.m. and handed the checks to the Supervisor. If there was a problem and he needed to come into the building he would do so but generally he sat outside in the car or in a taxi while the supervisor came out and picked up the checks. He would then drive off into the night. It was like clockwork. George had seen it happen dozens of times since he'd been hired and tonight would be no different. He sat on the couch in one of the offices to make a quick phone call.

"George, George, wake up! The boss is in the building." It was two o'clock in the morning and George had been asleep for the past hour. "He wants to see everyone downstairs in the lobby in ten minutes.

"George, George, did you hear me, man?" George sat up straighter on the couch and rubbed the sleep from his eyes. He looked into the face of John, a co-worker. Straining to rub the sleep and exhaustion from his eyes he replied, "I heard you, I'll be right down." "Well, hurry up because everyone else is ready to leave and you're holding us up from spending this money," John said. He waved the check held in his hand. George got to his feet quickly and then went in the bath room where he splashed some water on his face. The boss! Coming here at this hour, he thought! What did I do wrong now? He wondered if he would be fired for something stupid. Maybe it's a blessing in disguise. It's not the worst thing that's ever happened to me. He'd often guessed it would come to this end. He'd always been afraid of moonlighting.

He took the elevator to the first floor and walked toward the small group of workers now gathered in the lobby. "Bonsoir boss," he said. "It's morning George." The boss said as everybody laughed. He knew full well that George had been asleep. There was little that went on in the building that the boss did not eventually find out about one way or the other.

For example he knew the idiot Chuck had stolen a VCR from the classroom on the fourth floor. And he knew that it was still in the building's supply closet wrapped in a black garbage bag. The boss also knew that two of the employees were stealing meats and other items from the kitchen and taking the food home. And that one of the men had taken a stock of toilet paper and paper towels from the school and anything else he could sneak out of the building. It was a frustrating business in that respect. Some of the men were dishonest no matter how well they were treated. You just had to catch them and fire them. Already he'd fired six people in the last 12 months. Tonight would be no different. One more employee was being let go. In fact, to save himself from embarrassment, the man had already left the building. He'd received his two weeks regular pay and two weeks of vacation pay and he was no longer an employee of Apex Building Maintenance, Inc. The man had been fired because it had been reported that someone had been seen peering from an upper floor office in the school and looking into the windows of the buildings on the opposite side of the street. A peeping Tom, he'd been observed kneeling or in a chair at the window of the darkened room.

The boss read from a letter as the men looked around at one another questioningly. In turn they shrugged their shoulders to indicate that none of them was the culprit. But the boss was giving nothing away. Nothing. He let them squirm as long as he could and then admonished them for their sloppiness in cleaning the elevators and the garbage area each night. There had been complaints about that too and he wanted it stopped forthwith or heads would roll.

Then he returned to the topic at hand. The man responsible for the recent crime was careless. In the stairwell of the sixth floor he'd left evidence of his capers in a bag along with personal papers identifying him. No doubt he'd forgotten to take it when he'd left and by chance one of the day staff had found it. When security opened the bag they discovered man and the links. Inside were powerful binoculars. The boss now let that sink in and moving his eyes from one employee to the next he gave them the name of the disgraced man. He then let everyone know that as a result of this incident he was demoting the night supervisor. It was his responsibility to know these things and since it could have cost the company a very lucrative contract he had to take definitive action. The former supervisor would receive the same pay but he would have reduced responsibilities and that did not include overseeing employees. He'd be just another cleaning man. Then he announced that until he'd found a temporary replacement. He, himself would be doing the supervising and maybe it would remain that way. Perhaps he would not try to find anyone else, he'd told them.

"So all of you had better shape up or you'll be shipped out of here faster than I can say shipped!"

They knew he meant what he was saying. They knew the man. He was kind and gentle to a fault and he would give one the shirt off his back but he was not to be trifled with when it came to the job. He would fire without ceremony. They had watched him do it many times. Especially the older ones among the crew.

Finally, reiterating his concern for the building's electricity bill he boss instructed everyone that the lights in all of the class rooms and offices needed to be kept off unless the room was being cleaned. Turning to George he asked if he was nearly through with his work. George mumbled something about having another hour or so worth of work left. The Boss handed him his check. "You need to hurry son," he said. He reminded him that he would soon be the last man in the building. He then turned and walked through the glass doors and into the night. George breathed a sigh of relief that the man had not gone up to the 2nd floor to check his work. Or, to the 8th floor for that matter. George had hardly begun his work. He'd fallen asleep on the couch the moment he'd sat there nearly two hours ago. Yes, he was going to be in the building alone again. Or almost alone!

Not long after he returned to his work on the 2nd floor Smalls came up in the elevator and asked if he would come down to the first floor to put the security chain and lock on the front door. Bill Smalls was the last to leave the building and George would be alone until seven in the morning. He looked at the clock in the corridor and was surprised to see that it was nearly 4 A.M. Following Smalls down to the first floor he took the lock and chain from the cabinet. He felt strangely uneasy that Smalls was leaving him alone and he tried to make conversation with the man. At last the man said he had to leave. "Have a nice weekend," he said to George as he walked through the glass doors and into the street. "See you on Monday," he called. But George only faintly heard him. He was already walking toward the elevator. He needed to hurry to the 2nd floor to complete what was already turning into a rush job. He wasn't too concerned about the 8th floor; there were only two bathrooms and the lights to put out and he'd be done. Maybe, he wouldn't even mop the floors. There were often classes and employees in the building on Saturdays. Later, if anyone said he'd been negligent he could blame them. Who could dispute his word on a weekend? Admittedly, it would not be a good job. He didn't like to do things that way but maybe no one would notice. If they did perhaps they wouldn't mention it to his boss. He hoped also that they wouldn't notice that he was shirking the other part of his responsibilities. It was the part that required him to sweep down the east stair case every other night and to mop it every third night: especially on Fridays. Could he get lucky again? Just once more time?

At exactly 5 A.M. on Saturday morning Georges Hodges stepped from the elevator and into the lobby of the building. He had his lunch bag with him and the soda he'd bought from the deli. He'd left it in the fridge in one of the offices and it was chilled. It had taken him three hours to complete his work and he was glad to be finally on the first floor of the building. He felt safest there. At least there were telephones easily accessible and occasional pedestrian traffic in the street. If need be he could summon help from the window. He still had not shaken the feeling of uneasiness. Maybe it was all in his head but at least for now, just being on the first floor he was closer to the exit and nearer the rest of humanity. He thought for a second about taking the lock off the door but concluded that it was too dangerous to do. He was alone and he had no weapon to defend himself from an intruder.

He smiled as he thought of his employer. Yes, he was happy on this job and he meant to keep it. He would do a better job on his floors starting next week. There hadn't been that many complaints lately, he concluded. He felt pretty good about that part although he fully expected some complaints to be made on Monday. To be fair he knew what he'd done and he also knew what work he hadn't done and the latter outweighed the former by a long shot. But he'd just wanted to get through the night. He couldn't put it in words but he wasn't exactly feeling the atmosphere in the building. All he could say was that something was not quite right. Maybe it was that story about an employee watching people with binoculars. It was creepy and weird. In all his days he had never heard such illness. Not even in his country where people were known to do some sick and evil things to others under the guise of government leadership or religion. He didn't even want to speak the name. It was totally frightening. But in his heart George knew the feeling he had didn't have anything to do with windows or binoculars. He had had this feeling before coming to work. And as far as religion was concerned well, he didn't understand it. He knew from his mother that there were many good things about it. It's not about evil, she had told him. She'd said that it was a beautiful thing and that it was only simply a dogma such as Christianity or any of the many other beliefs that exist in the world. In fact he'd just heard that the very word religion was a Greek or Latin word meaning almost the opposite of what most people have been taught. He preferred the term Spiritual. But who was he to question the norm? "Don't judge it until you understand it," mother had often told him! And she had been right. He was finding that out more and more as he grew older. His mother had been one of the original people to arrive in Miami. She'd wanted to come years earlier but something always prevented her. After years of contemplation she'd made the trip via Montreal. George had come years later by the same route. He was glad he had. There were also lots of friends and family living in Miami. Like most immigrant communities theirs was a close knit one. Closeness had its drawbacks but it helped to have that kind of support in a strange land. The jobs he worked not only supported him here in the States but it gave him the opportunity to send money back home. That was the way it had always been. If you are able to send money or help, then you do. A few American dollars still went a long way in most countries of the world. A very long way.

About two hours remained before the morning man's arrival and George Hodges couldn't wait for his tour to end. He had forgotten that on Saturdays the man arrived a half hour later. Somehow that last half hour seemed to go by slower than the other eight.

It was like that every Saturday morning he worked and this one would be the same. He spent a few minutes reading the newspaper but he was unable to concentrate. He turned on the radio and listened to several stations before becoming frustrated. He was getting better at understanding what people were saying but he was far from understanding the myriad of accents and meanings of English words and phrases. The music was not any better. He loved the music but he understood almost none of the lyrics or their meanings. George was totally lost whenever someone used a slang and could not at all come to grips with the meaning and the intent of curse words and phrases. He took them as he heard them and it was not a pleasant feeling when someone once said, "Oh screw you, George!" "Screw me," he replied? He repeated the words twice more. You, screw me," he'd shouted at the man in disbelief! They had used the "F" word and George had nearly fainted dead away. It took some serious explaining to get him to understand that it was only a street expression that some people in America often use. He was not to take it literally. Finally, he got a sense of what the phrase meant. Or, he almost understood. It had taken the balance of that night to recover from the shock of it all and he never again turned his back to the man. George was happy when the man was given his walking papers.

Sitting at the front desk, he faced the street and looked out at the occasional passerby.

As the morning progressed he felt more and more alone inside the building. He'd have felt safer on the street. At least there were a few others out there. But inside with almost all the lights off it was almost like being in a morgue. He hated the atmosphere and he began humming.

To contribute to the eeriness every fifteen minutes one of the two elevators would automatically shut its doors. It would then ascend to the 9th floor before descending once more. The doors would again open as though the elevator was discharging passengers and the other elevator would then ascend to do the same. It was annoying and although it was not noticed when the building was occupied by hundreds of folks it took a while to get used to when one was alone in the building. They were on a timer and there was no way to stop them from this needless repetition. They could not be disabled because it was a fire hazard to do so. George always expected someone to step out of the car when the doors opened. Of course, no one ever did. Well, almost never. He'd been in the building more than once when someone from the day staff worked late and neglected to tell security. It was always an unpleasant surprise to hear footsteps coming from the direction of the elevators or to hear the echo of footsteps as they trod across the polished terrazzo.

George tried in vain to stop his mind from wandering. He wasn't afraid of being alone. At least that's what he had told the boss when he took the job. Unafraid or not, it was comforting to know that at least he could sit at the desk and see anyone walking the long corridor from the west side of the building.

That side of the building had an exit and it was locked and alarmed. But there were two areas he could not see. He could not see anyone approaching from the stairs almost directly behind him. Nor, could he see anyone coming from the dark theatre directly to his left. It was unnerving but it was the job. He looked down at the weekly sign -in ledger. Noting there was nothing unusual about the building. As far as he could tell everyone who had come in had signed out before 11 P. M. This was the cut off time for everyone and even the groups from outside the College had signed. There were no night classes on Fridays and Mr. Bishop had drawn a line straight through the space reserved for the professor who taught classes in Room 402. It had been an uneventful night.

Once again George unfolded the daily newspaper and tried to read the sports section.

He heard footsteps! No! *It* was his imagination playing tricks on him. George looked down at the Sports page in front of him and tried to concentrate a little harder. But he HEARD footsteps!

There was nothing wrong with his ears. Someone was walking on the stairs behind him and of that he was certain. He jumped up from the chair. He had been reclining in the swivel chair and his head had been resting against the wall below the security panel. He stood and listened again. The footsteps ceased! George thought about going to the stairs and calling. Maybe someone had fallen asleep as he had done earlier and had woke up to find themselves alone in an office or classroom. Maybe there were some kids in the building doing something they had no business doing and just waiting now for an opportunity to sneak out unnoticed. That would explain things, he thought. But a late worker have used the elevator and anyone working above the second floor would have done the same. If there was someone working late in an office, wouldn't security have known? He looked at the ledger again to be certain all the available spaces contained a signature. Everyone should have been out of the building. Just then, he heard the footsteps again. George was panicky. Beads of sweat formed on his forehead and he felt goose bumps on his neck. He had thoughts of running out of the building. He could do that easily enough. Just leave. Get out while he was still safe and unharmed. After all he was close to the door. He didn't owe the boss any more than he'd already given. He was nobody's martyr. All he had to do was use the key to unlock the chain. No one could blame him for saving himself and the boss would understand. That darned chain, he thought. I should have taken it off earlier, he muttered to himself. Wasn't it illegal to have the door chained? He'd heard it was illegal. Someone had told him that much. Maybe it was the security guard himself or one of the other workers.

He was sure that the college Business Manager alone insisted on it being there. There had never been a mechanism for locking the double glass doors. They had been installed in the early 1970's at the time the College was built and perhaps those were safer and less turbulent times. Certainly in terms of the crime in the City. No one would have even thought of breaking in and entering the place. They would not have dared. Nowadays, even the day guards were apprehensive about this section of the city. As a matter of fact, they felt so uneasy they kept a baseball bat under the desk to further emphasis their concerns. George didn't understand that one because during the day there were hundreds of others in the building. The bat wasn't there to use but only as a deterrent. To frighten, he'd been told.

But George wasn't a fighter and he certainly did not want to get that up close and personal with anyone intending to do him bodily harm. No, the baseball bat was no good to him. There was only one thing he could do. He had to call the boss. The boss had all but fired the supervisor just that night. Could it be that the man had somehow gained entrance to the building and had been upstairs stealing the school's property or vandalizing? Did he intend to harm George? It was certainly no secret that he didn't like him He'd often referred to George as the boss' flunky. This WAS America and he'd read those stories about disgruntled employee coming back to the job and killing their co-workers. No, he didn't want to call the boss. It had been after 2 A.M. when the man left the college and George hated to disturb him. He knew he would have to call him at home because no one would ever answer the business phone at nearly six o'clock in the morning. His mind afire and his thoughts in a quandary as he contemplated his next move. It was still dark outside and he realized he could not leave the building. His job depended on his presence inside the plant. One cannot simply abandon one's post, he thought to himself. That was unthinkable. Besides, what if the person had an accomplice who was waiting outside the building for just such an eventuality. With no one at all to call for help they could enter and vandalize with impunity. They could destroy the place and he'd be to blame. Then what?

Again, George heard footsteps. They were getting nearer and could not now have been above the second floor. He had walked down those steps many times and he could envision whomever it was as they paused on the widest landing. Would they take time to notice that he had not swept the stairs or mopped them that entire week? What was taking them so long to get to the first floor? It was deliberate. They were deliberately punishing him and making him sweat. He knew the deal. It was a wide staircase but it didn't take THAT long to descend. In fact, he'd counted the stairs many times. There were exactly thirteen steps from landing to landing with the middle landing being the narrowest and shortest. Then, the last flight of stairs leading to the garbage area and to the loading zone had an extra step. Any normal sized person would only have to take about five or six steps before they were through the open door and into the lobby. Here, depending on their choice they could turn left to the elevators and the restrooms or turn right seven steps where they'd come face to face with security. In this case a petrified and perspiring Georges Hodges.

He could take the suspense no longer. George Hodges quickly collected his coat and small carrying bag and headed for the last bastion of safety on the first floor. It was one room and it was located to the right of the elevators and nearest the restrooms. The room had formerly been used as a lounge for students. There was an electricity control closet there and security placed their things on hangers and in a corner.

It wasn't very secure because only recently someone had stolen a switchblade knife from the pocket of the evening man. They'd discovered it was the evil deed of one of the cleaning crew. The man had actually lied and tried covering his foul act by saying that the knife had fallen from the guard's coat pocket. He had every intention of giving it back to him but he'd put it in his pocket and forgotten about it until he arrived at his apartment The man had been fired for his true intentions. Insecure as the room was George knew that he could lock the door from the inside. And he knew that there was a telephone in the room. The room also had one extra added feature in that the walk-in closet also had a lock on its door. He could take the telephone inside the closet and use the overhead light to see how to dial his boss' number. He would not need to turn on the telltale light in the outer chamber. With these things running through his mind George headed for the room. He turned the knob of the door and eased it open, shutting it with just as much ease. Finally, he locked it. He could hear himself breathe deeply. But he was still sweating bullets as he took the telephone and tried to take it into the closet. The cord was about a foot short. He had no time to lose. Quickly he dialed nine and then his boss' home number, listening and counting the number of rings with bated breath. The rings had almost reached seven when a very sleepy voice answered. "Allo, oui," the boss said. George was beside himself with relief. How did the man know it was him? He must have ESP. He then remembered that it was his boss' habit of answering his telephone at home in French. Once he'd asked him about it and the man had told him that it was because he had a lot of friends who spoke French and they often called him from abroad. Here in the USA it wasn't quite 6 A.M. but in Europe and Africa it was six hours later.

"I'm sorry to call you at this time of the morning, George explained. But there's someone in the building." "Of course there's someone in the building George," his boss answered. You are there, aren't you? Or at least you'd better be there." "Oh, yes I'm here boss," George replied! But there's someone else here too and I thought everyone had signed out and left." "What time is it George and what do you want me to do?" "It is 5:58," George said, looking at the clock on the wall. He hurried to add. "I'm in the little room. You know the one near the elevators. I've got the door locked and I hear footsteps coming down the stairs. Can you come over here," a terror- stricken George gasped? "No! I most certainly cannot come over there. Do you think I'm a police officer or some kind of a hero? No George, I'm your employer and I'm telling you to call 911!" "NO! George almost shouted back.

I know, I mean I know you're my boss but I can't call the police because they'll ask too many questions.They might want to see some I.D." His boss could hear the desperation in George's voice and he quickly recovered himself. He remembered that he had hired an undocumented employee and he was as much at risk as George. "Okay I'll call the police, but I'm not coming there unless it is absolutely necessary. I don't believe there's anybody there but I'll call 911, so you'd better be right about this. Call me back in five minutes."

The boss hung up the phone and turned on the light on his night table. Looking at the clock next to him he said aloud: "dammit!" Still swearing to himself he dialed 911.

The operator answered. "911 May I help you?" "Yes ma'am you may," he said.

Giving his name he then explained the problem and gave the address of the College and his employee's name. After he hung up he sat there glancing up at the time every few minutes and wondering if maybe he should have rethought his decision to place an undocumented person in the late night position. But he had never dreamed anything serious would happen there. Now, it appears that something might be going on and a person with limited English efficiency skills was ill - equipped to deal with the situation. Sure, HE could understand the man and speak with him in the language he was most familiar with but how many others did he know who spoke French? Many police officers spoke Spanish but French was a different situation.

Quickly, he swung his bare feet to the floor and sat up. "Allo, he answered as he picked up the telephone. For once in his life the boss had answered on the first ring, George thought to himself. "I'm sorry I took so long to call patron but the police were here and they walked with me throughout the entire building." George hesitated as though he was reluctant to talk. "AND GEORGE," the boss screamed impatiently? "AND!" "They didn't find anybody here." George said at last. "It was a rat sir, he continued. There was a big rat near the exit where we set out the garbage. I don't know how it got there but it was a very big one and I know it did not come in since I've been here because I didn't put my garbage outside. My bags are still there in the corner. I was waiting until the morning man arrived before I set them in the street." The boss knew George was lying. He knew the whole business of getting the trash out of the building while there were still other workers there as support and he supported the idea. If it made everyone feel safer he was all for it. But to George he asked simply, "how many times have I told you that it is not a question of blame? Let's find a solution to the problem. That's all I care about George! Solutions!"

"Anyone can make a mistake and anything can happen that we cannot control. The question is what can we do about it?" "I don't know patron. Maybe..." "Never mind," the boss said cutting him off. "Are you alright now and will you be okay until Phil arrives in an hour?" "Yes, I'll be fine," he assured his employer. George hung up the phone.

He'd completely forgotten that Phil would be the replacement for Mr. Bishop on weekends. Mr. Bishop never worked weekend. It was a pity. George didn't care for Phil. George was not at all, just fine. He was worried and more frightened than before. He had lied to his employer. The police officers had not found a rat. It fact, they had only smelled one. They had walked through most of the building. That much was true but they'd found nothing. One of the cops had merely suggested to the others that the mysterious 'walker' might have been a rat. And only then after he'd seen the boxes and trash cans at the back entrance. The cops had found it amusing that George seemed to be afraid of this possibility. They had laughed openly as soon as he'd requested in his broken English that they place a squad car outside the college for a few hours. "What do you want us to do, baby sit you," they had asked him?

It was embarrassing that he had almost answered- yes. Yes, I'd like that, he wanted to say. I'd like it very much.

Instead he kept his mouth shut because he knew that baby-sitting would not have helped him.

Something else was going on and it had nothing to do with burglars. It had to do with George and his personal life. Something he had once done to someone. It had happened a few years before he came to this country and what he'd done was not very nice.

The person he'd offended had sworn revenge and now it was time to pay for his foul deed. That he had left his country immediately following the incident didn't matter. It was here and it was now. That's why the cops had heard nothing. The cops may have been confused but George Hodges knew the difference between the pitter- patter of rat feet and the sound of human footsteps. Or, in this case almost human footsteps. He had to find a way to right this terrible wrong. To placate the spirit that was now stalking him. Then again it might have nothing to do with that incident. He searched his head, trying to find some other incident in his life where he had wronged someone. The closest he could come to that was the time he had argued with a man from India. It had happened just down the street from the college. George had gone there to purchase a few things after work. One of the owners, a man from India or Pakistan had accused him of stealing and George emptied his pockets on the counter to prove the man a liar. Maybe the man had died and being of the Hindu religion had now petitioned Karni Mata to ask the god of Death to incarnate him as a rat. The way he had done for her dead relative almost seven hundred years ago. George was now grasping for straws and trying to connect the dots in any way he could. He had to find out. He had to know why he was being stalked and tormented in this way.

When Phil arrived he found George standing outside the building. He was smoking a cigarette and pacing up and down in front of the school. George lied again. He told Phil that he had decided to get some fresh air. It was stuffy inside and it only made him sleepier. He wanted to be there to chase away the early dog walkers to keep them from fouling the sidewalk. It was another lie but George didn't care if Phil believed him or not. The morning man looked at him with a queer look on his face. Then he repeated: "stuffy?" The building is air conditioned George." But George did not respond. He walked inside to gather his belongings. Before he left the building he set outside the two cartons he'd collected from the eighth floor. It was time for him to go home.

His mind was occupied with thoughts of the supernatural and he wasn't exactly thrilled about going home. He hadn't been happy about living there since he first began hearing footsteps in the hallway outside his room. The house itself was full of people from his country and although he didn't know several of them very well he had mentioned the footsteps. They'd just shook their heads in mocked ignorance but he could see that they knew. There was something they were hiding from him. If only he could call his mother or someone who was wiser in these matters.

He had heard of someone right here in the city who might be able to help him but it entailed a whole ritual of things he had to prepare himself to do. And it was scary stuff because once you embarked on this path there was no turning back. It was all or nothing. That was the way of the world he'd come from. Once you begin a task you must complete it. You can't go around changing your mind just because you're bored or because things seem to be taking too long. People in this country could afford themselves that luxury. But in his country it was another story. Americans didn't understand these things. They are such children. They are so naïve about worldly matters George thought to himself.

George Hodges headed for the number 2 train to take him to Brooklyn. He knew that he could never stay alone in the college again. He would just have to work something else out with the boss. He was an understanding man. Otherwise, George decided he'd have to leave the job. He didn't know how long he could continue evading the inevitable meeting with destiny but he didn't want to be alone again. He could never be alone again. At least not as long as his problem remained unresolved. Not as long as he was being stalked and watched. It might have nothing to do with him being alone. It could happen at any time and anywhere. He'd heard of cases where things had happened to someone while they in the middle of crowds. Maybe he shouldn't take the subway home. There might be an extra passenger on board the train: one who didn't need to pay a fare to ride. If so there would be two undocumented souls riding to Brooklyn and George was but one of them. As he crossed the street he was still thinking these thoughts. He momentarily forgot the sanitation truck he'd seen picking up trash in the block and as he crossed the street at the corner he never saw it turning the corner. The driver of the truck didn't see George either. But he felt the awful thud and the bump of the front wheel.

FIN

Message On The Subway
M.O.T.S.

Maurice P. Fortune

With all the money being spent on upgrades by the Metropolitan Transit System to improve what they considered to be the most important areas of the city, Hanley wondered why things always took so long to be completed in Harlem. At least this was the impression he had. Most Harlem residents agreed with his take on it. No matter how large or small the job, work lingered for weeks and even months with little or no progress.

The latest example was no different. The escalator from the lower 3rd level to the top floor had been down for six weeks or more. Cordoned off in haphazard fashion, it was easy to see that serious repair work had not taken place in days. The infirm, the elderly, exhausted mothers with baby carriages were forced to climb the long flight of stairs and then struggle two more flights to street level. It was unconscionable that the MTS had now proposed yet another fare increase.

This one would be the cruelest of all. Even school kids would not escape their greed. Gone would be the free passes and the half fares for the elderly. All would be forced to walk farther and to wait longer. The weather was not a consideration. No more bus shelters would be erected along the routes to protect passengers from the elements. There was not even a hint of fair play left in the cuts. Simply by providing transportation MTS assumed they'd be doing their paying customers a favor. Further customer consideration was unnecessary. Consideration promised but never delivered. Sort of like warmed over, day old Won Ton soup from the Chinese restaurant. It was soggy and didn't taste good but with a little effort customers could make it go down.

It was no wonder Hanley' d seen a young man jump over the turnstile and run onto the train just as the doors were closing at the 135th Street station. There were televised news reports that turnstile jumping was climbing in every borough. What did anyone expect to happen? Where would youngster just 12 to 17 years old get two dollars and seventy -five cents to pay a one-way fare? This was not rocket science! There aren't enough cops to enforce the laws, Hanley noted, shuddering when he accepted the obvious answers. Robbery and theft. What else?

He was momentarily detracted from the other scene playing out in the car. Only moments earlier a man had boarded the train and taken a seat across from him. Obviously homeless, he was dressed in tattered rags. Everyone on that side had deserted the car as soon as the man sat down. Some nearly trampled others as they ran to the far side. Or, braving danger and police fines others opened the doors between the cars to flee the intruder. How dare he insult their noses and their sensibilities with his presence! It was unfair of him to rob them of the few minutes of downtime they were enjoying as they chatted, relaxed, texted and listened to I-pods. It was enough that they had to endure the sight of his slovenly lack of self-discipline. They didn't have to smell him did they? Throwing up their hands in abject horror and disgust they turned away their faces!

The scene reminded Hanley of the film, "The Ten Commandments." De Mille had portrayed two women, mother and daughter returning to their former residence. They appeared on the streets wearing rags. Their faces were covered. This was a sign that they had leprosy and the town's folk screamed, "LEPERS, LEPERS!" The poor unfortunates were stoned and driven from the city. Of course, in real life New York City -2010 things were somewhat different. There was nothing leprous about this modern day character. His crime was homelessness. HOMELESSNESS, Hanley had wanted to scream, is NOT contagious! It's a lot of things in this city of millions where one could make a living collecting the unused and still edible fruits and vegetables that are thrown away outside super markets and fruit stands every day. Or, where the cooked restaurant foods that are discarded as garbage would be enough to feed an army of soldiers. Homelessness is unnecessary, undemocratic, un-Christian and wrong but it is not infectious.

The man's clothing looked dirty and his body too but these can be washed. He had a hoodie over his face and his shoulders were bent but when dignity has been restored shoulders can be straightened. Hanley supposed, this was but another attempt to hide himself. To hide any semblance of the person he had been in times past. Back when his world was different and his hope had not been thrown to the ground like an old piece of gum on a subway platform. Gum that gets trampled on again and again, day after day, until it too becomes hard as cement and a permanent part of the structure. No one seems to notice that it never gets scraped or power - washed away and those who do keep their mouths closed and their eyes refocused.

As the man sat there Hanley tried to see his face, but it was carefully concealed. His efforts to hide had succeeded. They always do a good job, Hanley thought. Riding the trains and walking the indifferent streets of New York City had taught him that there are two types of homeless people. One is bold and demanding. They are menacing as they approach others. They demand to be helped in some small way. A dollar, a penny, a bit of something to eat. Even when they accumulate enough for a meal, they continue their harangue. Eyes wide and penetrating, they are always menacing. Hanley had seen people insulted and threatened when they didn't comply with a request for a handout. But he understood that this too was only a cry for help. Just another way to let the world to see their pain. They too are crying out and are only saying: "Look at me! Don't sit there pretending not to see that I am suffering!"

The other kind is proud. They will hold on to a few shreds of dignity at any cost. They never look anyone in the eye. Keeping their heads turned they block out the rest of us, never wanting the world to see through the mirror to their soul. The mirror they fear will expose the shame they feel at being seen in their present condition. They will never understand that most of humanity lost the ability to see that deeply long ago. Even to react to anyone's tears but their own.

This man belonged to the latter group. His face was well concealed. He hadn't done such a good job in tying the strips of dirty rags around the equally dirty sneakers on his feet. Just walking he appeared in grave danger of tripping and falling on his face. He probably would have done so if he hadn't been moving in a slow shuffle. A shuffle that said, "Say what you will, I don't care anymore. I've taken all that life has thrown at me and I quit. I opt out, and you can all go screw yourselves!" Most of the other passengers in the car never realized that just by accepting the stranger's miserable condition, they too were playing a role in his defeat. Perhaps even their own defeat.

Lost in these thoughts, Hanley stared out the window. His train was making local stops. Facing south he could see and feel the vibrations of a southbound 'D' Express train. It roared down the tracks as it drew nearer and nearer. For a few seconds the machines were neck in neck, both headed in the same direction.

As the trains reached the same speed it appeared for a few seconds that his train was not moving. That he could reach his hand through the windows and touch the passengers seated inside the express train. Of course he could do no such thing but it was a strange sensation and Hanley made a mental note to find out if there was any scientific reason for it. With both trains moving at what seemed like breakneck speeds it was difficult for the passengers on either to actually catch more than a fleeting glimpse of one another.

He'd talked with other subway riders and they too, got the same impression.

This sensation only lasted for a moment before the express train, gathering speed blew down the track. It out distanced the local as both headed for the next stop.

To Hanley this seemed an unnecessary show of speed. Sort of like the final seconds of a game. With his team ahead by 20 points a player on the winning side decides to slam dunk the ball over the head of an opposing player. Suddenly, the trains veered- one to the left and the other to the right. Entering the 125th Street station both screeched to a halt: steel tires against steel rails. It was one final assault against an overworked and archaic underground rail system.

He sat there in his seat waiting for the usual on rush of passengers but it never came. Not a soul boarded his car. Soon the doors slammed closed and both trains and their passengers were on their way south to the next station.

At 116th Street the young fare-beater Hanley had seen sneak onto the train at the 135th Street station disembarked. Hanley had seen him then and the kid seemed still a bit wary as he sauntered down the platform backpack strapped to his shoulders. With jeans too low on his backside they revealed the maroon under pants that suffered laundry neglect. He looked both ways as if he expected at any time to be arrested for his absence of discretion. But there was no police officer in sight. Relieved, the young man increased his pace. Nearing the turnstile and the street exit his head turned just as the local train passed. It was just in time for his eyes to meet Hanley's - eyes that seemed to say, "thanks for understanding. Thank you for not being cynical and judgmental."

It took only a minute for the train to race from 116th Street to 110th & Cathedral Station and it was here that the indigent man rose from his seat. He shuffled from the car and onto the platform. Hanley wished he could see the man's eyes. Wished he could ask him if he could help in some small way. He didn't have much to give but in this case he'd gladly have given most of what little there was in his pocket. And maybe his coat too. He had others in the closet at home. He could spare one and besides it wasn't so cold outside. Not yet anyway. He wasn't going to freeze to death before he got back home. Hanley said nothing. He'd learned the hard way that in New York City one must be careful to mind one's own affairs.

Say nothing and usually people will return the favor. Or, the bane. Whichever one prefers to call indifference.

He sat there with only his mind moving. Like a kid with a remote control in his hand; image after image slashed through his consciousness. There were pictures- hundreds of them. But like commercial television there was little of interest. Only the image of the homeless man. His was an image that, like a re-run sit com, played over and over again in Hanley's sub-consciousness.

Now that he'd left the train what would the man do? Where will he go and will there be anything there for him to eat? Signs posted in nearly every car asked passengers not to give to mendicants. But why were there so many homeless folks riding the trains? And what of those who were only seeking shelter in the subways and would never ask anyone for a handout? It was common knowledge that the city's homeless shelters were dangerous and filthy. Every New Yorker knew that many homeless people braved the weather in all seasons rather than subject themselves to the torture of the shelters. Hanley had overheard the conversation of two homeless white guys in the late sixties. Their biggest fear was not of being robbed or beaten but of being raped. Both bemoaned their lack of sleep in the City's shelters. Sleeplessness due to cell phones ringing throughout the night.

And it wasn't just abuse from other homeless people, Hanley had been told. Those who ran the shelters were insulting and rude. They treated homeless people as if they were the scourge of the earth. Dictating to them, ignoring them. Dehumanizing them to the point of absurdity. Both men and women flee the shelters. It was safer on the streets and riding the trains and buses.

He recalled seeing a young woman on the train with very dirty hands and clothes. As she made her speech about her condition she got down on her hands and knees. She crawled on her elbows with outstretched hands as she begged for money or food. It was one of the worse scenes Hanley had ever witnessed riding the subways. Although he'd given the woman a dollar it had taken days to push it from his mind. He was still thinking about that as the 'C' train headed south to the next stop.

He noticed an envelope on the floor. He hadn't seen it there before the train arrived at 110th Street. No one had boarded the car at that station and only one passenger had got off: the homeless man. He must have dropped it. It might even be important to him. Very important, Hanley thought.

Maybe it was a letter informing him that he'd been accepted into some government run program for housing and shelter or for public assistance. He finally decided to pick up the envelope when the train lurched to a stop at 103rd Street. There, three or four people boarded. Hanley sat down again and the envelope lay there untouched and unnoticed as several passengers stepped over it. They continuing to their seats.

A rider stepped on the envelope and the dirty mark of her shoe became a permanent part of the already dirty piece of trash. Others sat in the empty seats on either side and Hanley watched with curiosity as one of the women sank down into the chair that had been occupied only minutes earlier by the homeless man. What would she say or do if she knew he'd sat there? It was like that in the city. People make such a big deal of feeling important. They preach cleanliness and then they go outside and touch, feel and sniff the rear ends of strangers and even dogs they've just met in the park. They sit on the ground and lie on the benches where rats and raccoons feed. Where worm-filled birds roam and nest. It's all such a farce. What's going to happen is going to happen and no one will be protected from germs in a place already filled with them

He laughed. He was no different from anyone else in that respect. Here he was criticizing humanity while he sat there reluctant to allow anyone, even strangers to see him get out of his seat and bend to pick up an envelope from the floor. But he couldn't allow it to just lie there. It might really have great significance to the man. As soon as the train doors slammed to a close and headed to the next station he stood up. It would be 96th Street and Central Park West and here Hanley would get debark the train and hurry down the platform to the 97th Street exit. He had a doctor's appointment at 12:45 and he was already late. Hanley stood. Walking quickly to the exit door, he poised himself above the envelope like a new father. He didn't want anyone to see him pick it up but he knew he wanted- knew he had to do it A voice behind him said, "excuse me sir but you dropped something." Hanley thanked the woman. Bending, he picked up the dirty envelope just as the train reached 96th Street. Holding it in his hand he walked down the platform. He stuck it in the pocket of his jacket as he climbed the stairs by twos. There was no time to glance at the writing on the front. He was late and he had no idea of the protocol or penalty when one arrived late at this doctor's office. He was Hanley's new doctor and this was only the third visit. The doctor had prescribed a cholesterol - lowering medication but he was already taking three other pills to control blood pressure and Hanley had been reluctant to add a fourth. He'd had the prescription filled but had not taken a single pill. He wondered what the doctor would say about that. Well, it was his body and he wanted to have more information before he began taking statins. He'd heard that there could be very serious side effects from these drugs. Well, there will be no need for blood tests to determine if the pills are working, he thought. Not today, anyway.

With ten people ahead of him in the office he signed the ledger at the desk. He stood there for a minute waiting for the other shoe to drop. He half expected the triage nurse or somebody to tell him he was too late and they'd have to reschedule. When no one said anything he took his place as the eleventh patient. He was annoyed with himself for not arriving on time although he doubted that half an hour earlier would have made much of a difference. There was nothing to do but wait and he took a magazine from the table and leafed through it until he came to a story about two Puerto Rican men.

Felix and Rob, or Robert were ex-cons. Felix would eventually be given a kidney by his friend Rob but would then be sent back to prison for a three year sentence. It was a good story. The human interest type that Hanley most liked reading and as he read, it took his mind back to the man he'd just seen on the train. Now, this man was the epitome of human interests. Hanley wished he knew something about him. A little something about his past and how it came to be that he found himself homeless. Something terrible must have happened. Surely, the man has or had loved ones who care about him. And why weren't they reaching out and helping? Why was no one helping this man and thousands like him all over the United States? Hanley next thought of the time he had spent as a contractor for the State of New York. He had worked in the State mental institutions and he'd been shocked by the numbers of unoccupied buildings on the huge property. No longer used, they'd been vacated abandoned and left to rot. They were situated on manicured grounds that looked like pictures of college campuses. It would take so little to put them in shape and to place them at the disposal of some agency or charitable organization willing to help alleviate homelessness in the city. And he'd heard that there were just as many unoccupied city - owned buildings that could do the same. It's a crime, he thought. A crying shame. He thought of the envelope in his pocket but before he could reach for it the doctor poked his head in the doorway. "Mr. Hanley," Dr. Patel said. He held the door open and moved aside so his patient could enter.

The doctor's visit was over. There would be another appointment in one month. In the meantime he should begin taking the cholesterol drug. And to make things easier, he could take the drug at any time during the day that he wished.

As long as he did so every day. Hanley preferred to take it in the morning along with the other drugs. This way he wouldn't forget and he wouldn't over dose. Forgetfulness had been the only excuse Hanley could offer for not taking the medication. He was relieved that Dr. Patel hadn't seemed particularly upset when Hanley asked for a clear explanation of the side effects. He'd heard that there were doctors like that but he'd never before been a patient to a physician who thought patients should just do what they were told and shut up about it. After all, doctors know more about patients than patients know about themselves. Even one they've never before met or examined.

Now, out of the doctor's office he walked quickly. He had a few things to pick up at the Gourmet Grocery and then he could be cavalier about the rest of the day. With nothing special planned, he just wanted to get back uptown before the rain began. Rain was predicted for evening and it would be heavy at times. It would continue throughout the night.

When Kenneth Hanley came up out of the subway station it was after 5 P.M. He was carrying two shopping bags in one hand and one in the other and he was tired. Once again he noticed the broken escalator. He passed it without disdain.

He reasoned they were still waiting for some special part to arrive before it could be repaired. Then too, maybe it wasn't the fault of MTS. After all they let those jobs out to contractors and so many things can go awry. Perhaps, the contractor hadn't yet received payment. But that it was not working was an inconvenience and that thought only added to his exhaustion.

At 96th Street, he'd taken the first train that came into the station. It was the B local and at 145th Street, the climb from the 3rd level underground platform had been tough. Especially carrying three bags. It was growing darker as night came earlier now. There were only a few weeks remaining before the end of the year and the air was growing noticeably more frigid. It was raw but not in the bone chilling way that January and February can be. It was almost as if nature was saying: I'm giving you one last chance to get your act together before I bring in the hawk of winter.

He had a sudden yen for something sweet tasting and he stopped at the pharmacy to buy candy. Deciding on a Cadbury Bar with fruit and nuts to indulge his sweets fantasy, he paid the young clerk. He stopped just inside the swinging doors and broke off a piece. Slowly, he allowed the taste of the chocolate to melt in his mouth and the last of it to trickle down his throat. Hanley continued down the avenue toward home. The street was almost deserted and he looked at the time on his cell phone before hurrying the short distance.

It is nearly 5:30. Someone should be here, Hanley reasoned. Perhaps they had all been detained as he'd been. Sometimes, it depended on whether one took the train or a bus. Most times it was the luck of the draw: six in one hand and half a dozen in the other. Hanley preferred the train. Once you've taken the bus a couple of times you run out of things to see. But there is always some drama happening on the trains. There are singers and musicians, dancers and comedians, poets and even beggars. Yes, there are always beggars and the homeless. Sadly, the homeless never go away. He thought of the man on the train yet again.

Hanley took off his coat, put the groceries away and grabbed an apple. He'd forgotten to wash his hands and when he came out of the bathroom he was about to reach his hand into his jacket pocket for the rest of the candy when he remembered the letter. The image of the faceless, hooded man on the train came rushing into his thoughts. He wondered where the man was now that it was dark. Had he re-boarded the train and then gone to the last stop. And if so, what then? Did he get off and take another train in the opposite direction. Harley knew that this was the normal routine for vagrants.

Some said that an underground community exists somewhere in midtown. The homeless gather there and the place is like Dante's inferno or something close to it. There, lived the rejects of society. The ones who, no longer able to cope, had fallen along the wayside. It was they said, a place of makeshift cardboard shelters, plastic garbage bags and shopping carts. There were no rules there. Just survival of the fittest or the unfit. But who knew the truth? Maybe this was only just one more tale on the long list of rumors circulating in the city. Another tale to rival the one about the huge albino rats living under skyscrapers in the sewers of the city. Rats much larger than adult cats. Rats that fear nothing! Not even man. Rats that don't even fear the alligators and snakes released as youngsters by their former pet owners but grown to adulthood in the dark and unused subway tunnels that stretch for miles and miles in the city. There, they live out their lives in the bowels of this giant metropolis. Stories say they lurk in the shadows of the transit system where they exist on garbage and human waste.

He'd once been told by a friend who survived the horror of homelessness that the nights are the most difficult time. The friend had told him how he'd ridden the trains and prayed for the night to pass quickly. Prayed that the terror of darkness would end its reign and give way to the safety and sanity of dawn. Even the morning company of strangers was preferable to the feeling of being not just alone but vulnerable. Like prey in a jungle. Only this was a jungle of concrete and tall buildings with stores of plenty that most folks can't afford to shop in but haven't the guts to say so. Night, his friend had told him brings out the hunters. Hunters who stalk the homeless. Hunters who are not satisfied just watching them in their misery the hunters stalk, abuse and maim. The hunters probe and steal. Occasionally they kill - just for the hell of it or to satisfy some sick version of mercy killing now terribly out of kilter. It makes them feel real manly and important as they slink off unnoticed into the night and back to their own miserable lots. It was a sad story but fortunately Hanley's friend had survived to tell his tale. Now, Hanley wondered how the poor man he'd seen on the train earlier would fare.

As he looked at the front of the envelope in his hand Hanley sat there on the side of his bed in stunned silence. Yes, the envelope was old and dirty. The rear flap had been folded but the back was left unsealed. At some point it had got wet and was stuck to a portion of the inside pages. Whomever had unglued it had been careful not to destroy the writing. Hanley could tell that much about it. But what caught his attention was the handwriting on the front. It was not in print. It was written in cursive.

And whoever wrote it was expert: If you should find this please be good enough to send it to Heaven. Thank you!" That was it. Hanley read and re-read the words. "If you should find this please be good enough to send it to Heaven. There was no name or return address. For a full ten minutes he sat there on his bed wondering whether or not he should open the envelope and read the pages inside. Would it be considered an invasion of privacy? There were laws protecting people from such things. But could this be considered meddling? This was something he'd found on the train. He'd even rescued it from oblivion. And although he knew who had dropped it where would he find the man?

Hanley's final thought was this: Suppose the man was an Angel. Hanley had heard about such things as Angels visiting Earth in the guise of ordinary human beings? Hadn't God sent two Angels to Abraham and then to his nephew Lot before He destroyed Sodom and Gomorrah? That certainly is how the story is told in the Bible. It's right there in Genesis. Hanley had heard the story dozens of times at his mother's side as they sat in the little Church on Sundays. Later, he'd read it himself a few times, and discussed it with friends.

He knew he had to read the letter. Maybe it would tell him what the front actually meant. If it was someone's idea of place called Heaven. A new concept or an old one he'd never heard. After all, he'd been brought up a Christian and had attended several different denominational churches. So many religious sects have their own practices and dogmas. Heaven could mean many things to many people and just by following a few instructions he could be fulfilling someone's dying wish. Slowly, he opened the flap on the back, carefully pulling the pages from within. The letter was written in the same beautifully formed hand. It reminded Hanley of the historical documents he'd seen visiting museums as a youngster. The copies of the Constitution of The United States, the Declaration of Independence with the fabulous signature of John Hancock.

Dear Angel it read.

My name is unimportant. If you have not already guessed my identity do not be alarmed. One day you will know who I am and who you really are. But those revelations are for the future. Right now I am writing this letter to let you know that you are loved. To tell you that you have not been deserted and to let you know that there are many who watch you as you progress through this life. Not as spies to clock you're every word and move. They recognize that you are human and you must have your space. They recognize that the flesh is weak and that you have needs and foibles like everyone else. But it is because you have had the courage to pick up this envelope and read it that you have been selected to carry forward the message of love and peace that is so essential to all who now walk the Earth. You have no special responsibilities or rules and regulations that you must perform in order to do this. You need only do what you have done and then pass this letter on to someone else in any manner you chose.

I ask only that you do that one thing. If you do it you will have accomplished and carried forth your end of this bargain. What happens to the letter afterwards will not be your cross to bear. You may leave it on a bus or train. Drop it in a mailbox, hand it to a friend or stranger or simply leave it on the doorsteps of a Church, Synagogue or Mosque. But, whatever you do. Please do not burn or destroy it or let it sit idly in a drawer. Like the air you breathe it must be circulated to continue its good works.

Now that your hand has touched it, this will be especially important to you. Part of you will now be borne along on currents of the wind, the way good words and good works circulate the universe. If you do not do your part you will undo all the good that has come to all those who've read it before you. This is why you have been selected. Only those of whom we are absolutely certain, will be given this responsibility. Have no fear. You will know what to do and where to place the letter when it is time. I have purposely kept the letter short. Not because I would not like to remind you of the sickness and plague that you know exists in the world. Not because I would not like to mention the sufferings of the young and elderly in the world. Or of the hurt you see and of the pain you feel as you pass the homeless and the diseased, the drug and alcohol addicted, the mentally ill and the miserable.

I have kept it brief to further emphasize to you that your current woes shall also be brief. They shall all pass away in the blink of an eye and what follows will be more wonderful and glorious than anything you've ever known or imagined in your lifetime. And when it comes, I want you to always remember those among you who have not yet been so blessed. That they too will find hope in a kind word or gesture that you can provide if only you will continue taking the time to embrace them. If only you will remain firm in your convictions and not let negative forces deter or detain you from the course for which you've already demonstrated a propensity. Please continue to take a moment to give back and extend your hand. Please take a moment to look back, to share, to laugh, to love and to hope. And most of all, never give up on yourself or on others. There is, as you've already discovered, some good in everyone.

May Heaven Bless you and the Ancestors continue to watch over you as you follow your heart and your dreams.

There it was. Not a word more. Not a pen stroke less. It was done, and Hanley felt a warm glow come over his body. Truly, he'd been surrounded by an aura and its presence was overwhelming. He felt a tear trickle down his cheek and he thought again of the man on the train. He wasn't so poor after all. Perhaps he was not even homeless. In fact, he was quite wealthy.

Wealthy in the knowledge that he'd brought peace and happiness to someone just as the letter had brought to him. Perhaps, this is what the man does. Hanley thought. Maybe he is an Angel and has a special mission here on Earth, to spread these messages wherever he travels. Perhaps, this is why he never shows his face. After all, anyone would clearly recognize the face of an Angel. This last thought brought Hanley to his feet and he stood up, reaching for his coat. It was still not quite 7 P.M. Rush hour in midtown. Workers would be leaving to join the mad dash home. If he hurried he could take the bus or train and ride downtown. Maybe, he'd see a friend or a stranger to whom he could hand the letter. He wasn't sure what it all meant. Especially the part about he'd know when the time came. And what was written on the face of the envelope was still a mystery. Please send this letter to Heaven. The words reverberated in his head.

He hoped that whomever he gave it to or found it would take the time to read it just as he'd done. It was such an important message. But the letter had absolved him of all future responsibility.

Surely he would see someone. Hanley walked out the door just as one of the kids came in. "Where you going Pop Pop," she asked him? "Oh, I'll be right back, my sweet," Hanley answered. But he didn't come right back. He walked and walked and rode the buses and the subways. Each time he left the letter on a seat it remained there. If he put it on the floor it was walked over and stepped on.

He might have left it lying there and gone on but he felt it was too important for that. After all, he had been given leave to do just that. He'd been absolved of all future responsibility. But he, Hanley had to "know" someone picked it up just as he was sure the homeless man had known he would do. Of course! That's It! The man knew Hanley was watching him! He'd known it all the time. That was the reason he got off the train two stops before Hanley. He wasn't concerned that someone else would pick up the envelope. The letter was meant for Hanley!

He knew I needed help and he dropped it there purposely to see if I was willing to bend a little to receive it. All I have to do is find a mailbox and drop it in as the letter says or put it on the steps of a religious place. Whoever finds it will find Heaven on earth. Not Heaven in Heaven. I'm still alive! We're all still alive and we haven't crossed that bridge yet. Maybe when we do there'll be another letter to read. Or, some friendly face to help us go the last mile of the journey. He remembered the death of his best friend who had told him just days before he passed about his own dream. The friend had dreamt of his mother and she'd told him that when he died he would not see her.

Not for a little while. She'd told him that there would be a kind lady on the other side to help him. His friend had seemed so relieved about that prospect and it had helped Hanley deal with some of the sadness and hurt he was feeling at the time. It had helped him even more after the friend died. Surely, it was so. He hadn't thought of it until that very moment. The day was nine years to the very day his best friend had died.

It was nearly ten o'clock by the time he got off the "C" train and walked up the steps to the first floor of the platform. He passed the disabled escalator for yet another time in 10 hours. But this time he didn't notice it. His thoughts were somewhere else. On the way home he had sat on the train determined to drop the letter in the first mailbox he saw. If he got off at the rear of the train he reckoned he would pass two such boxes on the street. But at the 110th Street stop something strange happened. The train slowed and Hanley, already looking out the window thought he saw a familiar figure on the platform. He stared in disbelief. There he was, the same man he'd seen earlier that day. And he was talking with another man.

The stranger who had dropped the letter. Leaping from his seat Hanley rushed to the door. He stuck his head out and looked back in the direction of the two men he'd just seen but he didn't see them. But he had seen them! He was sure of that! The man had been dressed in rags but the difference was that he did not have the hoodie pulled over his face. He'd been talking with another hooded man.

And he'd looked squarely into Hanley's face, almost as if he wanted to speak. Words were unnecessary. In a few moments the door closed and Hanley sat down again. He wondered if the men had boarded the train. The train continued uptown to 116th Street but Hanley still could not tell if the man was on the same train. He was tempted to get up and walk back through the cars. If he saw the man he would approach him and thank him. That's all, just tell him he'd read the letter and thank him. But remembering that he could be fined for his impulsiveness he waited.

When the train slowed for the 125th Street station. Hanley saw a hooded man. But it was not the man he'd hoped to talk with. It was the OTHER man from the bench on 110th Street and he was walking toward the middle of the car. Hanley knew why the man was there. The stranger took a seat at the door and kept his eyes down. His head was covered. Two more stops and Hanley rose from his seat to exit at his own stop. As he left the train he let the envelope slip from his fingers. It fell to the floor and landed inside the car just as the doors were closing.

Hanley walked swiftly along the platform. Soon he was almost jogging and trying to keep pace. He watched as the hooded stranger got up from his seat and took a few steps. Bending, he picked up the letter.

In an instant the train continued down the endless miles of steel subway track. It was headed to the Bronx or wherever 'C' trains travel through the long dark tunnels of New York City on a journey to a place some call Heaven.

THE END